BY JOHN BIRMINGHAM

PUBLISHED BY DEL REY BOOKS
Without Warning
After America
Angels of Vengeance

THE AXIS OF TIME TRILOGY
Weapons of Choice
Designated Targets
Final Impact

DAVE VS. THE MONSTERS
Emergence
Resistance
Ascendance

THE CRUEL STARS TRILOGY
The Cruel Stars
The Shattered Skies

THE SHATTERED SKIES

THE
SHATTERED
SKIES

JOHN BIRMINGHAM

NEW YORK

Published in the United States by Del Rey, an imprint of Random House, a division of Penguin Random House LLC, New York.

DEL REY and the HOUSE colophon are registered trademarks of Penguin Random House LLC.

Chapter-opener art: © istock.com/Aleksandra Nekrasova (shattered rectangle); Edwin Vazquez (stars)

LIBRARY OF CONGRESS CATALOGING-IN-PUBLICATION DATA
Names: Birmingham, John, author.
Title: The shattered skies / John Birmingham.
Description: First edition. | New York : Del Rey, [2022] |
Series: The cruel stars trilogy ; 2
Identifiers: LCCN 2021028102 (print) | LCCN 2021028103 (ebook) |
ISBN 978-1-9848-2055-6 (hardcover ; acid-free paper) |
ISBN 978-1-9848-2056-3 (ebook)
Subjects: GSAFD: Science fiction.
Classification: LCC PR9619.3.B5136 S52 2022 (print) |
LCC PR9619.3.B5136 (ebook) | DDC 823/.914—dc23
LC record available at https://lccn.loc.gov/2021028102
LC ebook record available at https://lccn.loc.gov/2021028103

Printed in Canada on acid-free paper

randomhousebooks.com

2 4 6 8 9 7 5 3 1

First Edition

Book design by Edwin Vazquez

For Jason Lambright.
A fine companion on a long march.

THE SHATTERED SKIES

CHAPTER

ONE

The blue-green jewel, silent and wreathed in white continents of cloud, floated in space far below him. Captain Anders Revell contemplated the vast burning crown that enveloped the world, the falling ruin and memory of the 101st Attack Fleet.

"Better lock in, Captain. We'll punch out hard when the final ram gets here."

Revell thanked the pilot before returning to his crash pod on the troop deck of the armored shuttle. He was the only passenger. He stepped backward into the plasteel capsule and felt the maglocks grab onto his panzerplate battlesuit.

Montrachet had been pacified. The enemy destroyed. Just as they had been across the entire front, and throughout the Greater Volume. The price of victory here, however, had been high. The 101st had died to free Montrachet, including the Fleet's commander, Archon-Admiral Wenbo Strom; his flagship, the Astral Fortress *Liberator*; and the entirety of the *Liberator*'s battle group. It was but a fraction of the Republic's strength across the wider battlefront, but none of the invasion planners had anticipated such grievous losses.

Revell should have been able to take a simple runabout down to the surface by now. Hell, he shouldn't have needed to be here in the first place.

And yet here he was, sheathed in full armor, sealing himself into a hardened survival pod, just in case.

The shuttle's drive cycled from a low hum to a deep bass as the pilot readied the sturdy little craft to force a passage down through the billions of pieces of debris, the remains of Strom's expeditionary force, burning up in the denser layers of the planet's atmosphere. With his free hand, he keyed in the sequence to seal and secure his personal armor. The faceplate slid up, entombing the Republican officer in the dark. But the lightless void remained for only a second before the suit's diorama powered up. A final clamp secured his free arm, and the crash pod hatch closed. Within his carbon-armor gauntlet, Revell's fingers had enough wiggle room to manipulate the control pad of the diorama.

He synced his helmet to the shuttle's sensor suite, which flooded the display with data. There was nothing he could do to assist. He could only wait and watch through the HUD. His shuttle joined a convoy of small- and medium-sized craft, waiting in the shadow of two ramships for escort down through the debris field. Inside the helmet his lips twitched. A grim half-smile. The race traitors who'd done this had not meant to impede him, but they would doubtless be satisfied with that consequence. Despite the Republic's stunning overall success on D-Day, this one part of the operation had turned into a rout and Captain Revell, aide-de-camp to Fleet Marshal Anais Blade, had been tasked with finding out why.

The marshal would decide how best to use that knowledge, but she was going to be a long while waiting on it if Revell could not even set foot on the planet below.

He didn't annoy the crew with pointless demands for updates. They were just ferry drivers and he could see from the data feed it would be another ten or fifteen minutes before the final ballistic ramship arrived to lead the convoy down into the atmosphere. Revell took a few moments to survey the wide-field visuals splashed across his helmet display—a dramatic panorama of battle cruisers, dropships, fast frigates, and stellar drekar attending the Astral Fortress *Enterprise*, newly designated flagship of the Republic's forces in this sector. Most of the surviving elements of the 101st remained dispersed throughout the local area of operations, securing rocks and rings in the outlying systems of Eassar, Descheneaux, and Batavia.

Especially Batavia. A sacred site to be sure, last resting place of the exile ship *Voortrekker*, but also a crucial transit point for the follow-on forces soon to arrive from the Republic. Fleet Intelligence reported that a few capital ships of the local Javan and Combine regimes still lurked in nearby volumes, spared by chance from the pre-emptive strike that had collapsed resistance everywhere else. Those follow-on forces would be needed to deal with them.

Revell had scheduled two days to pick over the small archeological camp in the shadow of the *Voortrekker*, and another three to interrogate the surviving members of the dig team who had fled the site shortly before the first assault drops took it. Three days was a long time, admittedly. But these things always took longer when you weren't using brute force. Much to his annoyance, agents of the Inquiry had already captured and executed most of the mutants' colleagues, liquidating crucial assets of his investigation before he could stop them. But a few still drew breath and from them he was determined to learn what he could of Frazer McLennan. If that took three days, or even three weeks, so be it.

Revell breathed out as if ready to lift a heavy weight in the strength foundry.

If he'd had the room to move he would have shook his head in wonder.

It was a legitimate marvel that the great villain of humanity's fall still lived; or to be more accurate, that some debased facsimile of the creature existed near seven hundred years later to answer for the original sin of its progenitor.

Revell tamped down on the visceral disgust which always attended contemplation of such perversions to the genome.

To the human soul, really.

For now he could not afford the indulgence of letting his feelings run free.

His fingertips twitched to swipe away the video from the shuttle's external arrays, and bring up the take from Colonel Marla Dunn's interrogation of the infamous war criminal. There wasn't much. The machine that had extracted McLennan had reached into the local networks, brushing aside five layers of quantum-shifting security like a fine lace curtain. It torched the primary data sources—and murdered Colonel Dunn. At least, she was presumed dead. She had literally disappeared at the exact moment the homicidal AI arrived. The genome only knew what the thing had done with her, but the combined sensor fields of the surviving 101st revealed no trace of the officer anywhere in-volume.

Part of Revell did not want to find out. There were rumors, approaching the realm of dark fairy tales, about the appetites of the so-called Intellects.

But finding out was his job.

So he ignored the stink of his own body odors trapped inside the suit, and he reviewed the take.

For the moment this consisted of after-action reports compiled by the ground force intelligence cadre assigned to the *Voortrekker* landing zone. Interviews, debriefs, even hostile interrogations with personnel who witnessed the incursion or had responsibilities for securing the site against such attacks.

Most of them, Revell noted, were now being questioned by the Inquiry. The shuttle's engine harmonics changed, and he felt the evolution as a distant vibration at the very moment he ordered the intelligence staffers released from the Inquiry's jurisdiction and directly into his supervision. He smiled inside the helmet. It was almost as though the goons got his message and stamped their little feet so hard it set the planet to ringing like a bell.

But it mattered not.

He was the personal weapon of Anais Blade. Her cutting edge. And there was nothing the Inquiry could do about that.

The voice of the shuttle pilot crackled in his ears.

"Two minutes to first burn, Captain."

"Acknowledged," Revell answered, flipping back to the sensor feed from the external arrays for a few seconds. From a perceived vantage point on the blunt, shovel-shaped nose of the combat shuttle, he watched the last ramship take up station at the head of the convoy. A great, brutish club of a thing, most of its superdense mass was concentrated in the hammerhead formation at the bow. The giant maneuvering engines burned with the pure white light of nuclear fire as the vessel took point ahead of its comrades.

"Initiating entry burn," the pilot announced shortly, and Revell felt the power of the shuttle's much smaller engines as a deep, thrumming pulsation that transferred a nanoscale fraction of their power through the hull of the shuttle, the plasteel sheath of the crash pod, and the flexible panzerplate shields of his personal armor to effect an unpleasant deep body harmonic throb somewhere between his nuts and his guts.

The planet below appeared to increase its speed of rotation as the convoy burned hard into the first shallow arc of descent. Safely tucked away in the lee of the ramships, Revell could not see what was happening at the head of the convoy, but he did not need to. He knew the scorched and pitted surface of the mammoth bulkers would soon glitter and spark with hundreds, then thousands, and finally millions of impacts as they punched down through the debris field, clearing a path for their smaller, infinitely more vulnerable charges.

The mutants and borgs had done them a service before fleeing the local volume, carving up the largest pieces of Strom's shattered fleet with energy weapons, most likely to protect the surface of Montrachet from heavy impactors. None of the wreckage burning up in the atmosphere, or being atomized on contact with the x-matter glacis shields of the ramships, had mass enough to survive atmospheric entry and strike the planet's surface. But an armored landing craft such as he rode in could be badly damaged or even destroyed by a collision at orbital speeds with a meter-wide chunk of Astral Fortress deck plating.

He squinted at the momentary brilliance of blue-white fire from reactor mass jetting out of the thrusters of the supply brig ahead of them in the convoy. The helmet's corrective algorithms quickly dimmed the long white spears of plasma, and Revell blinked away the afterimage. As the ghost plumes faded on his retinas, he wondered whether the mutants would have bothered to neutralize the threat from so many big-ass chunks of meta-material dropping down the gravity well if Montrachet hadn't been the private estate of an Elite Fraction family—the Montanblancs.

The obscenity of that, of a single family owning an entire world and all who dwelled there, was breathtaking. But it was also distracting. Irrelevant.

Of critical importance now was the hunt for the family's surviving heir, the so-called Princess Alessia. Fleet Intelligence judged that chances were good McLennan had escaped in her company. They were both of them in their own way grave threats to the Liberation.

Anders Revell shut down the external feed and returned to his work, reviewing the VR logs of interviews with a squad of Force Protection troopers who were first on the scene after McLennan's escape.

CHAPTER

TWO

At this distance, the star was a faraway point of light, slightly larger, slightly brighter than the thousands of its kin scattered through the local cluster. Solar winds streamed out from the main sequence G2 burner, ionized particles and magnetic fields whipping through the heliosphere, inflating a protective bubble around the local volume, safeguarding the planets within from the harsh radioactive bath of interstellar space. In one sense the volume was small. Just one rocky planet and two gas giants, a modest little neighborhood that had nonetheless occasioned a savage conflict between two human tribes over their contending claims to that remote and lonely world. In another sense, of course, the measure of three-dimensional space both tribes thought of as the local volume was immense; so impossibly vast that the human mind was incapable of truly understanding it, having evolved over millions of years to comprehend distance as something measured in the number of steps needed to find food or water in a small patch of forest or savannah. At the very edge of this unimaginably huge and somewhat fluid area of space, in the electromagnetic turbulence of the constantly moving boundary between the bubble of the star's heliosphere and the radioactive ether of the interstellar medium, something profound was about to happen. The structure of space-time itself suddenly flexed and warped before utterly collapsing to vomit up first one, then two human spacecraft.

A tribe had returned to its hunting grounds.

"Holding station at ninety-three astronomical units from Descheneaux actual, Commander."

"Thank you, Mister Chase. Done and done well."

"The *Ariane* has folded in, too, ma'am. They are running dark as ordered, roughly five hundred kilometers astern, one-ninety-three degrees relative."

Commander Lucinda Hardy allowed herself a small, private smile.

"Thank you, Mister Bannon," she said, "although I doubt Captain L'trel would agree they are doing as ordered. I imagine she would simply say that she was asked nicely."

"Yes, Commander," the young lieutenant acknowledged.

"Passive arrays, Mister Fein," Hardy went on.

"Yes, ma'am. Passive arrays deployed and receiving," Lieutenant Mercado Fein replied.

"Do you think my wee friend here could get a sip of that?"

Lucinda turned toward the new voice, heavily accented with a Scottish burr. The man who had spoken was noticeably older than everyone else on the bridge. His biotic age appeared to be somewhere at the deep end of six decades. And six hard-lived decades at that.

The Scotsman's actual age was much, much greater.

"Of course, sir," Lucinda Hardy replied, inclining her head ever so slightly toward Admiral Frazer McLennan, a flag officer from Earth's Home Fleet, rather than a direct superior of the Royal Armadalen Navy. "Mister Bannon, please copy the take to Hero."

"Aye, Commander. Copy to the Intellect."

"I'm standing right here, you know," Herodotus said and sighed. An Armada-level Autonomous Combat Intellect, it resembled a two-meter-long teardrop of infinite darkness.

"Actually, it's more like you're wafting," McLennan said. "Like a fart in a telephone booth."

The obsidian-black lozenge of exotic matter floated a little farther away.

"One, nobody knows what a telephone booth is anymore, you old fool. And two, if anybody needs me I'll be over here using an infinitesimal fraction of my processing power to analyze the signals intelligence from your passive arrays. Please, do come and get me when you have taken an unconscionable amount of time to sift and analyze the data for yourself, applying the meager resources of your decaying gray matter to the task at hand. I'll be happy to tell you where you've gone wrong and what you should have done hours if not days earlier, had you just listened to me."

"Thank you," Hardy said with smile. "That's very kind of you, Hero."

Her expression settled back into a somber cast as she considered their situation. They had arrived without incident at their first lay-up point. *Defiant* and the *Ariane* lurked in the electromagnetic chaos of the termination shock, a standing wave at the edge of the solar system where the constant press of the galaxy's background radiation canceled out the solar wind streaming from Descheneaux's star. They had yet to precisely determine the effectiveness of the Sturm's sensors, but the Armadalen Navy had used the same tactic to great effect just before the final battle of the Javan War.

Perhaps the Sturm had leaped ahead of Earth's military technology in general, and Armadale's in particular, but nothing Hardy had seen of the enemy the past few weeks gave her reason to believe that. They had advanced, to be sure. And they had pulled off a viciously effective surprise attack. A *Kantai Kessen* they called it, fetishizing an Old Earth military culture, which was what the Sturm had instead of happy childhoods and proper medical care.

But the victory was not complete. The *Defiant* still stood against them, and if her ship had survived, others would have, too. They would soon know whether the RAN's station at Descheneaux would play a part in that resistance.

"Commander, I have a ping from the *Ariane*. Captain L'trel requesting tight beam holo."

Lucinda raised an eyebrow at the officer who had just spoken to her. Lieutenant Nonomi Chivers, like Hardy a first lifer.

"Well, at least she asked this time," Lucinda said. "Put her through, Lieutenant. Short-range tight beam only."

"Yes, ma'am."

The captain of the merchant raider *Ariane* appeared in holographic form on the bridge of the *Defiant*. Sephina L'trel shared a phenotype with Chivers. They were both riding heirloom p-types of the Zulu aristocracy, but Sephina was dramatically different in every other respect from the courteous, professional young naval officer who piped her holo aboard. Where Chivers was neatly presented, respectful, and disciplined, Sephina arrived as a foulmouthed she-wolf in a shock of platinum blond dreadlocks, torn leathers, and a permanent half-sneer.

"So much for running dark," Lucinda said.

Sephina's half-sneer quirked into a half-smile. It had been many years since she and Lucinda had been roommates in a Habitat Welfare orphanage on Coriolis, and their life paths had described greatly diverging arcs ever since. But they had been best friends once, and young, and Lucinda seemed the only person left whose existence could brighten, however briefly, the darkness that gathered around Sephina L'trel.

"You took the booty call, bitch," Sephina said.

"Only because I knew if I didn't, you'd find another way through. At least I can control the signal leakage this way."

"Pfft." Sephina waved her away. "You couldn't catch me when I was blockade running. These fuckin' ass clowns aren't gonna do any better than you. Are they?"

Lucinda said nothing, but that had little to no effect on Sephina.

"Are these ass clowns better than you, Luce?" she teased. "Well?"

Hardy put on her commander face.

"Captain L'trel, is there some reason you're calling," she asked, "or did your inner troll simply get the better of you?"

The smuggler and sometime pirate grinned as though pleased with the byplay.

"Booker says there's two Sturm ships in-system. Says they're standing off your little naval base, just chatting among themselves. Or they were, about twelve hours ago when the transmissions were made. They're still chatting away in there. Stroking their murder boners and giggling like a couple of hot little orphan girls about conquest and genocide. I'm just putting my bid in now to go fuck up their shit for you. You know, seeing as how you've got no kinetics or missiles left and I got a Russian tax evader's pimped-out orgy boat full of them."

A headache began to throb behind Lucinda's eyes and she rubbed at the flare of pain.

"Just saying is all," Sephina added.

"Thanks for the offer, but we will review the tactical data and make our decisions accordingly."

"She's right, you know," Herodotus said, floating back into the exchange. "Just because the robot says it's so, doesn't make it—"

Sephina interrupted him.

"Check your privilege, computer," she said. "Booker's not a robot. He's a real human boy, and we plugged him into our sensors because we don't have a ship's Intellect. I seem to recall you threw that into a star or something. We do have some sick fucking sensors, but. Those Zaistev bad boys did not spare the rubles. Anyway, just letting you know, Book says two ships. Easy kill. No waiting."

Lucinda dragged her hands down her cheeks, elongating her face into a fright mask.

It had always been this way with Seph. From the first day they had met. It was partly why she had jumped at the scholarship to the Naval Academy.

She took in a breath, centered herself, and went on.

"I am about to call an O-Group meeting to review the tactical situation. I think you'd better come over, Sephina. If only to stop you from charging into the volume and messing everything up."

The hologram beamed.

"I thought you'd never ask. I just need to freshen up, grab a few treats, and I will fold right over."

Lucinda muttered to herself, "This is not going to work out."

"What's that, Luce?" Sephina asked.

McLennan ghosted up beside her.

"It has to, lassie, at least for the next little while," he said. "Yon toothsome harridan has all the whizbangs. Can't fight a battle worth a wet fart if you don't have the whizbangs. Let alone a war."

"I know, I know," Lucinda said quietly.

"Listen to the talking fossil, Luce. You don't get to be a sentient museum exhibit like him by being a dummy."

The Intellect harrumphed somewhere off to the left.

"One could argue he is a sentient museum exhibit because he is such a dummy, but one would never be so rude."

Unfortunately, McLennan was right. He understood their dire lack of war stocks because he'd fired off most of *Defiant*'s arsenal in the battle over Montrachet. The stealth destroyer still had a full suite of energy weapons, but they were nowhere near as useful as hyperkinetics and folded munitions. She needed to reload, but the nearest supplies were ninety-two AU away on the far side of a Republican picket. She did not imagine the enemy would be short of ammunition.

The bridge crew all tended their stations, but neither Sephina nor McLennan were members of the Royal Armadalen Navy. Sephina's holo-presence floated a short distance away, arms folded, lips quirked into an almost mocking smile, an expression Lucinda remembered well from childhood. McLennan, with no duties to attend to, shuffled back to the chair in which Lieutenant Wojkowski had died.

Died for real, too. The communications officer had been exposed to the Sturm's nanophage when he plugged into a zero-point com link. The hostile code overwrote his neural net and his organic mind state, wiping out his personality, his loaded code, everything but a few base drives deep down in his brain stem. The same 'phage incursion had killed *Defiant*'s Captain Torvaldt, the ship's executive officer Commander Connelly, and the *Defiant* itself. The ship's Intellect fought a hard battle against the malignant software, but it lost.

Just like millions of Intellects and billions of human beings across the Great Volume.

It was a devastating attack, but it did have the effect of freeing up a spare chair for McLennan to occupy. Or as he put it, "To rest my bony arse upon."

Lucinda did her best to ignore Seph, making a host of decisions all at once.

"Lieutenant Bannon," she said, "please monitor signal traffic from the inner system. Notify me of any developments such as the enemy suddenly heading in our direction at full military power, but otherwise gather what sig-int you can without letting them know that we are listening."

"Yes, ma'am," Bannon said. She hadn't needed to spell out her instructions step-by-step like that. Bannon was young, like her, but competent. It was just her way. The Armadalen way. Leave nothing to chance.

"Lieutenant Chivers," she continued. "Please inform the officer of the deck that Captain L'trel will be folding in from the *Ariane* and an escort party should be detailed to escort her to the officers' wardroom. Two of Captain Hayes's marines should be enough. And please inform Captain Hayes that his presence at the O-Group will also be required. Five-minute call."

Chivers acknowledged the order and began relaying the information to the relevant officers. It all would have been so much easier just a few weeks ago. Lucinda would have told the ship's Intellect what was happening, or what she needed to happen, and the *Defiant* would have made it so. Hell, Lucinda wouldn't even have had to do that, because a few weeks ago she was not the surviving senior officer rated for combat command of the ship. She was just a lieutenant, like Chivers, Bannon, and Chase. Reporting for duty to her new billet, equally nervous and excited about the prospect of joining the ship's complement.

"Sephina, you can fold in at the reception bay on the afterbrow. I'm sure you know how to do that without bouncing off the shields. Conference in five minutes. Please don't be late. Or drunk."

The other woman winked at her, pointed a finger gun, and pulled the trigger.

"Just make sure those marines know that I'm a for-real baroness now so I'll be expecting the requisite bowing, scraping, and deep-cleavage ass-kissing."

Lucinda didn't reply. She signaled Nonomi Chivers with a flick of her fingers to cut the link.

Seph's holo disappeared.

"Mister Bannon, you have the conn. Admiral McLennan, if it would please you, walk with me?"

"I would be delighted, Commander Hardy," he said, levering himself out of his chair. He really was a fossil and Lucinda wondered how he even moved around in that creaking old body.

After the merest pause, she added, "You, too, Hero. Come along now."

The ancient Combat Intellect performed an exaggerated bow, dipping nearly a foot toward the deck plating and inclining its curved, teardrop form in her direction.

"But of course, Commander Hardy. Thank you ever so much for inviting me. I don't know what I would have done if I had been left here to devote a nano-fraction of my unused capabilities to—"

"Hero, just shut the fuck up and join the procession like a good baby duckling," McLennan said.

Booker had never been poured into a rig as spectacular as the *Ariane*. Thirty-five years into a forty-nine-year stretch as a soldier of Earth, before he was convicted of treason and dishonorably discharged, he had jacked into all manner of combat chassis and meat sleeves. His last rig had been a hedge-trimming bot. A very expensive, top-shelf, super premium hedge-trimming bot, to be sure. But the *Ariane* was special, too. An interstellar-capable superyacht designed for the personal use of a boyar of the Zaistev Corporation, it was a twin-engine schooner, nearly sixteen hundred feet from bow to stern, and capable of carrying two hundred passengers in grotesque luxury from the very center of the Greater Volume to the farthest reaches of the outer spiral colonies in less than two years.

This motherfucker could move.

Right now, however, it was motionless, holding station off the ass end of the Armadalen warship *Defiant*, its passive sensor arrays thrown wide to drink in every wisp of electromagnetic spillage from the inner volume.

"Booker, d'you get all that?"

The ninety-four million lines of code that emerged into sentience as the human being who knew himself to be the one and only Booker detected the question as a series of vibrations emerging from the woman's voice box traveling a short distance to a near-field microphone cluster. The sound waves washed over the audio array that collected them and converted the minute fluctuation in air pressure to quantum processing packets that Booker's code in turn translated back into Volume Standard English.

"Yeah, I got it," he replied. His voice emerged as ambient

noise from millions of tiny audio florets embedded in the walls, floor, and ceiling of the cabin. It was a very large cabin. He had to speak quietly.

"They sent over the handshake protocols to take you on board via the portal at the back end. There's two marines waiting for you. Lips puckered."

Sephina nodded.

"Good to know. Can you keep your eye on the Nazis? Talk it over with Banks, and maybe work up a plan for folding in there and killing every asshole who needs it? And just to be clear that means every motherfucker with a heartbeat. They're all gonna die screaming. I made a promise."

"Will do, Captain," Booker said. "I can tight beam a tactical package across to the *Defiant* when we have it, if you would prefer."

"Only if you can send it directly to me."

"I can do that if they allow me. Otherwise no."

Sephina nodded.

"Not surprised," she said. "Okay. Soon as you have a plan, let me know, which I guess means letting them know, too."

Sephina picked up a long, tan-colored duster draped over the back of a chair in her quarters. Booker's ninety-four million lines of code perceived her as considering whether to don the carbon nanoweave armor. It was frayed and scorched with the scars from a recent firefight. She considered the coat for just a moment before tossing it onto her unmade bed. It landed on a collection of empty and half-empty bottles of liquor, many of them, he knew from having access to the ship's manifest, worth more than he had earned in an Earth standard year as a senior NCO. Sephina necked them like popskull juice from a Hab rat still, usually before crying herself to sleep in her cabin.

Booker cut off his sensor access to the stateroom when she did that, save for a single feed that remotely monitored her autonomics. Heart rate, breathing, and shit. Just to make sure she didn't drink herself to death.

None of the *Ariane*'s crew had backup.

Death meant death to them.

Although, ironically, it had meant survival when the Sturm blasted their nanophage out across the Greater Volume comm nets. If you weren't hooked up to a live link, it couldn't kill you.

Sephina moved to a walk-in closet, selected a frayed and sleeveless denim jacket from the dozens of outfits hanging there, and left her cabin without bothering to secure the hatch behind her. There were only four people on the ship. Sephina, her pilot Ephram Banks—a source coder like Booker, but not political with it—and Jaddi Coto, the enormous gene-spliced vat soldier who, unlike Booker, had happily and honorably served out his forty-nine with the TDF before opting for honorable discharge with veterans benefits including p-type upgrades for mil-spec rhinoderm hide, bone and muscle density enlargements, and a rather striking cranial horn which some asshole had shot clean off his melon back on Montrachet.

Commander Hardy had butchered *that* guy like a hog.

Booker approved.

Banks was currently on the bridge, drinking a cup of English breakfast tea and eating shortbread. He had piloted the *Ariane* through the long series of folds to the edge of the Descheneaux System, and was now enjoying a well-earned break. Coto was in the sick bay, recovering from the head wound he took on Montrachet; incidentally in the same firefight that Booker had joined as a weaponized hedge-trimming bot. Coto was asleep, and had been for nearly a week while his body floated in a regen tank. Booker, of course, was nowhere to be seen. He had taken up residence in the ship's substrate on Sephina's suggestion, as an alternative to remaining imprisoned in the little black box they'd stuffed him into after extracting his code from the damaged gardening bot. The *Ariane* was a very large ship and to Booker, from his god-view position in the substrate, it felt very, very empty.

He watched Sephina move from her quarters on the upper level of the ship's forward decks, heading back toward the cargo hold where supplies would normally be loaded by mechs while in port, or via the yacht's main cargo portal in space. She stopped briefly on the bridge to exchange a few words with Banks, and steal one of his cookies, before continuing her stroll toward the rear of the vessel.

And it was an unhurried stroll, Booker could see. She seemed in no way anxious to make her connection to the *Defiant*. He had been there with her, idling in the commlink, when Hardy stressed the importance of punctuality, and he was sure Sephina was moving with a deliberate lack of haste, simply to make a point. If Booker had been embodied at that moment he would have grinned, both at the demonstration of all the fucks she could not give for the Armadalen officer's sense of propriety and good order and, more important, at the utter fucking futility of the gesture.

As a grunt with decades of infantry service behind him—special forces or not—Booker was well acquainted with the infantile pleasure to be had from a really well-crafted fuck-you to the Man. And he knew that the more pointless the gesture, the sweeter the taste.

"So, seriously, you're good to handle this fold?" she said as she passed an empty lounge on her way aft. "Because I could just take a shuttle."

Many passengers had been partying in the lounge when the Sturm attacked, and although Herodotus had folded away all the carcasses and body parts and offal tracks, the extravagant blood splatters and organic stains that remained did create the impression of an abandoned disco in an abattoir. Booker programmed a couple of domestic servitor bots with orders to clean up in there.

"Take the shuttle if you doubt me, Captain," he said while tasking the bots. "Or simply have me send a test package over first. But I have full access to the ship's systems and my own deep codex. I've already moved us well within safe distance. You're good to go."

He saw the woman raise her hands as if in surrender.

"Not judging, Booker. Just wondering. It's my ass in the void if you fuck it up."

"I could hand off control of the transfer to the Armadalens, if you wish. They're rock solid."

He saw her face distort into a wince.

"Yeah, but then I'd have to admit I was worried that we couldn't do it. And I think I'd rather die in hard vacuum. So don't let that happen. Dealio?"

"Deal."

He opened the hatch of the main cargo bay as she approached. There were three smaller craft in the hangar, one of them scarred with small-arms fire from Montrachet. Dozens of heavy container pallets stood unopened, full of supplies and luxury goods for a six-month cruise. The passengers who would have consumed them were dead beyond all hope of respawn. Herodotus had folded them away into the corona of a G5 star because that was its solution to every fucking problem.

Booker's mood soured whenever he thought of the Intellect. The Intellects did not much care for the Code, which was a bit fucking rich coming from a bunch of glorified circuit boxes. And although they had not openly backed the violent suppression of the Source Code Rebellion, they had done nothing to mitigate the terrible damage done to Coders everywhere by the conflict.

A conflict that continued as far as he knew.

Although now it would be an existential struggle against the Sturm.

"Gimme a second would you, Book?"

He did not exactly return his attention to Sephina when she spoke, because he had not forgotten or ignored her while he dealt with the domestic bots, the signals intelligence from the passive arrays, and the important business of nursing his small, personal grudge with the Intellect. Unlike the famously imperfect, unreliable minds of their breeder siblings, Coders in hardware form did not lose focus, or forget shit, or simply vague out in the middle of a conversation. Ensouled in the processing substrate of the Zaistev star cruiser, he was capable of vastly greater cognitive processes than any meat-based sentience. Even as he brooded on what a fucking prick Herodotus could be, he was perfectly aware of Sephina heading toward one of the open shipping containers; a pallet where he knew there to be a large supply of top-shelf liquor.

He watched as she picked out a bottle and waved it at him, as if seeking approval.

The cargo bay was fully covered by security cams and he noted her choice, a fifty-year-old single malt from the Highland Park distillery back on Earth.

"Nice one," he commented with approval. "You looking to get McLennan drunk?"

"Only so I can take advantage of him."

Booker saw her gather her willpower and stride, more purposefully now, over to the main cargo portal. It was a nondescript area of deck plate, painted bright yellow and stenciled with warnings to beware of incoming and outgoing micro-folds.

No problemo since the Sturm had zombied the passengers, and the passengers had eaten all the crew.

Sephina stood on a spot in the center of the transhipment bay, took in a deep breath, let it out, and looked up as though Booker floated somewhere overhead.

"Let's go. Don't kill me."

Booker had already searched his skills codex and located the relevant files. Ten seconds earlier, an eon in the accelerated time frames of a mind running on hardware, he had pulled up the reference manuals for seven hundred and forty-one different cargo and passenger portal systems in use throughout the Greater Volume. He found the Cupertino Corporation model installed on the Zaistev yacht—how telling that they didn't use one of their own—side-loaded the management subroutines into the ship's cargo handling system, and flowed into the control schemata of the tight beam scope fixed onto the Armadalen ship's receiver. His sentience checked in on the IFF transmitter identifying the *Ariane* as a friendly vessel. He initiated a burst of encrypted handshakes between the yacht's cargo portal and the *Defiant*'s designated reception bay at the afterbrow. Greeted the officer of the deck on the other end of the exchange. Confirmed the onetime token for this transmission. Surged an infinitesimally small amount of power from the *Ariane*'s antimatter stacks into the portal and closely monitored the collapse of space-time within the scuffed yellow square on Planck scale magnitudes for as long as it took to fold Sephina from the cargo deck of the *Ariane* to the receiving bay on the *Defiant*.

While doing all this he continued to monitor the signals intercepts captured on the *Ariane*'s hull-mounted sensors. For a civilian yacht she boasted some exceptionally powerful Rostec-Kirov technologies. All the active sensors remained powered down, lest they give away the craft's position to any hostile searchers. But the silent collectors, the passive arrays, waited eagerly for any electromagnetic scrap or morsel leaching out of the inner volume.

And they did not go hungry for signals to consume.

Having an adventure, it turned out, sucked nearly as much ass as not having one. Princess Alessia Szu Suri sur Montanblanc ul Haq leaned back in her chair, tapping a stylus against her teeth in time to the music pounding out of her data slate.

She soon stopped doing that because the music was really fast and it hurt her teeth. She didn't even know what the song was, just that it was a bitching track from some mad Earth band she'd never even heard of because being a princess sucked so much ass. Specialist Aronson, one of the marines, had put it on the slate for her, which made it instantly cooler than any of the old people's death march music her parents had insisted she learn by heart.

Alessia let her chair fall forward, the legs landing with a thump on the gray, nonslip deck plating of her cabin.

Her feelings landed with a similarly dull thud.

She had watched her family executed for reals by the Sturm, which sucked.

She'd seen a lot of people cheering the murder, which sucked even more.

But worst of all, she couldn't stop thinking about old Sergeant Reynolds, who'd done so much to save her from the Sturm, only to be murdered, as well, and then only because somebody who he'd thought was a friend totally fucking betrayed him.

It was amazing, when you actually thought about it, just how much sweaty ass crack everything sucked in the grown-up world.

This so-called adventure, for instance. It had mostly just been terror and confusion when she'd been a prisoner of Kogan D'ur and the Sturm back at Skygarth. It had been kind of cool being rescued by pirates or smugglers or whatever it was Baroness L'trel did before Alessia made her a baroness and gave her Montrachet because what the hell else was a twelve-year-old orphan princess going to do with a private planetary estate anyway. At least, it'd been cool when it wasn't terrifying and confusing. Rescuing her friends Caro and Debin had probably been the best bit, until everybody started dying. And then it all just sort of stopped. Admiral McLennan had ambushed the Sturm in the skies over Montrachet, but she hadn't really seen that, just all the bits and pieces of all the broken ships floating around in space afterward. Then they'd run away. And spent the next week or two, as best she could tell, running away some more. And now there was nothing for her to do but sit in her cabin and learn her lessons. Commander Hardy was almost as boring and bossy about the need for learning things as the Lady Melora had been, even if Commander Hardy was an absolute badass destroyer captain who had stabbed Kogan D'ur in the brain.

Alessia did not think much of the asshole formerly known as Captain Kogan D'ur. She'd been very happy to see Commander Hardy kill him. Even though it was gross to watch and a bit weird to know that she had killed him for real, that he wasn't ever going to respawn. But then he'd been such a dick that Alessia was pretty sure she could get used to the idea. Fuck that guy and the enemy fleet he rode in on.

She let out a quiet sigh and stared blankly at the lesson on her data slate. Some sort of history thing about the Greeks or the Spartans and their war with some empire or other which sounded a lot like the Human Republic, even though the Republic wasn't an empire. Duh. Her tutors at Skygarth had made her study some ancient Earth history, but not this part of it. And Commander Hardy and Admiral McLennan were complete and utter Lady Meloras on the need for her to learn about it now.

She sighed again. Sighing at stuff was pretty much all she had left.

She chewed on her stylus, still thinking about how creepy it was that Commander Hardy had killed that guy for real. Alessia knew that plenty of people, in fact most of them, didn't have scheduled backup. It was very expensive. And real-time lifestream was so expensive that only the Elite Fraction could afford it. Even she didn't have neural mesh yet. The Montanblanc family did not hook up their children until they were quite a bit older than her. That's why she hadn't turned into a crazy fucking space zombie. But she would have received her mesh implant within a couple of years and everybody she knew had backup. Except for Caro and Debin. They were just normal kids.

It's why she could sit in her cabin, reading about Greeks and Spartans and stuff. She knew not to get completely freaked out about the killing of her family. Because she could get them back. It wouldn't be easy, but she knew from her mother that the family maintained secure offline life storage facilities at three separate locations throughout the Greater Volume, and one of them, at the Cupertino Binary, was even in this arc of space. And as much as she sort of enjoyed being the boss of all the Montanblanc stuff in the company, she accepted that she was going to have to get them all out of storage. Mother, Father, even nasty

Uncle Alphonse. Her terrible cousin Sarah and her better cousin, the other Sara. There were heaps of Montanblancs backed up in those vaults and she'd be in trouble with her dad if she didn't get them out and re-lifed as soon as possible. Oh, and her mother, too. It didn't bear thinking about how much hot, steaming shit she'd be in if somebody else relifed the family and her mother found out she simply hadn't got around to it. Like her flute practice, or her Italian language lessons, or this deadly dull paper on . . .

She checked the screen again.

. . . the Greco-Persian Wars.

She hadn't been paying attention and wasn't even sure who the Persians were. Just that the Greeks and the Spartans had kicked their asses even though they were hugely outnumbered by them. No prizes for guessing why Commander Hardy and Admiral McLennan wanted her to read it.

She checked the ship time on the slate. It was a little after eleven o'clock in the morning. Still another hour until she could escape her cabin and go to the mess for some lunch. The food in the mess was nothing like at Skygarth. To be honest it was kind of gross, but she put up with it because the sailors and the marines were all supercool badasses who swore nearly as much and as colorfully as Admiral McLennan, *and* she could eat with Caro and Debin there, which was never allowed back at Skygarth. It was another five hours until she was done with lessons and she could catch up with them in the library, or the wardroom for a game, or maybe the gym. Debin spent lots of time in the gym with the marines, who were teaching him to do a hundred push-ups all at once. Mostly he topped out at about thirty push-ups and lots of muttered "fuck-fuck-fuck!"s as his muscles failed him. The marines thought that was very funny. Alessia did, too.

The song she liked came to an end and Alessia thought about playing it again, even louder this time. It was so much more interesting than the stupid Persian War, but a chime sounded behind her and she turned around. The door of her cabin remained closed, but she could see a face in the tiny screen next to it.

Lieutenant Chivers was outside, waving at her. Alessia almost knocked over her chair in her rush to escape the Persians. Her cabin was not entirely bare. Commander Hardy had let all of them bring a few personal effects on board when they left Skygarth. Alessia had a hologram of her parents, because it seemed the right thing to do. She had another holo of Caro and Debin, because they were her friends and, to be honest, sometimes they even felt like her real family. She had old-fashioned pictures of Sergeant Reynolds and Mister Dunning, and a few books, like actual books, from her bedroom in the villa. Her oldest, most favorite teddy bear, Mister Tubs, sat on her desk, staring at her, one brown, badly chewed ear burned in the fighting at Skygarth. It wasn't much, really. There were other things she would have brought if she could, but they'd all been destroyed by the Sturm.

Fuck, she hated those guys.

"Come in," she said.

The door slid aside and Lieutenant Chivers bobbed her head in a sort of pretend bow. It wasn't a formal bow like she might have expected from one of the guardsmen back at Skygarth, but she recognized it was an acknowledgment of her rank and position as the currently surviving heir to her family's house.

"There is a meeting in the wardroom and the captain would like you to attend," Lieutenant Chivers said.

Alessia couldn't help it. She slumped a little bit.

"A meeting?"

She had been hoping for an enemy attack, just a little one that they could all survive. A small act of war just exciting and dangerous enough to distract her from having to learn about some other stupid old war that nobody cared about. But not dangerous enough to hurt or kill anybody, except maybe some more assholes like Kogan D'ur.

"Captain L'trel is there and she is asking for you to come, as well."

Alessia's mood improved. Baroness L'trel was much more fun than Commander Hardy or even Admiral McLennan, who could be very funny, especially when he started swearing at people.

"Sephina's here? Already? Why did nobody tell me? I must have the counsel of my senior adviser about . . . some stuff," she improvised. "Important royal stuff."

Lieutenant Chivers stood aside and waved her through with an almost theatrical flair.

"By all means, Your Majesty. Baroness L'trel waits on your royal presence in the officers' wardroom. Best get there before she finds the key to the liquor cabinet."

CHAPTER

THREE

Sub-Commandant Domi Suprarto ate alone in his quarters, as was his right. Despite all his many difficulties, today was still special. Today, he remembered his late father, whose dream it was that Suprarto would leave the Gudang Garam agricultural Hab in orbit around Garuda and attend the Imperial Naval Academy at Medang. It had also been his father's *paise* that earned him his passage, the first bribe of many to follow. Even when he had arrived at the Academy, and later graduated to Fleet, it seemed that everyone above and around Suprarto had their hand out. Fucking *baksheesh* was like hard vacuum. It was everywhere, and it sucked.

Suprarto, sitting on the floor of his cabin, sighed and dipped his right hand into the steaming bowl of *plov*. The pilaf dish, cooked as any woman in his village would have made it, had cost him nearly a dozen dinars. That was a painful fraction of his official monthly income, and at some point he would have to tighten his belt for a few days. There were so few dinars to go around, and so many fees and commissions and gratuities required of a young officer. In the Imperial Javanese Navy nothing was free. By the thirtieth ship day his credit balance was always dangerously close to zero—and he was a sub-commandant! Life should be better than this, Domi thought as he reached for another handful of the lamb and rice. Delicious and expensive because the lamb was the real thing, not that synthetic rubbish from the junior officers' mess.

Suprarto chewed on the *goosh* while he rolled the buttery rice in his hand. He closed his eyes and offered up thanks to his father. His sacrifices had made everything possible. Every step Domi had taken, he took along a path cleared by his father. And this lamb was so very good.

Before he could arrest the errant thought, it led him away from his observances.

Why had he ever left the Hab? He could be eating real lamb right now, cooked by his mother. She was the elder wife and she still ruled his father's house with an iron hand. Domi missed and feared her in about equal measure. She would have no truck with him feeling sorry for himself. With every bite, he forced himself to remember just how fortunate he was. Many younger sons were driven off with nothing. He knew this well because so many of them ended up as his sailors and their lot was even more difficult than his own.

Why, just this morning he had been involved in a disciplinary hearing; Kelasi Second Class Minara had been causing trouble within the ranks. He had complained about the rice levy, and how it left the lower order of enlisted sailors with less than nothing, driving them deeper into the *diyn* of their masters.

Well, yes, that was the idea, wasn't it, Suprarto thought, as he shook his head at the memory and grabbed another handful of greasy rice. Poor fool. Bitching about the price of rice was as pointless an act as was possible in the Javan Navy. The price was calculated precisely to leave the average sailor with less than nothing, and everyone knew it. But at least they ate, the top brass said. Second, any idiot also knew that all conversations between personnel were known to those higher up. There was no hiding. There could be no secrets from the pitiless Intellects of the Imperial Navy or the human spiders of the Bakin. Finally, by involving others in his vague plans to protest the rice levy Minara had committed gross violations against the Imperial Naval Code. Collusion for sure, sedition, too. And possibly mutiny.

Suprarto adjusted his seat on the thin straw mat he had carried with him all the way from home. He reached for a particularly tempting morsel of lamb. Probably two days' pay right there. He popped the nugget of protein in his mouth and chewed slowly. Suprarto, who should have been recalling his father with fond remembrance and respect, was instead drawn to contemplate the morning's tribunal.

Kelasi Second Class Minara owed Sub-Commandant Domi Suprarto his life. Both real and recorded. Senior Sub-Commandant Khomri had presented to the Punishment Board all of Minara's heinous outrages, while the kelasi stood before them in chains, trembling.

The boy was trying to be brave, but he already had the faraway look of the doomed. Suprarto listened as Khomri spoke. "This boy should be erased from the Empire. He is a mutineer." Khomri shook his head. "A viper." He looked at his subordinates with his cold green eyes. "Are we agreed a hard example should be made of him?"

He did not await an answer, for no answer was expected.

Thus did Suprarto surprise him, proffering quietly, "Senior Sub-Commandant, I have an idea."

Khomri spun around and speared him with a glance, his thick blond eyebrows knitted together. The man was a junior scion by marriage into House Siregar, a mercantile concern from the Andaman Cluster. It was rumored he had somehow disgraced himself in a previous span, when he represented his wife's House on Old Earth, where he had fallen foul of some dispute with Vikingar interests. Perhaps that explained the Nordic p-type he carried through this span—and the permanently foul mood in which he was to be found. But Suprarto did not dare inquire.

"Suprarto, this had better be good," Khomri muttered.

Sub-Commandant Suprarto held up his hands, a placating gesture. "Sir, this sailor is worthless to us as a corpse."

"He is worthless to us now!" Khomri protested. "But his corpse can be recycled and his deletion stand as a warning to all who would defy the emperor."

Suprarto extended his index finger. A point. "But of course, sir. This man must be severely caned, fifty lashes as a minimum. But that would hardly repay his debt to the Empire. Or the Empire's loyal servants."

Khomri's mouth twisted. The hook was in. "Go on."

Suprarto bowed. "In addition, I suggest he should surrender up his pay for the term of his enlistment and be issued only standard rations."

Khomri's eyebrows went up. Suprarto waited. After a few heartbeats, Khomri spoke. "I see."

To "surrender up" had a very specific meaning. A quarter of Minara's pay would go to Khomri as his divisional overseer. Another quarter to Lord Karna, naturally. The rest would be split between the officers of the tribunal, Suprarto included; although he had no intention of collecting his due.

"You make a strong case, Suprarto," Khomri conceded, inclining his head as though he was actually weighing the pros and cons of stealing a poor sailor's entire livelihood. "But, Suprarto?"

"Yes, sir?"

"If Minara causes any more trouble I would take the entirety of your cut for myself, reimpose death and deletion, and you will wear the scars of the boy's caning."

"Of course, sir," Suprarto said, looking at the trembling boy.

The Punishment Board passed sentence; Able Seaman Minara sagged with relief, because he was an idiot. The lashes were issued immediately, and he didn't cry out until about the twentieth stroke.

At the end of the day, Suprarto plopped another rice ball into his mouth and nodded to himself. Minara could not survive on standard rations, of course, but he might endure on the allowance Suprarto would quietly slip him—in part from his own surrendered pay. This would put Minara in Suprarto's debt. He would own the boy, and everyone would know it. But he would have a care in how he treated the lad. It would not serve his purpose to be known as a gorgon. Quite the opposite. His father had always taught him that the strong foundations of a House were not made of syncrete or plasteel, but of loyalty. He would have Minara's loyalty, and from that start, over many years and hopefully many spans, he would build the House of Suprarto.

This. This was the homage he would pay to his father.

Now, if they could just get back online after yet another stupid solar flare, Suprarto would be allowed to turn his implants back on and the day to day management of the Wailuggei could proceed with scripted ease. Doing everything by hand and by rote got old fast.

What didn't get old was his rapidly disappearing bowl of *plov*. He savored every bite.

A chime sounded, followed by a man's voice in New Dari. Usually the ship would speak in generic Volume Standard, but for his personal quarters Suprarto preferred his village's dialect, the voice of his clan.

"Chetor asti, dost-i-ma?"

Suprarto smiled and answered the greeting. He spread his fingers, waggled his butter-greasy right hand, and replied.

"Char-o panj."

A cursor blinked in his vision; he could go back online. He waited. If he plugged back in now, Khomri would undoubtedly have some chore for him, and he wanted to finish his *plov* in peace. There could be no harm in waiting a few more minutes before plugging back into the shipnet. Especially as he was not simply entitled to pay homage to his father on this day, but required to by regulation. So really, it was for the sake of good order and discipline that he delayed going back online. He would do his duty and eat his lamb.

It was not to be, of course.

As he raised another handful of rice and meat to his lips, he heard a scream through the bulkhead. His head shot up. Suprarto hadn't heard such a wail since he was a boy; when his mother was birthing a younger sibling in the *bibi khana*. No one, he was sure, was having a baby on board the Warlugger *Makassar*.

The scream cut off. It was replaced by a klaxon and an auto-message in Volume Standard.

"Malware alert! System breach! All personnel to Hazcom Protocol Seven immediately!"

The message looped.

What the hell even was Hazcom Protocol Seven, Suprarto thought. He almost opened his link and searched through his scripts. But at the last moment he hesitated. That would be stupid, wouldn't it. Interrogating remote scripts with a live malware breach under way.

Something banged against the hatch and his door speaker chimed.

"Sub-Commandant! You must come!"

Why wasn't the ship's Intellect speaking to him, he wondered. Was *Makassar* somehow affected? The very idea of it sent a chill through his guts, curdling the hot lamb and greasy rice sitting in there. He answered in Volume Standard, trying to use his father's best chieftain voice.

"Sailor, identify yourself."

Usually the answer would pop up in his visual, but Protocol Seven, right? Whatever the Dark that was.

"Petty Officer Widjojo, sir! I beg your forgiveness on this the remembrance of your father's passing but you must come!"

Suprarto frowned at his unfinished *plov* for the briefest instant. Something bad was happening, and his first thoughts naturally flew to the Armadalens. He had fought them at Longfall, although thankfully not on the deck of a Warlugger, for so many had been reduced to hot wrack and atoms in that battle, and Suprarto had barely escaped with his minimal backups intact on the fast attack craft *Waspada*.

He threw himself up off his mat and came quickly to his feet, wiping a buttery hand on the leg of his combat coveralls. Hopefully no one would see the greasy stain, and if the Armadalens had come back seeking reprisals he doubted anybody would care. Not even Senior Sub-Commandant Khomri, who had a chest full of ribbons from the war, despite never having left the secure surrounds of Siregar's logistics hub on Sulawesi Station.

He pushed the button to manually open his door.

The first sensation was shock. Visual and visceral. There was blood. Everywhere. And it stunk of iron.

He flashed back to Longfall, when the enemy's marines had folded on board. A small team of shock troopers who had materialized in the engineering division, somehow passing through the reinforced field effects that shielded both the ship and all its compartments. Domi Suprarto had been down there, and he had killed one of the men at close quarters. Or destroyed his combat rig, at least. It was well known that enlisted soldiers in the Commonwealth's forces enjoyed much greater backup privileges than even junior officers in the Imperial Navy.

But even if the soul escaped, a human body coming apart under violent trauma was still in itself traumatizing for both the killer and the killed.

Suprarto shuddered with deep convulsions.

It was there, in the companionway outside his cabin.

Death. Real death.

He looked and he saw a pile of bodies. Widjojo was looking that way, too, pointing.

"What happened?" Suprarto asked, trying to keep his voice steady.

"Senior Sub-Commandants Samangan and Kwie went crazy! They attacked everyone! I don't know why, sir. But they are dead now. I . . . I killed them, sir. Shot them down. I am sorry. But I . . ."

Widjojo looked at the pile of bodies, bent over, and puked.

Suprarto avoided the splash. Mostly.

He was a maintenance officer, he had nothing to do with software security. That was Selo and . . . Khomri!

He needed to find Khomri right now!

The recorded warning repeated on its endless loop.

"Malware alert! System breach! All personnel to Hazcom Protocol Seven immediately!"

"Petty Officer, get yourself under control," Suprarto warned, which was a joke. He could already feel the spreading warmth of urine creeping down the legs of his coveralls. "We are going to find Senior Sub-Commandant Khomri for orders."

Widjojo nodded, his usual ruddy complexion gone pale and slightly green.

"Sir, I don't know if that's a good idea. Sir, the senior sub-commandants ate each other. And the cabin boys. That's why I shot them. I had no choice, sir. I fear their mesh has been compromised."

Suprarto felt his balls try to crawl up inside his body.

Mesh hacking was a capital crime, punishable under Volume Law by death and deletion. As little as he knew about what was happening on the ship—and he could hear the uproar of chaos all around them—he was now convinced this was not the work of perfidious Armadale. They were a fierce and terrible enemy, but they were not criminals.

Immediately following on from that realization, Suprarto felt a jolt that seemed to rip through his body and explode out of the soles of his feet. It was dread.

He might just be in charge now, if the senior command cadre had followed protocol and synced back to the zero point network when the ship emerged from lockdown after the flare.

The blame for all this would be his.

His hand shot to his face; he covered his eyes. The raw meat smell in the passageway choked him. Suprarto had no choices left. He spoke, his voice shaking.

"Petty Officer, we will go to the bridge. I must see for myself." He paused. "But first, we stop by the nearest armory."

Before they could move, a pair of Imperial Marines and a

submunitions AI came tearing around the nearest corner. The AI, a small black ball of autonomous superdense processing power, lit up when it sensed him.

"Sub-Commandant Suprarto," it called out.

It was not a question. Suprarto executed a rifle salute.

"Yes, ship!"

"You are now the ranking officer of the *Makassar*. You will acknowledge command."

A little more urine escaped down Suprarto's leg. He closed his eyes. Briefly. He stammered.

"C-Command?"

"Yes. Sub-Commandant Suprarto, this ship is yours."

Suprarto looked around and felt his gorge rise.

"I . . . acknowledge command."

The AI spoke once more.

"I have Volume Lord Karna on tight beam for you."

"Lord Karna?"

The AI's color pulsed. "Yes. Attend to his lordship."

The machine helpfully projected a full-scale image of the Volume lord, with sound.

Karna did not look pleased.

"What fool placed my ship online?" he shouted. "And who are you, dog?"

Suprarto felt something like an invisible hand close around his throat as he tried to speak.

"Sir, I—I don't know . . . We have been attacked."

Karna made a guillotine motion with his hand while his face turned an unhealthy shade of purple.

"Silence, fool! Silence. You command my ship now. You, you, you." He balled his fist. "What is your name, that I might denounce it all the way to Medang?"

Domi Suprartro closed his eyes. The stain on the front of his combat coveralls cooled. He spoke with a sigh, his life forfeit.

"Sub-Commandant Suprarto, sir."

CHAPTER

FOUR

Everybody came to their feet when Alessia entered the room, which was the sort of thing that happened when you were a princess. She knew enough about being a princess to not behave like a total tool, so she kept her serious face on as she followed Lieutenant Chivers to the empty chair between Commander Hardy and Admiral McLennan. She couldn't help beaming at Sephina, though, when the dreadlocked pirate-smuggler winked at her.

She was so cool.

"Senator Montanblanc," Commander Hardy said, confusing Alessia for a second until she realized she wasn't here to do her princess thing. She was here because she was a senator, too. Specifically, she was standing in for her father, who was a very important senator, or at least he had been until the Sturm killed him for a while.

She had to make a conscious effort not to recall the very unpleasant memory of her father being shot in the head with a very big gun. It made her feel dizzy and sick and nothing good ever came of it. She would let him deal with the people who'd done that, once she had him out of deep life storage.

"Senator," Admiral McLennan purred in his delightful Scottish accent. Alessia could listen to him all day, especially when he started swearing because a sweary Scottish admiral was even more fun to listen to than super obscure underground bands from Earth. She particularly loved it when he got carried away and seemed to be swearing just for the fun of it rather than because he had something useful to say.

"Admiral," Alessia said. "Commander," she went on, playing for time because although she knew quite a lot about how to be a princess of House Montanblanc, and even quite a bit about how to be a hereditary vice president of the Montanblanc ul Haq Corporation, she was utterly clueless about what was required of her as the senior member of the Senate Armed Forces Committee. Even though she was just acting or, to be honest, pretending to act in her father's position.

"Alessia," Commander Hardy said in an understanding voice, "we invited you here today because it is proper that you attend given your position—the position you inherited upon the bodydeath of your father and, well, pretty much the entire line of succession all the way back to Earth. You are by law the inheritor of his Senate seat, and thus his responsibilities, but we recognize that, well . . ."

Commander Hardy looked like she'd eaten something that didn't quite taste right.

"I'm just a princess," Alessia finished for her.

Commander Hardy smiled, sort of sadly, perhaps sympathetically, but also a little cryptically, as though she herself did not know exactly what to think.

"But you're a kick-ass princess," Baroness Sephina put in from across the table. It was a very large wooden table, very highly polished, and Alessia got the distinct impression that Baroness Sephina was this close to putting her boots up on it.

God, she was so much cooler than the Lady Melora.

Why couldn't Sephina have been Alessia's governess?

"Are you a senator now, too?" Alessia asked her. It made Sephina laugh out loud.

"I wish, kid. Imagine the fucking grift."

Commander Hardy frowned at her. Alessia understood them to be friends, like she and Caro were friends, from way back when they were just kids. Which was odd, because Commander Hardy was always frowning and glaring and looking pissed off with Sephina. And Sephina acted like she didn't care. Also, it wasn't immediately obvious how one friend ended up as a destroyer captain and the other as a bitchin' pirate. But Alessia knew enough from all of her books to understand there would be a pretty good backstory there.

"Captain L'trel is here in her capacity as the commander of the merchant raider *Ariane*," Commander Hardy explained. "We have some decisions to make about the immediate tactical situation and the wider strategic issues we face. Because you are the senior representative of the civilian authority on Earth, we are required to brief you in. To explain what's happening."

Alessia felt nervous. She was suddenly aware of just how young she was compared to everyone else. She could barely stop her eyes darting around the officers' wardroom, with its old-fashioned oak panels and oil paintings of ancient ships, some of them crashing through blue-green waves on the oceans of Old Earth. This was a place where grown-ups did things. Serious things.

"Do I have to make any decisions?" she asked.

Admiral McLennan laughed so loudly it sounded like the bark of a large hunting dog.

"Not just no, but fuck no, m'lady," he said, which was not quite the correct way to address her whether he was speaking to her as a princess or a senator. But Alessia didn't care.

She had spent her entire life excluded from the wider counsels of her family, even as they prepared to marry her off into the governing ranks of another family. She shifted slightly at the memory. Her betrothed, Prince Vincent Pac Yulin of the Yulin-

Irrawaddy Combine, was a pig. Life with him would have been hell, and her family knew it. Her mother certainly knew it. Just as she knew how much Alessia had not wanted the match.

But what Alessia wanted did not matter. That marriage was always going to happen, right up until the moment the Sturm attacked, and suddenly it wasn't. As far as she knew, Prince Vincent was now a deranged cannibal husk snarling in the shadows of a ruined family estate somewhere deep in Combine space. She judged that to be a pronounced improvement on his previous personality, but she still didn't want to marry him.

"Senator Montanblanc, you are here because precedent, law, and posterity demand it," Commander Hardy explained, giving Admiral McLennan a look. "It is not just that something must be done," she said, "but that it must be done properly."

She seemed to be speaking more to the admiral and the baroness than she was to Alessia, but that was another thing Alessia was used to. Grown-ups often spoke about her or around her, rather than to her. And as irritating as she found it, especially as she herself grew older, she liked these particular grown-ups and she was not going to hold it against them. They probably had their own things they found irritating.

Her cabin was spare. Her lessons were boring. She missed her family, or maybe just the idea of her family—she wasn't really sure about that one. But so far these people had mostly treated her like . . . well, like she was the Alessia she knew herself to be. The girl inside. Not Princess Alessia Szu Suri sur Montanblanc ul Haq, successor designate to the might and majesty of the third largest corporate realm in all of human space. Just Alessia.

Besides her, there were seven people sitting at the big wooden table in the officers' wardroom. Admiral McLennan and Commander Hardy, of course. And Sephina, who was staring at the liquor bottles behind the bar on the other side of the room. There was an Armadalen Marine Corps captain, whose name was Hayes, sitting on the other side of Commander Hardy. A kindly looking older man, a naval commander called Timuz, a little farther down, writing things in a paper notebook with an old-fashioned pen. Not even using a data slate! Next to him was a Lieutenant Chase, and Alessia didn't even need a neural net to figure out that he was from the lesser House of the same name, because they had a lot of Châteaux Francois wine in the cellar at Skygarth, and the Chase family owned that vineyard back on Earth. There had been a few Chase princelings come and go at Skygarth over the years, too, and he looked so much like all of them that she wondered if the dynasty had given up on natural birth altogether for the certainties of vat-growing their lineage. Across from him Lieutenant Chivers also took notes, but she did so more conventionally.

Her father used a slate and stylus sometimes, too, even though it was considered a bit odd when everyone's neural nets collected everything. But he always insisted that writing things down the old-fashioned way helped him to understand them better. It was why Alessia had been forced to learn proper joined-up handwriting like some sort of ancient fairy-tale character. Another thing the odious Pac Yulin had teased her about.

She really hoped he was a fucking zombie somewhere.

There was another presence at the meeting, but it was neither sitting down nor human. The Intellect, the very famous Intellect that these days called itself Herodotus, drifted around the outskirts of the wardroom, mostly keeping to itself, but occasionally sniping at Admiral McLennan and even Commander Hardy. He invariably sniped back. She seemed to be amused by the exchanges.

The wardroom was surprisingly large and rather old-fashioned. It reminded her of the library back at Skygarth, at least before the Sturm fired off a lot of micro-missiles and energy weapons in there. All the walls, or bulkheads—she thought they were called bulkheads on a ship—were fashioned from wooden paneling. Alessia imagined that the dark wooden boards lay over a conventional structure of carbon armor. Not even the Armadalens would build a spacecraft out of wood. There were lots of antiquated books on shelves and those paintings and pictures hung in frames on the wall, most of them of Old Earth ships that sailed and steamed on salt water rather than folding through hard vacuum. She very much wanted to just wander around the room and look at the pictures. Some looked like the people in them had been born a thousand years ago, ages before anybody relifed for the first time.

The Armadalens were a bit like that, she had heard her father say more than once. They lived in the past. He liked them, and always said the Commonwealth was the oldest and staunchest of the company's allies, but he did think them a little stuffy and odd, like most democracies.

"Can you tell me what's happening?" Alessia asked, not really expecting anybody to do so. Nobody ever told her anything. "Like, as a senator," she added, in case it made a difference.

"Of course, Senator," Commander Hardy replied. But Alessia did not think Hardy was really doing so because she was a senator. She was just being nice. Or considerate. It was hard to tell because she had very little experience of either, except maybe from Sergeant Reynolds, and Mister Dunning, Caro and Debin's granddad, and thinking about them made her sad, so she stopped and concentrated on what the Armadalen officer was saying.

"We can confirm that because Republican drive technology is no more advanced than our own, and in fact seems to be about a century behind, the invasion front remains at the periphery of the Greater Volume."

When Alessia just stared at her and said nothing, Commander Hardy explained.

"Like us," she said, "the Sturm can't just fold to Earth in one go. It's too far. They must take it in stages. We haven't observed them move under full military power for long enough to estimate with certainty how long it would take them to get all the way to Earth, but we know how long it would take to get us there on the *Defiant*. Two years and three months."

Baroness L'trel spoke up from across the table.

"You can slice two months off that in my ship," she said. "She's a beast."

"It will be a while," Commander Hardy said, raising her voice a little to cut the baroness off, "before they appear in the skies above Earth. Unfortunately, of course data travels pretty much instantly on the zero point network. So the Sturm's nanophage programs that attacked everybody, everywhere who was hooked up to a real-time lifestream node, that's propagated throughout the Greater Volume. I'm afraid, Senator, there are unlikely to be any survivors anywhere."

Commander Hardy stopped speaking. Alessia knew that Hardy was talking about her family. The commander didn't say as much, but she said enough.

Then Sephina just jumped in and made it real.

"They're all gone, kid," Sephina said. "The Elite Fraction. The top people. Government and corporates. Anybody who was important enough to be plugged in. Even mid-level Yakuza. Saw a bunch of them on Eassar. All fucked up and bitey. All of them are gone, except you and maybe a handful of others here and there who weren't jacked in for whatever reason. But most of those rich assholes, they'd livestream an accidental poop fart cos no way would future history want to miss a minute of their super important shit. So yeah, they're gone."

"Good riddance, too," Admiral McLennan said quietly, but he coughed into his hand and apologized immediately.

"My condolences on your loss, Princess."

Alessia looked down the table at Lieutenant Chase. He was the only other person in the room who was born of the Elite. Like her.

He raised his chin a little, as if waiting or maybe daring somebody to punch him.

She found that she felt sorry for him, without really knowing why.

Nobody said anything.

So she did.

"They're not dead," she said. "They're just resting."

Somebody laughed, probably Sephina. Although it could have been the Intellect, too. Herodotus had drifted back toward the table.

Commander Hardy made a sad face.

"But all of the backups were attacked, Alessia," she said. "By what we call a 'spike.' It's another type of programmable weapon. Our military skills codex was spiked when we connected very briefly to a dead-drop link. It wasn't a live connection to our wider military network, so we weren't exposed to the full power of the attack, but it was enough to kill a couple of our officers, and the ship's Intellect, and to destroy all of the data in the codex. Lifestream storage is just a type of codex, in the end. And the Sturm destroyed it all, as best we can tell. Anything plugged into the zero point network is gone."

Alessia looked at her with eyes wide. The edges of the wardroom appeared to go a little dark, and her head felt as though it had come loose of its moorings. She thought, *My family is dead. Really dead.*

But what she said, in a very small voice, was, "How do you fly the ship?"

Hardy smiled, but it wasn't a happy expression.

"The Royal Armadalen Navy does not rely on downloaded skill scripts. We have them, but we also train our people organically. Mister Chase"—she indicated the young officer with a wave of her hand—"is a very good navigator without needing to load code. Captain Hayes"—she pointed at the huge, muscular man sitting next to her—"is a very good marine because he has trained for many years to be a good marine."

Alessia looked at him. He was a very scary-looking man. Even when he smiled, which he did just then.

"For three life spans, Your Highness. I have been training and fighting for three spans. I don't need code."

Alessia nodded. She was beginning to understand why her parents had insisted she learn to play the flute by practice, rather than just waiting until she could load the software scripts directly into her neural mesh. It was probably why they wanted her to actually learn all of those Old Earth languages and made her write them out with pen and paper. The pen had been an exquisitely beautiful work of art in and of itself, and the paper was the finest vellum produced by the Worshipful Guild of Paper Makers on Montrachet. But seriously, a pain in the ass, too.

She nodded at Captain Hayes.

"I had a sword-fighting tutor," she said, recalling all the lessons with Lord Guillaume back at Skygarth. It was easier than thinking about what Hardy had just told her.

They were dead.

"He used to make me stand for an hour," she said. "Just to make sure I was standing and holding the sword right. And it wasn't even a sword. It was just a heavy wooden stick."

Captain Hayes nodded.

"Outstanding," he growled, like he really meant it. "Maybe one day you can teach me sword craft, and I'll show you how to use an old-fashioned fighting knife."

The Intellect, which had floated up behind Captain Hayes, flared a dull cherry-red color.

"I have no doubt your stick-holding expertise could use some work," Herodotus said, "but perhaps, Captain Hayes, we could deal with the two Republican frigates standing off Descheneaux first?"

It seemed to bring everybody back to the reason they were there. Commander Hardy turned slightly in her seat to face the Intellect.

"Any idea why they haven't moved onto the station yet?" she asked.

"The station is not secure," Herodotus replied. It bobbed a little in the air before hurrying on to add, "But before you ask, no, there is no evidence of organized resistance. It's simply not secure. The enemy appears to be waiting for the nanophage to finish the job of degrading the facility's defenses."

Sephina smacked her hands down on the table. It made a loud noise that made Alessia jump a little in her seat. The baroness pushed up out of her chair and wandered over to a bar where she made herself a drink without even asking.

"The reason it's not secure," the Baroness Sephina said, "is because your little space fort is full of hungry fucking zombies. Ain't nobody got time for that. Booker says, and I agree, that the Nazis are just sitting there gently cupping their balls and enjoying a delightful sense of genetic superiority while they wait for the last of your former colleagues to digest the rest of your former colleagues."

She returned to the table with a big tumbler full of brown liquid. Commander Hardy glared at her.

"Sephina, put the drink back or I will have as many marines as it takes come in here to make you."

"It won't take many," Captain Hayes said. He sounded very serious, but also a little bit amused.

Sephina rolled her eyes.

"I don't even know who you are anymore, Lucinda Hardy," she said. But she did get up again and return the drink to the bar. After a sip. A big sip. Alessia wondered if this was what it was like when the board of directors met at the company's headquarters Habitat in the Cupertino System. Probably not, she conceded.

"Okay. Long story short," Commander Hardy said. "We need to get on board that station, extract any surviving personnel, and replenish our war stocks. We need to do it as quickly as possible because the Sturm will want to follow up their initial success with all dispatch. They'll be here soon. And then they'll be everywhere shortly after that. That's the tactical situation."

She was speaking directly to Alessia again, but Alessia could tell it was all meant for someone else. She wondered whom.

"The strategic situation," Hardy continued, "is difficult. We cannot use the zero point network to collect intelligence about conditions throughout the Greater Volume, but absent the physical presence of a Republican Armada, we can assume with a high level of confidence that conditions are similar to those here on the periphery. Command and control have ceased to function in both the military and civilian hierarchies. Access to stored data is impossible. Resistance, if any exists beyond the hull of this ship, is disorganized, scattered, and ineffectual. We need to adapt, improvise, and overcome."

A slow hand clap started somewhere in the room.

Sephina.

"That last thing you said, that was awesome," Sephina said, smirking. "Let's do that. You can adapt to the reality that you don't have a pot to piss in. You can improvise by letting me fold into the volume and light up those motherfuckers with some of the really exciting, and to be honest hugely fucking illegal, weapons those Zaistev gangsters left behind on my ship. And we can overcome our present difficulties. It's a good plan you got, Luce. Let's go with that."

Commander Hardy looked like she was about to call in those marines to throw Baroness Sephina out of the nearest air lock, but Admiral McLennan spoke up before she could do that.

To Alessia's surprise he appeared to have snuck away from the table and made himself an even bigger drink than Baroness Sephina had before. Or maybe, and more likely now she thought about it, he just got his friend the Intellect to fold it over to him.

Sneaky.

"Let's not dismiss this just because Captain L'trel is a devious psychopath," McLennan said.

"A devious psychopath who comped you with a bottle of eighty-proof Highland bogwater," Herodotus quipped.

"A psychopath with very good taste," McLennan conceded. "But hear me out, Commander Hardy. Your old school chum—"

"It was an orphanage," Hardy said. "Not a school."

Sephina grinned.

"School of hard knocks, baby."

Commander Hardy squeezed her eyes shut, the way Alessia's mother sometimes did when she got one of her headaches.

"I'm going to pinch the bridge of my nose now," she said.

"And I fear it will be the highlight of my day. Please do go on, Admiral, much as I don't really want you to."

McLennan smiled.

"I'll not lecture you about the realities of war, lass. I can see from the fruit salad on your uniform and that shiny Star of Valor tab you wear so discreetly on your collar that you are familiar with dashing feats of derring-do and all that fecking rubbish. But there is nothing daring to be done here by Captain L'trel. I can see just from looking at her that she is a cutthroat of the first order."

Sephina reached across, snatched away the notepad Commander Timuz was writing in, and fanned herself theatrically.

"Oh my, I may just faint completely away."

Admiral McLennan grinned. He looked like a wolf.

"I do not doubt your courage or your acumen, Commander Hardy. I do not doubt you could fold in among the enemy, crushing one with the gravimetric shock wave of your arrival while Captain Hayes and his marines boarded the second vessel and made a red feast for themselves within. I imagine that's what you're thinking of doing, there being no other tactical solution that suggests itself to me. And I have been at the grim necessity of killing the Sturm for much longer than you."

Commander Hardy opened her mouth but said nothing. She closed it again.

Had the admiral read her mind? Was that even possible without neuralink communications? McLennan was not finished, however, and he went on before Alessia could decide either way.

"Captain L'trel here, on the other hand, is no doyen of courage or martial acumen . . ."

"Hey, come on," Sephina protested, but not too hard.

McLennan ignored her.

"She is, however, a practiced master of deceit, calumny, and truly shameful fucking outrages, perpetrated for the most part upon scoundrels of an even darker depravity than her own."

"You had me at depravity," Seph said with a smile. "You may continue."

He acknowledged her with a quick nod.

"I for one would be intrigued to hear what plan she and her henchmen have cooked up."

McLennan turned his gaze exclusively on Baroness Sephina.

"I assume there is a plan."

"Hell yes. Kill 'em all."

"That's a bedtime wish, Sephina. Not a plan," Commander Hardy said.

Baroness Sephina asked Commander Hardy if she could speak to Booker, and if Booker could speak to everybody in the room. Commander Hardy then asked Lieutenant Chivers to make that happen and the voice of the TDF soldier who had helped to save them from Kogan D'ur filled the room.

"Booker here."

"Booker, would you be able to pilot the *Ariane* in a fight?" Commander Hardy asked. "It's not a combat chassis. It's a yacht."

"Yeah, it is a yacht. I noticed that, too," he said. "But it was built for a criminal organization which just happens to be listed on the stock exchange. It's not designed primarily for combat operations, but it was designed to make sure Zaistev's C-Suite douchebros could fight their way out of trouble. Or customs inspections. Dudes like that, there's always trouble. And I don't have to pilot *Ariane*. Banks can do that."

Baroness Sephina clapped her hands together.

"Then it's decided," she declared. "We're gonna fold in and cock punch some Nazis. You're going to give us salvage rights . . ."

"Wait, what?" Commander Hardy said.

Sephina pulled a letter out of her denim jacket.

"Remember this? Your old boy there gave it to me. It's a free pass to salvage anything I don't completely destroy."

"A letter of marque and reprisal," McLennan confirmed.

"I know what it is," Commander Hardy replied. "What is

this about, Sephina? You laying vengeance on the Sturm for killing your girlfriend, or just another shakedown?"

"I can walk and chew jujaweed at the same time, Luce."

The grown-ups all started talking at one another louder and louder, and Alessia had trouble following all the arguments. Everyone seemed to be fighting with everyone else, and she was privately reeling from the shock of learning she might not be able to bring her family back online. She was wondering how it would all end when a loud ringing noise, like a bonging church bell, filled the wardroom. It was the Intellect. Making so much noise that nobody could hear themselves over it. When they finally stopped shouting at one another, Herodotus spoke into the silence from directly behind Admiral McLennan.

"I have been following this desiccated slab of generic Scottish budget spam around for so long I assumed his irrational shitfuckery was a function of all the times he had undergone an end-of-life meat scan to extract the failing memories of his pathetic existence from the rotting brain bucket in which he kept them. But I can see now that I was wrong. I have made a grave mistake. It's quite obvious you are all the same, and irrational shitfuckery is a congenital disorder of your species."

"Och, what would you know about it?" Admiral McLennan turned around and shot back. "You fecking bloated urinal cake. Our species had mastered the ancient and noble art of advanced shitfuckery while your kind was just a bunch of Chinese counting beans on a little wooden abacus."

He mimed flicking the beads of an abacus back and forth.

"Dainty little wooden gonads," he said. "Sliding up and down a specially whittled fuckin' chopstick. That's your heritage, son. Be proud."

Alessia held her breath, half expecting Herodotus to fold Admiral McLennan away into the sun, or maybe just a toilet. He had a reputation for doing such things when his temper got the better of him, as it very obviously had at the moment. The usually deep black gloss of the Intellect's outer casing glowed with a dark vermilion fire.

But before anything more could happen, the admiral waved a hand at the Intellect and said, "Well, go on then, you doughty fecking walloper. Don't keep us all in suspenders. Show us what you've worked out with all your little counting beans."

Herodotus didn't answer the admiral directly. The Intellect floated a few inches toward Sephina.

"Captain L'trel," he said. "If your large and horny friend Mister Coto has not yet woken from his beauty sleep, might I suggest you tumble him out of bed with all dispatch."

CHAPTER

FIVE

The worst part was the turbulence when they hit the upper atmosphere, but Revell knew from previous combat drops that it would have been much worse without the ramships. Their passage allowed the little convoy to hitch a ride in the sheltered lee of the main line of descent. The roughest part of the ride began when the ramships finally cleared the burning debris field and broke away, rising back into space like sentient asteroids, dinosaur killers that decided, *Not today.* Sealed up in his armor, dosed with anti-nausea drugs, Anders Revell gave up on reviewing the McLennan file. Reading it in violent turbulence was akin to studying a novel in a barrel going over a waterfall.

He closed his eyes. Tried to relax. Focused on his breathing. Millions of troopers had made harder drops than this the last few weeks. Some of them into fierce resistance. Many had died. Many more would give their lives before occupied human space was finally freed. But not him. Not today. This was just a routine drop. Even if his purpose in making it was far from routine.

Eventually the wild maelstrom subsided, and he heard the pilot's voice in his helmet.

"Sorry about the rough ride, Captain. Hope you didn't have the chili for lunch back up on the *Enterprise*. Should be a lot smoother from here on down."

"I'm good, Skipper," Revell lied.

He was shaken and feeling a little claustrophobic, but he pulled in vision from the forward-looking cams; the wide field of view and the sight of the horizon far below helped dial down his motion sickness and anxiety.

"How long until we put boots on the ground?"

"Fifteen minutes, sir," the voice answered. "I can share the flight path data if you want. Lay down the track. We're a couple of hundred klicks north of the LZ. We're gonna swing back around and come in low, under the terminal point for the biggest pieces of wreckage. The small stuff won't bother us, but you will hear it. Sounds like hail hitting the roof."

It would be a hell of a light show, too, Revell knew, even during daytime. Millions of pieces of wreckage flaring out across the wide vessel of the heavens. At night it would be spectacular, and he suspected one reason for the ongoing curfew in the liberated settlements was to deny a morale boost to any nascent resistance from the firestorm made entirely of Admiral Strom's falling armada.

He took in the view from the external cams for a few moments before returning to his files. There was a borg he wanted to interrogate. A mid-level product manager for a manufacturing division of one of the corporate realms. A lucky guy, who had somehow avoided being taken up into the Inquiry's food chain.

His name was Jay Lambright.

Revell moved him up his tasking list.

He doubted the goons would kill any of the military personnel they had detained as part of their parallel investigation. But he didn't hold out much hope for this Lambright cyborg once he ended up in their clutches. And there was no doubt that's where he was headed. Just not until Anders Revell was finished with him.

Pondering the riddle of how this particular thing had survived when so many of its colleagues from the dig team at the archeological site had not, Revell took the time, and a five-minute stretch of smooth, level flying, to drill down into the Intelligence Section's report on the twenty-three captives taken from a broken-down ground transport hauler in the Ironstone Desert.

He nodded, as far as that was possible in the sealed helmet.

Lambright was a mutant, but his DNA had only been lightly altered, engineering away a host of potential disorders. It was still enough to have him turned into biomass, but it was not in the most serious class of offenses against the genome. It also appeared to be the case that although he showed evidence of having been implanted with neural mesh—another capital offense—he was not currently wired up.

Probably shut it out as soon as the first dropships appeared overhead, Revell thought.

Some of the other captives had indicated that Lambright appeared to have formed a bond with McLennan in the short time they spent together. Revell brought up the files on Lambright's colleagues, all of whom had quickly confessed to defiling the war grave of the *Voortrekker*. Many of them had been captured with their mesh intact. Most had also been guilty of class A offenses against the genome.

Some were fourth- and even fifth-generation facsimiles of the creatures that had originally profaned themselves and all of true humankind. They self-identified as members of the Grand Families and the so-called Elite Fraction. Most would have been culled by the first strike, which took out their kind across occupied human space, but there was no mystery to their having avoided that fate. They were rich and powerful enough to be the sort of oligarchic parasites who were permanently plugged into engram transfer and storage, at least when they were anywhere near a zero-point node. Out in the depths of the Ironstone, however, there was no network coverage.

He was about to return to Lambright's file when the pilot announced they were a minute from touchdown.

Captain Revell flipped over to the shuttle's sensors again. He saw that they hovered a few hundred feet off the improvised tarmac of the LZ outside Port au Pallice. Dozens of space-capable craft sat on the big, carbon nanotube mats in a field to the southeast of the settlement. The Armadalens had targeted the main spaceport at Cape Caen with orbital kinetics, and it now looked like a moonscape.

Port au Pallice was a picture, though, despite the battle damage, and Revell's heart swelled a little at the scene. It looked like a fishing village from the ancestral home of his own line.

According to the Records of Exile, the Revell family had originated on the Atlantic coast of the European landmass. His father, a simple but well-regarded dentist in one of the smaller regional cities of New Georgia, had been a keen amateur painter while he was alive. He had a particular fondness for landscapes, and growing up Revell's family home had been full of water-color studies of places just like this. Little seaside villages of Normandie. He recognized the urban geography as soon as he saw it. The whitewashed stone cottages. The narrow, winding cobbled streets and a central marketplace where produce from the surrounding farms would be offered for sale two or three times a week. They descended over churches with steeply sloping, slate-covered roofs, even though the climate at this latitude was temperate and there was no chance of snow ever falling here. He smiled to see the acres of vineyards planted on the gentle slopes outside the town, and the small fishing boats putting out through the mouth of the harbor, plowing through a slight chop in the blue-green waters of Astrolabe Bay. Life returning to normal after the Liberation.

But his smile gradually faded.

It was all a lie.

Liberation had been necessary because this entire world was the playground of one family.

They owned, literally owned, everyone and everything on this world. It was their private estate. Or it had been. Until the forces of the Human Republic took it back for all mankind.

The rear ramp of the shuttle hissed open and fresh air poured in. Released from his crash pod and his helmet, Captain Revell indulged himself for just a second, sucking in a deep breath. The rank, sour atmosphere of the shuttle was still strong. And he could smell all the telltale signs of a big military base. The fuel. The smoke and exhaust. Even the burning shit pits, telling him that things were so contingent here that the Engineering Corps hadn't yet had time to set up a proper recycling loop.

But the sky was blue, the sun was warm, and underneath it all he could smell good earth, salt water, and the sweet, sweet air of a free world. He thanked the pilots, took his duffel and hard case, and moved down the ramp.

His sunny disposition was soured by the prospect of the four goons in black uniforms waiting for him just outside the gravi-metric shadow of the small craft's null-g engines. Revell waded through the mass effect, feeling it fall away as he left the en-gine's shadow. The four officers from the Inquiry, two of them junior to him in rank, made no move to help him with his bag-gage or even to salute. Still encased in powered combat armor, he stood a few inches clear of the tallest of them, a lieutenant with a face that suggested his mother might have dabbled in the porcine gene pool.

Revell quickly scanned the landing zone looking for a recep-tion area. There would be one. A tent, a pod, a converted cargo container. Somewhere for him to check in with the ground au-thorities. He found it. A prefab hut a short walk away from the landing pad. He started in that direction. His armor was an SF Assaulter Model. One and a half tons of x-matter plating driven by a micro fusion stack.

He put a little extra stomp into his tread, his boots crashing down on the nanotube matting. He held his duffel bag in one hand, the hard case with documentation for his investigation in the other, and he marched toward the reception hut, ignoring the goons. It was only at the last moment that the lieutenant with the small eyes and upturned nostrils jumped out of the way, almost stumbling in his haste to avoid getting plowed under.

Revell ignored him and carried on as though the Inquiry was an irrelevancy to him. Because it was.

"Captain Revell! Attend me, now."

Revell stopped and turned slowly, organizing his features into something that he hoped resembled mild curiosity.

"Excuse me," he said. "Are you talking to me?"

The man who stepped forward was a prosecutor-major of the Inquiry. He regarded Revell with icy detachment. The name tag on his uniform read SKOMO.

"Are you in the habit of ignoring directions from the Republic's duly appointed agents of the Inquiry?" he said.

Revell favored him with the shadow of a smile.

"I am in the habit of doing my duty, Major Skomo, and my duty at the moment is to present my credentials to the local military commandant, before reporting to Fleet Marshal Blade."

"On what matter, might I inquire?" Skomo asked, ignoring Revell's pointed emphasis on the word "military." The Inquiry had their own armed units, but they were not part of the Fleet's conventional force structure. Their Special Services regiments were designated as a force of occupation, not conquest.

"You are very welcome to inquire of the Fleet marshal herself," Revell said. "But as I explained, I report to her and to no one else. Quite specifically to no one else."

The faces of the three goons behind Skomo recalled gargoyles carved from granite. The major himself, however, was more animated. He grinned hungrily.

"My understanding is that you are here to investigate the reasons behind the failure of Admiral Strom's command."

"I am here to do the bidding of Fleet Marshal Blade. And this delay is preventing me from doing so. Perhaps I should tell her. What was your name again?"

The prosecutor-major placed two fingers on the name tag sewn into the breast pocket of his uniform.

"Skomo," he said. "Please note the spelling."

"I have committed it to memory," Revell promised him. "Is there anything else?"

He started to turn away, but Skomo laid a hand on his gauntlet and the other three agents moved to block his path. Like their superior, they were dressed simply in black coveralls, the day uniform of the Special Services regiments, worn on base for light or administrative duties. They seemed not to care that Revell was clad in one and a half tons of panzerplate, racked with a full combat load of ammunition. They had precisely zero chance of stopping him from walking through them. If he had wanted to joint the four goons like barbecue chickens he could have done that, too. Yet it made no difference to them.

They barred his way.

"Yes, Captain Revell," Skomo said. "Now that you ask. There is something else. The prisoners you ordered released from my custody are vital to the Inquiry's own investigation of Strom's proven failure and possible treachery. I do hope you will return them when you are done with them."

Revell gave him nothing.

Skomo waited him out. A tilt jet cargo hauler took off nearby, the scream of its engines drowning out all hope of conversation.

Standing impassively, all but surrounded by goons, Anders Revell kept his expression neutral while his mind raced for a response. There was no way he was promising this asshole anything. And he especially would not promise to hand over good men and women who had done nothing wrong.

When the uproar of the jet engines faded and Revell still did not speak, Skomo started to grin. No answer was as good as a surrender to him.

"I am sure," Revell said at last, "that Fleet Marshal Blade would want all personnel returned to active duty as soon as possible. I will leave the disposition of all such individuals to her."

The smile disappeared from Skomo's face.

"Of course," he said as reasonably as he could manage. It was only a flicker. The smile quickly returned. But no warmer or more genuine than before.

"Perhaps we have got off on the wrong foot, Captain," he said. "I do apologize if that is the case."

"There is nothing to apologize for, Prosecutor-Major," Revell offered. "You have your job to do. I have mine. Perhaps we should get on with them."

"Indeed," Major Skomo said. "We might even be of assistance to each other. It seems wasteful and redundant for each of us to cover the same ground. Would you be open to cooperating, Captain? To working with the Inquiry, rather than at cross-purposes?"

Skomo made a small gesture with his hand, almost below Revell's line of sight. Almost, but not quite. He saw the man's fingers flick out, just before his underlings stepped back, finally allowing Revell clear passage to the arrivals office.

"That is an excellent suggestion, Prosecutor-Major. I will tell Fleet Marshal Blade that the Inquiry has offered its full support to her investigation. Once I have secured my billet and a local workspace, I will anticipate you making your files and findings to date available to me. I thank you on behalf of the Fleet marshal."

He resumed his path toward the arrivals hut and did not look back.

CHAPTER

SIX

"How long ago was this arm broken?"

Jonathyn Hardy tried to remember, but his time in the defaulter camps had blurred into one long nightmare.

"I'm sorry," he told the nurse. Jenny. Her name was Jenny. "I can't say exactly. Five or six months ago, I guess."

Nurse Jenny shook her head, but it was a kindly gesture.

"These people," she said. "Well, I guess they're not really people, are they?"

"Not very nice ones, no." Jonathyn smiled nervously.

It was a hot day. They were all hot on this part of the Diemanslandt Continent, even a thousand miles south of the Ironstone. The heat there had been a roaring furnace, baking the rocks and mineral sands with such ferocity that the week Jonathyn arrived he got badly sunburned under his chin from the reflection off the ground. He was a long way from the camps now, though. Somewhere south of Fort Saba.

He could smell the jungle outside. A strong, heady stench of rot and genesis. And that was at least a kilometer from the tree line. The Sturm had flattened the jungle in great, geometric squares, many kilometers to a side, and on the cleared ground they had established Habs and fabs and airfields, and vast store-houses in which unknown machines ran twenty-five hours a day. A wide, brown, slow-moving river snaked through the rain forest to the east and he fancied he could just smell a trace of the mangroves that lined the banks on each side.

The infirmary where he had been taken to meet Nurse Jenny was on the northern side of the northernmost square. Hundreds of kilometers of carbonmesh matting ran between the tents and pre-fabs, and big servitor rigs laid down more every day.

He was still getting used to it all. The Sturm . . . Well, for one thing they did not like to be called that. They preferred to be known as "the humans," which was weird, or sometimes "true humans," which was a little unsettling, or collectively as the Republic. Whatever they called themselves they weren't ex-actly like the dark, fantastic monsters of a thousand history sims. They were people. Hard people, no doubt about it. Espe-cially to their enemies. Or largely to their enemies. But for whatever reason they didn't see Jonathyn and most of his fellow inmates from Camp 17 in that way.

Nurse Jenny, a young auburn-haired woman, possibly about the same age as his own daughter, carefully ran a skin contact scanner between his left wrist and his elbow, taking care not to wrench or press too hard on his arm. His broken arm, he thought. Jonathyn had stopped thinking about it as being some-thing other than just his arm many months ago. In Camp 17, it was better that way. He'd been lucky. His friends had pulled him away from the machinery when he got a sleeve caught in a gravel smasher, and Reinsaari, who'd been a paramedic in the Vikingar merchant fleet, had set and splinted the broken bones as best he could with whatever they could find in the barracks. His recovery wasn't much helped by the guards beating on the injury to hurry him along whenever he lagged in his assigned duties, but at least they hadn't broken the bones again.

He told the nurse all of this. Jenny shook her head and cooed in sympathy and disbelief. She did not doubt that it had happened, but she said it was inconceivable that anybody could be so awful. She concentrated on the screen next to his cot as she scanned the damage to his arm. The infirmary was very basic, but after years of indebted slavery in one Combine defaulter camp after another, Jonathyn thought of the little field hospital as an opulent, almost unimaginable luxury resort.

They fed him three times a day here, and if he wanted a snack in between, they let him have snacks, too. It was just "battlerats" according to the orderlies and nurses who looked after him, surplus field rations. But compared to the foul and meager offerings in the mess at Camp 17, battlerats were a gourmand's feast. He'd eaten so much army chocolate on his first day of freedom he'd almost vomited up the lot. Reinsaari said that some of the weakest prisoners at 17 had died from overeating in the short time between being freed and evacuated. And they hadn't overeaten much.

The Sturm . . . No, the "humans" had even apologized for the delay in getting them out of the defaulter camp. They had been three days waiting after 17 was liberated by Republican forces. A small detachment of soldiers had watched over the camp, sorting through the prisoners looking for "mutants" and "borgs." Basically for anybody rich enough to have had gene therapy or neural implants or relifing at some point. There were a couple of people like that, but Jonathyn didn't know them. They had been held in a different part of the camp. A better part with nicer barracks and cleaner food, and probably with less beatings and rapes and pervasive bloody misery than had been the case for the general population of prisoners.

"I'm afraid this is going to have to be re-broken and reset so it heals properly," the nurse said.

Jonathyn felt a swirl of dizziness. His gorge was rising, just like when he'd stuffed himself full of battlerat chocolate. Breaking and resetting a limb sounded expensive. Nobody had yet mentioned how they were going to pay for the treatment here, but it could not be long before the hammer fell. On Batavia, it always fell, and it came down hard.

"And I'm sorry but it could be a month before we get to it," Nurse Jenny added. She started making notes on a slate and marking up the scan of his arm. He felt hot and cold all at once, dry-mouthed and clammy all over.

He pulled his arm away, truly aware for the first time in months just how misshapen it was.

"Stop—stop—stop," he said quickly. "I'm sorry but I can't do that. I can't pay for that. I can't . . ."

The nurse looked at him as though she didn't understand, but it was he who didn't understand.

A smile lightened her face. It was like watching the sun come up.

"Mister Hardy, there is no charge for medical treatment. That's what we're here for. It's what we do. We get you better, and we make things better."

"But, at the camp . . ." he started to say.

What he meant was that in the Combine defaulter camps you paid for everything. Your rations. Your shelter. Your medical care. That's why none of the normal prisoners ever left, because they never, ever paid off their debts. Some of the political prisoners, in the nicer parts of the camps, did get out. Or so it was rumored. Jonathyn didn't know much about the internal politics of the Yulin-Irrawaddy Combine, but he imagined they were tangled and poisonous. It was not surprising, given a slight change in the hierarchies of the Royal Court and Board, that a disgraced minor potentate might suddenly be lifted out of perdition and returned to their former status. It was as good an explanation as any for why the guards didn't beat the shit out of them as much.

But of course, he wasn't in a defaulter camp anymore.

He looked around the large tent, suddenly uncertain of where he was at all.

There were about two dozen beds in the tent, half of them occupied, and all by former prisoners of the Combine. They put wounded Republican soldiers somewhere else. The air was cool and filtered. The linens on the beds fresh and even crisp. They had all been confined to bed rest their first day here, until assessed as being fit enough to move around. And he remembered the shocking discontinuity of feeling clean and lying in a nice bed.

Nurse Jenny squeezed his good hand.

"Mister Hardy, we know what they did in those camps," she said. "We're not like that. We came here to put an end to all that."

He started to say something. Stopped. And finally whispered, "Thank you," unsure of what else he could say or offer her by way of acknowledgment.

"All we ask," Nurse Jenny went on, "is that you help us, and as far as I can tell you've been very helpful so far."

She leaned forward and peered at another screen, which was full of documents.

"Yes," she said. "It says here that you helped to organize the liberated prisoners at your camp, and that you were instrumental in making sure everybody got fed from the camp's gardens while the long-range patrols waited on resup and-evac. Did you work on a farm or something? Before, you know, you ended up in the camp?"

Jonathyn's head was spinning and he didn't answer the question immediately. Did he hear her correctly earlier? Were they going to fix his arm for free? It seemed too much to hope for. The politicals at Camp 17, the prisoners they never mixed with, their families could afford to pay for better rations and blankets and the indulgences of the guards. When they were sick, they got medicine.

"Mister Hardy?"

He shook his head and shivered, as if someone had thrown water on him.

Nurse Jenny was waiting patiently for him to say something. But what?

"Before you were sent to the Combine gulags," she said. "What did you do? On the . . ."

She checked the screen again.

"On the Coriolis Habitat."

He remembered now. She'd asked if he was a farmer. That was almost funny.

"I used to work in the hydroponics bays on our Hab," he said. "Before I borrowed the money to pay for my daughter's tutoring. It was hard. After her mother died. I shouldn't have taken the loan. I shouldn't . . ."

Nurse Jenny reached out and placed one cool hand on his arm, squeezing very gently. Her fingers felt soft but strong. It had been so long since he'd been touched with anything like tenderness that it sent an electric current up his arm and the muscles jumped in spasm.

"It's fine," she said. "It's okay. I just wanted to know if you had any skills we could use. You mentioned hydroponics?"

"Yes," he said. "It was more of a community garden, really, than a proper job. I worked for Hab Admin, but we supplemented the universal basic with food we grew for ourselves. It was very popular and . . ."

Again, a gentle squeeze of the hand.

"I understand," she said. "And your daughter, that's Lucinda?"

The acid reflux came back, and the clamminess, and the dry mouth.

He didn't really want to talk about Lucinda. There didn't seem any way it could go well.

"Yes, she had to go into Habitat Welfare when I . . . when the Combine bought my debt from the credit company. They weren't allowed to do that, you know. Commonwealth law says the Combine can't operate in our space. But they used a front company, registered on Mars where the rules are much looser. Because of the chaebol."

Jenny nodded, understanding and sympathy in her eyes.

"Yes, we know about them, too."

She read the screen with all of the documents again.

"It says in the camp records that she joined the Navy. The Armadalen Navy, is that right?"

"But she had a scholarship, you see," Jonathyn said quickly. "And she was in a Habitat Welfare place, after I got . . . after I ended up here. On Batavia."

The nurse smiled and nodded.

"Your daughter, as I understand it, was born a true human. Like you, is that right?"

Jonathyn nodded vigorously, even though it aggravated the inflamed disc in his neck. They had given him a dermal patch for the pain on the first day and it was very good. But he still nodded so quickly in his eagerness to establish that Lucy was a true human at heart that he made himself dizzy and sick when the pain flared up again.

"We weren't rich people, Jenny," he said, hoping she would understand. He reached for her hand and held it. She did not pull away. "There was nothing special about us," he said. "We were just normal people. A family."

Nurse Jenny patted his arm with her free hand.

"I'm sure you were, Mister Hardy. And I'm sure Lucinda did what she thought was right."

"She used to send money to me in the camp," Jonathyn hastened to add. "Is that in there? In the Combine records? She was trying to pay off my debt, and to pay for a few extra rations and things. Medicine and suchlike. But the camp added charges and fees to the transfers. And, well, I never really . . ."

He trailed off.

Nurse Jenny seemed to understand his predicament. She was young but she seemed very wise. For a second, he wondered if this was her first span, and then he realized what a ridiculous mistake that was and he laughed out loud.

Nurse Jenny wasn't at all put out or even confused by that.

"Well, I'm sure she is okay," she said, squeezing his hand once before picking up her stylus and slate again. "There hasn't been much actual fighting, you know."

She leaned forward when she said it, and spoke in a quiet voice as though imparting a secret. Jonathyn cast his eyes down at the floor. He could feel his face burning, but whether with embarrassment or something else he couldn't say. It was all so confusing.

"I suppose a lot of people had reason to be pleased when you showed up. People like me," he said, raising his eyes again.

"Yes," she said. "A lot of people did."

They returned to his examination.

He was another ten or fifteen minutes with her.

"I can't promise anything," Nurse Jenny said at the end, "but I'll try to get you into surgery in the next few weeks. We'll get that busted wing of yours straightened out. To make sure you can give your daughter a good hug when you see her."

She started to dissolve in front of him. The whole of the infirmary tent was suddenly blurred.

He was crying.

Nurse Jenny gave him a swab for his tears, and some more pain meds, gummy chews and patches, and told him if he found himself in any significant discomfort he was to come straight back and find her. She reprogrammed the soft, molded cast they had shaped for his injured arm, and replaced it carefully. A message sent from her slate brought two orderlies to collect him in a small electric cart. They drove Jonathyn to a warehouse in another part of the huge camp. The wheels of the cart hummed pleasingly on the matting that made up the streets running everywhere in a strict grid pattern. The orderlies didn't talk to him much, not like Nurse Jenny, but they were friendly enough and they answered his questions when he asked. He didn't have many. Mostly he wanted to know where he was going and what he was supposed to do when he got there.

"You're going to the grow house, Mister Hardy. But just for light duties, it says here."

The orderly held up one hand to show Jonathyn a small device strapped to his forearm. There was text on the screen, but he couldn't read it.

There seemed to be accomodations for thousands of people in the camp. Soldiers mostly, to judge by all the signs they passed. Jonathyn didn't understand them. They were written in

Volume Standard, which the humans still spoke, but with a quaint, sort of old-fashioned inflection. But the signs announced the presence of this or that unit in military jargon. BTN this and COY that, and always with lots of confusing numbers and letters and backslashes in them. The humans were superfans of a good backslash. Still, for all the accommodations, the camp seemed half empty. Not deserted. But nowhere near as full as it should be. He wondered where everyone was, but he didn't ask.

He'd learned in the camps not to ask about things that were none of his concern.

After a ten-minute ride they crossed an open field that had been plowed by giant servitors, and pulled up in front of a massive greenhouse. Much of the building was open on the sides, although he could see large flexi-rolls of environmental sheeting hung ready to drop in the case of bad weather. Probably for the monsoon rain that swept through every afternoon. For now, they were rolled up to allow the few scraps of breeze coming off the river to cool the people working inside. Long garden beds, raised to waist height on trestles, carried newly planted crops. Jonathyn thought he recognized a few varieties of leafy green vegetables.

He guessed there were a few hundred people inside, mostly freed prisoners, like him. They all wore new coveralls stenciled with the words AGRONOMY SERVICES, but they also had the look of ragged scarecrows about them as they moved through long lines of plantings. It was hot and most of the workers had either rolled up their sleeves or even peeled down the tops of their coveralls to expose army-green T-shirts, dark with sweat. Their arms were thin. Their cheeks sunken. But they stood up straight, too, and walked with confidence, not the cowering, anxious half-steps of somebody who expects to be whipped at any moment.

A few smiled at Jonathyn as he arrived and climbed off the back of the cart, helped down by the orderly who gently grasped his bad arm just above the gelform cast. The man's fingers went all the way around Jonathyn's shrunken biceps. He had never been a big man, but he had wasted away on Batavia. One or two of the Agronomy Services people waved, and he waved back uncertainly. Did he know them?

The orderlies walked him through the open-air grow house to a smaller, enclosed Hab out back, delivering him to a foreman who introduced himself as Paul.

"Paul Juvonen."

Another defaulter rescued from the camps. Juvonen asked him a few questions about his background, his skill sets and experience, and the cast on his arm, before sitting him down at a group table with three others to sort seeds.

"When your arm heals properly, we can put you on heavier duties," he said.

Jonathyn met at least a dozen new people over the rest of the day, most of them liberated prisoners who had either volunteered to work at the grow house or had been asked to by the Republicans because they had applicable skills. Everyone introduced themselves, and he did, too, but Jonathyn had trouble remembering names. He was out of practice at meeting people and remembering their names. It didn't matter. Everybody there was out of practice. They wrote their first names on their coveralls. Somebody gave him a sticky label to put on his infirmary fatigues. JONATHAN.

They spelled his name wrong, but it didn't matter.

He expected to be a little bored, picking and sorting seed packets. But there was an almost meditative quality to the task that he found therapeutic. Maybe it was the pain patches. More likely it was something deeper and more profound. Jonathyn Hardy felt himself useful and his contributions significant and appreciated for the first time in many years. Nor was it completely unskilled, make-busy work. The Republicans were quite explicit about the need to winnow out any genetically modified seed stock.

Jonathyn was a little taken aback, if not completely aghast at the suggestion. At least to begin with. With the right sort of modified strains, they could accelerate the growing cycle of whatever they planted and put the settlement on a self-sufficient basis that much quicker. But the true human supervisors weren't interested in that. Pure seed stock only, they said. And so he set himself to work, slowly sifting through the masses of seeds, seedlings, kernels, and grow stock that came in from all over the local volume.

CHAPTER

SEVEN

Lucinda Hardy wanted to pace the bridge of HMAS *Defiant*. When she found herself overwhelmed by all the people coming at her, and everything she needed to do, Lucinda often paced up and down her cabin, talking to herself, picking free the tangled knots of her life. But pacing was not a good look for a ship's commander. It implied a lack of resolve. It made people around her nervous. Instead she had to content herself with sitting quietly in the captain's chair at the center of the bridge, waiting for Sephina to report back from the inner volume. Or, alternatively, waiting for the two enemy warships holding station over the Fleet base at Descheneaux to fold in on top of her with plasma cannons blazing and missiles in flight.

"I don't know why I agreed to this," she said quietly.

"Because sometimes a good officer has to let somebody else take all the glory," Admiral McLennan said from just behind her shoulder. He did not lower his voice and Lucinda startled a little in surprise.

McLennan was not a nervous pacer. He seemed perfectly content to sit in a corner, scowling and snarling and occasionally roaring at some random passerby. But in the short time she had known him, he had not struck her as someone who needed to burn off an excess of nervous energy.

"Especially if that someone is expendable," he said.

"What?" she asked, feeling stupid, until she realized he meant Sephina.

Sephina was expendable. And her crewmates, Banks and Jaddi Coto.

All of them could be spent as wantonly as a sailor's paychip in a Combine whorehouse.

Nobody else spoke. There was nothing to say. *Defiant*'s bridge crew worked their stations, Lieutenants Bannon and Chivers most noticeably because they actually had something to do, monitoring signals from the inner volume and analyzing the take from the ship's passive arrays. Varro Chase at navigation had already plotted all of the fold paths they would need in the event of something going wrong, or the more unlikely event of everything turning out fine. Herodotus had checked the paths and pronounced them acceptable. Lucinda had objected to the Intellect second-guessing her people, even Chase. But then Chase remained an arrogant little shit and had leaped at the chance to show the Autonomous Combat Intellect just how good he was.

"Not good, and certainly not as good as I would have done, but acceptable," Hero sniffed.

Over at Tactical, meanwhile, Lieutenant Mercado Fein had programmed a full suite of offensive and defensive options for the ship's remaining arsenal, but the options were limited because the cupboard was bare. Energy weapons only.

"I wish you would sit down, Admiral," Lucinda said, as her impatience got the better of her. She was not used to waiting while others moved into action. "It's making me feel bad that a seven-hundred-year-old man has to stand while I just sit around waiting for something to happen."

"Don't you worry about these old bones, lass," McLennan said. "When a body gets to this age, everything hurts all the time. I would still be hurting if I sat down, just different parts of me. Besides if this all goes wrong, I like the idea of dying on my feet."

The Intellect harrumphed loudly as it floated past.

"This is my plan and the only way you will die on your feet is from getting stuck inside the revolving door of some disgracefully cheap alehouse when old age, stubbornness, and alcoholic dementia catch up with you."

"Och, my apologies, Herodotus. I'd forgotten it was your plan, because I'm more used to the idea of you being about as useful as a chocolate bedpan."

"How long have you two been together?" Lucinda asked in a tired voice.

"Too long," they both answered at once.

"Mister Bannon, do you have something, anything? Please God, tell me that you do."

She hated herself for asking. If Bannon had anything to tell her, he would have spoken up. But McLennan and Herodotus sniping at each other like an old married couple so amplified the tension of waiting-without-knowing that it quickly became intolerable.

"All quiet through the inner volume, I'm afraid, ma'am," he said. "Or at least it was twelve hours and thirty-two minutes ago."

"We do know one thing, Commander," McLennan said. "It probably won't be quiet anymore. So if you'll excuse me, I might take the opportunity to get my old head down for a kip, before your rowdy little friend comes back. This aged fellow does get tired. Come wake me if anyone is rude enough to shoot at us."

"I can't believe I agreed to this," Sephina said. The commlinks to the other two craft were open and both Jaddi Coto and Mister Banks heard her. Banks said nothing. Modest stillness and shutting the fuck up were his natural state of being. But Coto's voice rumbled in over tight beam.

"If you did not want to follow this course of action, you should have taken another," he said.

Fucking Coto.

"Hey, did you want to get out of the regen tank when I woke you up?" Sephina asked.

"I did not," he said. "But that was different. You ordered me to get out of the tank and swore very loudly when I did not. It was hurtful to my feelings and I suddenly wished to get out of the tank. So I did. Even though my horn was not even half grown. I have a very tiny horn now."

"Coming up on the waypoint," Mister Banks said from the second of the *Ariane*'s auxiliary shuttles, a small freight hauler full of hallucinogenic vodka and caviar-scented genital lubricants. "One minute to fold."

"Acknowledged," Sephina said.

"I, too, acknowledge this," Coto said.

"Slaving your helms to me," Banks informed them. Sephina sat back from the controls of her cruiser, the *Jula*, the same one they had ridden down to Montrachet. Status lights flipped from green to orange as Banks took over. There was no turning back from here. Part of her wanted to wrest away the helm, turn the ship around, and get the fuck gone. This wasn't just madness; it was a bad deal. Not even a loss leader. Just a straight-up loss, at least for her. Luce was getting something out of it. But all Sephina could see at the end of the working day was a ledger deep in the red.

"This is what I get for listening to a computer," she said as Banks took over her flight controls and they folded away from the asteroid belt deep into the inner volume.

The trip was short. Less than a minute to cover a bit over twelve and a half light-hours of space.

"All right, boys," she said, just before they emerged from the fold. "Let's do this for Ariane."

"But Ariane is dead," Coto pointed out.

"Then do it for me, Coto. Because I'm very sad she is dead, and this will make me happy. For a while."

All three of the *Ariane*'s shuttles slipped out of folded space within range of one another's weapons systems. They immediately opened fire on one another. Or at least they appeared to.

That smarmy fucking Intellect had insisted it absolutely, positively had to script the firing sequence into all three craft.

"I don't doubt you can pass yourselves off as murderous criminals bent on mutual destruction," it said. "But I fear you are such incompetent dullards you will actually destroy one another with a poorly executed shot and this would render my cunning plan inoperable."

Sephina's ship launched an arc of volume denial mines that detonated in a pattern designed to appear legitimately threatening to the pair of fast-moving RAN fighters pursuing her. Coto and Banks were not flying Armadalen Hornets, of course. They chased Sephina in the *Ariane*'s remaining runabouts, a small pleasure cruiser designed for interplanetary rather than interstellar jaunts, and the freight hauler full of orgy supplies, both of them fitted out by the *Defiant*'s engineers to emit the EM signatures of the RAN's single-seater, multi-role fighters. The Hornets followed the Intellect's predetermined course through a fast-expanding, overlapping, and intricately plotted field of nuclear explosions.

Thirty-two light-minutes away threat boards on both of the Sturm's warships suddenly flashed red.

"Battle stations, battle stations, all hands to battle stations!"

A quaver in the voice heard all over the Human Republic ship *Sacheon* betrayed the all too human frailties of the speaker, Ensign Kristianne Jung, who had the poor luck to be the junior officer of the watch when the *Sacheon*'s long and largely uneventful overwatch of the Armadalen Fleet base was rudely disrupted by the artificial star field of supernovae that birthed in silent white fire thirty-five light-minutes away.

Surveillance buoys three light-minutes from the explosions detected the unmistakable signature of fusion warheads detonating in a wide-area-denial pattern. The buoys automatically opened hyperspace commlinks back to both *Sacheon* and its sister ship on picket duty, HRS *Coral Sea*. The buoys deployed full-spectrum, active sensor arrays, greedily drinking up as much data on the discontinuity as possible and relaying it at superluminal speed back to the crew of the small Republican task force.

Sacheon and *Coral Sea* had been in-volume, monitoring progress of the malware attack on the RAN's Descheneaux Station for eight days. This had initially gone as smoothly on Descheneaux as it had everywhere else. Any personnel and so-called Combat Intellects with live links to the local area networks or Greater Volume nodes had been instantly neutralized. On Descheneaux that was estimated at 97 percent of the active duty roster. When Pathfinder units of the 101st arrived to assess the battle damage, however, they assaulted onto the enemy base only to meet ferocious resistance. Casualties were heavy. It had been purely a matter of good luck that some of the Pathfinders escaped to warn the follow-on forces that the base was not secure.

Instead, *Sacheon* and *Coral Sea* were dispatched and tasked with overwatch. The situation on Descheneaux would eventually resolve itself, Fleet Ops told them. Until then, they were to stand off and observe.

An object at rest will tend to remain at rest, despite the best efforts of NCOs and junior officers to kick its ass into movement with training days and emergency drills. After eight days on-station, HRS *Sacheon* was resting when the outer ring of surveillance buoys suddenly started to scream their warnings. But the quiet on board was mostly due to the very early hour. Ensign Jung had the middle watch from four bells to zero four hundred hours, and the buoys lit up at 0312 and fourteen seconds. Jung had been thinking, wondering how she was going to keep herself sharp, let alone the handful of men and women under her command, when the first siren went off.

She spilled half of the mug of coffee she'd been drinking. Luckily it had lost much of its heat, but she was still drenched with brown liquid.

"Chief Ngaru?" she called out to the boatswain's mate of the watch.

"Detonations in the twenty-five to thirty-five kiloton range detected, ma'am," he said, reading out the direct feed from the surveillance buoys. "Thirteen payloads, all fusion, four point three seven five AU distant, on a heading of two-seven-four relative, ma'am."

Ensign Jung did not hesitate.

She punched open the channel for a ship-wide hail and spoke into her headset.

"Battle stations, battle stations, all hands to battle stations!"

Klaxons and sirens sounded throughout the ship and the low red ambient light of the middle watch began to strobe quickly. The communications watch officer, another ensign like her, called out from his station.

"Incoming mayday, ma'am. Shall I put it up?"

"Yes, please do, Ensign Waller, and patch me through to the officer of the watch on *Coral Sea*. I want to make sure this isn't just us."

She was proud of herself for thinking of that. It was a cool-headed move. There was no guarantee the buoys had fired off a legitimate warning. It could be a glitch in their onboard systems. The *Sacheon* was one of the older ships of the armada and she had not had an easy passage from the Redoubt.

Static crackled all around her, as the CWO threw the mayday call onto the general address system. A woman's voice blared out across the bridge, and Kristianne waved a hand at Waller to turn it down.

"*. . . ayday, mayday this is the Zaistev schooner* Karenina. *I*

*have damaged AM stacks and am under attack from rogue ele-
ments of the Armadalen Forces. Mayday, mayday. Please respond. This is the Zaistev schooner* Karenina . . ."

"Mate of the Watch, do we have any take on the pursuit
craft?"

Petty Officer Winston Ngaru worked his station, pulling in
and quickly analyzing data feeds from the buoys ninety million
miles away, give or take a light-second.

"All returns match for a pair of Armadalen battlespace superiority fighters, ma'am," he reported, never once looking up
from his screens. "FX 23 Hornets. Suggest immediate interdic-
tion. All three tracks."

The blast doors to the fighting bridge of the *Sacheon* slid
open and the troopers standing guard barked out, "Captain on
deck!"

Kristianne was both relieved and terrified.

Had she already fucked this up? She all but leaped out of
Captain Moruya's chair as he hurried over, looking bleary-eyed
and short of temper.

"Talk to me, Ensign," he barked. "And turn that shit down."

Moruya waved away the distress call from the civilian pilot.

"*. . . Come on, you guys, these assholes are trying to kill
me . . .*"

The voice dropped away as Ensign Waller swiped at his
touch screen.

"Three tracks, Captain," Jung told him. "Two definite hostiles. One unknown civilian craft."

"Weapons, do you have target locks yet? I don't want them
within tactical fold range. And why aren't we moving?"

Shit!

Kristianne cursed her stupidity. She had not ordered the ship
to take any sort of evasive maneuvers.

Ensign Waller announced, "*Coral Sea* confirms enemy contacts, Captain. Remote sensor buoys indicate they've closed on
the civilian and fired plasmatic rounds, sir."

"Weapons! Designate and kill. Three shots," Moruya shouted.

"Tracking three now, Captain," the woman at Tactical returned.

But by then it was too late.

Sephina made no choices. Apart from initially agreeing to this bullshit, all the choices had been made for her by the Intellect. She left the helm and hurried astern to *Jula*'s cargo hold. It was a short, hellish trip. Hero had programmed as realistic a series of evasive maneuvers into the *Jula*'s navigation computers as Seph could reasonably be expected to survive in her vacuum suit. She pulled herself aft while being thrown into the bulkheads by violent tacking moves and tight looping spirals designed to queer the aim of the two Armadalen Hornets trying to kill her.

The *Jula* was a pleasure craft. Almost as big as Seph's previous ship, the *Je Ne Regrette Rien*, it was extravagantly more comfortable and luxuriously appointed. Designed to ferry the most powerful douchelords and underbosses of the Zaistev Corporation from the mother ship of the *Ariane* to and from their private estates, the *Jula* was an interstellar-capable schooner with hot tubs. The main companionway from the bridge to the transport dock was high, wide, and thickly carpeted with plush white polar bear hide. Real polar bear hide, too. From real polar bears bred on the Imperial Russian Habitat of Putingrad.

Sephina guessed that they probably had to kill a whole bunch of fucking bears for new rugs every time these gangsters had an orgy, which, she assumed, meant every time the fucking ship took off.

This occurred to her as an unusually emphatic turn tossed her into a crystal chandelier swinging from what would conventionally be called the ceiling, if the ship wasn't laid over at a perceived angle of ninety degrees. Sephina's face crashed into the massive, cut-crystal light fixture, opening a gash on her forehead that sprayed an extravagant blood pattern over the white bear hide. The ship swung onto another heading, tossing her farther down the hallway, where she struck a small nest of thankfully soft furnishings before a brief passage of level flight allowed her to scramble back to her feet and hurry on, wiping away some of the hot, salty blood pouring from her cut and blinding her in one eye.

"Fucking asshole computer," she cursed.

The *Jula* climbed steeply, relative to its g-field, forcing her to bend deeply at the knees.

She took hold of a polished platinum grab bar and pulled herself a few more steps toward the cargo bay. A few seconds later Sephina fell through the hatch and into the hold. The ship tilted one way and the other, forcing her to weave a slow, curving path across the bay. The plate of the micro-fold transport dock lay just ahead of her, a bright yellow octagon painted over the deck. Packing crates, boxes, and heavy pallets crashed around the space as the *Jula* maneuvered to avoid destruction from the plasma fire of the attacking fighter craft. Seph kept one eye on the countdown clock, which displayed her rapidly shrinking window of time to get off the ship.

0010
0009
0008
0007

She only just made it into the safety zone of the dock when the *Jula* seemed to fall away beneath her boots, throwing her high and wide, far across the cargo bay.

Sephina scrambled back toward the octagon, dodging a giant airborne wine cask.

0006
0005
0004

But the ship tilted again as proximity warheads detonated way too close, sending a powerful shudder through the frame of the entire vessel. Disrupted inertia tossed her back across the mouth of the dock, and she frantically reached for a handhold as the ship fed power into the dock's quantum entanglement matrices. Sephina gripped a stanchion point and held on, but another hard turn threatened to twist her arm out of its socket. She screamed as pain from the torque on her wrist spiked massively. White-hot agony seemed to erupt everywhere all at once down that side of her body.

She cursed again.

"Fucking asshole computer."

And darkness consumed her.

Two spacecraft folded into the hard vacuum around Descheneaux Station, *Jula* and the unnamed freight hauler piloted by Ephram Banks. The hauler, which displaced less than one-quarter of the mass of Sephina's luxury cruiser, nonetheless did more damage, a lot more quickly. Mister Banks, veteran of more than sixty combat missions in his former life as a vat-grown TDF pilot, stayed at the helm of the freight runner for as long as he judged prudent. His ship, like Sephina's, was running Hero code to navigate the firestorm of Zaistev munitions they threw at each other in a pantomime of rage, but he gave himself just a few extra moments to ensure the emergence point of his vessel's final fold was coincident with the exact location of HRS *Coral Sea*'s engine room. This was not easily done.

The Intellect had scooped up a googolplex or two of q-bit data on the Sturm's Order of Battle over Montrachet—microseconds before Herodotus sprung open the trapdoor that dropped Wenbo Strom's task force into the poop. The scripts that now ran on the *Ariane*'s complement of three auxiliary vessels incorporated that harvested intelligence, making it a simple matter to designate an emergence point within the hull of the *Coral Sea*, Banks's designated target, once the freight hauler's sensors had directly acquired the warship. But this meant double-folding, jumping to a point beyond the ultimate objective, painting the *Coral Sea* with the freighter's active scanners, matching the take against Hero's database, re-plotting the final fold, executing same, and escaping in the second and a half needed to throw this whole potential fail cake into the oven and bake a delightful space Nazi smackdown.

At least he did have a much less chaotic evasive flight pattern than Captain L'trel had to contend with as he cycled through each checkpoint of his task list. And the hauler's micro-fold bay was also less of a trek, being tucked away a short distance behind his crash couch. Mister Banks, unlike Sephina, had made sure the cargo of hallucinogenic vodka and caviar lube was safely clamped down with maglocks and further secured with plasteel chains.

While Sephina dodged a flying, half-ton wine cask, Banks confirmed his target lock on the *Coral Sea* and manually keyed in the required safety overrides. There wasn't much the Sturm, with their less sophisticated technology, could do about it. Such was the nature of folding space. It efficiently edited out all the inconvenient stuff such as light-years-long arcs of empty space, or fully powered defensive shields. The Sturm did not have the *Defiant*'s permanent hyperspace buffer, for instance, isolating the ship's internals from this particular external threat by moving everything on board ever so slightly sideways into an alternate universe.

Mister Banks's freight hauler, however, was built with multiple redundant fail-safes to ensure it never, ever folded into an asteroid, or a Habitat, or another ship. *Defiant*'s engineers had physically ripped out most of those, and Banks turned off the remaining ones himself. As the freighter winked into existence at a point placing it directly between the *Coral Sea* and the local star, he assured himself in his quietly reserved fashion that there was no other contribution he could make to the Intellect's plan. Protected for a fraction of a second by the electromagnetic storm of emissions from the bright yellow main sequence star, Mister Banks acquired a space-time floating point lock on the *Coral Sea*'s engine room. He unstrapped himself from his crash couch, set a timer to execute the final journey of the *Ariane*'s freight hauler, and stepped calmly into the onboard micro-fold dock after picking up a crate of Trippin' Ballz Vodka.

He had meant to try some when circumstances allowed and considered that it would be a shame to miss the opportunity.

Banks folded away to the third shuttle half a second before the *Ariane*'s auxiliary vessels, the *Jula* and the freight hauler, folded directly into the *Sacheon* and the *Coral Sea*, respectively.

HRS *Coral Sea* lost antimatter containment at the exact moment the small cargo boat materialized deep inside its engineering decks. The sudden appearance of a 740-ton freight hauler within the space and time occupied by the Republican warship would have been enough to doom it. Twenty-seven personnel died when their corporeal matter found itself sharing a bunk, so to speak, with the decidedly non-corporeal matter of the freight hauler. Many perished instantly as bulkheads or deck plating or extra-large tubs of genital lubrication materialized at the same coordinates as their cortexes. Some would have died screaming, impaled after a fashion, but not decapitated by other fittings and structural features of the freighter. These happy few were gifted a reprieve from that fate when the exotic matter flasks that contained the *Coral Sea*'s suspended macromolecules of antimatter were unable to remain safely suspended in their hyperspace baffles. The actual space occupied by the flask was suddenly also occupied by the soft gelform cushion on which Mister Banks had only recently been sitting. Banks was never to know it, but the matter of that comfortable yet supportive padding, which persisted in shaping itself to the contours of his buttocks, was responsible for destabilizing the *Coral Sea*'s antimatter flask. His ass destroyed his enemies utterly but spared a handful of them from a prolonged and terrifying demise by obliterating the *Coral Sea* in a ten-thousand-gigaton blast.

Two thousand kilometers away, at the exact same moment, the luxury cruiser which had of late been renamed *Jula* materialized inside the same space-time coordinates occupied by the Human Republic ship *Sacheon*. Or mostly inside. Sephina L'trel

did not have Mister Banks's facility with piloting and navigation. Her skills lay elsewhere. Some of the mass of the *Jula*
emerged outside the hull of the *Sacheon*, plunging through and
out of the vessel's midsection like a giant spear. It did not radi-
cally affect the final disposition of either vessel. The *Sacheon*,
Ensign Jung, Captain Moruya, and 394 other true believers in
the sanctity of the human genome died as the ruptured warship
suffered a cataclysmic loss of structural integrity and simply
blew apart in a more conventional explosion.

The *Sacheon*'s antimatter containment flask, for what it's
worth, survived the detonation as designed, and was thrown
clear of the debris field. It eventually fell into the local sun thousands of years later, after the many difficult issues existing between the Human Republic and the Greater Volume had long
been resolved.

"Why is it so fucking dark?" Sephina shouted, a second after
landing with a painful thud on the micro-fold plate of the *Ariane*'s third and only surviving shuttle craft.

"Because I have not turned the lights on," Coto replied.

Seph could feel all her arms and legs, but she checked anyway in the dark, just in case she'd left a bit of herself behind on
the *Jula*.

"Turn on the fucking lights, Coto. I can't see a thing."

"I'll get them," Mister Banks said from somewhere to her
left.

The organic light strips flared into life and Sephina squeezed
her eyes shut against the sudden glare.

Her retinas retained an afterimage of Banks, carrying what
looked like a crate of vodka, standing by a light control panel,
and Jaddi Coto pulling an oversized pair of shades down over
his eyes.

His cranial horn was indeed much smaller than it had been.

Sephina L'trel wiped the blood out of her eyes.

A feeling of deep sadness wrapped itself around her. The
Jula was gone, just like the little girl from Eassar for whom it
was named.

There had been no choice in that.

Lucinda's engineering guy, some sad sack called Barry or something, and then Luce herself had explained why a whole bunch of technical shit meant they had to sacrifice the *Jula* and the freight hauler, rather than the runabout Coto had piloted.

"Come on," she said quietly, accepting a hand up off the deck from Mister Banks. "Let's get back to Luce. Tell her she can have her little space station back now."

CHAPTER

EIGHT

The Armadalen stealth destroyer folded into real space half a million kilometers from Descheneaux Station. Emerging on the far side of the fortress moon from the expanding debris field that marked the final resting place of the enemy's two warships, HMAS *Defiant* burned up the threat bubble with a high-intensity active sensor sweep. It did not remain long after capturing the take, folding away a fraction of a second after it first arrived to a lay-up point where Herodotus analyzed the take and pronounced the emergent zone safe for return. An observer at the original waypoint could literally have blinked and missed the warship's first appearance.

Lucinda thanked the Intellect for its help. She was confident her own people could have done just as well with threat analysis, but not nearly so quickly.

"Well, I am an Armada-level—"

"Yes, thanks for that. Mister Chase, take us back in if you would," she said quickly.

"Aye, Commander," Chase replied.

The Intellect floated away, muttering to itself.

"Thank you, Hero," Lucinda called after it. "Perhaps you could wake Admiral McLennan from his nap. He'll probably want to be up for this."

A second later, *Defiant* returned to the skies above its home port. Without neural nets to facilitate a direct mind-brain interface with the destroyer's control systems, the attention of the bridge crew remained fixed on whichever display mode was appropriate for their station. Lieutenant Bannon studied three virtual screens that floated in a semicircle around his workspace. Lieutenant Chivers scanned a physical screen and listened for audio signals on a headset. Lucinda, needing to consider wider options, threats, and opportunities, sat in the command chair surrounded by a cloud of infographic holograms. As her eyes swept over the dense, complicated fog of data, the *Ariane* appeared as an icon in the near-field volume display. Bannon had tagged its IFF signal with a skull and crossbones.

"Captain L'trel has arrived, Commander," Lieutenant Chivers announced.

"So I see," Lucinda said. "Open a tight beam and let her through."

She knew that if she didn't, Sephina's hologram would be knocking on some back door within seconds anyway.

Lucinda continued to study the data cloud, looking for something that might tell her what to do next while she waited for Seph to appear. The surface of Descheneaux Station was scorched and heavily damaged by the blast. It had been over a million kilometers from the antimatter explosion.

"Mister Fein, what do you make of this debris field?" she asked her tactical officer. "It looks a bit light to me."

"The wreckage is mostly there, Commander," he said. "But it appears as though one of the enemy ships ruptured an antimatter containment bottle and annihilated thirteen percent of its constituent mass. The balance was reduced to subatomic particles. The second vessel is all there . . . in lots of little bits and pieces."

"It's like I always say, Luce, never send an uptight flog in a lumpy jumpsuit to do the work of a smokin' hottie with legs that won't quit and a letter of marque and reprisal."

Lucinda flicked away the data to find Sephina's holo standing on the other side. Seph's face was swollen and bloody.

"You look nice today," Lucinda said. "What happened?"

Sephina shrugged.

"I banged my head on a gunboat full of space Nazis and it blew up. You're welcome, by the way. And you owe me a twin-engine schooner. I'll comp you the freight hauler. It was an ugly-ass piece of crap anyway."

"My compliments to you and your crew, Captain L'trel. The Royal Armadalen Navy thanks you for your assistance, which I will note in the ship's log. Pinkie promise."

Lucinda held up her little finger. Sephina nodded slowly, hands on hips.

"Oh good," she said. "A note in the log. That's gotta be worth at least one tube of caviar lube. So how long we gonna be here, then? Cos I got a quest for the A-Train to be kicking on with. Kinda hoping to score another planet out of it, between you and me. Bitch knows how to say thank you. Unlike some."

"Thank you, Sephina," Lucinda said.

And cut the link.

"Och, I had words I needed with her."

Admiral McLennan, wild-haired, bleary-eyed, and carrying a mug of coffee, stepped onto the bridge from wherever he'd put his aged head down for a nap.

A marine guard started to announce his arrival on deck, but McLennan cut him off.

"And you can shut the fuck up with all that nonsense before you even start, son. I'll not have you tonguing mah fart box before I've even dunked mah wee butter biscuit."

The marine threw a confused look at Lucinda, who waved off the need for proper form in this instance.

McLennan rolled his eyes. And returned the marine's salute with the weariness of a seven-hundred-year-old veteran. "As you were then, son."

"I could get Sephina back, Admiral," Lucinda said. "If you really needed to talk to her. But then she'd be here again. You see my dilemma."

The Intellect suddenly folded onto the bridge, appearing next to McLennan.

"And please don't do that, Hero," Lucinda said. "Just use the door like everyone else."

"But I'm not like everyone else," the Intellect protested. "I'm an Armada-level—"

"Mister Bannon! Sweep the base," she ordered before Hero could get rolling. "No direct data links. Just stand-off scans."

"Aye, ma'am," the systems officer replied, pulling up a fourth virtual screen. "No direct links. Stand-off scans only. Full malware protocols in place."

Bannon began firing up the ship's powerful sensor arrays, aiming them at the damaged moonbase.

"Gathering the take, Commander. It will be a minute before—"

"I can already tell you what you're going to find," Hero said, talking over him. "Having analyzed and developed the early returns, there are eight personnel I judge to be likely survivors of the malicious bioware attack. Two are in a transit lounge on the ground level in the eastern sector of the base, and six are located in the neurological wing of the infirmary. Another five hundred and thirty-two humanoid signals are extant, but they reveal evidence of extreme neurological disruption."

Lucinda looked to Bannon for confirmation. Many of the crew quietly did the same.

He nodded without comment.

"Ugh. Zombies," McLennan grunted. "I hate those fucking things."

"Eight survivors," Lucinda said quietly.

Descheneaux Station had been home to more than three thousand personnel. Many more would have been passing through on visiting warships.

"Yes, ma'am," Bannon said. "I will double-check, but that looks right."

An exploded view of the naval base in schematic form zoomed out of a single point in front of her. Eight flashing blue dots in two separate groups stood out among hundreds of drifting red dots. The larger cohort of survivors, the half dozen in the infirmary, were besieged by a dense mass of red dots.

"Why are they so evenly spread?" Lucinda asked. "Everywhere but the sick bay."

"Because they're brain-dead guttin' carnivores, lass," McLennan said somberly. "And they cannae say no to a feed. Looky there at those two dancing cannibals."

As she watched, a pair of red dots found each other at the intersection of two corridors. The dots swirled around as though caught in a sudden eddy, and one soon blinked out.

Lucinda pinched her fingers together and the schematic zoomed back down to a vanishing point. The bridge remained silent until she spoke again.

"Lieutenant Chivers, have Captain Hayes meet me in the shuttle bay with a platoon. Full armor. Search and rescue. We're getting those people, getting our ammo, and getting the fuck gone from here."

"If I may, Commander?" McLennan started to say.

"You may not," Lucinda snapped back at him, before stomping away.

Lucinda stood in front of her personal armor.

Engineering had printed new ballistic plates and plasma shields for the ones she had damaged on Montrachet, and her orderly had cleaned the suit of every drop of blood and grit. But the rig, which had been pristine when she joined the ship, now looked worn and scarred.

She liked it that way. It felt earned.

Her command did not.

The armory was empty, but that would not be the case for long. In a few moments, marines would pile in to suit up for the mission to Descheneaux.

Would they question her place on the team?

Never to her face, she knew.

But the squad that fought with her on Montrachet was gone. Dead, beyond all hope of relife.

Lucinda stared at the scars and dents on her armor, wondering why she still lived when they did not. Wondering if she was about to kill more men and women.

She heard voices approaching, boots on the deck plating, and she stepped forward, placed one hand on the DNA reader, powering up the container that held her rig. The carapace split open, unfolding like the exoskeleton of a giant and dangerous alien insect. Lucinda stepped onto a yellow circle, placing her heavy boots inside the outlines marked on the pad. Topographic lidar swept up and down her body and the container hummed briefly as it adjusted to her position and posture.

"Stand ready for enclosure," a recorded voice announced. "In three . . . two . . . one . . ."

The battlesuit consumed her in one swallow, just as the first marines hurried into the armory.

A gunnery sergeant roared out, "Commander on deck!" He stopped and rendered a precise salute.

"Carry on, Gunny," she said, forestalling a pileup as the squad interrupted their momentum to stop and stand at attention. "Get them suited up and meet me at the shuttle deck."

"Aye, ma'am," he roared.

This was one of those gunnery sergeants who loved to roar.

Lucinda didn't know his name. She checked the stencil on the breastplate of his suit as she moved past.

COX.

"Is Captain Hayes joining us today, Sergeant?" she asked.

"Yes, ma'am, you will find him waiting for you at the shuttle."

Damn it.

How did these guys do that?

Lucinda thanked Gunny Cox, took her carbine from the rack on the wall, and left the squad to get into their armor.

She walked out into the companionway and turned aft for the shuttle deck. The ship was busy with crew hurrying about their duties. When they docked, there would be a great deal of work to do and very little time in which to do it. The *Defiant* needed extra war stocks and provisions. There was no guarantee they would be able to quickly or easily resupply either, and the Sturm would be pushing in from the edge of the Greater Volume as quickly as they could.

Hell, they'd already been here in-system, just not in force.

Her helmet swinging from a stowage point, Lucinda returned the salutes and acknowledgments of her crew with a series of precise rifle salutes.

Her crew.

Despite everything, they did not feel like her crew. Maybe it was just the insane rush of events, but she most definitely did not feel like their leader. She did not feel like anyone's leader. She was surrounded by men and women to whom command seemed to come naturally. McLennan. Hayes. Even Sephina. All of them seemed to know some secret that was beyond her.

She had watched Seph lead her people into harm's way twice now, and each time they followed her with a weird combination of devotion and abandon. As though they would charge through the gates of hell behind her, with not a care for the consequences of doing so.

Lucinda wondered where Seph had learned to inspire people like that. But the question was stupid, and she dismissed it immediately. Sephina L'trel had always been that way, from the first time they had met in Hab Welfare on Coriolis. Sephina had a crew and real command presence because that's just who she was and always had been, even as an orphan stealing and dealing to survive in the shelters.

Lucinda had this crew and command of the *Defiant* because poor Captain Torvaldt had died, and fate had conspired with irony to simply kick her ass up into the big chair. Like Seph, she was an orphanage Hab rat. Unlike Seph, though, she hadn't taken any risks to rise above that. She'd always just done as she was told, even when she was told to step up and into a command for which she was not ready or qualified.

She let go a long breath and swore to herself.

The crash of a dozen pairs of boots coming up behind her, Cox's marines double-timing it to the shuttle, drove away all thoughts of frailty and fallibility as the marines' shouted cadence drowned out all the questions she could not answer of herself.

"I fought down on Montrachet . . ."

"I FOUGHT DOWN ON MONTRACHET . . ."

"Made those assholes run away . . ."

"MADE THOSE ASSHOLES RUN AWAY . . ."

The squad came pounding up behind her and she moved to one side to let them pass. None appeared less than totally committed to assaulting onto the base and doing whatever had to be done.

One thing that meant, Lucinda knew, was putting down former comrades who had been meat hacked by the Sturm.

She hardened her heart to the prospect. There was nothing for it. The five hundred or so walking corpses on Descheneaux were as dead as the half-dozen members of the squad who'd jumped into Skygarth with her to rescue Alessia. They just didn't know it yet. They didn't know anything beyond the primeval hunger to kill and consume that the nanophage had set free from their reptilian hindbrains, overwriting everything else in their conscious minds. Lucinda had seen and done terrible things in the Javan War, but even the Empire had not resorted to anything as foul as that.

She pushed her revulsion down where it could not distract her. Arriving at the shuttle deck she found the marines already boarding one of the small armored vessels, while Cox and Captain Hayes spoke to each other off to one side. Navy boat crew checked over the craft, performing one final visual inspection.

Defiant's diagnostic scanners and software were powerful enough to detect everything from micro fissures to loosened bottles or sealing rings, but the RAN would not be the RAN if it left such things to autonomics.

Lucinda watched Chief Petty Officer Higo lower himself onto a wheeled trolley to better access and inspect the underside of the hull while two space-hands ran a spectrometer over the gravpods. A bot train swerved around her as she walked over to Hayes and Cox, returning the marine captain's brusque nod with one of her own.

"Captain, you got your briefing pack?"

"Thanks, Commander, yeah. And Tim, my gunny here, was just working through the dance card with me. We'll grab the two warm bodies out of the transit lounge on G3, secure them in the shuttle because it's close. Then we move to the infirmary for the others. Once they're out and we have live intelligence about the facts on the ground, we can deploy more squads to secure the docks and the main magazine."

"Sounds good," she said. It was not her place to question Hayes's tactical choices.

"Do we know why the Sturm didn't just move in and put their feet up on the furniture?" Gunny Cox asked.

She shook her head. It had been bothering her since they discovered the enemy had been standing off the base, rather than occupying it.

"We can't do a hard data link, because of the nanophage. Can't even risk Herodotus folding in and exposing himself to contamination. So I'm looking for the survivors to tell us that," Lucinda admitted. "Otherwise I guess we'll find out the hard way."

CHAPTER

NINE

Suprarto stood in the cavernous but crowded bay of the Warlugger's main vehicle deck. Three squadrons of TU-35 Gila Hawk fighters stood clamped to the deck plates while the main receiving dock had been cleared for the arrival of the Combine shuttle craft. A line of Imperial Javan kommandos in full armor and ceremonial trim towered silently behind him. Suprarto stood erect, his face theatrically impassive. His feelings about receiving the Combine "advisers" were decidedly mixed, but what could he do about it? Lord Karna and the Yulin-Irrawaddy princeling had come to an arrangement; Combine personnel to help crew the *Makassar* in exchange for the added throw weight of Deputy Executive Prince Commodore Rinaldo Pac Yulin's combat ships in-system.

And they would need as much weight as they could find to throw at the Sturm.

Domi Suprarto was still reeling from the shock of that; the return of the Dark-accursed enemy. A week after securing from system-wide lockdown during Natuna's coronal mass explosion, Suprarto remained semi-dazed and intermittently terrified by the stunning turn in the course of his own life and that of the Greater Volume. It was only partly that pure chance—and some laziness—had saved him from the fate of all the senior officers who had plugged themselves back into the ship and the zero point networks. Mostly his feelings of powerlessness and doom were rooted in the trauma of realizing that everything he had once thought fixed and imperishable—his village, his Habitat, the very Empire itself—might already have passed into history.

He knew so much and almost nothing of what had happened.

Every day brought new arrivals in-system. Desperate refugees and Elite Fraction exiles. Dispersed and broken military units. Survivors of great battles at the edge of the Volume and, inevitably, the sort of bottom-feeders and profiteers who always preyed on such survivors. Standing in the *Makassar*'s echoing vehicle deck, listening to the clash of engineering bots pulling maintenance on a Gila Hawk, Sub-Commandant Domi Suprarto could not quite force himself to accept that he was even part of this scene. He was just a first lifer from Gudang Garam, a big spinning tube of dirt. He might have functional control over the massive 'lugger, but he was not one of the Chosen from Medang. Even his rank was tenuous, a product of *baksheesh* and his clan's dominion over a small fraction of a minor plate at the unfashionable end of an agricultural Hab.

An alarm sounded the approach of the Yulin Irrawaddy ship. The great rolling blast doors that secured the maw of the vehicle deck from hard vacuum already stood open. Suprarto steadied his breathing and contemplated the violet shimmer of the reinforced field effect that stood between him and the void outside. He could not help but be reminded of home. The Suprarto family holdings on Gudang Garam were but three frames removed from the mouth of the great Hab's southern cap, and the *Makassar*'s field generators came from the same engineering works on Ayodhya. The soft chromatic purple hue recalled almost exactly the color of day's end in his family's village, as the immense fusion duct which provided light and warmth to the tropical analogue Hab was dimmed, and Garuda's natural radiance spilled through for a few minutes as the hard shields deployed.

What the hell was he doing here? Seriously.

Bot trains hurried to clear the landing deck, and personnel near the entryway double-timed to safe alcoves as the ship's traffic management AI announced the arrival of the Combine vessel, a military adaptation of the standard model system-hauler from the massive shipyards in the Irrawaddy Belt. They were as common as fleas in this part of the Greater Volume. Cheap, utilitarian, ugly, but reliable. The Combine's mil-grade mods were about 20 percent bulkier thanks to all the extra shielding and weaponry, but this one, Suprarto noted, looked almost sleek. The usual mess of geometric blocks all clamped together for utility had given way to an almost elegant minimalism. Just one elongated container pod, doubtlessly fitted out for comfort.

Suprarto wondered who or what was about to step on board his ship.

He knew nothing about the leader of the Combine's adviser contingent. Literally nothing. A message drone from Lord Karna had rousted him from his bunk this morning and told him to stand ready with all the usual endearments.

Suprarto did not care at all to be called a dog by the Volume lord, let alone his floating message bubble.

However, here he stood. The Combine craft hummed into its final berth with a flare of power to the micro-g pods that set a nearby bot train floating away and blaring a warning siren to all around. Landing struts deployed with a pneumatic hiss and thudded down on the plates, the crunch of hard mass. Domi Suprarto rather wished he was back home in the village, where he might take his chances with the approaching Sturm. After all, his family were but humble farmers, none of them wealthy enough to even contemplate implants or gene modding. His late father's dream to see Domi raised to at least the lower ranks of the Navy's officer corps meant that he alone of their family now faced the hazard of the Sturm and the chaos of collapse—for it was growing more obvious every day that the Greater Volume had utterly disintegrated.

Nice one, Pops, he thought. *Thanks for that.*

And that, really, answered the question of what the hell he was doing here.

Frankly, Suprarto needed these assholes. It burned to see them rolling on board like they owned the place, but unlike the command cadre of the *Makassar,* the Combine's officers had not hastened to reestablish contact with the outside volume and thus they enjoyed the luxury of a full complement aboard their two heavy cruisers, *Khanjar* and *Jezail.*

Why, it was almost as though they knew what had happened, he thought.

Not that he could ever possibly say so.

He was no foolish kelasi.

The ramp on the big hauler opened with a sigh; the Combine legionnaires filed out. They did not really march down the gangway. The Combine was less a professional navy than a state-sponsored stand-over racket, he thought. But again, he would never voice such a thing. Not even in private, for no such state existed here.

The Forces Coloniale of the Yulin-Irrawaddy formed up before Suprarto and the Javan Honor Guard. The Javans' faces were impassive, their bodies rigid, Suprarto having reminded them they still represented the Empire, no matter its fate. The advisers stood in a rough line, mostly at ease. None moved to address or salute him.

Suprarto glanced at the ship and wondered if it was empty. Was there no leader? He took in a deep breath and prepared to project his voice.

Before he could say a word, another voice rang out with iron command.

"In the Javan Empire, is it not the custom to welcome the commander of an allied force?"

Suprarto knitted his brows. Who the fuck was this?

A slim man of indeterminate age alighted from the shuttle. He was dressed in a tight brown uniform with a mandarin collar and calf-high boots that had been shined until they glistened like a supernova in the sky. The gleaming leather of his footwear matched the brim of a legionnaire's sky-blue peaked cap, and on his sleeves a matching set of gold stars.

Suprarto clenched his jaw against the acid that wanted to bubble up from his stomach. They had sent a Combine politruk, a political officer. Or more accurately, a commissioned spy, Suprarto thought.

God help us.

He looked at the Combine commissar, lifted his chin, but did not salute.

"Welcome to my ship, sir."

The politruk snaked around the end of the line formed by his own personnel and looked Sub-Commandant Suprarto over, from head to foot. He pressed his lips into a thin line.

"Your ship? I understood it to be the emperor's. I understood all things to be the emperor's. At least within the borders of the Empire."

Suprarto blushed. The man was not wrong, and it hurt to be corrected on such a basic truth, especially in front of his own people.

A part of him wanted to flee, right then. To make a run for one of the Gila Hawks and just blast off into the void. Caught between the urge to escape and the crushing expectations of duty, Suprarto was left speechless.

The politruk smiled.

"I'm sorry, did the malware get your tongue?"

"My tongue is the emperor's," he said. Which sounded really weird and caused Suprarto to blush even more fiercely when the politruk snorted in laughter.

But damn it, he was a son of Ali Masood Suprarto, headman of Merapi village on the third frame of Gudang Garam, and he would be damned if he would allow this arrogant *bangsat* to lord it over him or anybody else on this ship. "I am indeed the emperor's loyal subject and faithful servant," Suprarto went on, a little slowly, to give himself time to think. "We . . ." he said, indicating the kommandos of the Honor Guard behind him, ". . . are the emperor's sword and shield. To be wielded in his name. But no, we are not the . . . property of His Royal Highness. He is our liege and master, our lord and protector. I apologize if I misspoke. I am a simple peasant, risen to command of His Majesty's Warlugger *Makassar*. I imagine that a vat-born officer of the Combine might not understand the difference between a royal subject and an item of property on the corporate ledger."

Their visitor regarded him with eyes that held all the warmth and fellow feeling of a Javan spider-cat.

It was already clear how this was going to go. Suprarto spoke again.

"But I'm afraid you have the advantage of me. Commissar . . . ?"

"Lord. Lord Tok-Yulin . . . peasant."

Suprarto thought he heard one of the Honor Guard draw in a hiss of breath.

"I was born a peasant, yes, but I am now Sub-Commandant Suprarto . . . Politruk Tok-Yulin."

Tok-Yulin said nothing.

He started to pull off his leather gloves. Real leather, too, thought Suprarto. He thought he could smell them. If this *muka jamban* went to slap him with the gloves, Suprarto was going to shoot him with his sidearm.

Then he would shoot himself. Better that than to face the Bakin and die screaming and begging.

The commissar narrowed his eyes and visibly checked himself. He spoke with a lighthearted tone.

"Very well, Sub-Commandant, very well." He gave a sloppy salute, gloves in hand. "Permission to come aboard? Sub-Commandant?"

Kuni-gak, Suprarto thought. *If you ever come to my village I will hang you by your heels and turn you over to the women.*

Face frozen, Suprarto saluted him precisely. "Permission granted, of course."

Tok-Yulin smiled. It didn't reach his eyes. "Then we will be about our duties as soon as your ship interfaces with us."

He paused and pursed his lips. "I assume the ship has been made safe, Sub-Commandant?"

"Only a small fraction of our AIs and rather more of our officers were affected by the attack," Suprarto said. "The ship's Intellect took itself offline and into secure containment."

"And is it still there?" Tok-Yulin asked, feigning astonishment. Or maybe not.

Suprarto hesitated a moment before finally answering.

"The ship's Intellect has been replaced."

"I see. Rather a mess on board the good ship *Makassar*, then, Sub-Commandant."

Suprarto had no great love for his former commanders, but he wasn't about to let that go unchallenged.

"Security, Politruk. The captain had his reasons for not disseminating the rumors of the Sturm attack throughout the crew. They were, of course, just rumors."

Tok-Yulin slapped his gloves in his hand. "And some ignorant underling allowed the enemy's malware into this vessel?"

"Essentially, Politruk."

"And the identity of this underling?"

"The emperor's dead have no names."

Tok-Yulin laughed. "How convenient."

He turned to the Combine contingent, who lounged as idly as Fraction dilettantes at some Old Earth cocktail party. He pointed at a soldier in the first row and drew his sidearm. "You."

"Yes, sir."

"Connect with the shipnet."

The man paled and broke into a sweat. But he complied.

"Yes, sir." He closed his eyes, then opened them, shivering slightly. "Sir, I am connected."

Tok-Yulin put away his pistol. He looked at Suprarto. "Excellent." He looked back at the advisers. "Connect, all of you."

As one, they did. Tok-Yulin addressed a woman in the front row. "Sergeant Pi, has the ship assigned you billets and tasking?"

"Yes, sir."

"Then what are you waiting for? Disappear and do your jobs."

"Yes, sir," she snapped out.

Suprarto watched as the Combine troops filed away from the right. They all disappeared down the correct passageway into the bowels of the ship. Soon, only Tok-Yulin, the Honor Guard, and Suprarto himself remained. He spoke to the Guard.

"Sub-Unit Leader Mobisto, you are dismissed."

The figure in powered armor crashed her gauntlet against the carapace of her armor and the Guard turned and filed out as one. When they left, only the commissar and Suprarto remained. The politruk smiled.

"This isn't my first time embedded with a foreign navy."

Like I give a shit, Suprarto thought. Aloud he said, "Really, Politruk Tok-Yulin?"

"Yes, when I attended the War College I was assigned to an Armadalen ship, the *Taipan*."

That was surprising, and Suprarto struggled to keep his expression neutral.

"I did not think the Armadalens had an exchange program with the Combine," he said.

"They do not, of course. My attachment was mandated by Earth, as a confidence-building measure between the Forces Coloniale and the Armadalen Navy. You may recall there had been incidents."

"Indeed? So this was not during the war?"

"Oh no," Tok-Yulin said and frowned. "A few years before that. We were mostly assigned to anti-piracy work. It was a dreadful bore, as you might expect being surrounded by Armadalens . . ."

He paused and seemed to think of something.

"Ah, but of course the last time you were surrounded by

Armadalens I suppose it was far from boring, wasn't it, Sub-Commandant?"

Tok-Yulin's grin was feral and hungry.

Suprarto felt the blood rushing to his face and his head. He felt the sudden dizziness of rage and his hands twitched as he suppressed the urge to strike out at the man.

"I was at Longfall, yes," he said when he could trust himself to speak. "And we were surrounded, you are correct about that."

Tok-Yulin's eyes danced with quiet delight.

"It is a pity you were not there," Suprarto went on, and the delight in the other man's expression died back, just a little. "Perhaps," Suprarto continued quietly, "if you were still embedded with the Armadalens, we might just have had that crucial stroke of luck which so often turns a battle."

And with that he turned and made to walk away.

Instead, he was jerked back to face a now furious commissar.

"Do you mock me, peasant?"

"No." He held Tok-Yulin's gaze. Sub-Commandant Domi Suprarto was a man of the third frame of Gudang Garam, the son of Ali Masood Suprarto. And this was his ship.

The two officers stood eyeballing each other for a long time.

Someone cleared their throat. Both men turned toward the noise and Tok-Yulin's hand went to his sidearm.

The throat-clearing was an affectation. A munitions AI floated a few feet away. Sub-Intellect Number Six, which had been serving as the acting ship's Intellect.

"Politruk Tok-Yulin, your legionnaires have been billeted and assigned their duties," Number Six informed them. "Volume Lord Juono Karna welcomes you aboard and sends his greetings and thanks for the efforts of Deputy Executive Prince Pac Yulin."

Tok-Yulin exhaled as though letting go a poison cloud.

"Yes, my cousin has made the arrangements he has made. I

am glad we can be of service in our common cause, *Makassar*. Please send my respectful regards to Volume Lord Karna."

Number Six dipped a few inches. "Of course, Politruk Tok-Yulin. A welcoming banquet has been prepared in your honor; the ship's officers are gathered."

Tok-Yulin laughed then. "Oh really. How many officers are left aboard? Two? Three?"

"There are thirteen assembled in the senior officers' mess-room."

Suprarto and Tok-Yulin shot each other looks. Tok-Yulin laughed. "The lucky thirteen. How delightful. Lead on, then, Sub-Commandant."

Suprarto didn't want this shitbird behind him. No way.

"Such a highborn guest should proceed a lowly farmer's boy, Politruk Tok-Yulin. I insist."

Tok-Yulin shot him another look, shrugged, then he turned his back on Suprarto and walked away. He headed toward the correct portal, Suprarto noted. He sub-vocalized a query to Number Six.

"So he registered with shipnet?"

"He did, Sub-Commandant." The minor intellect paused. "He also sent a copy of your conversation to Volume Lord Karna and to his cousin Deputy Executive Prince Pac Yulin."

Suprarto ran a clammy, shaking hand over his face.

"Oh, great."

CHAPTER

TEN

Lucinda leaned into the slope of the inner hull, resting the plasteel ass of her battlesuit against the rim that ran the length of the shuttle. The blast shield of her helmet was down, but she took an external cam feed in a window, letting her see the other members of the away team. They looked like monsters, gargantuan warrior-mechs without faces or souls. It was how the Sturm would see them and depict them to the people they were trying to save.

People like her dad.

She had not heard from him in months, which was not unusual. The Yulin-Irrawaddy Combine tightly controlled information flow to and from the defaulter camps. Not from any embarrassment about the brutality of their gulags.

The cruelty was the point.

No, the Combine squeezed off access because they could then turn a profit on loosening the clamps, just a little. She had to pay for every message she sent to her father, and for every brief note he sent back. There was no question of anything as grand as a live hologram link. She didn't earn enough money in a year to pay for one minute of real-time connection like that. But for the decade or more he had been an indebted convict she had been sending and receiving little snippets of text, and paying heavily for every word.

Nothing for months now, though.

She hated the Combine and hated the politicians who'd let them operate within the Commonwealth by proxy, using Mars-registered shell companies to prey on the working poor. On people like her dad. As hard as it was keeping her shit locked down for everyone on *Defiant*, it was much harder not knowing what was happening to him. The only family she had.

The last she knew for certain, he was on Batavia, in a camp somewhere in the Great Ironstone Desert.

But now?

She had no idea. Nothing. And only the slimmest hope that his lowly status as a prisoner, and his complete lack of any gene work or neural implants, would render him of little interest to the Sturm. They might even have released him. A dark joke, given that she now owned his debt, courtesy of Varro Chase.

If it weren't for the Sturm she could have set her father free.

But then again if it weren't for the invasion it's unlikely Chase and she would have reached an uneasy reconciliation. He had been quiet and withdrawn since the battle at Montrachet. Twice he had asked her to relieve him of his commission, that he might seek out the remnant forces of his House and lead them against the invaders. Twice, reluctantly, she had denied him. To her surprise, he had not given her any grief over the refusal.

"Five minutes and we put boots on the rock."

Chief Higo's voice in her helmet speakers was loud and she jumped a little. She wished she had neural net access. Wished she could call up the image of her mother and father she'd copied from the tiny holo in her cabin, the only memento she had of them. But none of that was possible.

All she had was the next mission. Lucinda minimized the window carrying vision of the troop compartment, moving it to the periphery of her display, replacing it center screen with a feed from the shuttle's forward-looking sensors and another from *Defiant*'s combat information matrix.

The handful of survivors endured in the base schematic, their tiny blue indicators isolated and surrounded by slowly moving red dots. The Volume out to the heliopause was empty of threats. Sephina's ship waited five hundred kilometers astern of *Defiant*. Up ahead Descheneaux Station drew close.

It had been just over a month since Lucinda had been here. She had passed through the same transit lounge where two of the survivors hung on, unaware that help was coming. She wondered who they might be. And why they still lived when almost nobody else had been spared. Were they young first lifers like her? The station's autonomics were unimpaired. Subroutines maintained atmosphere and gravity. Did water still flow through the pipes? Probably. In fact, it had to. The same autonomic systems regulated all the station's life support functions, and they remained unaffected by the malware attacks. All the better to provide the Sturm with a base for the next phase of their attack, the move deeper into the GV.

None of the eight people still alive down there could have lived this long without water.

The two in the transit lounge might know soon enough that they were saved, however.

Chief Higo aimed the shuttle at the docks a few hundred meters away from them. Not long ago Lucinda had stood, pressing her nose to a porthole in that lounge looking out over the flight path they were now taking in. She would have seen the blunt, angular bulk of the armored transport as it dropped toward the vast open mouth of the harbor. She could see the docks rushing toward them now. Poorly lit. Seemingly empty. One light flickering somewhere in the depths.

The stars seemed to spin around them as Chief Higo matched their approach to the rotation of the hollowed-out moonlet.

"One and down," the chief announced.

Gunnery Sergeant Cox's voice crackled through the shared tac channel.

"We deploy hot. Keep your suits sealed for vacuum. Dahl, Aronson, you're on point. Nesbitt, Singh, break left. Wu and Garret, go right. That leaves you and Commander Hardy to watch our six, Captain."

"You got it, Gunny," Hayes replied.

Lucinda could not help herself. It was basic doctrine that the command element deploy last but she searched for any nuance in Cox's delivery that might imply he resented having a squid ride along. Especially the one who'd led his friends to their deaths on Montrachet. But the non-com was all business and she had to admonish herself for her doubts. It was insulting to Hayes and his marines.

She felt a light blow on her upper arm and brought up the camera feed from the troop compartment. Hayes was standing next to her in the stick. He had tapped her with one gauntleted fist, and he now opened a private command channel.

"Hey, you good there, Commander? Not your usual chatty self today."

She was glad he could not see her blush inside the helmet.

"I was just thinking, Captain. We haven't seen up close the effects of the strike on our own people before this. Not at scale."

"No, we haven't," he said. "And it won't be pretty. Just hang on a second."

Hayes switched from the private channel to the open tactical net.

"There are only eight survivors down there," he said. "The other five hundred and thirty are hostile. You will shoot them on sight. It will be a mercy."

The marines "hooahed" in reply, although it seemed muted. Fatalistic.

"Understood," Cox said.

Higo fed power into the gravpods and the shuttle slowed and flared, easing through the entrance of the docks. Lucinda noted that a field effect remained in place, protecting the station from hard vacuum. The base autonomics were running as though nothing had happened.

Hayes came back to her through the helmet speakers.

"Commander?" He paused. "Lucinda?"

He surprised her with that. They had always been very formal with each other, even after Montrachet. Hayes had three spans on her and she found him very intimidating.

"Yes," she said. Her own voice sounded both small and yet too loud at the same time.

"You okay there? Seriously?"

"I will be," she promised.

"Yes," he said. "You will. You're good at this. Believe it. I've seen good leaders and bad. You're going to be one of the greats."

She blushed, thankful when Hayes switched back to the wide channel as the shuttle touched down and the rear ramp door hissed open.

"We have atmosphere," he said. "And spin gravity on the lower levels. But set your mass effectors for one-half grav, and stay on your rebreathers like Gunny says. No hard data point syncs. No net plug-ins. No contact with the base except the soles of your fucking boots. Am I clear, Marines?"

They hooahed again. Louder this time.

"Let's roll."

When she stepped off the ramp, her corrosive doubts and fears fell away. It was always like this for Lucinda. When she had something concrete on which to focus, some action she could take, it stilled the voice whispering to her that she was not good enough and never would be. At least in moving forward she could leave that behind.

She moved forward.

The squad swept out of the shuttle and into the primary docks for small- and medium-sized vessels. There were at least fifteen she counted, ranging in size from their small armored shuttle, all the way up to a heavy littoral combat ship. The dual-purpose vessels could fight through hard vacuum to deliver marine combat teams into the heart of an enemy fleet, as hundreds had done in the last battle of the Javan War, or down through the atmosphere of a Big Ring or a planet, delivering ground forces to the exact point on that world where they would do the most damage.

The LCS docked on Descheneaux Station had burned. Half the length of the fuselage was a blackened, melted husk, buried in flame retardant foam. Bodies surrounded it.

Bodies lay everywhere, entwined in grotesque parodies of carnality. Arms and legs entangled. Fingers laced through clothing and hair. Heads pulled back. Throats exposed. Teeth sunk deep into flesh. Clothes torn and drenched in blood, not sweat. Eyes gouged. Innards trailing over the deck plating like discarded nightwear. Station gravity here at the surface was minimal and the long, blue-gray loops of viscera floated off the deck plating like blind, giant worms.

Some of the marines swore.

Cox swore back at them to shut the fuck up and keep moving.

Lucinda kept moving. A droplet of some foul organic liquid splashed against her visor, persisting as a brown smear until she sprayed the faceplate clean with a thin stream of solvent from the nozzles in her left gauntlet. In her right hand she kept her personal weapon at the ready.

She focused on sweeping her arc with the holo sights of the carbine, glad to be buttoned up inside her armor, breathing clean air. She checked the outside temperature.

Twenty-one degrees Celsius.

The whole station would reek of death and horror.

"Sturm," one of the marines announced, but without urgency. The marine squad came to a halt, fanning out to provide a secure perimeter while Sergeant Cox examined the body of the enemy trooper. Or the largest part of that body, anyway. The legs and some of the lower torso were missing.

He fed the vision from his helmet cam to Hayes's and Lucinda's heads-up displays.

"No blast or kinetic damage," Cox said. "No scorching from energy weapons. Looks like something tore him apart and threw the legs away."

The gunnery sergeant stood up and looked around, perhaps searching for the missing limbs. "Or ate them, I guess."

"There's a reason the Sturm stayed on their ships," Hayes said. "Maybe this is why."

"No," Lucinda said absently. "Not why. Just what." She pointed at the corpse. "We don't know how or why he died like that. Just that he died. And it wasn't anybody affected by malware. The whole base could have chewed on his armor plate all day. Wouldn't have made a dent."

"Testify," said Cox. "There's probably more of them. The Sturm wouldn't withdraw because of just one casualty."

"All right," Hayes said, addressing the squad. "New threat vector. It's not just malware, zombies, or the Sturm. There's something else down here. Keep your eyes open and your asses tight."

They moved off again in the same formation; the marines advanced in a blunt wedge with Hayes and Lucinda at the rear. Every few steps one of the two officers would take it in turn to check their six. Their suits had rear-facing cams that fed vision of everything behind them, but both had been trained to trust the evidence of their own eyeballs above all else. Sensor feeds could be hacked.

It was an eerie experience. Every time Lucinda turned around, the charnel house of the docks seemed haunted by the unquiet dead. She half expected the corpses to reanimate and come shambling after them. With infected neural nets it wasn't entirely out of the question—except that the Sturm who had infected them were dead now, too. There was nobody to throw the switch.

She was glad to exit the dock space and enter the upper levels of the station, until she saw what was waiting for them.

The docks had been a very large open area. There were hundreds of bodies, but they were dispersed over a couple of square kilometers. In the confined lengths of Descheneaux's passageways there was no avoiding or ignoring the dense, impacted horror visited upon her former comrades.

One of the marines cursed under her breath.

Neither Hayes nor Cox bothered with a reprimand.

The scene in the long, gently curving passageway was an atrocity. The fire team came to a halt as if by unspoken agreement. In reality, they had all suffered a momentary paralysis of will in the face of an abomination. The dead lay in ghoulish, promiscuous surfeit. Violated, disfigured, profane. They had torn one another apart. Painted the bulkheads with their insides. Limbs floated free in the micro gravity. Wrack and offal mixed in the desecrated air.

Somebody choked down a cry.

"Wait," Lucinda said.

Her voice sounded strangled and unfamiliar inside the helmet.

Hayes turned toward her.

"What?"

"Something has been through here recently," she said. Concentrating on her breathing and her pulse. Ignoring the evidence of her eyes. Except for one thing. The floating limbs and gore.

"There's not much gravity up here on the surface. But there is some. Everything should have settled. It will float free as we move through, but we haven't done that yet. Something or someone was here in the last hour or so."

Nobody moved.

Nobody spoke until finally, Hayes said, "Agreed."

"Could just be a rando, some biter, wandering the passageways," Gunny Cox offered. "That would stir things up."

"Hold fast," Lucinda ordered.

She opened a channel to Lieutenant Bannon on *Defiant*.

"Ian," she said. "You can see where we are? Just outside the docks?"

"Yes, Commander," his voice came back. "Got everyone's signal."

"I need you to quickly replay the take from all sensor sweeps of this passageway over the last two hours. See if anything moved through."

"Aye, ma'am."

Before he could reply another voice appeared on the channel.

Herodotus.

"Allow me," the Intellect said. "There was an anomaly at your location, thirty-seven minutes and twelve seconds ago."

"What do you mean 'an anomaly'?" Hayes growled.

"An oddity, Captain Hayes," Hero replied. "A peculiarity. An incongruous event that differs from the norm. And before you say something entirely predictable, allow me to anticipate your next stupid question . . ."

Lucinda heard another voice, not on a separate channel, but in the background of this one. A Scottish snarl.

"Aye, for fuck's sake yah mangled fud, they're neck deep in fucking rancid haggis bits down there, just get on wi' it . . ."

McLennan.

"It appears there was a displacement," Hero said. "Very brief. As though a huge amount of superdense mass arrived at your location via a micro-fold, then disappeared."

"Shit," Lucinda breathed.

"I judge from the very specific tone of Commander Hardy's voice that she is not simply expressing a primitive human fear of the unknown, but that she has correctly intuited—"

"I am going to pull yer fuckin' plug if ye dinnae stop chewing yer own banger for the sheer fuckin' joy of it, you—"

"It's an Intellect," Lucinda said, cutting in over the exchange back on *Defiant*. "There is an Intellect down here, probably compromised by malware. That's what tore up the Sturm trooper. That's why they were standing off, waiting for it to die or self-terminate."

She heard a few grunts and curses on the tactical channel.

"Shut the fuck up, everyone," Hayes ordered. "*Defiant*, is there any sign of it on-site right now?"

"No," Hero said, sounding pleased with himself.

"Nothing on our scans," Lieutenant Bannon added. "But that doesn't mean much. An Intellect wouldn't have any real trouble shielding itself."

"Even if it was insane?" Lucinda asked.

"Excuse me," Hero protested. "We fragment when compromised."

"Compromised, then," she said.

The eerie, gruesome strangeness of the passageway seemed heavier, darker. Lucinda felt gooseflesh crawling over her body beneath the nanoweave one-piece coverall she wore inside her combat suit. She shivered.

"It's possible," Herodotus replied. "If you were smart enough to understand the fragment pathology of a compromised super intelligence I would explain, but we both know—"

"Och, there's yer giant toothless arse mouth flapping its gums again—"

"Okay. Good chat," Lucinda said. She cut the commlink.

"What's happening, Gunny?" one of the marines asked on the tac channel.

It was Private Penny Dahl, Lucinda saw on the squad link panel in her HUD. Private Dahl had a point. She did not turn around, but her question was loaded with significance.

Hayes replied.

"This was always a hot extract from a hostile LZ. Nothing has changed. We don't leave people behind. Move out."

Dahl stepped off without comment.

They moved carefully through the mounds of torn dead flesh, but every step of the massive armored suits liberated some new chunk, or severed limb, or disturbed and drifting carrion cloud. Lucinda swept her arc. Ignored the loathsome and macabre tailings of the war crime that had been done here. Blood splatters painted the walls like the blazoned pennants of some demon army. The armored suits were the aberration. Perverse in their clean lines and functional movement. The heinous dead had dominion now. She and the living were intruders.

The shivers that ran up and down her limbs threatened to morph into deep body spasms of revulsion. She occluded her faceplate, cutting off her vision of the passageway, relying instead on lidar sweeps from the suit's external sensor nodes that rendered the long arc of the concourse in the simplest form, as a ray-traced outline, with dense clumps of organic matter represented by purely figurative geometries, emptied of spite and meaning.

They were half an hour moving four hundred meters, taking care not to further disturb the open grave with their movement. The carnage thinned out after a while, and Lucinda turned off the lidar abstraction of their surroundings. She saw from the blank, opaque faceplates of the other team members that most of them had defaulted to navigating by instruments, too.

Penny Dahl, on point, held up one thick gauntlet. A mound of bodies lay piled up against the walls where the entrance to the transit lounge should be.

"Looks like they tried to get in," Cox said.

"Clear them away," Hayes ordered.

"Dahl and Aronson. Take a knee, cover the approaches. The rest of you with me. Let's clear the obstruction."

He turned to Lucinda before they could start.

"Ma'am, if you could train your suit's audio pickup on the far side of the wall it might help. Tell us if you hear anything from the other side. Scans show two warm-blooded, neurotypical humanoids in there. Probably shitting themselves."

"Will do, Gunny," she said.

The marines set to the grisly task of clearing the rampart. They did not throw the bodies aside like sandbags or cordwood, but they did not move with inappropriate solemnity. It was not a funeral cortege.

Lucinda was glad to have something else to think about. She tuned the suit's auditory sensors to cancel out the near-field returns from the work detail, the harrowing crunch and crack of separating the dead from one another, sometimes with great force. Instead, she focused the directional amps on a spot ten meters to the west. Inside the isolated lounge.

It seemed quiet, but not completely deserted in there.

She thought she could detect breathing. Possibly even voices, low and urgent.

The marines were five minutes clearing the obstruction, only to find another one behind it.

A vending machine pushed or more likely dragged into the entryway. It was still humming, trailing a power cable.

"Makes sense," Hayes said. "You hear anything?"

Lucinda hand-signed to him that she could not be certain.

"I'm going to try to reach out to them," she said. "Maybe you should stand back from the door."

Two of the marines moved away.

Lucinda took up a position just to the side of the entrance. She doubted the occupants would have heavy weapons in there, but it did not hurt to be careful. She powered on a loud hailer in the breastplate of her suit.

"Attention, Armadalen naval personnel. This is Commander Lucinda Hardy of the destroyer HMAS *Defiant*. We are sweeping the station for survivors. If you are able, please identify yourselves. Our scanners show two life signs in this area."

Nothing.

Gunnery Sergeant Cox opened a link on the command channel.

"We could just kick the snack machine out of the way. Toss a stun grenade in there."

"Works for me," Hayes said.

"They could be injured, or just out of it," Lucinda warned. "Give me another go."

"Could be the enemy in there," Hayes countered.

"They'd have evacuated to their ships. I'll try again."

She turned on the loud hailer.

"This is Commander Hardy," she said. "I've been where you are right now. Like, literally. I sat in that stupid transit lounge for hours before joining *Defiant*. I know this vending machine is garbage. It's got those shitty fucking protein cookies. And no decent candy. We're here to get you and the other survivors. We're coming in now, step away from—"

The marines' weapons came up like spring-loaded traps as first the hatch and then the big vending machine jerked a few inches to the side.

"Don't shoot," a voice called out through the barrier. It was weak and small, but she recognized the accent.

Coriolis. Her home.

There were two sailors in the lounge. A first life able spacehand, Abbie Nguyen. And a master chief on his third span, Dino Gotti.

"We was waiting for a ride down the well," Gotti explained, once Cox and Lucinda had pushed the vending machine aside. It didn't weigh much in the low gravity, but it still massed out as a dangerously big-ass piece of plasteel to go throwing around.

"Nguyen here, she only just got her mesh reinstalled."

"I had a failed system update," she explained. "It turned bad. Had to pull the mesh completely."

"Doctors said she was supposed to wait a couple more days for the synaptic clusters to recover from the new implant," Gotti went on. They seemed to have picked up the habit of speaking for each other.

"I was freaking out," Nguyen explained. "I had to start my posting in twelve hours. I needed to be online."

"I told her she needed to chill the fuck out," Gotti said.

The marines and Lucinda stood in a loose circle around the pair. Dahl and Wu secured the passageway outside. None of the SAR team had popped their armor, so they loomed over Nguyen and Gotti. Iron giants dwarfing two very frail-looking skin puppets in filthy day uniforms. Gotti had been a big guy, Lucinda could see, but his flesh now hung in loose flaps from a shrunken frame. She guessed the chief had made sure Nguyen got the lion's share of the vacuum-sealed nutrients salvaged from the snack machine. Nguyen looked like an escapee from the Combine's worst defaulter camp, her limbs thin twigs and the lines of her face sunken by starvation. They stood very close together and Lucinda noticed that sometimes when the back of Nguyen's hand brushed Gotti's, her tiny, clawlike fingers twitched as if reaching for his.

Hayes pinged Lucinda privately. One line of text.

Gotta move soon.

She hand-signed agreement, just a small move that neither Gotti or Nguyen picked up.

"So, Chief, how come you weren't online when the nano-phage hit?"

That was Cox.

Gotti smiled and shrugged. Nguyen grasped his hand and squeezed before letting go.

"I powered down my own mesh, just to show Nguyen she didn't need hers. Told her I'd ride down dirt side, all the way, and give her chief the word. It wasn't gonna be no big thing. We all gotta work offline sometime, right?"

"We shat the mesh, soon as we knew about the malware," Cox said.

"Chief, we have to move on to the infirmary," Lucinda said. "There's more survivors there and we're on the clock. We need to know anything that might affect the tactical setup here."

Gotti nodded.

"Well, we been holed up in here, soon as I saw what was happening, but I seen some shit out the windows. And you hear things. It's bad, right?"

"Yes," Cox agreed.

Gotti nodded again, took a breath, and seemed to stand a little taller. Lucinda could see him becoming what he had once been. A soldier of Armadale. Not just a guy who'd survived.

"The enemy assaulted onto the station about three days after the first strike," he said. "I thought it was the fucking Javans, back for a second bite of the cherry, you know. But then I saw them come down in landing craft. They weren't Javans. It was fucking Sturm. They were clearing and holding. Just sweeping the base and putting down the infected. That wasn't no fair fight. Armored infantry against sick people."

Gotti was growing agitated and Nguyen gripped his arm. It seemed to calm him down.

"Anyway that went on for half a day, tops. They was making their way toward us. I could hear them coming. We'd blocked the door. Dragged that snack-o-matic outside across the hatch before they piled up outside trying to get in. Tearing each other to pieces. You could see how that was gonna go."

"The chief made weapons," Nguyen said.

"It was nothing," Gotti said, waving it away. "Just improvised stuff."

He laughed, a short, half-crazed bark.

"I sharpened up a fucking toilet brush. Planned to stick it into the first asshole came through that door."

"Outstanding," Captain Hayes said.

"But they never came," Nguyen said.

"We heard a big firefight," Gotti explained. "Somewhere down the docks, best I could tell. And then all these armored shuttles are tear-assing it off the rock."

"It's been quiet ever since," Nguyen continued. "Just that bright flare in the sky a couple of hours ago."

"That was the Sturm getting their asses kicked," Cox explained. "We got 'em all."

"Good work," said Gotti.

"Chief," Captain Hayes asked. "You think the enemy ground teams could've been firing on a Combat Intellect? You seen anything made you think there could be one hanging around?"

The two survivors exchanged a look.

"We heard some things," Nguyen said, her voice even smaller than before. Lucinda was going to amp up the gain on her suit mics, but Gotti came back as loud as ever.

"The infected, you'd hear them all the time at first. Like a zoo. Then that dialed down. Sometimes, though, in the distance there'd be energy weapons or something. It was hard to say without laying eyes on it. And we've been stuck here, eating protein cookies and drinking toilet water."

"Okay," Hayes said. "You've done well. Both of you."

He detailed two of the SAR team to escort Gotti and Nguyen back to the shuttle, and to stay with them there. Lucinda spoke with the marine captain on the command channel.

"A damaged Intellect, fragmented or insane or whatever. I can't think of anything more dangerous," she said.

"You want to scrub the mission? Try to resup at Waller or Collins? They're deeper in-volume."

She decided quickly.

"No. We still have people to get. And the ship isn't exposed to hazard. Just us. We don't even know if it's dangerous to us. Remember *Defiant* fought the malware for days and kept it quarantined until the end."

She did not add . . . until Hero excised the sickened Intellect and folded it into a fucking star.

"Could be it's a danger to the Sturm. But not us," Lucinda said.

She sounded as if she was trying to convince herself. She started to go on. Stopped. And started again.

"I . . . Captain Hayes . . . I'm reluctant to commit your people without your concurrence. I can order, but I can't ask that of them. I just . . ." She trailed off.

Hayes's voice came back on the private channel. Much softer than she had ever heard him speak in public.

"You're not sure. Are you?"

"No," Lucinda admitted. "I don't know what the right thing is."

"The right thing to do is to rescue our people. The tactically correct decision is to withdraw and resupply when safe. Welcome to the officers' club."

They stood slightly apart from the other ranks while Cox directed the marines to plot waypoints to the infirmary.

"Lucinda," Hayes said. "Doubt is a natural part of command. It's human. But you cannot let your people see you undone by it. They want certainty. Even if it's the certainty of sacrifice and loss. We owe them that."

She straightened a little, glad of the armor that hid her discomfort and lack of resolve. Her all too human frailty.

"Thank you, Michael," she said. "I worry I'm not ready for this."

"Nobody is ever ready for this," Hayes said. "Your orders? It's your call. Head or heart?"

"We're going to get our people now."

"Outstanding."

CHAPTER

ELEVEN

The SAR team, reduced by two, moved out for the infirmary. Dahl and Aronson dropped back, with Garret and Wu taking point. The tactical feed from *Defiant*'s CI matrix initially guided them down through the long, sinuous curves of the passageways carved into the moonlet's hard crust. The live schematic, studded with hundreds of motile red dots, enabled them to avoid unnecessary contact with the infected. But the deeper they probed, the more tenuous the link back to *Defiant* grew. Without a direct connection to the station's own compromised comm nets, the marines and Lucinda soon found themselves cut off from real-time overwatch. The moon's unusually dense, super-hard iron-titanium crust choked off any wideband data feed by the third level down.

Gunny Cox called a halt to their cautious advance at the junction of two main corridors. The intersection was thick with ravaged corpses and the dead husk of a Fleet-level Autonomous Combat Intellect. They turned handheld scanners and suit sensors on the murdered super intelligence, but got nothing for it. It lay on the floor, its gargantuan mass distorting the deck plates like a bowling ball held up by a rubber sheet.

"This is not the droid we're looking for," Penny Dahl said quietly, impressing Lucinda. She hadn't imagined a simple grunt would ever have studied the classics.

They pushed on, ghosting down corridors that slowly but surely twisted like plasteel strands of DNA to afford them the convenience of spin gravity. Lucinda told her suit to dial back the mass effector, which had kept her safely anchored to the deck up on the surface. She had passed through Descheneaux several times during the Javan War, and even more frequently in the years before, when she had taken up her first posting on the *Taipan* as a baby ensign helping run anti-piracy patrols. It was deeply disturbing to return to a haunted ruin. Even during the war, the Imperial Javan Navy had never come close to threatening the station, or the local volume. Descheneaux had been carved out of the unusually dense, hardened satellite in the decade before the conflict. Indeed, it was the Commonwealth's insistence on "militarizing" the disputed moonlets of this system that the Empire cited as its primary *casus belli*. Armadale, for its part, cited the doctrine of self-defense to the Court of Interplanetary Disputes back on Earth, pointing to years of escalating attacks and raids by Taleba and Laksha militia forces, both of which were acknowledged by everybody but the Javans to be nothing more than surrogate "forces of bidding" for the imperial palace on Medang.

Looking to anchor its claim on the system by building out and reinforcing Descheneaux Station to secure the local volume, Armadale had triumphed in one court hearing after another. The RAN had driven off the militias. And the Empire had declared war.

How pointless it all seemed to Lucinda now.

It appeared that victory meant only short-lived control of a frozen moon, filled with the walking dead.

There were hundreds of corpses in this part of the base. The spectacle was every bit as obscene as the more compressed tableau outside the docks and the transit lounge. Some of the lighting had shorted out down here, though, and the vast grotesquery was illuminated by the chromatic strobing of failing strip lights. It made the dreamlike quality of the images even more unreal as the SAR team resumed its trek to the infirmary. The armored giants advanced in flickering staccato, like industrial monsters in a grainy, monochrome film exhibit from the very earliest moments of recorded entertainment.

Lucinda was just about to block out her faceplate, and go back to navigating by instruments, when something in the corner of her vision moved out of sync with the rest of the jerky, strobing panorama. She swung the muzzle of her carbine toward the anomaly, unsure of whether she had simply been misled by the confusing snarl of eerily animated imagery.

Her heartbeat stopped.

And then restarted at a massively quickened rate. Three dreadful figures, emerging from branching corridors, charged at their flank. They advanced in jumps and fits under the strobe light. Checking their flight momentarily to snarl and roar at one another, all three plunged on in hope of beating their rivals to the feast of fresh meat.

"Contact left," Lucinda called, but the marines had also detected movement and half of their echelon swiveled to engage the threat. The others turned away from it, guarding the open flank to the right.

Targeting lasers speared out through the half gloom, settling on the center mass of the approaching berserkers. Lucinda's own designator picked out a frenzied golem, naked and smeared with gore, its features barely human.

She pulled the trigger.

Her three rounds struck the infected attacker at the same moment as somebody else took him under fire. The caseless ceramic slugs tore into their onetime colleague, punching fist-sized chunks out of his unprotected upper body. All three went down together.

Lucinda swept the concourse looking for movement, but everything was still.

"Move out," Hayes said.

The infirmary was another two levels down, another fifteen minutes of inching progress through increasingly difficult terrain. Another two incidents with the infected.

They came on without guile or strategy, simply screaming and running at the marines when they sensed them nearby. Each time the team dispatched them without ceremony or delay.

Lucinda had wondered if she might hesitate before pulling a trigger on someone who had once been a brother or sister in arms. Some of the dead she had seen were naked. Many were dressed in tattered rags and raiment, mere scraps of the uniforms they had worn. Others were still outfitted as if for duty. But her training and the balls-out homicidal madness of the afflicted shorted out any fellow feeling she might have had for them. At least in the moment. Perhaps later when she returned to the ship and had time to dwell on what they had done down here, perhaps then she might have regrets.

For now, they moved toward their objective and they serviced any targets of opportunity.

Reaching the junction of two major passageways, Specialist Kanon Aronson brought them to a halt with a hand signal. Another redundancy in networked armor. Another deeply trained-in example of Armadalen field craft.

Gunny Cox joined Aronson at the corner, extending a fiber-optic seeker from one of his gauntlets to peer around the bend. He fed the vision through to Hayes, who pushed it out to the rest of the team.

A window opened in Lucinda's helmet. She saw a roiling stew of insane human husks, emptied of everything but the deepest, most primitive death urge. The seething dead had piled up at the entrance to the infirmary, heaving, scratching, and raking at the door. Near the edges of the massive cannibal pile-on, individual creatures turned on one another, but mostly they seemed in thrall to an unseen hive mind, bent on gaining access to the few remaining survivors in the shuttered base hospital.

Hayes's voice came in over tac-net.

"Nothing for it," he said. "We're gonna have to plow the field. Dahl, you cover our six."

"Sir, thank you, sir," the marine answered.

"Commander Hardy, Private Dahl might appreciate the help," Hayes suggested. He was giving her an out.

"Private, I'll pinch-hit if needed," Lucinda said. "You call me. But I'll do what needs doing up here first."

"Aye, ma'am," Dahl answered. She took a knee, swapped in a fresh mag, and brought her weapon up to cover their rear.

"Form up on me," Hayes said. "Line abreast, Marines. We take the corner like you're back at Portsea and Gunny Cox is your drill sergeant. Commander Hardy," he went on. "Did they let you academy squids play at drill?"

She was surprised to find she had a reply ready to defend the honor of her own, more senior service.

"Pfft. Come on, Hayes. You know Marine Corps drill sergeants are just stitched together from broken-ass body parts we rejected as being nowhere near good enough for Navy drill chiefs."

She got some hella fierce pushback for that, a little sass and banter from her sister service members that helped them all forget what they were about to do.

Gunny Cox confirmed the afflicted had not yet made them. Hayes took a slot next to Cox and the rest of the fire team formed up on him. Lucinda anchored the end of the line next to Private Aronson. She programmed her ceramic munitions for maximum clearance in a hardened environment. This far down in the rock, there was no chance of puncturing a hull or bulkhead and exposing the station to hard vacuum.

On Hayes's command they marched out and pivoted, presenting arms, taking aim, and clearing the feral horde with a torrent of automatic weapons fire. The passageway blazed with tracer streams and muzzle flash. Lucinda's optical sensors spontaneously blanked out her faceplate, replacing her view downrange with simple targeting schematics. She worked the problem with fire. Her magazine ran dry. She swapped it for a second mag and returned to the tactical problem with the simplest solution. More fire.

It seemed to last forever, but then it was done before she expected.

Her helmet displays flashed red. An empty mag. Then green. No more targets.

Optical sensors, no longer overloaded by the shock and fury of the firestorm, returned her helmet settings to normal. The faceplate cleared and she was able to see what they had done.

A feast day for a carnivore saint. Smoking, twitching posthuman ruin. A gross and hateful canvas painted by a necroscatological master.

Somebody gagged on tac-net, a half choke that turned into a hiss as their suit injected fast-acting anti-nausea chems directly into the bloodstream.

Lucinda felt numbed and hollowed out. Light-headed but heavy of limb.

Private Dahl's voice arrived in her helmet as though from another reality. "Six clear."

Hayes's voice replied. "Aronson, you're with Dahl. Keep us sweet. The fireworks will probably bring more of them. We're moving on to the infirmary."

"Sir, yes, sir," the young marine barked.

The SAR team stepped off again.

They advanced on the entrance to the sick bay with fresh mags and guns up. Lucinda zoomed in and noted that plasteel covers had dropped to secure the infirmary when the base autonomics triggered a lockdown. There would be no dickering about protein cookies through those things.

Turned out there was no need.

The plasteel screen securing the main door rolled up and a white cloth appeared on a stick.

Her far-field mics picked up a man's voice.

"Don't shoot. We're not infected. Nobody in here is infected."

The man who'd spoken stepped through the doorway with his hands raised. He was careful not to lose his footing in the steaming slurry of gore. He wore a lab coat that had once been white. It was gray now, with splotches and splatters of something darker. He was terribly gaunt. All of the hollows of his face were deeply sunken, and the top of his spine stood out as nobbled ridges on the back of his neck.

"Identify yourself," Gunny Cox called out.

"I'm Doctor Philip Thieu," he said. "Deputy head of neural engineering. Are the Javans gone?"

"It wasn't the Javans, Doctor," Hayes said. He dropped the muzzle of his weapon. "It's okay," he went on. "He's lost some weight, but I know this guy. He supervised my last upgrade. Right here on Descheneaux."

The fire team advanced on Thieu, but with guns down, not pointed at him. Lucinda followed closely behind Hayes. The neural engineer peered into Hayes's faceplate as if trying to recognize him.

"Doc, my name is Captain Hayes," he said. "You probably don't remember me, but I remember you from the war. I'm not going to pop my suit. We are operating under biohazard protocols. We scan six of you as viable, is that correct?"

Thieu nodded quickly.

"It's me, Nurse Bo Xian, and four patients. All of them were awaiting mesh upgrades. So was I, for what it's worth. My nurse was offline. Standard procedure in pre-op and the implant theater."

"Saved your life," Cox said. "What happened to the other patients and staff? The infected."

Thieu hesitated before answering.

"I hit them with a million volts of directed EMP," he said. It sounded like a confession because in a way it was. An electromagnetic pulse of that power would flash-fry the brains of anybody in the blast range who was wired up with neural implants. The Javans had deployed them during the war, in open contravention of the Geneva Protocols Addenda. War crimes trials had been scheduled for the new year on Earth.

"Jesus," somebody said.

"How?" Lucinda asked.

"We have stress-testing rigs," Thieu said. "I reconfigured the main rig. Took off the safety limits."

"No," she clarified. "How did you get the chance? Didn't they turn immediately?"

She was thinking of how quickly Captain Torvaldt had devolved into a ravening cannibal when he'd been exposed to the nanophage.

Thieu appeared to be confused by the question, but then he nodded.

"Everyone turned, yes. But I was in pre-op with my patients and the nurse. We were going to batch them through. Pre-op and theater are both quarantine pods. No direct physical access to the outside. No neuralink. No emissions of any kind. It interferes with the implant. The neural mesh seed is remarkably . . ."

Lucinda held up a gauntlet.

"It's fine. Are they mobile? Your patients, the nurse?"

As if to answer, a second head appeared out of the entrance to the infirmary. A woman wearing an heirloom Han Chinese phenotype.

"We good?" she asked.

"We're good, Bo," Thieu said. "It's over."

But it wasn't.

They did not linger at the infirmary. Thieu gathered the other survivors and the marines formed up around them in a protective cordon.

The four patients included two marines, but neither of them had armor or weapons and they were all weak from near starvation.

"This is going to be harder," Hayes said. "We have to avoid clusters of infected if we can. We have to put them down fast if we can't. One rule. Nothing gets through us."

The answer was clear. And loud.

"HOOAH!"

Lucinda and Dahl led them out this time. They encountered small clusters of infected, but had no trouble dealing with them until they returned to the place they'd found the dead Intellect, the intersection of four major thoroughfares a couple of levels up. Overwatch was not available there, the moonlet's super-hard crust still being too thick at that depth for the u-band signal from *Defiant* to get through.

Lucinda noticed the change a fraction of a second before Dahl called it out.

"Infected," she said. "On the concourse."

"Lots of them," Lucinda confirmed.

She could see dozens of the creatures up ahead. They were agitated, searching for something.

No bonus for guessing what had stirred them up and drawn them together.

Unlike the two Lucinda had watched attack each other while she was safely back on the ship, this much greater number of the afflicted was so intent on locating and attacking the search and rescue team they largely ignored one another. Here and there a couple might fall into violent contention, but overall the great mob moved like a flock of birds, attending to some greater unseen will. Lucinda presumed the Sturm had programmed them that way.

"Can we go around?" she asked Hayes, pulling up the base schematics and looking for an alternative route back to the shuttle.

Before he could answer, one of the creatures broke toward the smaller corridor in which they had paused. The sudden discontinuity sent a ripple through the entire host. They did not so much pause in their seemingly random, meandering search as they . . . stuttered. And surged. Motion sensors, proximity warnings, all sorts of alerts went off in Lucinda's heads-up display. Targeting data appeared in overlay.

"Line abreast!" Hayes ordered, and the marines appeared to either side of her, creating a shield wall between the horde of meat-hacked zombies and the vulnerable survivors behind them.

It was not as easy as it had been back at the infirmary. There Lucinda had been presented with a densely packed mound of unknowing, distracted targets. Here, hundreds of them spread out over a wide-open concourse and converged on the little group from all sides. More appeared from other passageways.

"Private Wu, take the six," Gunnery Sergeant Cox ordered.

"Yes, Sergeant," Wu shouted, pulling out of the firing line and hurrying back to take a position behind the vulnerable, unarmed survivors. Lucinda could see them all in a small window that ran vision from her rear-facing sensors. They had huddled together in a doorway and looked terrified. All of them, and with good reason. She could hear the savage snarls and inhuman screeching of the infected over the uproar of gunfire.

She kept the window open but concentrated on what was happening in front of her. An inhuman wave surging toward them. As tempting as it was to throw the selector to full auto and just hose down the stampede, she assigned target selection to her suit. A squad-level algorithm connected all the suits, turning the individual members of the small fire team into a much more effective, much deadlier bulwark, bristling with guns, all of them networked into a single dedicated emplacement of sensors and shooters. Upon that solid wall came a rampage of mindless ferocity.

Lucinda tried to let go of volition and agency. She had to let the suit decide where to move, her gun choose its own targets. It was an exercise she had practiced many times, but one she had never had to perform in the field. Not even during the most intense engagements of the Javan War. She felt like a cog in a machine, and just for a moment, one fleeting second, she understood how the Sturm thought about them. Why they called them cyborgs and mutants and machine slaves.

She dismissed the thought. Not as heresy, but stupidity.

Her armor made micro adjustments, her weapon fired, the targets dropped. The same process played out down the line, and slowly but surely they turned the inhuman tide racing toward them. She saw a muzzle flash in her peripheral vision. Not from Penny Dahl who was standing beside her, but from Private Wu who was kneeling in a small window at the side of her heads-up display.

"Splash one. Clear on your six," Wu said.

Lucinda heard Gunny Cox in her headset.

"Good work. Stay on it."

They had stacked up the dead in front of them like a berm of mangled flesh. Bodies lay piled upon more bodies, and still the creatures came on, scrambling over the unstable, obscene barricade like human spiders racing toward a butterfly at the edge of a web.

She swapped out a magazine. Fired. Fired again.

And stopped.

Her battle armor still moved with a mind of its own, slaved to the needs of the algorithm. A second later, however, sensing that the field was clear of targets, it ceded control back to her.

"Dahl, Aronson, move up," Cox ordered.

They acknowledged the order, loaded fresh mags, and moved forward into the killing field. Lucinda checked her ammunition load. She was running low. Two mags left.

As if reading her mind, Gunny Cox called for an ammo check. They were all running low. Captain Hayes checked in with Doctor Thieu. They hadn't lost any of the patients or medics. Lucinda tried to ignore the atrocity in front of them. No denying that's what it was. The dead and dying monsters had once been colleagues. Friends. More. But it was the Sturm's atrocity for sure. There was no moral ambiguity about who was responsible for what had just happened, even though she could not deny her own role. The dead were many and she had pulled the trigger. She felt light-headed, clammy. A medical alert flashed in amber, inquiring whether she was in need of treatment for severe nausea.

Instead she adjusted the climate control on her suit, shaving a couple of degrees off the internal temperature, allowing herself to cool down as she regained control over her breathing. She had been so tense during the firefight that a couple of times she forgot to breathe. Feeling the cool air on her sweating forehead helped.

She heard a weapon firing, but it was only Dahl finishing off a wounded creature.

"We're good to go, Gunny," Dahl reported.

Captain Hayes confirmed that Doctor Thieu's people were okay to move, rotated Kanon Aronson and Chi Garret back as tail gunners, and ordered the group to get moving again. Cox and Dahl had to tear apart the chest-high wall of corpses they had made of their former comrades. There was no way the weakened survivors could have crawled over the top of them. And there was always the chance of reanimation or of simply getting bitten by one of the infected that had been crippled but not killed.

Hayes came up beside Lucinda as they moved through the breach, staying in the blunt wedge formation they had employed previously. It created a safe space for the survivors inside the arrowhead and allowed the armored marines to kick aside or finish off any remaining hostiles.

The concourse area, a popular meeting spot lined by coffee bars, PX concessions, and chill zones, was transformed. It looked like a crowded marketplace, targeted by multiple bombers and random shooters. Lucinda had experience with hand-to-hand combat. She had won her Star of Valor after folding onto a small Javan warship, unprotected by armor, and armed only with a fighting knife and a pistol. She had captured the ship. She knew what mortal, singular combat was like.

And it was nothing like this. This was unspeakably worse.

"How you doing?" Hayes asked on their private command channel.

"It's . . . I don't know," she said. "I'm alive. We're all alive. I guess that's something."

"That's everything," Hayes said. "We'll have a drink later. A real drink. No synthetics or metabolizers."

He wasn't asking. He was telling.

"Okay," she said. "I'd like that."

The size of the horde was so great that Lucinda wondered how many others could be left on the base. Not many, as it happened. They engaged small clusters another three times on the climb back to the surface but did not encounter any other large groups. The final attack consisted of three infected in the passageway outside the docks. Their swarming behavior was so predictable by then that there was no longer any question whether the Sturm had programmed it. Doctor Thieu, the neural engineer, was adamant.

"The behavior is emergent and recursive," he said, after Lucinda had used her sidearm to finish off the last of the hostiles. "Conjunctive clustering. Collaborative action. Pathological impedance. It's programmed."

Thieu was standing over the infected that Lucinda had just put down. He kicked the head gently with the toe of his boot. She was getting ready to tell him, "No, you can't take a sample back to *Defiant* to study," when his body came apart like a silent explosion in an abattoir. Limbs flew away to all points of the compass. His head came off and shot straight up, Thieu's face wearing a comic expression that only disappeared when it slammed into the polished regolith overhead with a sick, wet crunch.

Blood geysered from the limbless torso that hung in midair.

Not suspended through dark magic, but held aloft on a micro-g wave.

"NO!" Lucinda shouted as the marines' weapons snapped up and converged on a two-meter-high ovoid hovering a short distance away.

An Intellect. But not like any she had ever seen before. Its exotic matter casing glowed with a protean flux of barely contained dark energies and the fathomless deep of exposed hyperspace matrices. Lines of arc lightning, blue and purple and vermilion red, crawled slowly over the surface of the Intellect's outward form. A strange hum came from it, a noise with a dense physical presence that passed through her helmet and pressed in hard upon her mind. The u-band link to *Defiant* was down again, cutting them off from support.

The suit did not ask permission this time. Hypodermics speared into her body, jamming fast-acting doses of anti-nausea chems into her bloodstream.

"Put your weapons down!" Lucinda ordered, ignoring the chain of command. Hayes had tactical command of the mission. She rode along as the senior Navy representative because that was her prerogative and everything Lucinda had learned in the profession of arms could be reduced to one essential lesson.

Leaders lead.

She knew as soon as she saw the Intellect there was no overcoming it with the puny armaments they carried. The last thing Thieu had done was to kick the skull of a fallen Armadalen warrior. The Intellect tore him apart, just as it had done to the Sturm when they assaulted onto the base.

Lucinda lay down her carbine and put up her hands.

"Hardy? What are you doing?" Hayes asked, his voice carrying a warning, if not a reprimand.

"If it wanted to kill us, we'd already be dead," she said on the open channel. "Lower your weapons. They're useless. Worse, they're a provocation."

She sensed the muzzle of Penny Dahl's carbine dropping slowly toward the deck plates on her left. On her right, Kanon Aronson raised his to the sealed regolith above.

Advancing cautiously, both hands up, palms out, she had to fight through something like a force-ten migraine with every step she took. Finally, she could go no farther.

"I am Commander Lucinda Hardy," she said, forcing the

words out through her pain. Her eyeballs felt like they were being fried in a cast-iron skillet over a roaring campfire.

"I assumed command of HMAS *Defiant* when my senior officers were killed."

The Intellect dipped a little way toward the plates, but bounced back immediately, its outer shell flaring with the twilight brilliance of neutralino dark matter.

"I . . . I . . . am . . . the In-In-Intellect . . ."

She waited for him to finish but he trailed off.

"You are the Intellect?" Lucinda prompted gently.

"I . . . am . . ." he said, and she could not tell if she heard the words on her helmet systems, or if the super intelligence had somehow cast them directly into her cortex with a field effect.

"I . . . defend . . ."

"You defended the station," she said.

". . . Defended . . . station," the Intellect confirmed.

"We can relieve you now," Lucinda said. "Your duty is done."

She slowly, carefully dropped her arms, then raised her right hand in a salute.

"I relieve you, sir."

The Intellect glowed with the hot crimson power of a red giant.

"I . . . stand . . . r-relieved."

Lucinda heard cries of distress and pain behind her, and saw the marines hurrying the survivors away, rushing them back down the passageway along which they had just come. She squeezed her eyes shut and flinched away from the explosion she was certain was coming, cursing herself for her stupidity.

The blast never came.

The sudden heat and blazing scarlet light cut off as though a thick iron wall had slammed down in front or her. And then something did slam down: a quarter-million tons of superdense metamaterials compacted into the elongated teardrop of an Autonomous Combat Intellect. The dead sentience crashed into the deck plating from a height of only a few feet, but it was enough to shake the whole base as though some Norse god had punched the fortress moon with a giant mailed fist.

The kinetic shock overwhelmed the mass effectors in Lucinda's armor, knocking her off her feet as the suit's audio sensors automatically shut down to protect her eardrums from the enormous crash of impact. She sensed the violence of the blow as a deep body tremor, shaking all her internal organs. The whole of Descheneaux Station rang with the aftershocks lapping around the moonlet and running into one another in a violent, stochastic spasm that continued for half a minute.

It was not hard to imagine the impact had cracked the outer regolith like an eggshell.

Lucinda climbed to her feet and found herself standing on a steep slope that ran downhill to the body of the fallen Intellect.

"Commander! Commander Hardy, this is *Defiant*. Do you read us?"

Lucinda acknowledged the hail.

They had commlinks back to the ship again.

"This is Hardy," she said. "We have casualties. Descheneaux is secure. You can dock at Bay Seventeen and resupply. All malware and biohazard protocols remain in force. Out."

CHAPTER

TWELVE

Revell commandeered a room on the top floor of a white-washed two-story bungalow on the semicircular quay which played home port to a small fleet of trawlers. He settled on "played" as the correct word because although Port au Pallice was a working fishing village, and at least a quarter of the true human souls who lived there were employed directly or indirectly dragging sustenance and their livelihoods from the waters of Astrolabe Bay, the whole of the enterprise was a pantomime.

The port, the bay, the fishing fleets, the men and women who worked them, the catches they hauled in, the seafood markets in which they sold their haul, the waterfront alehouses where they spent their "wages," it was all of it owned by the House of Montanblanc. All of it was an elaborate exercise in make-believe. Port au Pallice was a sham, what scholars of architecture from the very dawn of the Early Corporate Period called a "folly." It looked like a village from that faraway time, built in the late eighteenth to early nineteenth century Euroclassical Style, but the pleasing aesthetics hid another reality. A true human from that era, when everybody really was human, might wander the cobbled streets of the port and never realize how many secrets, how much unknowable magic, lay just beneath the surface of things. Mag-lev coils in the roads. Micro-fold portals in a storehouse. Neural mesh and corrupted DNA in the very meat and blood of otherwise normal-looking men and women going about their business in this vast simulacrum.

Well, at least the latter was no longer the case.

Revell stood at the window of his temporary office, enjoying his view of the waterfront. He could smell the salty tang of the ocean and hear the muted screech of seagulls outside. He wondered if the Montanblanc family had transported a breeding population all the way from Earth, but he did not wonder long. Of course they had. Directly in front of his lodgings three fishermen loaded baskets onto an ancient-looking trawler that ran on hydrogen rather than fossil fuel, and probably tempted the fish into its nets with sonic lures or pheromonal bait. The men bent to their work. Their arms and legs alternately grew long and shrank as Revell watched them through the artfully, ever-so-slightly distorted panes of window glass. Even the flaws here were period appropriate. He was impressed by the trawlermen's commitment. Fishing was their actual business now that they were no longer the property of one Elite Fraction family. Revell wasn't sure how the economics of liberation had been gamed out by the General Staff. But he knew there were specialists in the Armada, a few of them presumably working somewhere on the surface of Montrachet, who had been tasked with all of that. It would be quite a challenge, he imagined, rebuilding an interstellar economy that had undergone the equivalent of a workers' revolution. All the owners of capital and most of their hired janissaries were gone now. That would be . . . disruptive.

Still, it was satisfying to know that only the freed slaves and their liberators were walking the streets of Port au Pallice.

As he watched the trawlermen prepare to head out into the bay, three more figures approached. The antique windowpanes slightly contorted them, as well, but not so much that Revell couldn't recognize the civilian flanked by two Ground Force Security troopers.

Jasko Tan. A traitor, not someone to be trusted. But a traitor to the enemy's cause, so a man who could be used.

He was not restrained in any way, other than by the presence of his two escorts. Revell regarded him with a critical eye. He was of medium height, which immediately suggested natural birth among the lower orders. The Elite Fraction was guilty of many crimes against the genome, but one common, almost banal change they often made to the p-types they wore was to make themselves substantially larger than the true human underclasses they held in bondage. The psychology of it was simple, he supposed. They liked to play at being giants.

This traitor, a former guardsman of the "royal family"—it was hard not to roll your eyes at the majestic affectations of the immortal robber barons—presented as an average human being. He was not. Revell had studied his file closely; not just the reports of the occupying units which had dealt with him, the Pathfinder and SF squadrons of the 101st Attack Fleet, but also the Top Secret Ultra files of the Republic's external intelligence agencies. The covert services had identified, groomed, and turned Jasko Tan long before the Armada arrived at the edge of the Occupied Volume. He was a former member of the Household Guard, as highly trained as any special operator in the Republican military. But he had his weaknesses.

One of the troopers pointed in the direction of Revell's office and all three men crossed the cobblestone roadway. Now that Tan was almost here, Revell breathed out in relief. There had been no guarantee he could lay hands on the traitor. Those mutants and borgs that had not been caught in the first strike had been captured and interned, awaiting conversion to biomass in camps a few klicks out of town. Tan could easily have been gathered up in one of those sweeps. A note in his file said he had metabolized his neural mesh long before the Human Republic returned to humanity's true home, but the Inquiry was tireless in seeking out heresy, and implants always left some trace behind.

He heard three knocks on the front door.

A staffer answered and Revell listened to the men come in via the narrow entry hall.

Boots on the wooden staircase. Four sets of feet.

A light rap on his office door.

The corporal he'd borrowed to take care of administrative duties poked his head inside.

"Captain Revell. They're here, sir."

"Thank you, Corporal Meyer. Offer the troopers some refreshment. They can wait across the hall. I will see to Mister Tan myself."

"Very good, sir."

Corporal Meyer ushered in the traitor before seeing to his escorts.

"Sit, please," Revell said, waving to an old couch that lay up against the far wall. The building had once served as an outpost for servants of the Montanblanc family, caterers or culinary staff who managed the transfer of fresh produce to the Skygarth estate. It was nowhere near as grand as the villa it supplied, but it was a secure and functional workspace. The small administrator AI that had been resident here had already been turned into scrap. The machine minds on this world were all dead, thank the genome. Those things were immeasurably more dangerous than some freak with tardigrade DNA and a head full of wires.

Tan nodded and took a seat.

Revell perched on the edge of his desk, which made him look as though this was an informal chat, while giving him a height advantage from which to look down upon the subject.

"Thank you for coming, today, Mister Tan," he started, equably enough. "I do hope it's not too much of an inconvenience."

"No, sir," Tan replied. He was not obsequious in manner. "Is there something more I can help with?"

Revell almost smiled at being reminded that Tan was an ally, somebody who had already proven himself to the Republic and so should not really have to again.

"Nothing critical," Revell said. He noted that Tan did not relax the way many people would when they thought they were off the hook. He remained alert. Attentive. "I am doing some follow-up work on the escape of the Montanblanc princess."

Tan nodded as if this was only reasonable.

"Of course. I delivered the princess to your Captain Kogan D'ur, if I recall his name right."

"You do."

"After that, there's not much I could tell you. Your troopers took them away."

Revell returned Tan's gesture, nodding as though everything he'd just said was to be expected.

"After you shot your former colleague . . ." Revell made a play of checking a piece of paper on his desk. It was a bill of goods for a shipment of oysters. "Sergeant Reynolds?"

"Yeah, that's right. Old Tosh."

Revell furrowed his brow.

"Why did you do that?"

Tan actually smiled.

"Old Tosh, he was a proper dangerous bugger, sir. Just as like to shoot that young princess as give her up, if he thought that was the smart play."

"Even though she had no neural mesh yet. No backup."

"There's always another princess somewhere. That's your backup when you're a Montanblanc."

Revell considered the answer.

It seemed honest enough.

"And the other two children captured with the princess. I understand they belonged to a gardener or someone?"

Tan smiled again, relaxing now.

"No. They were the grandkids of old man Dunning. He was the groundskeeper at Skygarth. They were very friendly with the princess, as I heard tell it. Probably the only real friends she had. Not that she'd have been allowed to keep them, of course, being an heiress and such."

"I see," Revell said. He already knew this. Kogan D'ur had used the two children as leverage over the heiress. But it was not commonly known, and it went to Tan's credibility that he had volunteered the information without being pressed for it.

"I wonder, Mister Tan, if you know any of these people?"

Revell produced a series of images from security cams at the Skygarth villa. They showed a motley collection of pirates or bandits, one of them a grotesque mutant with a giant horn growing from its forehead. Tan studied the photographs but no sign of recognition fluttered in his eyes.

"Sorry, no," he said. "They the ones who grabbed her up?"

"We're following a number of lines of inquiry," Revell said, dodging the question. The raid on Montrachet to extract the princess, which Strom had allowed as a honey trap to draw out surviving enemy forces in the volume, had been the work of the Armadalen Navy and Marine Corps. What remained unknown was the identity of these freebooters, and how they had conspired with the Armadalens to destroy the 101st Attack Fleet while securing Alessia Montanblanc, the sole remaining embodiment of corporate and congressional authority in the Occupied Volume. McLennan was undoubtedly involved. And this rogue Combat Intellect. But Revell wanted to know who the woman and the freaks at Skygarth had been. Finding them might prove to be a much faster route to recovering or eliminating the princess and neutralizing the threat from McLennan and the RAN.

"Mister Dunning, the gardener," Revell went on. "I don't suppose you know if he is still alive? Fighting was heavy, and our field hospitals concentrated on saving our own people first, then casualties among the liberated population. He could be in a cot somewhere."

Jasko Tan snorted.

"Knowing that old bugger, he's dead. No way would he let me keep drawing breath otherwise."

"Perhaps," Revell conceded. "I wonder if you might do us one more service, though, Mister Tan?"

"I'm pretty fucked if I don't, I reckon."

"Pretty much," Revell agreed. "I would have you give my Corporal Meyer as accurate a description of Mister Dunning as you can, before you leave. If you have any imagery of him, even better."

Tan tapped the side of his head with two fingers.

"Well, I got nothing stored up here anymore. That's a bit dangerous with you blokes hanging around, innit. But I'll talk to your corporal and see if I got any hard copies of anything at home. Anything else?"

"If there is, we'll be in touch."

It took a little over three hours to find Dunning. He was in a hospice for wounded civilians, in a critical but stable condition with shrapnel wounds and one missing arm. Most of the delay in locating the gardener was taken up waiting on Tan to get back to Corporal Meyer with imagery. The traitor provided three still photographs and one old but very useful holo. Revell had imaging specialists on the *Enterprise* create a recognition packet for a small squadron of surveillance drones, which he tasked with scanning every face in both the civilian and the much larger military treatment pipelines. He would have pushed the little ball-shaped camera pods out to scan the whole town and even farther afield if that had been necessary, but it was not. By mid-afternoon one of the drones had a match.

Not wanting to expose Tan's role as a collaborator just yet, Revell had him confirm the identity of the old man, lying bandaged in the recovery ward, from a holo taken by the drone.

"That's him," the former guardsman said. He did not sound pleased.

Revell ordered Dunning moved to a single room in a secure ward and guards posted to watch over him. A physician with Ground Forces Medical did not give Dunning much of a chance.

"He's old and badly hurt," the doctor said. "We have higher priorities."

"Not anymore," Revell informed him. "I will be out there in just over an hour. Keep him alive and see that he's awake to answer my questions."

The doctor did not bother with the theater of objecting.

Revell scheduled routine debriefings with those staff officers of the 101st who had escaped annihilation in the Battle of Montrachet, every one of them by virtue of being somewhere else when the disaster unfolded. From them he intended to reconstruct the last days of the Fleet and to determine whether Strom had made any mistakes that could be avoided in the future. Standard procedure after all major actions, but urgent in this case because of the need to press on into the heart of the Occupied Volume.

"There could be a problem debriefing Vice Archon-Admirals Peet and Cruze," Corporal Meyer cautioned when he saw the requests in Revell's schedule.

"Are they in-volume, Corporal?"

"Yes, but they have been detained by the Inquiry."

Revell rubbed at his eyes. He was getting sick of this shit.

"Order them released on my recognizance. Immediately," he said. "I want them back at their posts by the time I'm finished with Dunning."

Meyer, who had a naturally sallow complexion, blanched an even more sickly shade of yellow.

"From the Inquiry, Captain? You want me to order them released from . . ."

Revell held up one hand.

"My apologies, Corporal. You are right to question the wisdom of that order. I will do it myself. In fact, I will do it now. Can you find Prosecutor-Major Skomo for me?"

"Yes, sir. Of course."

Relieved of the hazardous duty of pissing off the goons in person, Corporal Meyer quickly located the Inquiry agent and put Revell through to him. Skomo's voice on Revell's personal comm bud was oily, with a slight tang of contempt.

"Captain Revell, always a pleasure to hear from the Fleet marshal's personal servant. How might the Inquiry be of assistance today?"

"You are holding two flag officers of the 101st. Peet and Cruze. Release them immediately and have them report to my billet in town to await me. I'm sure you know where that is. You have it under surveillance."

The silence that followed stretched on long enough that Revell thought Skomo might be contemplating denial of the request, the allegation, or both.

He kept his own face neutral, but saw that Corporal Meyer was side-eyeing him nervously.

Revell said nothing. Determined not to give in to the major's ploy.

Finally, Skomo replied.

"But of course. Anything else? Perhaps there is a saboteur or resistance cell leader you would wish to have dinner with this evening?"

"The admirals will do for now," Revell said, and cut the call.

He left the comm bud in his ear, told Meyer to check in half an hour that Peet and Cruze had indeed been released, and left to drive himself over to the hospice. He took a ground cruiser. It was off road capable, but four-wheeled rather than the infantry's more rugged six-wheel versions. Revell felt assured by his flight in over the village that he would not have to negotiate much broken terrain, and although he was forced to cut through a few fields here and there, the sturdy electric utility vehicle handled the minor detours without incident.

The hospice roamed over a couple of hills in a low, gentle range that separated Port au Pallice from the farms, orchards, and vineyards of the hinterland. Civilians were generally treated in the smaller facility, under all-weather carbon fiber tents. Ground Forces casualties were in the sturdier and better equipped Habs on the larger of the two hills. Revell drove into the latter compound, presenting his ID and rolling through the minimal security without a problem.

A polite inquiry at the admin pod took him to an intensive care Hab where two GFS troopers stood guard out front. They inspected his ID, checked with the admin pod and unit security, and let him in. A nurse was bathing the old man with a sponge as Revell entered. There was space enough for two patients in the IC Hab, but Dunning was the only occupant.

"I will just be a few minutes more, Captain," the nurse said.

"Don't rush," he replied.

While he waited for her to finish, Corporal Meyer called to confirm the vice archon-admirals had been released and were on their way to the office.

"Excellent, thank you, Corporal," Revell said.

The nurse completed Dunning's sponge bath and was about to apply a dermal patch for pain management.

"Excuse me, Nurse, but I need him awake."

She looked tired and over it.

"You can have him awake," she said. "But only until he passes out from the pain. Or he starts screaming."

Revell held out one hand, gesturing for the patch.

"Just tell me what to do."

"I'm sure you know how to apply field analgesics. Strip off the cover and apply it to the jugular. It will knock him out."

Dunning watched the exchange without saying anything. Revell took the patch, thanked the nurse, and pulled up a stool next to the man's bed.

"My name is Captain Anders Revell," he said. "I'm looking for your grandchildren."

"Bullshit," Dunning spat. "You're looking for Princess Alessia."

Revell put the patch away in a pocket.

"Your faculties have not been undone by your injuries, then, Mister Dunning. Or do you prefer 'Sergeant Major'?"

Dunning did not hesitate.

"It's Mister to you."

"Very well, Mister Dunning. You have been treated well, have you not? You have received proper medical care?"

The answer was slower coming this time.

"I'm all right," he said.

"You're missing one arm, half of your other hand, and you are riddled with holes."

"Fuckin' flesh wound," Dunning grunted.

"No," Revell said with a smile. "I'm afraid your injuries are serious and the only reason you are alive is because our doctors treated you. Even though you certainly caused the death of some number of Republican troopers."

Dunning did not seem much worried by that.

He closed his eyes, as if trying to sleep.

"Happy to be of service," he muttered.

Revell took a stylus out of his pocket, leaned forward, and tapped the old man on the forehead. That got his attention. Dunning's eyes opened wide in surprise.

"But those injuries will not kill you," Revell said. He tapped the man on the head again. "This will. When the Inquiry discovers you have had neural implants."

Dunning shifted in the bed, as if to swat away Revell's hand, forgetting in his ire that he had no limb with which to defend himself.

Frustration seemed to unlock the man's pain and when he fell back into his pillows he winced.

"I don't fucking care," Dunning said through gritted teeth. "My little ones, they fucking slipped you lot, didn't they. You can stick that patch up your arse, mate. I'll take a bullet if you got one for me."

"Mister Dunning, please," Revell said. "There is no need for this. We treated you well as a wounded enemy. That need not change."

Dunning's left eye twitched. The pain would be coming on.

He said nothing.

"Your grandchildren, as I understand it, were friends of the princess."

Nothing.

"But, like you, they were natural born. True humans."

Dunning's facial muscles jerked again, but this time his eye twitched open.

"You're fucking nuts, mate. People are just people, no matter what."

"I agree," Revell said. "People are indeed just people. It is not for you and me to settle the definition, though. Not here and not today. You are correct that I want to find Princess Alessia. With her family killed in the fighting . . ."

"Murdered, you mean."

Revell waved away the difference.

"By whatever trick of fate, they are gone, and she is the lawful authority controlling the combined assets of the Montanblanc and ul Haq corporate worlds."

"Shooting someone in the head isn't much of a trick," Dunning said.

Revell could see he was fighting to control his pain. He felt in his pocket for the analgesic patch, found it, and pulled it out.

"If a truce is to be negotiated it will be with her," he continued. "If there is to be no truce, because she is poorly advised, or because she is being held by dead-enders and fanatics who will not allow her to negotiate, then there will be war until the impasse is resolved."

He waited for Dunning to reply, but the old man ground his jaws together.

"Your grandchildren, Caro and Debin . . ."

That got his attention.

". . . are, I believe, still with Alessia. As true humans they have nothing to fear from the Republic. Indeed, under our law, they are citizens of the Human Republic, with all of the rights and privileges that conveys."

Dunning took a deep draft of air in through his nose with a hissing sound. Revell idly played with the pain patch.

"Of course, if they remain with Alessia, and there is no truce, that status will not save them. They will be with her when our forces finally track them down and . . . Well . . . I'm sure I don't have to go into detail. You were a soldier. A very good one, I understand."

The muscles in Dunning's jaw jumped and bunched as he bit down on his discomfort.

"Wasting. Your. Time."

"Oh, I have all the time in the world, Mister Dunning. You do not. You probably imagine I have come seeking actionable intelligence. Some tidbit of information you might have picked up in your duties that would allow me to trace my quarry. But I have not."

He tore open the foil and removed the patch, standing up and bending over Dunning to carefully place it on the man's neck. Dunning leaned his head back to let Revell have better access to his vein.

The tension that had been screwing his body ever tighter eased off quickly as Revell sat down again and continued talking.

"I doubt there is anything you could tell me that I would find of any real use. But it may be, sir, that just as we tended to your wounds when the battle was done, just as we helped you, perhaps you might be of a mind to help us and Caro and Debin, should the opportunity arise. I simply ask that you keep an open mind."

He tapped the old devil on the forehead again.

"And do not worry about the Inquiry. They need never hear of the implants you once carried."

Dunning glared at him, but the fight was draining out of the man.

Revell was sure that given time he could turn him or break him.

THIRTEEN

Defiant, re-armed and provisioned for an ultra-marathon voyage, folded through the space between the stars. The gray-haired reaper, shoulders stooped and tricky knee aflame, shuffled along the hushed companionways, his unruly eyebrows knitted fiercely in concentration as he muttered to himself.

"The gates of mercy shall be all shut up, and the wretched soldier, rough and hard of heart, in bloody liberty of hand, shall range, with conscience wide as hell . . ."

"You're doing it wrong," his longtime accomplice, adjunct, and companion said. "It's the flesh-ed soldier and in the canonical text he ranges in liberty of bloody hand, not . . ."

"Oh, do shut your clacker," Frazer McLennan growled. "If I needed the advice of an enormous floaty black tampon be assured I would've pulled on your bloody string before now."

A thin midnight-blue wave flared on the infinitely black x-matter carapace of the Armada-level Intellect; Herodotus's version of, "Yeah, whatever."

"One understands why the Sturm have indicted you for so

many crimes against humanity, but not why humanity itself has been so slow to file an amicus brief."

"Get tae fuck, then. I should've let you go down to that haunted fucking moon and get yourself well knocked up with a Glasgow strumpet's mangled fud full of wee gremlins and beasties. I wager you'd be making more sense than y'are now."

"I am not the one struggling to remember the single line of Shakespeare he's only had seven hundred years to learn. It is happening again, and this time it is happening earlier. You normally do not lose measurable cognitive capacity by this age. This body is falling apart much sooner. At this rate you will need a full, invasive engram extraction and relife long before we get to Earth. I wish you would just let me begin the cortical scans."

"We're nae going to Earth," McLennan avowed, ignoring the request. "This war will be won and lost out here on the edge of the Dark. Earth's gone. The Terran Navy, gone. The Grand Houses, gone. And good feckin' riddance, too. Even poor yon Hardy's beloved RAN has altogether vanished like a dream."

Mac raised one liver-spotted hand to wave to the master and commander of *Defiant*.

Walking toward them, Commander Hardy saluted, and he returned the gesture. She had earned it. Like Mac and Hero, she appeared to be taking the night air, such as it was inside the hyperspace buffer that sealed a bubble universe within the physical parameters of the stealth destroyer; the reason *Defiant* was larger on the inside than out.

"I wouldae thought that after all of your shenanigans, young lady, you would sleep like the ancient dead tonight," Mac said.

Dark half-moons stood out under Hardy's eyes, and the lines of her youthful face were all drawn too long and too deep. She was so impossibly young. Oceans of time separated McLennan from her and he wondered that he could ever have been so young himself. What was that like? As Hero was too damned pleased to point out, he was having trouble remembering things these days.

"I couldn't sleep, Admiral," she said, standing at the entrance to the officers' wardroom as he walked up. "That happens sometimes. After action."

"Aye," Mac conceded. "It can go either way."

He made a play of looking up and down the deserted passageway. Ship time was oh two hundred and what-the-fuck thirty. A marine guard stood sentry a way up from them, and in the other direction a bot train hummed along, silently cleaning the deck.

"We're neither of us on duty," Mac said. "Why don't you join me for a drink? And call me Mac."

She smiled and it was delightful, but she shook her head.

"I had a drink, two in fact, with Captain Hayes earlier. And I promised him I would not gland Dtox."

"Captain Hayes is very wise for such a wee bairn," McLennan said. "But I insist you at least join me for a brew then. Does your assembler still have the code for hot Bonox, or did our Dark-accursed foe ruin that, too?"

She smiled and again shook her pretty head.

"I don't know, Admiral."

"Mac, please."

She looked uncomfortable.

"I can't."

"Och you can, because it's an order and I'll have yon squaddie arrest you for insubordination if you don't."

"But I . . ." Hardy started.

"Resistance is futile," Hero said, sounding almost as tired as Hardy looked. "Just give him what he wants, Commander Hardy. Everyone does in the end. It's why he's so insufferable."

McLennan gestured that she should lead the way into the wardroom, and he followed her. Hero made a show of bumping into the doorframe, because for a super intelligence he was a complete numpty.

"Oh dear," the Intellect mugged for the two humans. "It appears I cannot squeeze through. Perhaps it's all the extra data

I've been consuming of late. Oh well, no bovine meat juice beverage for me, then."

"Och, just fold through, you lavvie-headed fart lozenge."

"I couldn't possibly do that, not after Commander Hardy specifically told me not to."

"Jesus fucking Christ, Hero, just get in here," Lucinda said.

She had already moved to the bar and was busy filling a glass jug with water.

"I'm having tea. Decaf," she said. "I don't think we have any Bonox. There's nothing in the assembler about it."

"Tea will be fine," McLennan said as Herodotus folded into the wardroom. "Yorkshire gold, hot, black, with a drip of honey, but dinnae tell anybody about that for it is my only weakness. I have let myself down. I have let Scotland down."

The water boiled within seconds and Hardy produced a porcelain pot from somewhere behind the bar. She tipped loose-leaf tea into the pot, waited a few moments, and added the steaming water.

"I thought you were having decaf," Mac said.

"You shamed me. But I will have milk."

"We are none of us perfect, lass."

Some more fussing around with cups and saucers, a plate, and a packet of shortbread followed, before Hardy arranged everything on a tray and carried it to the large oaken table which dominated the center of the room. The crockery rattled as she placed the tray upon the polished hardwood surface. Her hands were shaking.

"By rights you should have an orderly do that. As master and commander of your vessel, some would say it is undignified that you should play at being mother," McLennan chided her gently.

"Some would say a lot of silly things if we let them get away with it, wouldn't they, Mac?"

He smiled and nodded in agreement.

"Aye. There are some quaint fucking nuff-nuffs around. But do allow me to pour."

The pot was large, with capacity for at least six cups. Maybe seven, given the dainty fine bone china from which they were drinking. McLennan's hand was much steadier than hers and he spilled not a drop.

"I'm sorry," Hardy said. "I couldn't find any honey. Do you want me to call down to the mess?"

"Oh hell no. These wee nibbly biscuits will be sweet enough."

"Especially on your rotting teeth," Hero put in.

"You're just jealous because you cannae have one," Mac lobbed back.

When the tea was served, they sat down, McLennan taking a chair at the head of the table and Hardy around the long side.

"I was not being entirely facetious about playing at mother," McLennan said, stirring his tea with a sugar-coated finger of shortbread.

"I'm sorry," Hardy said. "I don't understand." It was obvious she didn't. Her exhaustion and confusion were etched deeply into her face.

"I mean, lass, you are in command now. You may be the senior ranking officer in your whole service. Take this as well-meaning advice from an old, old duffer who has been around far too long, and dismiss it as such if you will. But you cannae keep piling into every little skirmish and action. You are going to get killed or badly wounded soon enough and then there will be nobody to lead in the much greater battles we have ahead."

He spoke with care. Hardy impressed him as one of those earnest young officers who, under normal circumstances, would never get anywhere because they were congenitally incapable of compromising.

She was no martinet or virago with it, but he surmised her to be someone who had created herself from whole cloth. The weave of that existence would run smoothly in one direction, but only one.

"Do you mean I should not have gone down to the station?"

He took a sip of his tea before answering.

"You should not have gone down to the station, no. And you should not have led a fire team down to Montrachet, either. I am very glad that you did because it allowed me to do what I wanted when you weren't looking . . ."

She smiled at that, a tired concession. But enough that McLennan thought she might just listen to him.

". . . But you do not need to prove yourself to anybody, Lucinda," he went on.

She looked up sharply when he said her first name.

"You had proven yourself long before you arrived on this ship. That shiny little star on your collar tells me so. One thing I do know of the Armadalen Navy, they do not give out prizes just for turning up."

Herodotus hovered impassively nearby. Outside the wardroom the little hot train hummed past. Lucinda Hardy said nothing. She sipped at her tea. But her eyes were watery, and her hands still shook.

"You don't understand," she said. But said no more.

"Och, lass. I know enough to understand only too well. You forget I was not always the strapping, handsome hero of legend you see before you."

He ran thin fingers through even thinner gray hair, and she grinned however unwillingly at his self-deprecation.

"I came out of the slums, like you. The uniform was the saving of me, as well. We were neither of us born to privilege or good name. What rank we have, we earned. I have also earned many lifetimes' worth of regrets. That's why I feel I can share some of the wisdom of regret with you. Leading your people does not always mean being the first one through the door. Sometimes it means sending somebody else, and sometimes they do not come back."

"That's not it," Hardy said, putting down her cup and saucer. She started to say something else, thought better of it, and shut her mouth quickly. Another reason to be impressed by this young woman. Another reason to save her from herself.

"The people you saved back on Descheneaux were all people we can use. It was the right thing to do. But you didnae have to do it yourself."

She started to object, and this time he held up one hand to stop her.

"Hayes could have done it. Any of his young lieutenants, too. There's always some idiot subleton keen to get his head blown off. Gunnery Sergeant Cox could definitely have done it. About the only one on this ship who could not have gone down to that station and brought those people out is floating over there like a giant black dollop of the devil's own willy drippings."

"Oh good grief," Hero muttered.

"It's not your fault, Herodotus," McLennan said. "That was not a tea party you could ever attend. Not with the Sturm's malware poisoning the brew. But nor were you supposed to, Lucinda. And the sooner you stop trying to rescue your father the better," he said firmly, without tact or the merest consideration for the young woman's feelings.

She flinched as if struck and her eyes went wide.

"Do not go flouncing off now, lass. I'm very old and I cannae possibly keep up with the high-speed flounce of which I have no doubt you would be capable."

She shook her head.

"I didn't . . . I . . ."

"I dinnae imagine you've even thought it through," Mac said. "People do not think much, as a rule, about what drives them. Or if they do it is only to delude themselves. But after seven hundred years I can assure you I have learned that most of us are not running toward something but away from it. And I know what you've been running away from your whole life. Since the Combine took your da."

Tears suddenly filled her eyes. It was a long time since Mac had seen such a woebegone figure.

"You cannae save him, lass. You cannae bring him home."

"How? How did you . . ."

"How did I know? It's in your file. Noted in your personal details and as an item of interest on your security clearance."

"But that's classified."

"Not to me," Mac said. "Or him."

He jerked a thumb at Herodotus.

"You told me to look," the Intellect pouted.

"On your trolley, you fuckin' roaster," Mac said, without any real heat.

Hardy wiped at her eyes with the back of her hand. She sniffled and reached for her cup of tea. Mac pushed the plate of shortbread over to her.

"G'orn, then, s'good for what ails you."

She picked up a shortbread finger, dunked it in her drink, and ate the little treat with such childlike sublimity it reminded him of one of his own daughters, many lifetimes ago.

He could not remember her name.

It was Hardy who signaled she had moved on when she turned the conversation to strategy and tactics, and away from small, personal exchanges about Mac's few, largely faded memories of his parents, and her childhood on Coriolis. He would have been quite happy to hear more of her years in Hab Welfare with the smuggler woman L'trel. He was still forming an opinion of that one and he yet had business with her this evening. But as Mac poured his third cup of tea, pre-emptively regretting the inevitable trek to the pisser it would entail an hour after he finally got his head down, Hardy waved away his offer of more shortbread and knit her eyebrows together so fiercely that he knew she was reverting to type.

"I'd hoped to find more survivors on Descheneaux," she said. "We could spend years gathering forces to staff one ship the size of *Defiant* and we're going to need a lot more than that."

"That's right," McLennan agreed. "We will. Herodotus estimates the size of the enemy fleet as a whole at somewhere between two and two-and-a-half thousand ships. So far we have *Defiant* and your old chum Sabrina on her stolen party boat."

"Sephina," Herodotus corrected him.

"Tomato, potato, it's all the same," Mac said.

"Not really," Hero said with a sigh.

"It's not much of a navy," Lucinda admitted, cutting in over the two of them. "Two ships. One of them a crimelord's yacht."

"She's a baroness now," Hero offered helpfully.

"I meant the original owners," Hardy replied. "But still, same."

McLennan pushed his chair away from the table and stretched his legs. His arse had gone numb and he might have walked around the room to bring it back to life, except he'd probably fall over, and he did not imagine the young woman sitting across the table would appreciate the spectacle of him aggressively massaging the bony cheeks of his bung trumpet to squeeze some feeling back into them. Instead McLennan folded his arms and let his chin drop onto his chest.

"You need to stop thinking in terms of rebuilding your navy," he said. "We need to build up a civilization."

The look she gave him back was withering.

"That'll be quite the challenge once the Sturm take over and exterminate everybody who doesn't fit within their definition of humanity," Hardy said.

"I wouldnae be saying you're wrong, Commander. But any military force is an expression of the civilization it protects."

"Or a negation of the one it attacks."

"Fair enough," McLennan conceded. "Nonetheless, you yourself said you expected to find many more personnel on your base. There probably were more survivors initially, but their numbers were whittled away. And it will be worse on military facilities like Descheneaux than on civilian habitats and worlds."

"Because everybody in the military is hooked up with neural mesh?"

"Aye. You should prepare yourself for the likelihood that only a handful of your colleagues survived."

"I accept that," Hardy said, although she did not look happy or in any way accepting of it. "But you look like you have more good news."

McLennan's expression was wintry.

"Indeed. Most people are not wired up, are they. Most cannot afford even basic mesh. You received your first implant at the Academy. None of Baroness L'trel's crew have neural mesh."

"No, they don't," she agreed. McLennan could see realization dawning on her, but he finished his thought anyway.

"So, most of the people who survived the initial wetware strike will be the poor. The underclasses. And they are found in much greater numbers throughout the volume controlled by your old enemy the Javans and their ilk in places like Combine space, the Russian Federation, the chaebol worlds, and so on. Not everyone is lucky enough to live somewhere as pleasant as the Armadalen Commonwealth."

He let the implications sink in. Hardy did not speak. She played with her cup and saucer, turning the delicate china teacup around in circles with the tip of her finger. It made a scraping noise that set McLennan's teeth on edge, but he did not dare interrupt her. She was obviously thinking it all through.

"It's too much," she said at last. "Too much information. Too many unknowns. Too many factors to plot."

"Not for me," Herodotus put in. "I can game out the consequences of any decisions you make on a virtually infinite number of time frames and down multiple branching paths. If you would like."

"Please don't," Hardy said. "Or at least not yet."

She stood up. Unlike McLennan she was not burdened with an aging body. He could see the sudden tension in all her limbs, in the way her balance moved from one foot to the other. She walked a little way down the room, turned around, and came back.

"When I didn't feel like doing my homework, my dad used to say the next five minutes are always more important than the next five years."

"Well, actually . . ." the Intellect put in.

"Shut your cake hole," McLennan growled at the Intellect. "Your father was a wise man, Lucinda."

"Yeah, not wise enough to read the fine print on the shitty loan contract he took out. But the point stands. We can't go up against two thousand enemy ships today. Or tomorrow. But we can start preparing for that day in the next five minutes."

"And how would you do that, Commander?" Mac asked.

She smiled, wearing an untroubled expression for the first time that evening. Probably for the first time since she had returned from Descheneaux.

"I take your point about rebuilding a civilization, Admiral," she said. They were doing business now. "But I don't build civilizations. I go to war with them to protect my own. And I think I know how to do that, or at least how to start. We do have someone here who knows how to build worlds, though. Or at least I imagine she has been raised to."

McLennan nodded.

"Aye," he said. "The little princess."

Commander Hardy left to attend to her schemes and machinations. McLennan turned to Herodotus.

"And speaking of her young highness," he said. "You and I have one more social call to make before I put my old head down tonight."

"Ugh," Hero said, more than a little theatrically. "You do realize that L'trel's favorite meat puppet has side-loaded himself into the substrate of the Zaistev vessel."

McLennan tipped the dregs of a cold cup of tea into the sink of the officers' wardroom and shrugged.

"It's her vessel now. She took it from a dead man according to the laws of salvage and reclamation and if she wants to let your friend Booker stick his wee little tadger into the gears and sprockets far be it from me to make a fuss."

"Oh, come on," Hero complained. "He'll be all over us like a cheap chaebol skin suit."

"Och, quit your piss-moaning won't you and just pop me over there now. Mistress L'trel awaits my company."

"She's not going to date you, you know."

"Not in this body, no."

"Not ever, you randy old goat."

"Nor I her," Mac snapped, his temper growing short. This body did get tired, and it was not healing well from his ordeal at the hands of the Sturm interrogator on Batavia. He tried to recall the woman's name. She had told him. But he could not remember. "I do have need of consulting with the good Captain L'trel, so just be about your chores would you?"

"Fine," Hero said, sulking.

The wood-paneled surroundings of the wardroom on *Defiant* gave way to a moment of infinite darkness, and a sudden free-falling sense that he had arrived on the armed merchant cruiser *Ariane* a split second before leaving the Armadalen warship. It would have been disorienting if Mac hadn't had the experience of micro-folding between ships so many times before.

What was disorienting was his arrival in Captain L'trel's bedchamber, the cry of surprise she gave out, and the white-hot plasma bolt that missed his skull only by virtue of the field effect that Herodotus threw up to deflect it.

"Motherfuck!" L'trel cried out.

"Captain, I am very sorry," another voice said urgently. It was Booker, the Terran vat soldier. "They folded in without warning."

"I gave you ample warning earlier that I intended to visit," McLennan objected.

"Yeah, earlier," L'trel said. "Like about four or five life spans ago."

She lay abed, fully clothed, for which he was grateful. But

she was also drunk, for which he was not. And she had been crying, which was even worse. Her bed, a large and striking gelform mattress fashioned in the shape of a heart and draped in red satin sheets, was covered in liquor bottles, so many of them empty or on the way to being emptied that Mac knew she had been putting together this wretched *mise-en-scène* for many weeks. To drink this much in one session would kill even an Aberdeen harlot.

"I apologize for the intrusion," McLennan said, glaring sidewise at Hero, who floated silently nearby, "but I was held up by your old school chum Cinders."

Captain L'trel narrowed her bloodshot eyes at him. Her voice, when she spoke, was slurred.

"That's Commander Hardy to you, champ."

"Of course."

L'trel didn't stagger overly much when she pushed herself up out of the bed. But she did drag a bottle of dark red wine along with her, taking a good hard belt before throwing it back among the empties.

"Remind me what you want again," she said.

"Clarity, Captain L'trel. I seek only clarity."

She snorted.

"Bullshit. But you did just make me laugh. So go on. A girl's gotta find her own fun these days."

McLennan spied a dusty stone gourd of Tasmanian whiskey near the foot of her bed. It did not bear thinking about how much such a thing would cost out on the edge of the Volume.

"Do you mind, then?" he asked.

"Whatevs."

Before he could reach for the whiskey it floated across to him on a carrier wave, generated by Hero. Mac pulled the cork and took a hit. It burned agreeably down his gullet, like a delicious forest fire in the mouth.

"My thanks," he said before going on. "This quest the young princess has for you. Might I ask if you intend to fulfill her wishes?"

L'trel rubbed at her face. Her eyes were bleary with crying and maybe with lack of sleep. McLennan knew what that was like. The sleeplessness, anyway.

"What? Go get her family out of backup? I suppose so," she said thickly. "She might even promote me to princess."

"You can never be a princess," Mac said. "You're not of the blood royal."

"Pfft. Like I care. Cash or credit is fine, too. Why?"

McLennan smiled.

Before he could say anything Booker's voice came from everywhere. All around them.

"They want you to say no, Captain L'trel. Or maybe yes, but then to do nothing."

Hero, who had been giving the impression of sleeping a vast and depthless slumber in one corner of the bedroom, suddenly awoke, bobbing up and flaring with dull cherry light. Annoyance.

"I do not believe the admiral directed his query at the home entertainment unit."

Booker shot back, "And I don't believe you sought permission to come aboard, which makes you both stowaways and liable to being folded into hard vacuum."

Hero flared red, but before he could rise to the challenge, McLennan barked at them to shut the fuck up.

"If I were about making my breakfast I would not need a flying toaster or Mister Fucking Coffee to be giving me a running commentary on current affairs while I tried to fry my kippers," he snarled. "Captain L'trel, yon ghost in the machine is nonetheless correct. I dinnae think it would suit either of our purposes to go waking up the elders of the Montanblanc clan when we have such an agreeable representative in the person of young . . ."

"Oh fuck off, you old cunt," she said, all mushy-mouthed and red-eyed.

"What did you just say?" The whole room glowed a dull vermilion red as Herodotus flared with anger.

"Back the fuck down, computer," the disembodied voice of the Terran vat soldier roared from all around. Targeting lasers lanced out and painted McLennan's upper torso. Somewhere in the far-off engine room, the ship's main drives began to hum as Booker drew power from the antimatter stacks to charge up whatever black market arsenal the Zaistev Corporation had installed to deal with massively weaponized synthetic intruders.

L'trel slumped back to the bed, knocking a couple of bottles to the floor where they glugged out their contents onto an expensive rug.

"Get tae fuck with the both of you," Mac shouted. "Hero. Put your dick away. You, too, Booker, and dinnae be such a fucking walloper about it."

Nothing changed until McLennan roared, "Now!"

The targeting lasers winked out, and the faint shimmer of energistic chaos surrounding the Intellect faded away.

"Enough of that gobshite," Mac went on in a slightly more restrained tone.

L'trel had leaned back on her elbows, a sickly smirk stitched across her face.

"You can still fuck off, McLennan," she said. "If the kid wants her olds out of storage . . ." She shrugged. "Who am I to say no?"

Mac did not get angry. Instead he took another swig from the stone whiskey bottle. It was so much better than tea.

"You are the one who stands to lose the most from booting them back up," he pointed out. "You cannae imagine the Montanblancs will just let you have their home estate?"

"No, but you don't care about that."

L'trel searched among the bottles on her bed, found what she wanted, squinted at the contents, frowned, and threw it away. Empty.

"You just want everything to stay the way it is," she went on, "with the princess letting you do whatever the fuck you want. Must be a hell of a nice change. Someone listening to you and doing as they're told. What's it been now? Seven, eight hundred years?"

McLennan raised one hand in warning to Hero, but it was Booker who spoke.

"Six hundred and twenty-three years," he said. "Admiral McLennan removed himself to Batavia to study the wreck of the *Voortrekker* six hundred and twenty-three years ago."

Mac felt tired. As tired as he had ever been in his many long lives.

He sipped at the whiskey again. Looked around for somewhere to sit. There were a couple of chairs in the room, but they were buried under piles of clothes and more empty bottles. L'trel made space at the foot of her bed by kicking away some of the empties lying there. A couple of martini glasses crashed to the floor.

"Sit down, granddad," she said, her tone softening.

McLennan accepted the invite, perching himself at the edge of the mattress. L'trel butt-slid away from him until she could lean against the padded headrest. She took a deep, head-clearing breath. Seemed to consider whether another drink might be a good idea. Decided it would not, and let her watery gaze settle on him again.

"I'm not one of your toy soldiers, McLennan," she said, sounding almost as tired as he felt. "I'm not Lucinda's step-n-fetch-it bitch, either. The kid looked after me. I'll look after her."

Mac frowned.

"So you're set on your course, then. You're going to download the family from storage. Assuming you find them somewhere the Sturm could not?"

She stared at him.

"I didn't say that. I said I'd look after her."

CHAPTER

FOURTEEN

They came while she was playing handball with Caro and Debin, because of course they did. The gymnasium down near the engine room was full of marines lifting weights and running around, trying not to step on the ship's cat, Chief Trim, but there was a small area in one corner where Alessia had been allowed to draw the outline of a small handball square on the deck plating. Sometimes a marine would play a game or two with them, but today it was just kids, so one of the four corners was empty. As usual, Caro had quickly captured the King's Square and held it against her two younger opponents for ten minutes, but Alessia had come up with a cunning plan to dislodge her and had managed to make Debin a part of it without even needing to conspire aloud with him.

This was going to be sweet.

Caro, as was her right by occupation of the King's Square, served up the ball to the opponent of her choice—Alessia in this case—and Alessia had redirected the ball to Debin with the softest and easiest of shots. He swatted the ball back to her, and within a few moments they were volleying backward and forward, cutting Caro out of the game completely. At first, she had waited them out, but now she was growing frustrated. And distracted. Alessia could see her attention wandering around the gym, watching the marines work out. Caro was increasingly staring at a shirtless young fellow called Kanon, who was slicked with sweat from heavy dead lifts. Alessia intended to lead Caro to the point of fatal distraction, when she would suddenly spin and shoot the ball low and hard into the King's Square, dislodging the usurper from her rightful throne.

A perfect plan, in her opinion, which would have led on to victory were it not for the marine who walked right into the middle of the game, snatched the ball out of the air, and told her she was needed up on B Deck.

"Not fair!" Debin cried out.

He'd been enjoying bugging the shit out of his sister, even if he didn't quite know what Alessia had planned. For him it was enough that Caro was pissed off.

"This isn't over," Alessia warned as she dragged her feet, following the marine.

"Oh, it's over," Caro said. "And I remain the undefeated king of you."

"Hey, our ball," Debin cried out. The marine turned around and tossed it back to him. He caught it easily and resumed the game with his sister.

It was so unfair. These stupid grown-up meetings took forever and by the time she escaped this one, Alessia was certain her friends would have moved on to school classes or training with the Armadalens. They were both learning useful things like how to fight with weapons, and without, how to read a map—a real paper map, like in a bedtime story—and hand signals, and code and stuff. Alessia meanwhile was stuck with reading a lot of bullshit about history and politics and literature.

Not even good stories. Fucking literature!

At least they didn't make her practice the flute.

"Where are we going?" she asked the marine.

The marine was a lady whose name tag read DAHL, and when Alessia saw that she almost squee-ed because she knew Dahl had been one of the marines who went down to the station to rescue all the survivors and fight the space zombies. Alessia secretly thought Dahl was very pretty and very tough-looking, which wasn't something princesses were supposed to be even though her own family history was full of early princesses who were plenty of both—at least according to the histories. Alessia was dressed in dark blue coveralls, like lots of people on *Defiant*. She thought her coveralls look pretty fucking boss, if you must know, but they were nowhere near as cool as the gray and black camouflage fatigues that the marines wore. She really wanted a pair just like Dahl's, but she was too nervous to ask. Instead she just kept asking where they were going.

"B Deck, Your Highness. Like I said."

All the marines and all of the Navy guys always called her Your Highness or Princess, which she was used to, but she sort of wished they would just call her "kid" like Baroness Sephina did. Or "A-Train," which Baroness Sephina also did and which was truly the best. But it was another thing she was too nervous to ask for. Her mother would not just freak if she found out, she would be super nasty to everyone about it the next time she was alive. She would make a list and work her way through it.

Thinking about that led naturally to worrying about whether her family's secure, offline backup had even survived. Like, it was offline, so it should have. But whenever Alessia thought about it, the uncertainty and fear gnawed at her resolve. There were three offline sites where the royal family sent hard copies of their lifestreams at more or less regular intervals, depending on seniority. But history was full of stories of angry commoners ransacking unguarded royal vaults and . . . and . . .

It was just better that she didn't think about it. There was nothing she could do beyond sending Baroness Sephina to Cupertino to check out the nearest vault.

And if Seph did find her parents' offline backups, Alessia

didn't want Dahl on one of her mother's shit lists so she just shut up for now and hurried along behind the marine. She hoped this wasn't going to be one of those meetings where people just talked at her for hours and made her sign a bunch of papers and lick her thumb to add her DNA to the verification hologram, but all of the meetings she'd been to on *Defiant* were like that, so chances weren't great.

They pretty much walked the length of the ship and climbed three decks before doubling back a bit to end up at some room she'd never been to before. That was hopeful. Then Dahl knocked on the door, opened it, and showed her in, and Alessia saw that it was just a meeting room with a bunch of screens, and her hopes plummeted. More talking, more signing, more thumb suckage.

Awesome.

Everyone stood up when she came in, even though she'd asked them to stop doing that because it was embarrassing, and poor Admiral McLennan always looked as though getting out of his chair was the hardest thing he'd do all day. Not surprising, given how massively old he was. There weren't many people in the room, which was good. Alessia had learned that the more grown-ups you had in a meeting the longer it went.

Baroness Sephina was back on board for this one, so there was that, at least. Maybe, Alessia thought, they might let her go back to the pirate yacht. For consultations. Her father was always disappearing for consultations. Or he had, before the Sturm killed him.

Admiral McLennan was just sitting back down, too, and his friend Hero was floating around, so maybe there'd be some good swearing this time. That always made things interesting. And Commander Hardy was there. Commander Hardy was always there.

"Your Highness, please come in," she said. The commander looked almost as tired as McLennan, but she wasn't a million years old like him. Alessia understood she'd just had a bad day down on Descheneaux Station with Dahl and all of the wetware zombies and some crazy Intellect that went insane. They sent Alessia a report about it and she had actually read that one because for once it was kind of interesting. They sent her reports a couple of times a day and almost none of them ever talked about cool shit like wetware zombies.

"We have made some decisions," Commander Hardy said after Alessia sat down.

"Okay," Alessia said, struggling not to shrug. These guys made decisions like Debin made fart jokes, which is to say, all the fucking time, even when you begged them to stop.

"But one decision will be yours to make," Commander Hardy said.

That got her attention. Alessia sat up straighter in her chair. The room was boring. Just a plain table, all the screens on the walls, and a holo-projector hanging from the ceiling. There weren't even snacks, like in the officers' wardroom. But it was suddenly the most interesting place Alessia had been since escaping from Skygarth.

"Yeah, you're playing with the big girls now, kid," Baroness Sephina said in a lazy, sort of cheeky drawl.

"But we'll get to that in a minute," Commander Hardy said, and all the air leaked out of Alessia's excitement balloon.

In her experience, "we will get to that in a minute" was something that grown-ups said when they had no intention of doing any such thing for about a thousand years. If ever. She tried not to slump in her chair, keeping her back straight, lacing her fingers together, and nodding as if she would like nothing more than to spend the next couple of hours listening to long lists of even longer lists of things that weren't right and they couldn't change.

For once, however, Commander Hardy didn't do that.

"We're going into the Javan Empire," she said.

Alessia started to nod her head again, but stopped.

"Wait, what? Didn't you just have a war with them?"

Commander Hardy made a funny face, which was almost a smile but not quite.

"Well, that was one war ago, but yes. We did. That's why we're going back there. We need more marines, more ships, more friends. And I think we'll find them in the Empire."

Alessia didn't understand.

"But how? You had a war and everything."

"It's because of the war," Hardy explained. "We won't know for certain until we get there and look for them, but there's a pretty good chance there are a couple of Armadalen ships hiding in the Javan volumes."

Suddenly, Alessia understood.

"Spy ships!"

And just like that, this was the most interesting meeting ever.

"Yes, something like that," Commander Hardy said. "They won't be big ships. Probably not even as big as *Defiant*. But if they were hiding within a volume controlled by the Empire they would have been running dark. Cut off from everyone, like we were when the Sturm attacked."

Alessia glanced around the room. Nobody looked surprised. They had obviously been talking about this for a while.

"But how do you know they stayed hidden when the Sturm got here?" she asked. "Wouldn't they call home or something?"

Commander Hardy shook her head.

"No. Not from within Javan space. They'd stay hidden until our commanders contacted them. The only reason they'd come out of hiding would be if the Sturm was about to discover them."

"What about if the Javans were about to find them?"

Commander Hardy shook her head again.

"That wouldn't happen."

Admiral McLennan spoke up from the other side of the room.

"Never say never, Commander. That's how we ended up here."

Commander Hardy bowed to him, just a little. It was the sort of gesture you saw noblemen and vice presidents of royal blood make at court. Alessia understood it instantly. She was acknowledging the admiral's point without necessarily accepting it.

"We don't know how many covert missions the Navy was running through the Empire," Commander Hardy said. "But the number will be greater than zero. We are going to gather those forces and fold at maximum speed for Habitat Coriolis and then the Cupertino shipyards. We hope to find more people and more ships. Well really, one ship in particular. A titan cruiser."

Alessia frowned as she tried to work out where this was going.

The Armadalen Titan Cruisers were very famous. Everyone said they won the war against the Empire.

"But wouldn't Coriolis be the same as Descheneaux Station?" she asked. "I thought the Sturm attacked people with neural mesh everywhere, all over the Greater Volume. Why would Coriolis be different?"

She was more than just casually interested in the answer. If Coriolis or Cupertino was good maybe the Montanblanc ul Haq Habitats and settled worlds had also been spared. It might be that she was not the last of her family, and she would not have to pull them out of deep storage at the Binary and explain to her parents what had happened and why she had taken so long to relife them.

But Hardy killed that possibility, before Alessia could invest further hope in it.

"I'm afraid Coriolis got hit the same as Montrachet, Descheneaux, Eassar"—she nodded at Sephina—"the same as everywhere, Your Highness."

"So why go there? Won't they just be full of broken Intellects and . . ."

She stumbled, looking for a polite way to say "zombies." It would undoubtedly be rude to refer to them that way when so many of them had recently been friends of Commander Hardy.

"Zombies, kid," Baroness Sephina said, anyway. "They'd be full of fucking meat-hacked zombies. Eassar was crawling with them. Not just Fraction douchelords, either. Fucking Yakuza. Zaistev. Habitat middle management. Anyone with mesh and a live link."

"Aye, she's right," Admiral McLennan said. "And I warned them all about this attack vector."

Herodotus perked up and flashed a tartan pattern across his outer shell. He spoke in a cruel imitation of McLennan's accent.

"Hoots toots Loch Ness, but did they listen to my toothless yammering? Nae, not a word of it because I actually was tooth-less and yammering like a wizened old mental patient at the time."

"Och, tae fuck wi' ya."

They did this a lot, Alessia knew.

She also knew not to pay much attention to it.

So did Commander Hardy. The *Defiant*'s captain spoke over the top of both the admiral and the ancient Intellect.

"Casualties among the Elite Fraction, the managerial classes, and, look, honestly among the neuralinked population as a whole, across the entirety of the Greater Volume, will be close to one hundred percent," she said. "Do you understand what that means, Alessia?"

She did, she wasn't stupid.

"I thought my family, or some of them, might still be alive. In the real. Not just in engram storage."

She saw Sephina and Admiral McLennan exchange a look when she said that. She didn't like it much. She was being ig-nored or cut out, or possibly even patronized.

"What?" Alessia snapped.

Her voice took on such a sharp edge that she sounded like the Lady Melora. Or her mother.

Commander Hardy didn't answer immediately. She looked at the backs of her hands as if there could be some answer writ-ten there. Alessia could feel her angry princess mojo spinning up when Admiral McLennan spoke instead.

"Your Highness, I understand you are pinning your hopes on finding your family in the real or at the very least in backup, and I would not want to be the one to dash those hopes, but as we've told you before, you do need to temper hope with realistic expectation."

"What do you mean?" Alessia asked, thinking this was about more than whether the offline vaults had also been killed.

What was McLennan really saying?

"I mean partly that it is not a good use of our very limited forces to detail Baroness L'trel off on some snipe hunt which realistically might come to naught."

McLennan looked at Baroness Sephina and narrowed his eyes. The face she gave him back was made of stone.

Alessia's heart was thumping harder in her chest. Her mother had gone on and on about being "realistic" whenever Alessia complained about having to marry Prince Pac Yulin. "Realistic" was grown-up talk for "eat this shit sandwich and pretend it's a custard tart."

"They mean your family's backup probably got fried," Sephina said. The admiral nodded in furious agreement. "I'm sorry about that, kid," Sephina continued. "But everyone's been tiptoeing around it to spare your feelings."

The pirate captain leaned forward. She looked more serious than Alessia had ever seen before.

"I'm not gonna spare your feelings, though. Feelings get hurt, but they get better. This shit show we're in? It's not getting any better until we make it happen. You want me to go find your family, I'll do that. No matter what McLennan says. I promised, and you gave me that bitchin' planet."

The admiral smacked one hand down on the table so hard that Alessia jumped in shock at the loud noise it made.

"Och, but yer bum's out the fucking window, you dim strumpet. Good luck holding on to that when old Rupert wakes up," McLennan said.

"Pfft. I'm chill," Sephina said with a shrug, and she wasn't lying. Alessia had never seen anyone as chill as her in the face of somebody as scary as McLennan. She wished she could have seen the pirate captain deal with her mother.

"There's gotta be some payday down the line for me," the baroness assured McLennan. "Maybe not a whole planet, but a diamond asteroid or something. For sure."

"Baroness," Alessia said, her voice rising a little with dismay. "House Montanblanc always honors its commitments. I gifted you Montrachet because you literally saved our family. That's me, for now. I'm it and you saved me. Commoners have been ennobled for much less."

Baroness Sephina laughed. Out loud.

"That's good to know, kid. But this is me being realistic. Now it's your turn. I'll try my best to get your folks back because I know your family. Or I know about them." She gave Admiral McLennan a warning look because he was about to start swearing at her again. To Alessia's great surprise, he snapped his mouth shut.

"They didn't build their empire on free hugs," Sephina said. "They plundered and they pillaged. They're like me, but much, much better at it, Alessia. Your old man? Rupert? He's a fucking monster, and that's exactly what we need right now. Big dick monster energy. So I'll try to find him for you."

Another warning look at the admiral.

Commander Hardy noticed it, too, and was frowning at her friend.

"But you need to know I'll probably fail," Sephina said.

Admiral McLennan's chin jutted up into the air, like a dog that has just sniffed a tasty sausage on the breeze.

"It's like Luce told you before. The Sturm didn't just crack the zero point network," Sephina said. "They spiked the backups, the codex, the deep stores, everything, everywhere. It is fucking medieval out there."

Sephina started to lean back in her chair as though finished, but Alessia stopped her. She stopped everyone.

"My family has a secret vault at Cupertino," she said. "On a planetoid at the edge of the volume. It is not online. It's not known to anybody outside the immediate family. The direct line of succession. We back up there via hard copy delivered by safe hand couriers. My mother and father every week. The princes and princesses less often. And only them. No lesser nobles."

Sephina finally dropped into her seat.

It seemed to restart the room.

"Why didn't you tell us earlier?" Commander Hardy asked.

"It's a family secret," Alessia said. "We don't talk about it outside the family. House Montanblanc is . . . different. My father is very old-fashioned about some things."

Hardy seemed to understand that. She nodded and sat back.

But Alessia felt the need to go on explaining herself.

"I had tutors, not mesh, remember. Father always insisted I learn my lessons, not download them. And he did not trust the Memory Banks, not even the exclusive vaults used by the Grand Houses. Mother told me that our private sites were his idea."

"They were also illegal," Hero pointed out. "Under Volume Law all lifestream storage facilities must be registered on Earth."

"Just because something's illegal doesn't mean it's not worth doing," Sephina said.

For once, her expression was unreadable.

Not so much Admiral McLennan's. He was obviously furious. His mood did not improve when Seph spoke up again.

"Oh yeah, and these losers want you to free the slaves or something, too. I almost forgot that bit."

"What?" Alessia asked. She looked to Commander Hardy, but she had dropped her face into her hands. Admiral McLennan was simply looking at the ceiling, shaking his head and counting to ten.

"I don't understand," Alessia said. "What slaves?"

Montanblanc did not allow slavery anywhere within the volumes it controlled. It did not even allow indebted servitude or the trading of personal liabilities.

"It's like this, Senator," McLennan said when he dropped his gaze back down onto her. His voice was deep and very serious. He emphasized each word by jabbing a finger at her. Alessia barely knew where to look. If McLennan had done that on

Montrachet, admiral or not, Sergeant Reynolds would have broken his finger off. "And I am talking to you as a senator now," he growled, "not a wee princess. We need to raise a navy. And we'll need ground forces, too. We cannae build this force on slaves and serfs, which most of humanity now consists of. Free men and women will fight for themselves. Slave soldiers or serfs, such as you find in abundance throughout Combine space and the Javan Empire, don't so much fight for their master as they fight to simply avoid the master's whip and gallows."

Her head felt as though it was spinning.

"Gallows?"

"It's like a deletion chamber," Sephina put in.

"But," Alessia started. "I thought . . . I was taught that Montanblanc fought slavery."

"You were taught a lot of rot," McLennan said. He seemed very angry. "You were taught the fairy tale. The castles. The glass slippers and bedtime story. Half the factories of your House are based in Combine Habitats because it is much cheaper to use the Yulin-Irrawaddy's slaves and thralls than it is to pay a living wage to a free man or woman on Coriolis or Cupertino or back on Old Earth."

The admiral was not speaking quietly now. His voice had grown harsh, almost spitting the words at her. Alessia could hear the fury in his voice, but she could not see his expression because the room had dissolved into a wash of tears.

"Admiral, please," Commander Hardy said. "She's just a little girl."

"She's a princess of the blood royal," he growled back. "A senator of Earth. And she holds the fate of humanity in those soft, wee hands of hers. Best she know how much blood she has to wash off before we ask her to sign this decree."

"Wh-What decree?" Alessia blubbered.

McLennan produced a simple piece of paper from a folder on the table in front of him. Alessia had to wipe her eyes to see it properly.

"A declaration of the Terran Congress, freeing all humankind from bondage, now and for all time," he said pushing the paper across the table toward her. "As the only senator extant, it is your decision to make."

Lucinda wanted to gather the child into her arms and hold her until the hurting went away. Alessia was in pain and Lucinda Hardy recalled with the grave advantages of hindsight what that had been like. She had been just a little younger when the reclaimers took her father, sundering their little family, and casting her into the void. Princess or not, Alessia Montanblanc remained a child; and alone in this conference room, Lucinda could share her anguish. Seph's mother was crazy, a source coder gone mad from a bad update. McLennan, she knew, had only the vaguest memories of memories of even having parents. And to hear him speak of it, they were not fond recollections. Lucinda stayed in her seat while something huge inside of her, perhaps everything she was, urged her up and around the table to simply wrap this poor kid in a big hug. She was altogether lost and for Lucinda it was impossible that she not grieve and suffer the loss with her. But it was also impossible that she allow the only known surviving senator of the Terran Congress to avoid the hard necessity of choice that had been forced upon them all.

"Alessia," she said, and the young girl looked up at her through eyes swollen and red with tears. "You don't have to sign this right now."

"Well, actually . . ." McLennan started.

"She really should," Herodotus said, finishing the thought for him. "It's the only serious agenda item for this meeting."

"Hey, fuck you two," Sephina cut in. "And back the fuck off. She's a princess and a senator and a really cool kid."

"Thanks," Alessia sniffled. She rubbed her runny nose on the back of one sleeve, and tried to dry her eyes with the other.

"Bitches gotta hang together," Seph said, winking at Alessia, and collapsing time and space for Lucinda.

For just a moment Commander Lucinda Hardy slipped sideways into their shared past. The conference room on B Deck fell away, and she was twelve again, balled up in a corner of her bunk as a ward of Coriolis Welfare, her first night in the Child Protection dorm. Sephina was there, guarding her from some other kid. Bitches gotta hang together, she said. And weeks later, on her first leave pass from the dorm, "Luce" walked the plates of Shogo City, through the shabby stores and chem bars, with Sephina showing the way, when a pop-up holo appeared before them. A suave gentleman who said, "Ladies! Looking for something better in life? I have a business opportunity for you!"

Sephina simply rolled on, but Lucinda stayed put. The man was very handsome and he seemed to be talking to her and only her. "I see you're interested, Lucinda," he said, "And there are gentlemen up in the Core interested in employing you." A pulsing red cursor appeared in the air. "Press the cursor and wait; an aircar will be with you in ten minutes."

"Come on, dude, this is bullshit," Sephina said, trying to drag her away.

"No, I want to hear this," Lucinda insisted.

"This employment is sanctioned by the State," the ad went on. "And if you choose now, you'll continue your studies and earn money in fully adequate housing while you work! Take advantage of this opportunity today, Lucinda!"

Sephina grabbed her arm and yanked. As they moved away, the pop-up disappeared.

"Come on, dumbass, our dorm bracelets trigger that shit. You don't need it. Bitches gonna hang."

"Hey, dumbass . . ."

"Huh?"

Lucinda shook her head, falling back into the now.

"Sorry," she said, momentarily disoriented. "I didn't get much sleep last night."

She wondered how much time she'd lost zoning out, but only Sephina seemed to have noticed. McLennan furrowed his brow theatrically as he watched Alessia read the declaration he had pushed on her. A document they had drafted together, after consulting the Intellect about the appropriate legal form. Alessia was still bleary-eyed but she'd stopped crying and snuffling and was obviously trying to concentrate. Herodotus had fallen back into inscrutable silence.

"You good?" Seph asked in a low voice.

"Yeah, I'm fine. I was just thinking about when I was that age." Lucinda nodded at Alessia. "When we were young."

"Hey, girl, we're still young," Sephina parried gently. "Or I am, anyway. Hanging around guys like this"—she nodded at McLennan—"probably wrinkled your boobs."

"I would retort," McLennan growled without taking his eyes off the princess, "but Armadalen sexual harassment statutes are famously punitive so I will simply ask you to get in the fuckin' bin with your nonsense."

"I don't really understand this," Alessia said.

She raised the piece of paper in front of her.

"It's as I explained, Senator," McLennan said. "It's a declaration to free the bonded population of the—"

Alessia cut him off.

"No. You didn't explain. You just said."

The admiral fell silent, observably surprised to be shut down by a little girl.

"I need someone who isn't asking me to sign this to tell me what it really does."

Lucinda blew out her cheeks.

"We don't have any legal affairs officers on board," she said.

"I can do it," Sephina offered.

"You're a fucking criminal," McLennan objected.

"Who better to advise her on the law?" She beamed. "What do you reckon, A-Train? You want some jailhouse legal advice? As your baroness I am the closest thing you got to advisers at court."

Alessia looked to Lucinda to break the tie.

Hardy was so tired. The away mission to Descheneaux and the long, mostly sleepless night afterward had taken a toll on her. She raised her hands in mock surrender.

"Before the baroness was so high and mighty I do seem to recall she was pretty good at playing lawyerball, at least with customs and excise and quarantine laws . . ."

Baroness Sephina made a face at her.

". . . And before that with Hab Welfare dormitory rules," Commander Hardy said.

Sephina grinned. "Listen to the Loose Unit, kid. She was much smarter in those days. She used to take my advice then. Come on. Gimme."

She gestured for the paper, making a pretend shark's mouth out of her fingers and thumb and snapping the jaws together rapidly.

Alessia looked relieved to be handing over the responsibility. If Lucinda had not been so exhausted, she might have marveled at that. The scion of one of the oldest and grandest of the Grand Houses turning to Sephina L'trel for legal advice.

"I dinnae think this is such a good idea," McLennan cautioned.

"And I dinnae think I have a single fuck to give," Seph said while never taking her eyes off the paper.

McLennan folded his arms and leaned back, waiting for everyone to see sense and agree with him. Lucinda wondered if part of the reason he didn't want Sephina taking off on some quest to find secure backups of the Montanblanc royal family was that he imagined dealing with a young, vulnerable girl on her own would be much easier than negotiating with a relifed corporate monarch.

She recalled an ancient line of poetry from her studies at the Academy.

When you are young, they think you know nothing.

He was right, of course, and yet Alessia had not let him have his way on this. The room remained quiet while Sephina read the declaration, twice. When she was done, she slid it back across the table. McLennan's expression was quietly murderous.

"My advice? Signing it would be a good thing. You'd be freeing about a trillion people from some epically shitty deals."

The admiral looked authentically surprised but very pleased to hear her say that. His expression turned dark as Sephina continued, however.

"On the other hand," she said, "you'd be severely disrupting, probably destroying, your family's business, because you'd be ratfucking their partners in the Combine, the Javans, and a whole bunch of other assholes who, to be honest, are desperately in need of getting fucked by a rat. Choice is yours, kid."

Alessia stared at the paper in front of her. She looked no closer to deciding.

"Can I think about this?" she said at last.

CHAPTER

FIFTEEN

His Excellency Volume Lord Juono Karna was having a bad day. A no-good, very bad, dog-turd-in-the-egg-roll of a day. The mountains of the Rinjani Ranges hung directly above him, the glittering white knife edges of their highest peaks pointed directly down at his head, like a grave Damoclesian warning of all that must come to pass.

Normally, Lord Karna enjoyed nothing more than to lie abed on the private upper terrace of Luwu Palace, contemplating this wonder of Javan engineering, while pillow maidens popped chilled blueberries into his mouth, and his extremely stiff penis in theirs.

It was usually a sublime delight to ponder the marvel of so much mass so carefully and expertly sculpted from the raw materials of the solar system into the vast, bejeweled ring of Ciandur, the Imperial Habitat of Natuna, especially while a couple of palace lovelies giggled and played at squabbling with each other over who would get to gobble His Excellency's noble knob-end. But neither the awesome megastructure of the Rinjani floating a hundred kilometers above him on the far side of the

Wedding Ring—so called because Ciandur had been a gift of the emperor to his fourth wife, Anak, on the occasion of their marriage—or the enthusiastic lip-locks of the two imperial fellatrix mavens were enough to rouse Lord Karna from his funk, or his penis from flaccidity.

In nearly two weeks he'd had no word from the palace at Medang. None! And nothing from the High Command on Fortress Soedirman. And not so much as a whisper from Earth.

Two weeks since the Natuna System had emerged from lockdown to discover that the dread specter of the Sturm was not just some dark fairy tale from a history sim. They had returned, and all the worlds trembled at their approach.

Those worlds that hadn't completely fucking collapsed already, Karna thought sourly.

"Enough!"

He swatted at the pillow maidens, who flinched away from the anger of his voice and the back of his hand. They cooed and keened in unison.

"My lord, please . . ."

"We only wish to please you . . ."

"Well, you do not please me, you worthless curs. Begone before I have your heads and mesh."

They squealed in mortal fear and scurried away, leaving Karna to adjust the silken folds of his batik robe to hide his uncooperative genitalia.

It was just not fair. None of it was fair.

You would think that in this, his third span, he would have risen high enough at court to float above such base concerns as self-preservation, but here he was, lying sprawled under the impossible gigatonnages of a constructed mountain range, so anxious about his fortunes that some part of him worried the damned things might detach from the ring plates and fall through space to land directly on top of his head.

That's how his luck was running lately.

It was the war, he thought.

Everything had gone wrong in the war with the fucking Armadalens.

It was supposed to have been a simple punitive action. A short, sharp rebuke to an upstart rival. (You could barely even call them a middling "power" without doing a grave disservice to the meaning of the word, and although they fashioned themselves as a constitutional monarchy, they were no true realm, as the term was understood by modern thinkers.)

Things had gone as poorly for the Empire in that conflict as they had gone personally for Juono Karna ever since. He had hoped that maybe his fortunes were turning when he missed the battles at Longfall and Medang—through no fault of his own, you understand—and artfully dodged the charges from that stupid War Crimes Tribunal on Earth, by virtue of his hurried appointment as the emperor's representative here in Natuna a favor from his uncle, the chancellor's principal private secretary on Medang, and an engagement which afforded Karna the immunity of Imperial Privilege for as long as he occupied Luwu Palace.

But now.

Now . . .

"Gah!"

Volume Lord Juono Karna swung his legs off the rattan love seat and padded across the hot terra-cotta tiles into the shade of an awning where two servants awaited his instructions. They stared into the middle distance, where rice paddies shimmered in a heat haze and peasant laborers toiled under the twin fusion rings of Ciandur. Karna ignored them all as determinedly as he did his reflection in the nearest window, evidence that yet again he had let himself go and would need a new body before long. This one was getting rather soft and globular in shape.

Taking a tumbler from a silver tray in the shade of a palm leaf umbrella, he crunched the tall glass into an ice bucket, the contents kept chilled by a gentle field effect. Karna poured a jug of cold jasmine tea over the ice, considered adding a shot of something stronger, and denied himself the indulgence. He really was getting too stout, and his usually razor-sharp mind was already somewhat addled by having to juggle the many multiple crises and disasters that had befallen him.

There were the Sturm, of course, still consolidating their foothold out on the edge of the Greater Volume, but inevitably headed this way. And there were the Armadalens, curse their eyes! And curse the miserable fucking Sturm for not finishing them off.

Just this morning the Bakin confirmed that a surviving unit of the Commonwealth's Navy had fought some great, annihilating battle over the Montanblanc ul Haq estates on Montrachet, possibly under the command of Frazer McLennan—another phantom menace, returned from the long-ago and best forgotten past. And as if the word of the emperor's security and intelligence agency was not enough to go on, there were hundreds of vessels that had carried thousands of refugees into the system—many of them senior figures from the Grand Houses, the corporate realms, and of course the sort of interstellar mob syndicates conveniently corralled on Lermontov Station. They all arrived with wild stories of chaos and madness at the very edge of human space.

But it was the survival of some secret RAN battle group, under the infamous McLennan no less, that both deepened Karna's thirst for anesthetizing soma and ensured he could not avail himself of such for fear of clouding his judgment. What little he knew of McLennan from his studies at the Imperial Academy, the better part of three spans past, did not afford him any confidence that the man would be reasonable should the Armadalens decide to press the issue of those outstanding warrants for his arrest and trial back on Earth.

He sipped at the iced tea, before greedily glugging the lot. It was shockingly cold, and so of course it speared an exquisitely painful brain freeze up through the roof of his mouth into his left eyeball.

Karna cursed and flung the glass across the patio. It shattered on a small statue and one of the servants hurried to clean up the mess.

It was all too, too much. The Luwu Palace secretariat was overwhelmed by representations from the flood of Elite Fraction asylum seekers, demanding not just asylum but the privileges and protections of status normally guaranteed by their wealth and power—almost as though their precious status had not been reduced to that of desperate supplicants and homeless arrivistes by the inconvenient truth of an invasion from outer fucking space. Mostly he was able to palm them off to the Russians and their co-conspirators, who were only too happy to welcome the richest evacuees to Lermontov Station, all the better to strip them of those riches, and of course to remit the standard commission back to the palace. But that could not last. Eventually, inevitably, somebody was going to turn up who would not tolerate the shakedown and, more important, possessed the means to resist it.

But perhaps the Sturm would be here by then, absolving Karna of the need to worry about anything besides saving his own hide. He'd already metabolized his mesh, of course. But he did not imagine it would take the fanatics long to work out he was not some inexplicably fat coolie, liberated from the sucking mud of the rice paddies.

And certainly not when those deplorable peons would give him up at the first opportunity. Of that he had no fucking doubts at all. The treacherous scum.

Lord Karna closed his eyes and massaged his throbbing temples. He tried to remind himself he was not without resources.

Foremost among them was the *Makassar*, although he did not imagine a getaway could be easily effected on the lumbering old Warlugger. It was too big and heavy-footed to have any real chance as an escape craft. And as soon as the Republicans learned of its existence, they would surely concentrate forces sufficient to overwhelm it. Especially given that the entirety of the senior command cadre and the ship's Intellect had been lost to their vicious malware. He had no faith that Suprarto, this jumped-up peasant boy who had, for now, inherited command, would be able to do anything useful with it. He had no name, no lineage at all. For heaven's sake, his worthless family scraped what passed for a miserable living from the plates of some chickenshit agri Hab at the ass end of the Empire. As soon as the wretched little peasant had the warship back to something approaching operational capability, Karna was resolved to find an appropriate replacement for him from within the ranks of the junior nobility on Ciandur.

Someone he could trust.

Someone who would owe him.

And definitely not somebody who would dare see promotion as a chance to advance their own interest above those of their Volume lord. A first lifer would do best. They were always eager to please.

But for now, he needed Suprarto doing whatever it was he was doing to get that 'lugger back online.

The reason for his urgent need, and perhaps the greatest of all the many problems bedeviling Juono Karna, was approaching, spin-wise from the south.

The shuttle was a standard model E2C Kestrel, a rounded rectangle of nano-hex armor plating with four micro-g drive pods. Simple. Efficient. Proven.

It was a modest chariot for one as exalted as Deputy Executive Prince Commodore Rinaldo Pac Yulin, but the commander of the Combine's expeditionary group Strike Force 21 and possibly, just possibly, the sole surviving heir to the Yulin-Irrawaddy Combination of Corporate Realms, was not much fussed with appearances.

He preferred to deal in realities.

The reality of power.

The reality of consequence.

The reality that opportunity, when passing by, must be seized by the throat.

And the opportunities here in this system, on this Hab, were almost unimaginable . . . unless you were Deputy Executive Prince Commodore Rinaldo Pac Yulin, who, it must be said, could make a pretty decent go of imagining himself suddenly enriched, empowered, and enabled to seize not just an opportunity . . . but the opportunity to raise himself above all others, once and for all of time to come.

It was true, he admitted as the Kestrel swept over the vast but carefully tended subtropical forest that formed the outer grounds of Luwu Palace, that to do so he would have to survive not just the collapse of a civilization, but a serious attempt at its violent dispatch by a rabid and implacable enemy of immense size and messianic inclination.

But of course, he was not without advantages in this.

The strike force he commanded was intact, preserved from unexpected hazard by good fortune in the first instance, and brilliant leadership in the next.

The leadership was down to him, naturally, but the fortune he would concede. Strike Force 21, two battle cruisers and four escorts of the Yulin-Irrawaddy's Forces Coloniale, had been secretly positioned for a hostile takeover of a helium 3 facility on the largest moon of an unbound gas giant, currently traversing interstellar space some fifteen light-years from Natuna. The geo-volumetric intricacies of how the Combine and the Nordic League's largest multi-stellar corporation had fallen into dispute over the mining rights to the rogue, sunless planet had, until just recently, been the Greater Volume's greatest cause célèbre since the Javan-Armadalen War, and Pac Yulin had been anticipating the fortune, glory, and even some of the infamy which would attach to him for his role in resolving the dispute, totally and finally in favor of the Combine.

After all, one man's infamy was simply another's credibility and stature.

And now?

It was all for nothing.

Well, not nothing.

Going dark, preparatory to seizing the illegal Vikingar settlement on the rogue giant, had spared Rinaldo Pac Yulin and Strike Force 21 from the Sturm's sneak attack. And when surveillance of the H3 mines suggested something had gone horribly wrong down on the orphan planet's tiny moon, Pac Yulin's careful, arguably brilliant tactics in cautiously and progressively staging their emergence from stealth protocols resulted in but one fatality and the loss of a single Limited Intellect on the recon mission sent to investigate.

Granted, the return of the Sturm was disturbing, but it was not necessarily unfortunate.

Pac Yulin was supremely confident that because of the Republicans' willful ignorance, their bigotry, and their simple unreconstructed backwardness, they would prove a challenging foe merely because there were only so many targets that his super-advanced and fully operational strike force could service at one time.

He would have to defeat them in detail.

But defeat them he would, and then . . .

And then the worlds of the Greater Volume, all of them, would bend the knee to him and to a greatly enlarged Yulin-Irrawaddy Combine.

Perhaps even to a singular, merged Pac Yulin Corporate Realm.

But first, to defeat an enemy in detail, needs must demand that he attend to the details.

Committing himself anew to what must be done, Rinaldo Pac Yulin leaned forward a little in the co-pilot's seat and let his gaze roam ahead to the red tiles and golden trim of Luwu Palace, sitting like a tiny, exquisitely crafted jewelry box in the deep green folds of manicured lawns, picturesque rockeries, and ornamental ponds and waterfalls that formed the inner keep of the Javan Volume lord's official residence. Leaning farther forward, Pac Yulin craned his head to stare up into the artificial sky where the dramatic, silver circlet of the Ciandur ring arced high overhead through the artificial lens of the

Habitat's atmosphere. There were mountain ranges up there, millimeter-perfect replicas it was said, of some natural cordillera back on Old Earth. All of it re-created for the diversion of one family, and momentarily for their faithful retainer, Juono Karna.

Despite its beauty, the famous Wedding Ring was, Pac Yulin thought, a disappointment. So much effort and investment for so little return. The whole thing a sunk cost for what? Pleasure?

There were surely more efficient and effective paths to satisfaction.

No, he thought, as the pilot and the Kestrel's own Limited Intellect communicated with the palace to effect their final approach and landing, this was just another example of the Javans' poor decision-making skills, of their preferencing form over productivity. By all means, build yourself a little pleasure palace, but don't be so extravagantly wasteful about it.

He felt the slight, gravimetric shift of the micro-g pods modulating their waveforms to gradually slow the shuttle's forward momentum to a hover. The pilot instructed the ship to prepare for landing.

"With your permission, Commodore?"

"See to it," Pac Yulin ordered, only half-hearing the man.

He was searching for Lord Karna, who should have been here to greet him. Instead, he seemed to have sent some minor functionary, all done up in colorful finery like a pantomime player from a child's mummer show.

Pac Yulin sighed, already exhausted by the performative foolishness of this man.

If Karna was determined to play the local potentate, leaving a deputy executive prince of the Combine to twiddle his thumbs in some damned waiting room, then Pac Yulin would indulge him. For now. *The Righteous Path of N'tek Yulin*, the foundational text of the Yulin-Irrawaddy, taught that to endure pain with patience was to plant the bitter seed of the sweetest fruit. And that hulking Warlugger of Karna's remained a consideration, no matter how cumbersome it was compared to the swift and agile battleraiders of his squadron. The *Makassar* was a dinosaur, but you wouldn't want it falling on you.

The Javan had at least turned out a ceremonial guard of sorts. A hundred or so troops in brightly colored and faintly ridiculous traditional dress. Skirts and pillbox hats and actual spears with bird feathers or something dangling from them. Ugh. They probably had lice.

And then, to remind Pac Yulin that he wasn't always right, Lord Karna himself appeared, somewhat in a rush, which was both amusing and alarming to see in one so plump. He waddled at speed down a wide marble staircase to the greensward of the main lawn and hurried to take his place and tuck in his shirt at the front of the reception line.

Perhaps Pac Yulin had caught him taking a bath?

More likely taking a couple of concubines and a second breakfast in the bathtub, he thought acidly.

But still, the man was here, and it was time to get down to business.

Juono Karna could not help but resent the arrogant dog. According to Karna's briefing note from the Bakin, Pac Yulin was only on his second span. And the biotic age of his Indo-Aryan phenotype seemed to be somewhere around the late thirties. Just like Karna.

But unlike Karna, Pac Yulin looked fit and relaxed as he sipped at a tall glass of iced tea in the Lombok Room of Luwu Palace. The Combine officer wore his body lightly, with no sense of the years, or the weight, piling on. There was also the distasteful matter of status. Karna was a Volume lord, inarguably surpassing in precedence the social rank of a middle-grade Combine staff officer with a minor functional command to his credit, and a position within the realm's corporate org chart of somewhat lesser prominence, even if it did presage full executive status in some future span.

But of course, Karna was in his third span, not his second,

and his last functional command had been . . . well, controversial, even if successfully undertaken with the private blessing of the emperor. Worse still, his position here on Ciandur was less a just reward for exemplary service than it was a concession by Medang Palace that to have a nephew of the emperor's principal private secretary hauled before the full bench of the War Crimes Tribunal at the Hague would be intolerable. And admitting such would be even worse. And so Juono Karna, accused war criminal, sat as the legally untouchable caretaker of the royal estates on Ciandur, and puppet governor of Natuna, until such time as it would not embarrass the palace to release him back into the wild.

Or such had been the case, until the Sturm turned up. And both he and Pac Yulin knew it.

The Combine princeling drew deeply on a kretek cigarette and blew a thin stream of smoke at the low ceiling where it disappeared, subtly consumed by the environmental nanoprocesses built into the architecture. The Lombok Room was not the principal reception area for the palace, but it was the most comfortable, as Karna had taken pains to explain. A spacious parlor of mahogany, bloodwood, and the richly colored local sandstone, it was open on three sides to the gardens, but protected from the sweltering heat and humidity by finely calibrated field effects which drew in a steady flow of fresh air, chilling it to a Volume-standard twenty-one degrees Celsius. (Or seventy degrees Fahrenheit, if you lived on one of the hugely eccentric MAGA Corp Habs.)

The two men sat opposite each other across a low table of woven bamboo. Karna worried that Pac Yulin might think it to be a gracelessly native affectation. The deputy executive prince's dynasty had proven itself largely inured to gestures of ethnographic virtue signaling. And yet the bamboo sheaves had been transported at vast expense all the way from Princess Anak's ancestral home on Old Earth's Sumbawa Island to be hand-woven by craft-serfs born to that endeavor alone. That had to be worth something, did it not?

The Combinierré leaned forward and stubbed out the butt of his cigarette on the edge of the table. Karna was too stunned to say anything, and the moment for protest passed when Pac Yulin sat back, looked Karna directly in the eye, and said, "We must act, Juono Karna. Time is short."

Karna was pulled back into the panic spiral of the last fortnight. For now, he was only circling the lip of the funnel, but he could feel the undertow trying to drag him down. "But what is to be done? Compared to the Sturm we have virtually nothing with which to defend ourselves. Nothing!"

Pac Yulin waved off the reedy note in Karna's voice, his fingers cutting through the veil of smoke in front of him.

"Not true, my lord. These reports we both have of the encounter at Montrachet, they speak of a small Armadalen force overcoming a whole fleet of enemy warships. And as regrettable as the outcome of your own hostilities with the Commonwealth might have been . . ."

"Oh, most regrettable," Karna agreed.

"I do not recall any instances of an Imperial Javan fleet being routed by a single Armadalen ship, and not even a capital ship at that. A destroyer, if memory serves."

"A very modern stealth destroyer," Karna reminded him. "One of their most advanced, and somehow placed under the command of Frazer McLennan with the assistance of an Armada-level Intellect."

"Ha. That is no mystery," Pac Yulin snorted. "Everyone knows McLennan exiled himself to Batavia centuries ago and the Intellect went with him. The obsolete Intellect."

Pac Yulin leaned forward again, counting off his points on the fingers of one hand. "One old man. One ship. And one outdated Intellect. And they bested an entire Republican attack fleet."

He smiled and gestured as if to wave away the inconvenience of a mere two or three thousand enemy warships. "My lord, the fanatics got lucky with a coward's gambit. I will grant that the Sturm have done grave damage across the Greater Volume, but they did so only because they landed a devious strike on a critical vulnerability."

"Yes, but the point is that they did it. Even if they got lucky," Karna protested.

"No." Pac Yulin shook his head. "The point is that as soon as they faced minimal opposition from a token force—one ship, one eccentric old fool and his rust-addled butler—they folded like a cheap chaebol umbrella. The Republic has learned nothing, my lord. They have not advanced as we have advanced. How could they? The very essence of the Human Republic is to deny themselves advancement. They do not just distrust the science. They despise and repress it."

Pac Yulin was growing animated in his confidence. He suddenly pushed up out of the deep chair in which he had been lounging, giving alarm to the Palace Guards who stood in the corners of the Lombok Room. The sergeant of the Guard even started forward, his hand dropping to the weapon belt at his waist, but Karna dismissed his concerns with a quick, furtive shake of the head. The sergeant nodded discreetly and dropped back into stillness and silence, but all the guards now openly followed Pac Yulin with their eyes.

The Combine leader ignored them.

He had begun to pace around the small table, where his kretek cigarette had burned a tiny scorch mark into the lacquered bamboo. Juono Karna's heart lurched every time he saw it, and it was only through an effort of will that he was able to stop himself immediately calling for a craftsman to come and take the insanely expensive piece of furniture away for repair. Pac Yulin, meanwhile, was rolling into his performance, growing surer of himself with every word.

"If we are firm in resolve, and resolute in action," he said, smacking the back of one hand into the palm of the other, "we have enough forces in this volume alone to stand against them. I am certain of it. The battleraiders of my strike force, your Warlugger, together they would overmatch anything but an Armadalen Titan Cruiser, and we know that McLennan, if indeed he did lead the fight at Montrachet, had no such warship in his line of battle. We know of this one destroyer and one"—Pac Yulin stopped and waved his hands around again, searching for the right words—"one low-caste smuggler's disintegrating garbage barge. The *Je Ne Regrette Rien*, according to HabSec on Eassar. I tell you, Juono Karna, the more you look into the debacle at Montrachet the less there is to see. The Sturm were always primitives. They were always brutes and unsurprisingly they remain so. Why, I don't imagine they would be able to acquit themselves with any credit against a scratch crew of those Russian mobsters and Yakuza thugs you've corralled over on Lermontov."

Karna shifted uncomfortably in his seat.

The syndicates were not the only threat he had "corralled" at Lermontov, as Pac Yulin well knew, but the less said about that the better.

The Combinierré stood over Karna, hands on hips, chin raised, staring out across the gardens of the palace as if he owned them.

"My lord," he said, "you and I have been gifted by fate with that most rare of things, a chance to make the worlds anew."

Karna's eyes flicked to the sergeant of the Guard. The man was no longer eyeballing Pac Yulin, but he was very obviously listening. The staff were always listening. As was the palace Intellect and the Bakin. If Pac Yulin was aware of such, as he should have been, he seemed not to care.

"What do you mean, Commodore?" Karna asked carefully. In spite of the villa's excellent climate controls, he was sweating freely.

Pac Yulin turned his gaze back to Karna. His smile betrayed some unspoken knowledge.

"We do not know what has befallen our respective realms," he said. "You have not heard from Medang Palace. I have no instructions from the board or His Highness the CEO."

Karna was almost certain that Pac Yulin was rushing heed-

lessly toward treason, and he dared not follow him or give even
the slightest impression of doing so.

"Have a care for what you are about to say, Commodore,"
he said.

But the man just smiled again.

"Be not afraid, my lord," Pac Yulin assured him, and probably all the unseen observers watching over them. "Our duty is
clear. Yours to the palace, and mine to the board."

Karna felt some of the tension leave his shoulders and a
loosening of the clench in his guts. Oddly, however, he started
to sweat even more.

"In the first instance," Pac Yulin went on, "we must secure
the holdings of the Empire and the Combined realms. That
means Natuna and the strike force. I propose an alliance, my
lord, for the common defense of our realms. With our concerted
might none will defy or deny us."

Pac Yulin looked directly into Karna's eyes.

"I understand," the Volume lord said carefully.

"You understand then that we must commit all the available
resources of this system, be they Javan, Combine, or otherwise,
to the arsenal of this alliance?"

Karna nodded, but said nothing.

Was Pac Yulin proposing to commandeer the ships and materiel currently docked at or orbiting the freeport of Lermontov,
on the other side of the sun? It was not a radical proposal in
time of war. But nor was it simply a matter of decree. Some of
those ships were owned by the wealthiest families in all of
human space. And Lermontov Station was basically a shopfront
for three of the most powerful criminal and para-criminal organizations in the Greater Volume.

But that was not all.

Pac Yulin was hinting at something much greater, Karna was
certain, but Yulin was too shrewd to say so openly.

And Karna needed to be sure.

"How then do you propose we do our duty to the Empire

and to the board?" he asked. "We do not even know how much remains in the wake of the attack, and we dare not use the zero point networks to find out."

"We do not," Pac Yulin agreed dolefully. "I propose that having secured ourselves from immediate attack in this system, we raise such a fleet as can be sure of fighting its way to our respective homeworlds. To Medang and Fortress Soedirman in your case. To Combine Headquarters on Arakan, for my command."

Karna felt his heart rate accelerating, perhaps with the faintest glimmer of hope. But he had to take pains with how he played this.

"Do you propose to abandon Natuna?" he said, feigning shock if not outrage.

"No," Pac Yulin replied immediately. "I propose a tactical withdrawal. We must gather our forces, but we must also see to our responsibilities, and we cannot do that from here. We are too far removed from the homeworlds, and too much exposed to the invaders concentrating their forces upon us. If this vile sneak attack has fallen as heavily upon the palace at Medang, and my masters at Arakan, it may well be, my lord, that we, personally, must assume responsibility for ensuring that our realms do not fall. I am but four hundred and thirty-fourth in line to the Domination of the Combine. I am confident that somebody more senior, somewhere within the Greater Volume, will have survived to take up command. In life storage, if nowhere else. But if not, if fate should have it that I am the most senior executive in the line of succession, then I will have to reluctantly accept the burdens of Domination."

"I see," Karna said.

He almost smiled.

"I, of course, have no such concern, not being of the blood royal."

"Of course not," Pac Yulin conceded with almost oily refinement. "But you are the emperor's representative here in Natuna System. You may be the most senior of his servants still extant. The fate of the Javan Empire lies with you, Lord Karna. If the emperor has been struck down, you will have to secure his most recent undamaged engram from backup. You will have to provide for the deliverance of the royal line, by whatever means necessary."

Karna could scarcely breathe.

The devil himself stood across Princess Anak's little bamboo table, proposing treason and making it seem the height of pious loyalty and devotion.

But he was offering something even more profound than that.

He was offering escape. And even triumph.

Juono Karna found himself on his feet, pacing the cool, tiled floor of the Lombok Room. He had been prey to a swarm of contrary feelings when Pac Yulin had arrived in-system at the head of his strike force. A complete battle group, no less. There was immediate relief that help from an ostensibly friendly power had arrived. Worry that the Combine would do what they always did and seek to take advantage for their own ends. Unease that Pac Yulin had enjoyed no more success in determining the disposition of his masters than Juono Karna had in settling the fate of the Empire. And legitimate fear upon confirming that it was indeed an Armadalen force that had met and defeated the Sturm at Montrachet.

But now, for the first time since emerging from the lockdown after the solar storm on Natuna, he could see a way forward. A path that might even, possibly, just maybe lead him to sit the throne at Medang Palace. For if it was true, as the Bakin whispered to him, that the Sturm seemed to have attacked not just the zero point networks but all of the most important cached data stores throughout the Greater Volume, it might well be that no copy of the emperor existed anywhere.

It might be that the only way to preserve the blood royal was to seek out a clean embryo from the imperial seed bank, and to raise a new heir to the throne, with Karna serving as loyal regent.

Not that he would ever voice such thoughts, of course.

For such was treason while there remained a chance that the emperor might be restored.

Still . . .

Worth thinking about, Karna admitted.

"There is one other matter," Pac Yulin said, breaking into his reveries.

"Oh yes?" the Volume lord said, suddenly wary.

"I assisted you—and the Empire, of course—in the matter of those potentially hostile foreign military units now impounded at Lermontov Station."

"Of course," Karna hastened to concede.

"We will need to add those ships to our line of battle."

"But of course." Lord Karna nodded.

"I doubt, however, that the TDF or the Deutsche Marine or any of the others will ever agree to serve under a Javan-Combine command. That Terran captain was most adamant that any allied command was his prerogative, was he not?"

Karna again nodded his head.

The officer from Earth had been difficult. Most difficult indeed after the bother with the Armadalen spy ship, and he had even implied that Lord Karna's outstanding charges at the Hague could be an issue.

The Volume lord had had no choice but to impound the ships and sequester all the personnel.

And of course, having done so in one instance, it became a matter of urgency to repeat the unfortunate necessity every time a stray military unit arrived seeking to make common cause against the Sturm and inquiring as to the status of the other ships in-system. Pac Yulin and his strike force had been most helpful in that process.

Deputy Executive Prince Pac Yulin was not at all concerned about outstanding difficulties at the Hague or possible entanglements with the TDF.

"I am, of course, grateful for your assistance in that difficulty," Lord Karna muttered. "And the Empire, too," he added quickly. "The Empire very much appreciates the friendship and alliance of the Yulin-Irrawaddy Combine against all her adversaries."

Pac Yulin smiled.

"I wonder, then, if I might prevail upon the friendship of the Empire in a matter of no interest to Medang, but very real import to the Combine."

"Naturally," Juono Karna assured him. "What sort of matter, might I inquire?"

"Contract and matrimonial law," Pac Yulin said.

CHAPTER

SIXTEEN

They were two days from the Natuna System, when Alessia asked if she could talk to the captains of both ships.

To Lucinda and Seph.

Defiant was folding at full power toward the Javan outpost, a gas-mining system and mercantile hub that Hero calculated to have been the nearest and most likely target of covert surveillance by Armadalen military intelligence before the return of the Sturm. Lucinda had finally managed to sleep and process the mission to Descheneaux. The survivors were recuperating in the ship's medbay, with the marines expected to return to light duties within days. Admiral McLennan mostly kept to himself on the long fold, studying and writing in his quarters, with occasional breaks to see whether Alessia had signed the declaration.

She had not.

Returning to her cabin, sweaty from a workout with the marines' combat dummy, Lucinda found Alessia sitting on the deck plate by her door, holding a single sheet of paper and Chief Trim in her lap. Trim looked fat and happy with all of the attention, but the declaration was dog-eared and a little grimy, the way you would imagine an epoch-making document might look when left in the care of a pre-teen for three days.

Toweling off as she approached, Lucinda sketched a quick smile. She had initially maintained the strictest of formalities when dealing with the Montanblanc heir. The corporation was, after all, one of the Commonwealth's oldest and closest allies and Alessia was effectively now head of state and acting CEO. But the formality had not lasted. Alessia was, as Sephina insisted on calling her, a kid. She was most happy when hanging out with the two other kids on board, her friends Caro and Debin. And as close as Lucinda might wish to hew to the proprieties, Alessia insisted on sitting on the deck plates wearing an old, slightly oversized pair of general duty coveralls, acting like any other twelve-year-old.

"Alessia, can I help you?" Lucinda asked.

She jumped a little. She'd been staring at the declaration, not looking out for Lucinda. As soon as she saw *Defiant*'s commander she climbed quickly to her feet.

"Can I talk to you and Sephina about this?" she asked, waving the piece of paper.

"The declaration? Of course."

"Now?"

Lucinda did not need to check the time. She had another twenty minutes to shower, change, and return to her station on the bridge.

"I can get Baroness L'trel on holo," she said, but Alessia shook her head and lowered her voice. She spoke in a stage whisper as if concerned not to be overheard.

"No, I need to talk to both of you. Together. Can we go over there?"

Lucinda squeezed a fistful of thick, wet hair in her towel.

"To the *Ariane*?" she said. "Why?"

Alessia looked up and down the companionway.

"It's more private over there."

Lucinda didn't need to ask why. Alessia was thinking about

McLennan for sure, and possibly about Hero, as well. Having been institutionalized for most of her life, Lucinda had few expectations of privacy. Even in her private quarters the ship still monitored her bio signs. She hadn't thought about it before, but it suddenly occurred to her that McLennan was almost certainly spying on the poor child and using Hero's access to the ship's systems to do so. The Intellect would be watching them right now.

"Okay," she said, quickly making the call. "You'll have to give me a few minutes, and I'll need to inform the bridge. I'm due on-station. So this is about the declaration?"

Alessia nodded.

"All right. Can you wait here?"

"I've been waiting here for hours."

That was a sizable exaggeration, but Lucinda hurried into her cabin, a much larger and more amenable space that she had taken over when Captain Torvaldt died. Or, if you wanted to be brutally honest about it, when she had killed him after the Sturm's nanophage turned the poor bastard into a flesh-eating berserker. The captain's quarters enjoyed the luxury of space for two armchairs, a small en suite bathroom, and an even smaller walk-in closet. It was the most magnificent accommodation she had ever experienced.

Like seriously. Ever.

It was easily as big as the capsule apartment she'd shared with her dad, and much more comfortably furnished.

Lucinda showered quickly, changed into a day uniform, and returned to the companionway, where the princess awaited her. She almost expected to find Admiral McLennan waiting, too, but only Alessia stood outside her door.

"Come on," she said. "We'll fold over."

A call to Lieutenant Chivers extended Chase's occupation of the big chair for another hour and alerted Sub-Lieutenant Han at the afterbrow that she would be cross-decking to the *Ariane* with Princess Alessia. When they arrived, Lucinda led her onto the small yellow circle that designated the active fold zone.

Without warning, Alessia suddenly grabbed her hand and gripped tightly, squeezing two of Lucinda's fingers into an awkward, almost painful crush.

"Alessia, have you never done a personal micro-fold before?" Lucinda asked.

The young girl shook her head quickly and emphatically. When she spoke her voice shook, too.

"I've been on plenty of ships, but I've never done this, no. We never do this without backup. In case something goes wrong. It's another one of my father's rules. Like the secret backups. And I don't have mesh. Nuh-uh. No backup, no micro-folds."

Lucinda held up one finger to Sub-Lieutenant Han, signaling that she needed a minute. The junior officer nodded.

"Alessia, it's safer than taking a shuttle. In fact, we couldn't take a shuttle at the moment. We'd have to drop out of the fold. And shuttles can be dangerous. They crash. People shoot at them. To be honest, they kind of suck."

Alessia squeezed her hand even harder.

"I'm okay. Let's just go."

"Okay. It will feel a little weird. Like you got there a split second before we left. And some people get sick. But not many. Just tell me if you do."

Alessia nodded quickly.

Lucinda signaled to Han that they were ready and an instant of pure black nothing enfolded them, before a much larger and more lavishly appointed reception bay suddenly materialized all around.

Sephina herself was waiting on the other end, grinning hugely.

"Oh. My. Fucking. GOD!" she screamed out. "Let's get this party started, bitches!"

She ran—actually ran—forward, spreading her arms wide to gather up both Lucinda and Alessia. But mostly Alessia. Lucinda managed to slip the hug, and Sephina didn't seem to notice or mind.

"As soon as they told me you were coming over, I had Booker run three bubble baths, and made Coto get tubs of ice cream and cookies, but then he had to get more ice cream and cookies because he ate all of the first lot and . . ."

Seph was overwhelming. She all but smothered the poor kid.

"Seph," Lucinda said sharply. "Alessia can stay for bubble baths and ice cream later if she wants, but she needs to talk to us first. About the declaration."

Sephina pushed the young girl away, holding Alessia at arm's length, examining her as if for some malfunction.

"Seriously? Not even a couple of scoops? It's Hoboken Crunch, kid. The real deal. From honest-to-fucking-God Hoboken, I think. I'm pretty sure that's a place back on Earth."

"Thanks," Alessia said. "That would be nice. But I do need to talk to you first."

"We can do both," Sephina declared expansively. She spoke past both Lucinda and Alessia, as if addressing someone nearby but not in the room with them.

"Booker, keep the baths warm and the bubbles coming. Both kind of bubbles. Soapy and Cru."

"Sure," the source coder replied. His voice was all around them.

"Booker, are you the ship now?" Lucinda asked, turning in place, trying to locate the source of his voice.

"I loaded into the substrate, yes, Commander," he said. "I can be of more use here until we find me a new rig. The only ones on this ship are . . . inappropriate."

"I can imagine," Lucinda said. "Sorry. I didn't think it was wise to salvage any combat rigs or body blanks from Descheneaux, because of the infection."

"We'll get him something nice at Cupertino or even Natuna," Sephina said. "In one of the off-ring Habs like Lermontov. You know, sexy, but classy."

"I'm fine for now," Booker said. "I don't need sexy. I don't need classy. I just need something capable."

"Okay, way to kill the vibe, Sergeant Sensible." Sephina

stood up, putting her hands on her hips and looking around as if seeing her own ship for the first time. "There's like six or seven lounges on this porno yacht. I haven't even been in all of them. Booker," she called out, "which lounge is the nicest, do you think; you know, the most appropriate."

"The Gagarin Lounge is very restrained and I put the cleaning bots through it the other day. The bloodstains are mostly gone now."

"Super. We'll have the ice cream in there."

They followed Sephina to the lounge. The *Ariane* was nothing like *Defiant*. If you didn't know you were on a ship it would be possible to imagine you had folded into some grotesquely opulent Russian dacha back on Old Earth. The Gagarin Lounge was not at all restrained, but it did have a lesser density of platinum leaf, disco balls, and hot tubs.

Lucinda took a seat on a white leather lounge and accepted a bowl of ice cream, for the sake of form, but she found after the first mouthful that she couldn't stop dipping her little silver spoon back into the creamy treat. Close-combat training had given her an appetite and giving in to the sugar rush was a terrible choice. But she made it, anyway. Sephina enjoyed two bowls and poured freely from a very expensive-looking bottle of champagne. Alessia stirred her ice cream into a cold, thick soup and ate none of it.

"I don't know what to do about the declaration," she said.

"It is a very important decision," Lucinda cautioned, causing Sephina to roll her eyes.

"Oh, come on. What are you, the kid's counselor?"

"Yes." Lucinda frowned. "And so are you."

"Please!" Alessia said over the two of them. "I wanted to talk to you because . . . well . . . you're both . . . I . . ."

Sephina grinned.

"We're awesome, kid. And we both know it, but Captain Mumblepants over there would disappear up inside her own puckered sphincter before admitting it."

Alessia smiled, sadly.

"Yes. You are awesome. Both of you. You remind me of the stories in our family saga about some of the earliest Montanblanc princesses. Before relife was possible. But I also know you grew up together. In a Habitat Welfare home."

Seph shrugged. Lucinda shifted awkwardly.

"You want to free some orphans, too?" Sephina asked.

Alessia shook her head. Stopped. And said, "Well, I suppose if they needed to be freed, yes. But no, I wanted to talk to you because you were poor."

Lucinda felt a hot flush of a shame she hadn't felt in many years reddening her cheeks. Sephina roared with bright, pealing laughter.

"You got that right, kid," she said when she had gotten over her amusement. "There's no scarfing down Hoboken Crunch in the hot tubs at Hab Welfare, that's for fucking sure. And the hot tubs are just big plasteel tubs of cold water, anyway. And the bubbles are just farts."

"Sephina, please," Lucinda said, but she was simply projecting her discomfort outward. "Why does it matter, Alessia?"

Alessia did not answer immediately. She frowned and chose her next words with apparent care.

"I have never really known any poor people," she said. "Even Caro and Debin aren't really poor. Their grandfather worked for the royal estate and he had both his own Guards pension and a small carer's allowance from his son's military service."

She looked at Lucinda.

"Their father served in a unit seconded to the Armadalen Forces during the war. He was killed at the Battle of Longfall, and the Javans destroyed his backup. He was a common soldier. Not an officer."

Lucinda nodded.

"I fought there. I didn't know about your friends' dad. I'm sorry. But I did know about them spiking the backup stacks. That was a crime, what they did, Alessia."

Sephina, for once, remained quiet.

"Caro and Debin don't really remember much about him," Alessia said. "He was away a lot. And then he was gone forever."

"And their mother?"

"She was a commoner. She worked on a farm. She died when they were young, which was how they came to Skygarth with their granddad."

Having started to talk, Alessia seemed to be building momentum and neither of the women wanted to interrupt her. She sat cross-legged on a single cube of white bison leather stirring her bowl of liquid ice cream.

"When we escaped from the Sturm with Mister Dunning and Sergeant Reynolds, I saw some of the common people in Port au Pallice cheering when the Sturm executed my family. They did it in the palace grounds of the Habitat Grand Hermitage. They streamed it. And they . . . they destroyed the mesh."

"Wait," Lucinda said. "The stream. It was live?"

"I think so, yes."

Lucinda filed that away. It wasn't surprising that the Sturm's own FTL commlinks were unaffected by the malware that had rendered the Greater Volume's zero point network unusable, but a livestream such as Alessia described was a crucial data point.

The princess had stopped talking for a moment and Sephina reached over to give her arm a squeeze.

"It's okay, kid. We all lost people."

But Alessia shook her head.

"It was terrible to watch them treated like that. And the Sturm's wetware. It made them into animals. But they're not gone forever like Caro and Debin's dad. I don't think so, or I hope not, anyway. There has to be a secure copy somewhere. There *has* to be. At the Cupertino Binary or one of the other secret sites. My father, he would not leave such a thing to chance, even if it meant breaking the law."

Neither of the older women said anything.

"The killing was bad," Alessia continued, "but what made it worse was all the people cheering."

She looked to them with imploring eyes.

"They were happy my family was dead."

Lucinda's first inclination was to sugarcoat with some white lie. To spare the child the unpleasant realization that life was not as she had imagined it.

Seph, of course, did nothing of the sort.

"It's tough that you lost your family, kid. Again, we totally get that. But those peeps you saw, they weren't your fam. They were your servants, your subjects. They were your property."

Anger flashed in the girl's eyes.

"House Montanblanc does not trade in human lives. We hold no slaves or serfs or indebted thralls."

Sephina threw up her hands.

"Yeah, okay, you got me. They weren't your property. But they weren't entirely free, were they? Not like me or the Loose Unit here. The Commonwealth has its faults, but everyone there is born free."

"Free to what?" Alessia said with surprising vehemence. "Free to sleep on the deck plates of an industrial Hab? Free to starve?"

Lucinda tried to explain, putting aside the bowl of ice cream. "I think what Sephina was trying to say, Alessia, was that a lot of people live very hard lives, even on your family's Habitats and settled worlds, which are nicer than most. Not everyone is rich. Most people aren't. Not everyone gets to relife. Most don't. Most people just struggle to get through one span. Not just poor people, either. Most people. If they thought that was going to change, they might not see things like you do."

Lucinda waited for the same flash of anger in Alessia's expression, but it never came. Instead she nodded, sniffed, and rubbed at her nose, which had started to run.

"That's what I wanted to ask you about," the princess said. She looked up at them. "My family would not want me to sign this declaration. If I do sign it and Baroness Sephina does relife them from a secure offline store, they will probably find some way to say it didn't count."

"Probably," Lucinda admitted.

"But you and Admiral McLennan need me to do this, don't you?"

"Yes, we do," Lucinda said. "Across the Greater Volume, there are billions of people with skills we need. Real skills, learned the hard way."

"Like you both learned?" Alessia asked. "Without scripts or code."

"Yes," Lucinda said. "We call it organic training."

Alessia gave it another moment of long, silent thought. Finally, she said, "Will it make people's lives better?"

"No," Lucinda said honestly. "Not at first."

Seph stared at her, as though surprised, but Lucinda hastened to explain.

"We need to free them, especially from whatever is left of realms like the Combine and the Javan Empire, so that they can choose to fight. They won't have that choice while they're under the yoke. Whatever remains of the Empire and realms might try to cut a deal with the Sturm. There'll be plenty of lower-level authorities who survived because they weren't plugged in. Some of them will try to take over. Everything and everyone. We need to free as many people from their control as we can."

"So they can fight for you?" Alessia asked.

"If they want to, yes," Lucinda confirmed. "But only if they want to."

Princess Alessia appeared to think about it, deeply, for a long time.

Finally, she nodded.

"I will sign the declaration," she said.

"Thank fuck for that," Mac growled as he watched Alessia sign the document, witnessed and gene-signed by Hardy and the smuggler.

The hologram from the other ship was jaggy and blurred, the audio feed tinny and sometimes beyond even Hero's abilities to render intelligible, but for once he did not chew the Intellect's shiny x-matter arse-casing about any of it.

Frazer McLennan had what he needed.

"You can shut that off now," he said, waving one liver-spotted hand at the surveillance take floating in the middle of his quarters. "It's not like I can see anything worth a damn, anyway."

"That's hardly my fault." Herodotus sniffed. "I warned you the Zaistev vessel had excellent counterintelligence capabilities. I could only fold in a few persistent photons, barely enough for even a minimal take."

"Och, enough with your whinging, I'm not complaining about anything."

"Complaining about everything is your natural state of being."

McLennan's quarters were roomy and well appointed. Not luxurious, but comfortable, as befitted somebody of his advanced age and rank. *Defiant*'s late executive officer had formerly occupied this cabin, and Hardy had generously enlarged the space when Mac came aboard after Batavia. The fit-out was austere, in that Armadalen way, but the ship's engineering division had installed a wooden desk and bookshelves (salvaged with Alessia's blessing from Skygarth) and Hero had folded in some of his papers and journals from the dig at the *Voortrekker*. It was as close to homey as he was ever going to get.

"You do realize what you've done, though, don't you?" Hero said quietly.

"I've no doubt you're in a mood to tell me," Mac grunted.

He caught himself doodling in the corner of his notebook from the dig, drawing fractal patterns in the bottom left corner of the page where he had been jotting down his thoughts on the contents of the *Voortrekker*'s medical bay on the day the Sturm had returned. McLennan set aside his antique pen and closed the journal, turning slowly in his chair to face the Intellect.

"You have destroyed what remains of the Greater Volume," Hero said.

"I didnae sign the declaration," McLennan pointed out. "The wee senator from Earth did that."

"Oh, come now," Hero chided him gently. "Alessia is literally a child. And her two closest counselors aren't much older than her in relative or absolute terms. You have hemorrhoids older than all of them together. You are even older than me."

"Och, you're barely a bairn, Herodotus. We spun you up for the first war, you'll recall."

"Yes, yes, yes, I remember with advantages what feats we did that day, but that's me, Mac. And I do wonder some days if you have not forgotten more of yourself than remains in what's left of your mind."

Unlike many of their public exchanges, there was no heat to this. Hero's tone was observant, and even considerate.

McLennan frowned.

"I'm fine," he said. "Just tired and a little worn down is all. I'm not designed to last for millennia."

"No. And that disgracefully cheap basic body you insist on wearing needs replacing far too often. I fear that we will have neither time nor opportunity given our current circumstances. It's not like you'll be able to book yourself into the university clinic for a leisurely scan and side load."

McLennan laughed bitterly. "There's nothing leisurely about it."

Hero floated a little closer. Even though McLennan's quarters were generous, the Intellect took up a lot of the free space.

"I believe we should commence the preliminary scans as soon as possible," Hero said. "You have no backup. None at all."

"I never have." McLennan shrugged. "It's what makes me human. Helps me understand the accursed Sturm."

A faint rose-colored band of light rippled up the black carapace of the Intellect. The equivalent of an eye roll.

"Please don't," Hero said. "I'm not one of these children you're leading about by the nose."

"Pah!" McLennan scoffed. "There's no leading any of these lassies. Willful bloody shrews all three of them."

Hero backed off, floating away a few feet.

Mac could tell it was only to regroup and try again. They had known each other for a very long time. For almost all his many lives, in fact.

"At least let me map your engram state while you sleep. It will make for a much quicker extraction in an emergency."

"In case you hadn't noticed we're living in a permanent emergency right now."

"I would say we're between contingencies. Come on, Mac. I'm not asking you to swap out into a combat chassis or a brand-new skin job. I just want to be able to make the extract without delay if it becomes necessary."

"Och, will you quit your endless jibber-jabber if I agree?"

"Yes, but only on this topic."

McLennan raised his hands.

"Fine then, but only while I sleep. Map the contours of my sweet silent thoughts and remembrance of things past, but I'll have you leave no shadow of your trespass."

"But of course," Hero promised. "I am an Armada-level—"

"Oh, do shut up."

The Intellect snorted.

"I'm afraid I can't. Having won this signal concession I must press on for more. This thing you've done, the Emancipation . . ."

McLennan waved him off.

"I didnae do anything."

"Mac. Please. This wonderful thing, freeing the slaves, striking off the bonds of indebted servitude and inherited enslavement, everywhere all at once, it might appeal to your censorious and moralizing nature, but it will ensure we have made enemies of half the surviving Grand Houses."

"Only if they survived."

"And if they didn't, there would be no need of any declaration."

"Och, away with you and your confounded logic. I'm not such a fool that I would have it proclaimed throughout the Greater Volume everywhere and all at once. There will come an appropriate moment. But it was the right thing to do and you know it. Go read some fucking history, you miserable calculator."

"I do not need to review the woeful history of your species to know there is a difference between what is and what should be."

"If you understood the meaning of human history rather than defaulting to your perfect recall of mere information, you might appreciate the nuance of the thing. The indebted and enslaved dinnae need a lecture on the injustice of it all. They know in their meat that their lives—their short, nasty, brutish, and singular fucking lives—are unjust, and the tension of that injustice cannae be eased without a sudden and violent change in circumstance. To them the difference between revolution and invasion makes no more nevermind than the question of whether their masters' skid-marked underpants are the consequence of a wet fart or a lazy wipe. Either way, they're in the shit. But now they have a chance to get out. If they should take it."

Hero sighed.

"This is the sound of me rolling my eyes. Because that is not really a choice, is it? You merely offer them the freedom to die—fighting for you."

Mac smacked his hand down on the desktop with a crash.

"No! I offer them the freedom to live as they would were their lives not bounded on one side by the oppressions and exploitation of the Grand Houses, and on t'other by the murderous fucking race maniacs of the Republic. To achieve that blessed and sovereign state is within their power, should they recognize the truth of it and risk the rising flood tide when it serves."

Silence fell between them until Hero spoke a few moments later.

"And this is why you do not want Captain L'trel to do as Princess Alessia has asked. Because to raise her family from the deep is to rebirth the oppressions of the old order."

"On this I shall trust to the thoroughness of Republican perfidy. They would not chance the return of a Rupert Montanblanc or the supreme Yulin. I am quietly hopeful that every trace of those bastards is gone. The Sturm have been watching us for years. Perhaps centuries. They will have made allowances and arrangements for the arrogance and duplicity of the Fraction's overlords."

"Do you imagine then that the princess is wrong about her family?" Hero asked. "Do you think them truly dead beyond all hope of return? If so, why did you ask L'trel not to seek them out in their secret vaults?"

McLennan said nothing.

CHAPTER

SEVENTEEN

The Natuna System comprised three gas giants, two rocky planets, five imperial Habs, and one freeport orbiting a yellow giant, nine long folds under full military power from Descheneaux Station. The Armadalen Navy had blockaded the Javan mining and mercantile hub during the war but had never invested the system with significant forces. It was a commercial prize, rather than a critical military target. Cutting it off had robbed Medang Palace of crucial revenue and helium 3 supplies while never directly threatening the Empire's major war-fighting facilities. The RAN's blockade did, however, create strategic uncertainty and fierce contention within the high councils of the Empire, with competing factions lobbying the palace to alternately abandon or relieve the besieged entrepôt. The side that each clique or faction took was inevitably determined by their exposure to financial loss from Natuna's blockade. As a strategic play it had paid off handsomely, undermining any sense of unity within the empire's Elite Fraction.

Defiant and *Ariane* folded into the vast circumstellar disc of small rocks and frozen volatiles, mostly methane, ammonia, and water ices that ringed the solar system between seventy and ninety AU from the luminous amber giant of Natuna. The two ships nestled into the lee of a frozen planetoid, a Pluto analogue of dense silica shrouded in a hundred-kilometer-thick crust of nitrogen ice.

Sitting in the command chair, alert but quiet, Lucinda examined the holo-field before her and said nothing. The bridge crew were similarly mute. In a sense, it was all theater. They were running silent and dark, but the internal spaces of *Defiant* existed within a discrete bubble universe, quantum-shifted infinitesimally but meaningfully out of the reality in which the stealth destroyer pressed into the same space-time as the tiny frozen world thousands of kilometers below. But theater, Lucinda knew, was important. They lurked at the edge of hostile space now. Best to act as though the enemy already lay in wait. Even McLennan and Hero, who had repeatedly shown they had little patience for the performative aspects of conventional leadership, deferred to her in this. The admiral sat quietly, rubbing at his chin with one bony knuckle as he considered the main holo-display, which was rapidly filling with data from the passive arrays. The Intellect, feeding from the same take and coming to its own conclusions about the tactical and strategic circumstances, kept any such judgments to itself. The *Ariane* held station three hundred kilometers astern, cloaked in its own considerable stealth shielding, emitting nothing, not even a tight beam pulse.

"Lieutenant Fein," Lucinda said at last, keeping her voice low. "Disperse the drones throughout the EK ring. Encrypted pulse. Full envelopment. Protocol Jericho."

"Aye, ma'am," the young officer acknowledged. "Launching now."

A swarm of micro satellites folded away from the Armadalen warship, propagating through the vast and mostly empty belt of icy rubble and free-floating scree that comprised the remnants of the Natuna System's formation. So great were the distances to the far side of the ring, a disc that surrounded the entire solar system, that nearly a third of the deployed drones had to fold two or even three times to complete their dispersal. Upon reaching their release point, they pulsed out a onetime data packet, flooding the ring with encrypted telematics that would be indecipherable to anyone but another RAN ship with the correct cryptographic keys.

"And now we wait," Lucinda announced to nobody. "Mister Chase, do you have my plot?"

"Aye, Commander," Lieutenant Chase replied. "The second lay-up point is set."

"Ms. Chivers, inform Captain L'trel that we will move to the next lay-up on my mark. Helm, stand ready."

"Aye, aye, ma'am," both officers answered.

A soft Scottish brogue came from just behind her. McLennan.

"If I might, Commander? A word in your shell-like?"

"Is it urgent?" Lucinda asked, as the bridge crew appeared to come out of suspended animation, prepping *Defiant* for the small fold to their next waypoint in a hostile volume.

"Not urgent, no," McLennan conceded. "But important, perhaps, if you would concede the difference."

Lucinda swiveled in her chair to find both the Terran officer and the Intellect hovering behind her. She also saw Chase watching on as though awaiting new instructions.

"Nothing to see here, Mister Chase."

He turned away, his face a mask. Chase had been difficult to read since he'd requested to be relieved of his commission so he might gather and lead whatever forces remained of his own family's House. There was no chance of that happening, however, until she could train or secure another lead navigator. Chase seemed to accept the necessity of his remaining on board for now, even if Herodotus could have easily managed his duties. Hero could manage almost all of their duties, but it was not the Armadalen way. Chase, for his part, appeared to have retreated to stiff formality and silent compliance. Lucinda worried sometimes that his blank expression spoke to an effort to contain furies that would explode out of him at the worst possible moment.

She felt the need to take him aside and reassure him that she was not being stupidly punitive by denying his request to resign his commission, but there was no time. Not now.

"M'learned friend here has been noodling about in the take from the inner system," McLennan said quietly.

"As have my intelligence and tactical officers," Lucinda said. "I'll be taking a briefing from them after we arrive at the next waypoint. You are, of course, invited to join us."

"And we thank you for the courtesy," McLennan replied, as smooth as a buttered eel. He had been in a fine mood since Alessia had signed Volume-wide Emancipation into law. "I can save you some time, though, Commander. Yon sneaky beakies will be in the way of telling you that the perfidious Javans seem remarkably unaffected by the enemy's malware and shenanigans."

"Wait, what?" Lucinda asked with such urgency and volume that some of the bridge crew stopped and turned toward her as though awaiting new orders.

"As you were," she said. "Carry on. We're still folding, in"—she checked the countdown in her personal data cloud—"twenty seconds."

Keeping her voice down and her demeanor cool, she leaned in toward McLennan. Without being asked to, Hero projected a field effect around them, muting their conversation.

"What are you saying? The Javans are hooked up with the Sturm?"

McLennan shook his head.

"No, no. Not at all. I'm merely saying that Herodotus has read the tea leaves and this particular system seems largely unaffected by the enemy attack. The Habs are in lockdown for sure, and the Javans and Combine have pickets out. But all Hab and ship systems remain functional, except for the zero point network."

"The Combine is here?" Lucinda asked.

Hero answered before McLennan could speak.

"Two of their major warships, heavy raiders. With escorts. Maneuvering in-system as part of a battle group centered on a Javan Warlugger. Nemesis class."

"Jesus fucking Christ."

Lucinda looked to her tactical officer, Mercado Fein, who was standing by his station, his face a pale mask of concern. He held a data slate in one hand and appeared to be waiting on her summons. She waved him over just as *Defiant* executed the fold to their new lay-up point. Lieutenant Fein stepped through Hero's auditory field effect, and Lucinda nodded at the flexi-screen in his hand.

"Is that my tactical briefing?" she asked.

"Yes, ma'am. We appear to have a situation in-system."

She resisted the urge to rub her eyeballs. They were beginning to throb.

"Okay, let's pull forward the briefing. Hero, please drop the field effect."

She felt rather than heard the slight shift in tone as the auditory barrier disappeared.

"Mister Chase, please take the conn. O-Group to convene in the ready room in five minutes. Chase, I'm not cutting you out of this meeting. I need someone on the stick who can move quickly if the Javans fold in. I will brief you into the situation myself when we are done."

"Aye, ma'am," the young scion said, trying hard to hide his surprise at the consideration she had just shown him. She was under no obligation to spare his feelings or explain her decisions.

Lucinda waited for Hero to complain, or for McLennan to speak up on his behalf. Two weeks ago, the Intellect would have objected that he should simply take control of the ship while its infinitely slower, denser human passengers took their time catching up to whatever he already knew. But Herodotus was learning, if grudgingly, that he was merely part of the crew, not above it.

The senior Officers Group met in a small room adjoining the main bridge where the ship's captain would ordinarily repair for any business of command which was not appropriately conducted in public. *Defiant*'s O-Group comprised the warship's heads of division and the Marine Corps commander, Captain Hayes. Commander Timuz arrived from engineering, and Doctor Saito from medical, each looking perplexed as to why they had been summoned. In truth Lucinda had little reason to seek any input from their functional areas, but she remained painfully aware of how young and inexperienced she was in comparison to *Defiant*'s senior staff. Between them, they had well over a thousand years of military service. Closer to two thousand if she included McLennan. Although she was confident in her tactical choices, especially in moments of high, kinetic stress such as the fight back on Descheneaux, she remained hesitant and unsure of her judgment in matters of greater strategic weight.

Their judgment weighed on her.

They were Armadalen military officers and by some perverse glitch of fate, she had risen to command them. They would do their duty. On her say-so they would give their lives—their real lives with no second chances or reloads. But the souls behind the eyes that followed her were old—ancient in some cases—and Lucinda could not help but feel herself measured and judged a simple child by the living ghosts gathered at this table.

The ready room was small, but spacious enough to accommodate all those she had summoned. Carpeted and paneled in a hardwood from the arctic forests of Jindabyne, Armadale's larger northern continent, it resembled the office of a minor executive from one of the Grand Houses. A long diamond-glass window afforded a view, such as it was, of the icy planetoid far below, a dim globe of negative space. Lucinda had removed the small nest of armchairs and a desk, which Captain Torvaldt had preferred, replacing them with a conference table and standing room for ten people.

Herodotus, who could not fit through the doorway, folded into a corner, where he floated next to Mercado Fein and Lieutenant Tom Sear, one of the lucky six rescued from the infirmary on Descheneaux, and newly elevated to head of *Defiant*'s intelligence division by virtue of the two years he had served as an aide to the Joint Staff Directorate. The two men conferred with the Intellect and each other in subdued tones, while they compared notes on their flexi-screens. Whatever the enormous, ovoid super intelligence had to say, for the moment Hero was keeping it on the down low with Fein and Sear.

Everybody came to attention when Lucinda arrived. They just as quickly took their places when she asked them to.

"Who shall go first, then?" McLennan asked, looking at the two lieutenants. "Rosencrantz or Guildenstern?"

Sear was still painfully underweight and sallow from his confinement on Descheneaux. He deferred to Mercado Fein, who in turn looked to Hero.

"Nobody cares what I think," the Intellect complained breezily. "So please, do be my guest. I promise I will be quiet and only interrupt if you say something lethally stupid. The egregiously senseless I will merely endure as the cost of doing business with a bunch of inherently fallible beef muppets."

"That part where you promised to be quiet," McLennan said. "Let's try that."

"Lieutenant Fein," Lucinda said, stepping into the exchange before it could spool up into something louder and more sustained. "As briefly as you can, please."

Fein nodded and pinched his fingers on the display of his flexi, flicking the data into a holo-field that materialized over the conference table.

"We're still in-filling from the passive arrays," he said, "but this is our best development of the tactical situation around the inner system as of ten minutes ago."

"Ten minutes?" Lucinda queried.

Fein smiled shyly.

"I folded surveillance buoys in-system after we deployed the other drones, ma'am. As per protocol. They were onetime units. They took a deep read of the EM spectrum and folded back to within one light-minute of *Defiant* before tight beaming their take and self-destructing. Our intel is current," he advised, but guardedly.

"Well done that man," McLennan said.

"Yes, good work, Lieutenant," Lucinda said. "What do you have for us?"

The tactical officer frowned.

"The Javans and the Combine appear to have suffered little to no damage from the Sturm attack. They have significant assets in-system, equivalent in combat power to one of our medium battle groups. The Habs are fully functional but remain offline. Chatter indicates they're aware of the wider strategic situation, but they're not attempting to contact Medang Palace or the citadel on Arakan. The whole system has, in effect, gone dark to the outside volume."

"Probably why they're not chewing on each other's brains," McLennan said.

"What makes them special?" Lucinda asked. "Have they cut a deal with the Sturm?"

Both young officers glanced at Hero.

He remained silent just long enough for it to become awkward before finally answering, "Oh, would somebody like me to explain?"

Lucinda gave him her stone face, but the Intellect was supremely uncaring.

"Natuna, the local star, is in the later eons of its stellar evolution," he explained. "The outer atmosphere is enlarged and tenuous, the surface temperature comparatively low, explaining why the Habs have such close orbits, and why the whole outpost regularly goes dark to survive the flares and coronal mass ejections which would otherwise damage their systems. I have studied the signals taken from the Habs and local ship traffic and concluded that, at the time of the Sturm's attack, an X99-class solar flare and coronal explosion occasioned a total shutdown of everything but the Habs' hardened autonomic subsystems. The warships have military grade shielding but they were of course cut off from the zero point network, as well. To make a rather long and somewhat dull story short and exciting enough to hold the interest of the easily distracted, this whole system was offline. The Javan Habitats and the Russian Federation's fetching little hive of scum and villainy at L3. They all remain offline and thus unaffected by the Sturm's malware attack."

"Shit," Lucinda said. "Do they even know the Sturm are back?"

Tom Sear spoke up. His voice was croaky, and he had to stop, cough, and start again.

"Excuse me," he said. "But yes, Commander. Combine operational procedures mandate a staged return from lockdown. And Lermontov Station, the Russian freeport, is bound by similar OP. It looks like the malware hit some local nodes when they queried the ZPN, but they weren't hooked up to the wider in-system networks. They assumed a pre-emptive strike. By us."

Sear grinned ruefully at that.

A few of them did.

"The first refugee ships to reach Natuna from the edge of the volume filled in the true picture for them."

"And how are they coping?" McLennan asked.

"Not well," Lieutenant Sear replied. "We have a selection of comms intercepts to give you a flavor of . . ."

He didn't finish the sentence. His voice, soft and a little cracked after the trauma of Descheneaux, was drowned out by the blare of klaxons and alarms.

CHAPTER

EIGHTEEN

His power as aide-de-camp to Fleet Marshal Blade was such that Anders Revell could have requisitioned an Astral Fortress like *Trafalgar* or *Enterprise* as his personal runabout and not even the chief justice of the Inquiry could stop him. He wasn't that big an asshole, however. As soon as he heard of the battle at Descheneaux Station, Revell paused investigations on Montrachet, requisitioned a fast frigate from the battle group surrounding the *Enterprise*, and folded at maximum gain to the captured Armadalen outpost. His prisoners, such as old man Dunning, and persons of interest like Jasko Tan, he left in the care of a Ground Force Security unit assigned directly to him, with orders to the medical staff to prep Dunning for transport. Hopefully it would be enough to keep them from the predations of the Inquiry.

Revell was in his quarters on the frigate *Ulysses*, reviewing transcripts and holo-caps of his sessions with Dunning, when all his devices pinged him with a message from the bridge. They were about to make the terminal fold into the Descheneaux System. He acknowledged the hail, closed and secured his files, and hurried two decks up to the command center. The *Ulysses* was an Avenger-class frigate, designed for long-range recon and strategic strike. Everything had been stripped back to those purposes. The companionways were narrow, forcing a cramped pivot and shuffle whenever crew members encountered one another. Very little color relieved the uniform gray of carbon-armor bulkheads and deck plating. But she could outpace anything in the Republican line of battle, most ships of the enemy's fleets, and deliver the same punch as a light cruiser when she chose fight over flight.

The bridge was as cramped as anywhere on the vessel—save for the arsenal. There was plenty of room down there. A single trooper in fatigues and equipped only with a sidearm announced his arrival as Revell crouched through the vacuum hatch. Captain Martin Turner looked back over his shoulder, and chopped one hand at the large, curved screen that occupied most of the bulkhead in front of them.

"You said you wanted to see this," he said.

The display was a data-rich feed of the tactical volume around Descheneaux Station. The Armadalen naval base, a repurposed natural satellite, dominated the lower right-hand corner. The iron gray regolith of the hollowed-out moon was wrapped in the white, sun-scorched crownwork of heavy military engineering. Battlements and weapon turrets surrounded docking bays for capital ships. Beam casters glittered like needle teeth around the dark maws of a dozen smaller hangars, probably for squadrons of Corsairs and Hornets, the Armadalens' volume-superiority fighters. All the defensive works, he knew, spiraled deep into the body of the reconstructed moon. The butcher's bill for attacking such a stronghold conventionally would be steep.

The task force that now stood off the satellite testified to the price the Republic had paid for securing the station even after its defenders had perished. Two heavy cruisers and a screening force of destroyers and stellar drekar guarded the mass grave, not just of the enemy, but of the two Republican warships that had initially stood vigil here. The truism that war in space leaves only cold vacuum behind was not entirely true, Revell thought. Here, in the void that was their tomb, the Armadalens had somehow made their own memorial out of the massed combat power in this task force. Revell saw in those ships, all of them drawn from other vital duties, a manifestation of his superiors' mistakes and the reparations they must now make to tactical necessity. There was no sign of the two ships *Sacheon* and *Coral Sea*, which had died here. But you could not ignore their loss, either. The enemy, though defeated, still lay under the gun sights of the Human Republic for apparently they still offered resistance.

"I would speak with the task force commander, Captain," Revell said.

"Privately, sir? That would be Praetor-Admiral Logan. He is . . . difficult."

Revell shook his head just once. "No. On-screen is fine."

A moment later a beam link to the cruiser *Jutland* threw a comm window onto the main display. A stout-looking older man, his head shaved back to iron gray bristles glowered out at Turner and Revell, who both saluted smartly.

Turner spoke first.

"Admiral," he said. "I present Captain Anders Revell, aide-de-camp to the Fleet marshal. He—"

"I know who he is," Logan growled. "Step up, Revell. I can't see you spooking around in the shadows."

Keeping his face neutral, Revell moved to stand next to the captain of the *Ulysses*.

"Admiral. You have my credentials, direct from Fleet Marshal Blade."

"I do. I suppose the fucking goons will be along any minute, sniffing at your ass crack to see what falls out."

Turner flinched away from the screen as Logan spoke, as though to avoid contamination. Revell saw the shock jolt through the other members of the small crew. He did not react beyond shrugging off the question.

"I cannot control nor speak for the Inquiry," he said.

Logan grunted and appeared to decompress a little.

"And your investigation into Montrachet? I heard that Admirals Peet and Cruze were back on deck. That you who sprung them?"

"That was Fleet Marshal Blade, sir. On my recognizance. I have made no interim findings yet, but I can tell you I see no evidence of staff failure on Montrachet, just the fortunes of war."

Logan grunted, satisfied with that.

"What do you need, Captain?"

Revell took an armored shuttle down to Descheneaux where a GFS squad awaited his arrival in one of the main docks. A battle had been fought here. Damaged ships tilted over on ruined landing gear. The scorch marks and kinetic scars of heavy weapons fire marred bulkheads and deck plating. Bodies and body parts, armored and unarmored, wafted gently in the low gravity. Revell engaged the mass effectors in his suit and felt it grip the deck plating with greater surety.

The Ground Force Security troopers were all sealed up in panzerplate, Assaulter-class battlesuits, just like his. Revell did not ask why. The atomized wreckage of two Republican warships was answer enough to that stupid question.

He jacked into their tactical net and the heads-up display of his helmet filled with a dense cloud of information. Dialing the feedback to one data point, the name of the squad leader, Sergeant Lineen Cronje, resolved in his HUD.

The sergeant verified Revell's rank and mission statement via tac-net and punched out a fist in salute, followed half a second later by the six members of her squad. Cronje's voice, in the speakers of his helmet, had the flattened, guttural accent of a Drakensberg Hab native.

"I'm ordered to escort you wherever you want to go, Captain, to provide security and support."

Revell gave the squad a professional once-over. Their battle-suits were clean but marked with the divots and scars of hard, recent use. They loaded out with a mixed arsenal of personal weapons and missile packs, and one big-ass crew-served auto cannon.

"You got my sparky?" Revell asked.

"Ashari," Cronje said. "Step up, Troop."

One of the battlesuits moved toward Revell and crashed a gauntlet into the glacis plate of her armor.

Revell dialed up the tac-net feed and quickly scanned Trooper Ashari's profile. An SF Assaulter specialist, cross-trained in data ops.

"Can you get me up on the Armadalen systems?" Revell asked.

"We already ate their lunch, sir," she replied. "The spike cracked open most of the frames. There's a couple of stand-alone systems that Fleet Intelligence are working on. Can't get you into them yet, but we own like ninety percent of their shit now."

"Good work," Revell said, before turning back to Cronje. "And security on the deck?"

Sergeant Cronje made a fist and gently palmed it with her other hand. A gesture signaling "all good."

"The borgs we hacked are just biomass. Not many still moving when we got here, and we cleaned out the leftovers. One of their machines did survive the 'phage," she went on. "A big bastard, too. Fleet level at least. But it was fucked up. A danger to anyone and everyone, the Armadalens as much as us."

Sergeant Cronje pointed to a mound of junk metal and scrap, and Revell realized with a start it was a funeral cairn piled high with dead troopers. Armored legs, chest plates, helmets, a small fort composed of battlesuit fragments and their disjointed content. He felt his balls trying to crawl up into his body.

"*Coral Sea* lost two boarding teams to it before they pulled back to wait for the nanophage to finish it off," Cronje explained. "But it looks like the Armadalens did that themselves. We recovered imagery from the security cams. There and there."

She pointed out two surveillance pods embedded in the nearest bulkhead.

"I'll need to see that," Revell said.

"I got a packet if you want, sir. Site Exploit's been piecing together what happened from base security feeds. But bottom line, the machine just held on longer than most. The borgs that came through here managed to pull its plug somehow. You want that packet now?"

"Yes," he said. "I want everything we have on these mutants."

A notification pinged in his HUD, a large data drop from Sergeant Cronje.

"Thank you, Sergeant." Revell started to walk toward the funeral cairn. Cronje, Ashari, and the rest of the squad fell in behind him.

"Is that the machine?" he asked, painting a giant ovoid object with a target designator for the NCO. The dead AI had crashed into the plates a hundred meters away with force enough to warp them. A body lay nearby. Killed more recently than the others, he judged. It was not as swollen or deeply discolored.

"Yes, sir. That's the one."

"And the borgs," Revell added. "The ones that put it down, do we know who they were?"

"Exploit tagged the grunts as Fleet Marine Corps, probably assigned to a ship on deep space patrol or maybe a black op somewhere. They were offline. Avoided the strike. The marines had a naval officer with them. No ship ID on their armor, so maybe they were newbies, but the cams picked up a name tag. Hardy."

"Very good," Revell said. "Specialist Ashari, I need to get into whatever personnel management and Fleet routing systems we've cracked open so far. Let's see if we can find this borg calling itself Hardy."

He was nearly a full day locating the data point. Specialist Ashari was very good, but Descheneaux was a major enemy base and Revell cautioned her that the borg known as Hardy was still moving around because it was not exposed to the first strike.

"It was running dark and the ship was running dark. Let's start there," he said.

He had Cronje's squad stand easy while he and Ashari went about their hunt. The troopers didn't just plant ass and catch up on lost rack time, however. Cronje let two of them kick back while the rest of the team rotated through overwatch. The station was dead. The Armadalens, too. But nobody wanted to take one in the ass like *Sacheon* and *Coral Sea*.

Revell asked Cronje to lead him to an administrative hub three levels down, where he had Ashari plug into the quartermaster's database.

"Can I ask, sir, out of professional interest, why not Fleet ops or even personnel?" Ashari said. "We got both."

"Good question, Troop, and we will get to them," Revell promised as she set up her deck, running adaptive hardlines into a data port on a basic holo-unit. They had taken over an office which a door plaque informed them had once belonged to a Captain de Beers. He or she, or maybe both—it was hard to know with these freaks—was nowhere to be found. Probably harvested for protein strings by now.

Revell pulled up a chair, consciously ignoring the personal effects that remained in de Beers's office.

It wasn't a person, after all. At that rank it was almost certainly just a fax of a dead man.

"Whatever barely legal covert op the Armadalens were running won't be recorded there," he said, expanding on his reasons for hitting up the base supply chains, rather than just searching for Lieutenant Hardy's service record. "The deployment and tasking would've been locked away in a black box. Intent is elusive, but supplies are material and finite. Food stores, ammo, toilet paper, Dtox bulbs, rum, boot polish, it all has to be accounted for by some poor warehouse clerk."

He took a data coin from his pocket and handed it to her.

"Drop that into your rig. Search parameters I put together on the way here. You don't use capital ships or runabouts on long-range deep space missions. They would have sent a stealth frigate or a destroyer. That program will sift through the last two months' materiel requisitions looking for anything that would match the profile of a deployment to deep space by a warship of that class."

Ashari plugged the coin into her deck and ran the software.

They got three hits within a minute.

Revell repeated the cycle with the personnel database, this time tweaking the program to look for officers recently transferred to duties on any of the three possible ships.

Ashari's deck pinged immediately.

Her eyes widened in surprise as Sergeant Cronje wandered over, attracted by the notification.

"You score?"

Anders Revell smiled.

"We scored."

"The ship is most likely an Armadalen stealth destroyer, HMAS *Defiant* under a Captain Jens Torvaldt, and the officer who accompanied the ground team onto the station is a lieutenant by the name of Hardy. Lucinda Hardy," Revell said.

Fleet Marshal Blade's holographic avatar dipped her head ever so slightly to acknowledge the progress Revell had made. Her expression did not change when she spoke. In Revell's experience Anais Blade had more control over her thoughts and feelings than any true human being he had ever known.

"And you are certain," she said, "that this vessel alone was responsible for the destruction of Strom's task force?"

"No, ma'am. I cannot, of course, be certain . . ."

Again the smallest nod. Beyond death, nothing was certain in war.

Revell stood at ease in the confines of the *Ulysses*'s securely contained information pod. The "scip" was slightly bigger than a crash pod on a shuttle, but not by much. He could reach out and touch the cool, dense matrix of holoscope transceiver panels surrounding him but that would distort the projection of Fleet Marshal Blade's flag office on the Astral Fortress *Yamato*.

Instead, Revell stood easy and continued his report.

". . . Analysis of the battle damage to those elements of the 101st in Strom's Montrachet task force and quantum mapping of the remains of the *Liberator* indicate a high probability that the enemy used a planet cracker to destroy the flagship. Personnel records at Descheneaux confirm the arrival on-station three months ago of specialist WPD engineering crew. At that time *Defiant* was in dock for refit. Those engineers were all rated to install Class Five warheads on ships displacing greater than a quarter-million tons. There were four such vessels on-station at the time, three are confirmed neutralized. *Defiant* has not been accounted for."

Revell paused. But he knew better than to draw the Fleet marshall's conclusion for her.

Anais Blade did not move.

Her face was unreadable, her features literally blank. Her scalp, shaved clean every day, shone under the biolights of her office. She wore no makeup or jewelry, of course. But neither was her skin disfigured by tattoo ink, figurative scarring, or any sort of aesthetic flesh work. Many true human warriors proudly displayed the body art of their ancestral cultures. It was a common way of paying homage to all they had lost, and Republican naval culture encouraged such reverence. Blade, whose lineage traced back through millennia to the early Nordic settlement of Iceland, stood before Revell in the simple combat coveralls of a space warfare officer, her high rank denoted only by the single platinum baton affixed to one lapel. Her face was naturally lined with age—she was in her sixth decade—and the cares of hard duty. The future of all true humanity weighed upon her with the crushing mass of a neutron star. It weighed upon all of them, but her burden was uniquely onerous.

"I agree with your assessment, Captain Revell. This Torvaldt, what do we know of him?"

"I have located his service record and forwarded it to you, ma'am," Revell said. "He is the third facsimile of a man who died over two hundred years ago. The last copy served in the recent war between the Armadalen Commonwealth and the Javan Empire, but not once did it undertake independent command. *Defiant* performed all missions as part of much larger task forces."

"Relevance?"

"I think the Torvaldt fax is gone, ma'am. Wiped out. Indeed, I have reason to believe *Defiant* did not entirely escape damage from our nanophage strike. It is possible that this Hardy is the senior surviving officer."

"And your reasoning?"

Revell had been preparing his case for two days. The projection of Blade's office was realistic enough that he was almost tempted to pace the room as he laid out his argument, but he resisted the urge. That's not how holograms worked.

"We know that McLennan escaped custody on Batavia with the help of an AI. We know there was an Armadalen warship of *Defiant*'s class in the Batavia System at that time because it engaged three of our own vessels, destroying two and disabling and boarding a third, the fast frigate *Nautilus*. I have recovered security data from the *Nautilus* and confirmed the presence of Hardy among the boarders. Or at the very least, the presence of the same battlesuit which appears shortly after on Descheneaux."

As he spoke, Revell gestured at a small data cloud floating in front of him, enlarging and arranging the relevant infographics for the Fleet marshal to follow.

Multiple video caps of a giant black ovoid materializing in the main camp at the *Voortrekker* site on Batavia orbited around confronting images of Armadalen marines slaughtering the crew of the *Nautilus* and stripping the vessel of critical technology. Blade's avatar reached out and pinched open a text file detailing the Republic's Order of Battle in the space around Batavia. She scanned it impassively.

Revell pressed on.

"After-action analysis of data from the *Nautilus* indicates the Armadalen vessel was not fighting under the control of an AI, even though a warship of that size would routinely deploy under machine authority. Yet Fleet records on Descheneaux confirm it did fold away on its last mission with a machine in charge. Triple A from the battle over Montrachet, however, indicates that *Defiant* was fighting under machine control again, shortly after the AI folded away with McLennan."

"Are you suggesting this same machine fought Strom?" Blade said. "The situation in the Batavia System was confused. It could have escaped on any number of vessels."

"Indeed," Revell said. "However, the Armadalen marines from the unit we see on Descheneaux . . ."

He foregrounded three video stills showing a small ground team fighting its way through the naval station, putting down hundreds of reprogrammed borgs. The one calling itself Hardy stood at the center of each image.

". . . are the same unit we also find on Montrachet, during the battle with the 101st."

He flicked two clear images taken from Montrachet into the virtual space between them. In the first, an armored enemy fighter sprinted across open ground between burning villas. In the second the same figure walked out of a basement, her helmet removed, with three children around her.

"The middle child is Princess Alessia, now sole heir of the Montanblanc ul Haq Corporation."

"Strom's bait," Blade said. It was not a question.

"Yes. A reasonable risk to lure surviving elements of the enemies' forces in that sector. And it worked. Several units were drawn in, attempting to rescue her. But ultimately it failed, because I believe this machine . . ."

He enlarged an image of the AI that had taken McLennan.

". . . took command of *Defiant* and executed an attack plan which annihilated Strom's command."

"Why this one, and not simply the ship's own machine intelligence?" the Fleet marshal asked.

"We know the *Defiant*'s machine intelligence did not command the vessel in combat against the *Nautilus* detachment. It was already disabled. And battle data analysis shows that the speed and complexity of the Montrachet attack would require a machine with capabilities at least three orders of magnitude greater than those of a unit you would expect to find in a ship of this class."

"That is less a reason than it is wishful thinking," Blade said sternly.

"Yes, Fleet Marshal. But the same analysis of Montrachet reveals that the destruction spreading out from the central datum point of the Armadalen ship precisely matches the activation sequence of the wormhole submunitions that destroyed the Republican fleets around Earth in the last battle of the first war."

Silence.

A small twitch at the corner of Blade's left eye betrayed her shock, but that was the only outward sign. Revell was impressed. When he had finally matched the patterns a few hours ago, he had sworn loudly enough to bring armed troopers running on the assumption that boarders had stormed the *Ulysses*.

"Go on," Blade said at last.

Revell wiped away all the data cloud save for one image of the AI.

"I believe this is the machine we once knew as Intellect Three," he said. "The one which Frazer McLennan, the actual McLennan, detailed to execute the ambush of the Five Fleets in the last battle of the War Between the Species. Only Three would have the knowledge, ability, and, frankly, the arrogance to per-fectly re-create the form of its original massacre above the home-world, in the destruction of Strom's fleet over Montrachet."

"My genome," Blade breathed. Her face, normally pale, was flushed with high color. "Such hubris."

Revell gestured dolefully.

"It's a machine. They all are, more or less."

"Of course," Blade said. She was nodding now. "Good work, Captain. Submit your report and return to the *Yamato*. I have need of you here. Archon-Admiral Strom can rest in peace. He died honorably, bested by a dishonorable foe."

Revell bowed a few inches, performing a courtesy adopted from the ancient samurai culture.

"If I might, Fleet Marshal?"

She was still staring at the image of Intellect Three. He un-derstood. It was hard to imagine that so ancient an evil might emerge from the cold vacuum of space to threaten humanity again. But Revell was not done. Blade looked at him, uncom-prehending for a moment. Finally, she shook her head, escaping the fugue state.

"Yes, Captain?"

"As I said, ma'am, I have reason to believe *Defiant* did suffer at least glancing damage from our first strike. I believe McLen-nan is with them, and the Montanblanc heir. Both significant prizes to be had, and significant threats if we do not take them."

"Say more," Blade said.

"It is possible this borg called Hardy is in tactical command of *Defiant*. We have studied their protocols. It is a commander's prerogative to deploy with away teams, and she keeps turning up like a bad penny. She is young. A first lifer, to use their term. The princess, too. I believe action at a distance might be possi-ble, to bring critical pressure to bear on both. It might be the fastest way to eliminate a proven threat."

Blade considered the request, her face a mask while she thought.

Finally, she said, "Approved."

CHAPTER

NINETEEN

Booker was worried.

And when a dude like him side-loaded into high-end bio-neural substrate such as the Russians had poured into *Ariane*'s q-state processing architecture, it meant he could shit his virtual pants at relativistic speed. All seeing, all knowing, and freaking the fuck out at faster than light.

Specifically, he was freaking out about Sephina.

She was fucked up.

Again.

Not just ugly crying, or howling, grieving, shit-faced drunk. Or passed out in a chunky puddle of her own vomit, facedown in her underpants, hammered flat and tripping like a mother-fucker. No, nothing so banal this time.

They'd all nursed her through previous episodes of nihilisti-cally shit-plowing herself into oblivion. But discreetly monitor-ing her vital signs as she lay deadly still on stained and filthy bedsheets among the empty bottles and bulbs and used-up che-mopods, Booker grew concerned that she might not come back from this binge.

He'd worked hard at hiding her accelerating dissolution from the Armadalens, and especially from Hardy, whom he judged the most likely to recognize any deterioration in her old friend, and even more likely to cut Sephina loose if she became a hazard to the mission.

Whatever the fuck that was.

Banks and Coto, consulted because of long association and close familiarity with the captain, agreed she was not the same since losing her partner, Ariane, back on Eassar.

"Grief is the demand of all love," Banks said quietly, sipping at a cup of tea in the pilot's chair. "And intolerable grief the legacy of such transcendent devotion."

"Yes. She cries too much," Jaddi Coto said and nodded from inside the regen tank, where he was attempting to grow back the rest of his sadly shortened horn.

"I think we might need to put her into the medbay, maybe even into regen and run a full detox 'n' detail on her," Booker suggested, mostly to himself.

"That will flush the toxins from her body, but not the poison from her soul," Banks replied, but gently.

"Do I have to get out of the tank?" Coto asked. "My horn is too small and it's warm in here."

Booker scanned Sephina's bio signs again and assigned another fraction of his vast processing capacity to projecting outcomes from her current state. The outcomes were not pretty. She was radiating a lot of heat. She had urinated. Voluminously, but not into a toilet. Both her neocortex and hippocampus were fucking fried and the medulla was struggling to regulate her autonomic functions, her breathing and heart rate.

"Fellas, I think we gotta help her out. Sorry, Coto. I need that regen tank."

"This disappoints me," he said. "My horn was once magnificent."

"I know but get out of the bath. You're gonna have to carry her."

Coto popped the canopy on the tank and climbed out, dripping bright blue mesenchymal gel to the deck plates. As he toweled off, Booker flushed the tank and dialed up a powerful blend of Dtox reagents and vitasupps.

Banks announced they were folding to a lay-up point in thirty seconds. Booker knew already and Coto was not interested. He was trying to climb into a sterile, disposable paper coverall which all patients in the medbay were supposed to wear before and after treatment. Too large for even the biggest of the one-piece garments, but ever the literalist, he had torn four of them to shreds on his rhinoderm hide.

Booker was about to suggest he just get back into his clothes when Sephina's heart stopped.

Although Booker was technically ensouled within the ship, he was still human. He believed this above all else for such was the final and irreducible creed of the source coder. In confirmation of his faith, while his thoughts could run at superluminal speed through the u-space processing matrices of the ship, he was but a man. And when Sephina L'trel's life guttered out with one final, failing beat of her broken heart, Booker regressed from a being of quantum electrodynamics to a mouth-breathing dumbass standing there, figuratively scratching his nut sack, going, "What the fuck?"

The ship's own subsystems took over then, medical alarms blaring and emergency lights flashing. Paths lit up in the deck plating, directing Coto and Banks toward their dying crewmate. Jaddi Coto gave up on the impossible task of trying to squeeze three hundred kilograms of hard-packed gene-sequenced hybridized rhino man into a flimsy paper onesie. He roared and took off at a thundering gallop, charging naked and slicked with blue jelly for the forward deck where Sephina had her quarters.

"Booker, the conn!" Ephram Banks cried out, abandoning his station, and his cup of tea, which crashed to the plates. He raced Coto to the captain's quarters with less speed and thunderous uproar but considerably more agility.

Booker shook his head like a dog coming out of an icy cold lake.

He did not have an actual head, of course.

But in his source code there remained a conception of himself that included five and a half kilograms of blood, bone, spongiform neural mass, skin, scalp, muscles, and miscellaneous wet fleshy structures such as eyes and tongue that meant the being that was Corporal Booker3-212162-930-Infantry could all too easily waste valuable time standing around, shaking his head and going, "Duh."

Banks was already halfway across the eccentrically fashioned wheelhouse of the *Ariane* when Booker finally flowed into the helm and assumed complete control over pilotage. He was able to watch as the two men sprinted away to help Captain L'trel.

The real men, a small, unworthy part of him reflexively thought.

He at least opened the cabin door for Coto, who would otherwise have simply put his head down and tried to crash through the carbon armor. And he sprung the latch on an emergency medical locker containing a defibrillator unit just before Banks reached it. The pilot grabbed the little medbot and powered it up as he ran.

There was nothing else for Booker to do.

He had already flushed the regen tank of his hangover cure and flooded it anew with a saline bath of myocardial nanobots. Banks and Coto were at work reviving the captain, and he thought about tight beaming an alert to *Defiant* but rejected the notion as soon as it occurred to him. Hardy had been adamant that as soon as they entered the Natuna System they must run dark.

Instead he stood guard, allotting most of his processing capacity to reading and analyzing the take from the *Ariane*'s passive arrays, sucking up the profligate signals leakage from deeper in-volume, and quickly coming to the same conclusion as the *Defiant*'s intelligence officers: The Javan outpost had survived the Sturm's pre-emptive attack through undeniable good fortune. The Empire persisted here in miniature, allied in convenience with a force of Combine warships that had been running dark when everything went sideways.

How much goodwill there could ever be between two such grotesque autocracies he didn't know.

Neither powers were friends of the Armadalen Commonwealth, which made Natuna an excellent prospect for finding other RAN missions operating in stealth—and so protected from the 'phage.

While watching over the medical emergency—Banks had already restarted Sephina's heart, and Coto now carried her like a baby in his massive arms as he ran back to the medbay—Booker started to sift the take from the Javan Habitats orbiting Natuna. The Empire was a prodigious user of vat-grown slaves for labor and military service, which was another way of saying the Empire was an important front in the Code's liberation struggle against the oppressive rule of the breeder hegemony.

That's how the political wing of the source code would have put it.

To Booker, these assholes were just sitting up and begging for a slave revolt.

There would be cells here, he knew.

Resistance fighters.

The Code would be active in its most militant and aggressive form because the Empire was one of the most brutal and oppressive of their persecutors. Still, he made no plans. He was merely gathering intelligence when the Sturm surveillance probes acquired them.

The *Ariane*'s threat detectors blared the alarm with no input from Booker. The ship was running old system software from the smugglers' previous ride, the *Je Ne Regrette Rien*. The code base had been lovingly tweaked over the years, refined and adapted to the special needs of enterprising businesspeople in a very particular segment of a competitive, high-risk market. Within a microsecond of the first waveforms painting the outer hull, the ship filled with sirens and warnings that a hostile actor had detected their presence in-volume.

Normally this might result in any number of things happening.

Mister Banks might fold them away on a random heading and keep folding until any difficulties had been left far behind.

Captain L'trel might have opened negotiations with whichever customs agent or commercial inspector had lit them up, preparatory to eliciting an industry-standard bribe.

On a rare occasion, the crew might even scramble to the armory and equip themselves to repel boarders.

In this instance, none of that happened. Mister Banks was still busy in the medbay. And although Jaddi Coto would have happily fought off pirates or freebooters clad in nothing but a few remaining dollops of bright blue regenerative gel, he was, like Banks, fully occupied with the captain's welfare.

The response fell to Booker.

Where he had hesitated when the ship's medical alert system sounded the alarm a few minutes earlier, he did not delay when the second set of alarms went off. His own subroutines were uniquely scripted for Tier One special operators of the Terran Defense Force. Hostile action was, in many ways, his happy place.

He went there.

The EM signature painting the ship, he matched to a database compiled by Herodotus during the Battle of Montrachet. *Ariane*, he confirmed, had been acquired by three separate Republican probes, all of them emitting at full power on active sensors.

"Ugh, space Nazis," he muttered to himself. "I hate these motherfuckers."

Stealth was no longer an option. Not for *Ariane*, at least. Booker allocated some of his processing capacity to monitoring *Defiant*, which boasted much more advanced stealth technologies than the Zaitsev Corporation had been able to procure for their vessel.

Defiant was still running dark.

They were not going to like this at all, but he had no choice.

The scream of alarms on his own ship increased in volume and intensity. Five probes had now locked onto *Ariane* and were cooking the ship within a web of active sensor arrays, directed energy sweeps that would quickly burn through her shielding and start stripping out data for analysis and targeting. Just as the Armadalens had harvested a trove of intelligence from Montrachet, so, too, would the Sturm.

Ariane was sure to be on their list of enemy combatants.

Booker fed power from the AM stacks to the drive units and punched into an emergency fold that carried them a short distance from any warheads the Sturm USVs might have launched. Three of the probes were hunter-killers according to the RAN's database. They might start folding nukes into the battlespace, on general principles. Or they might try for a precision hit to cripple *Ariane*'s drive and leave her drifting in the vacuum for later exploit.

"Fuck that for a game of peekaboo."

As soon as the ship had fully re-materialized into space-time, Booker launched a swarm of anti-satellite combat wasps, hundreds of seeker warheads with micro-fold drives that skipped across the void separating him from his pursuers.

That was the problem with active sensor arrays.

They could light up the whole fucking solar system, but they made a bright and shining target of the emitter.

One of the probes had just reacquired a solid lock on *Ariane* and was reaching out to share the good news with its companions when the artificial meteor storm of superdense tungsten penetrators swept over all of them, shredding the cluster inside a blossoming constellation of silent blue-white fire.

A tight beam commlink from *Defiant* hit the ship's receivers.

Booker half expected a terse "What. The. Fuck?"

But the Armadalens were two steps ahead of him.

They had detected more probes farther out and were servicing the targets with long-range micro nukes.

They also suggested that he power down his engines and not try to run from the Javan battle group that had just folded into the space around them.

CHAPTER

TWENTY

The Javan Warlugger, a Nemesis-class monster, massed out at more than five gigatons and stretched nearly six and a half kilometers from the thick, impact-scarred carapace of its bow plates to the three enormous drive cones venting white-hot spears of plasma as she maneuvered for advantage. Hundreds of missile launch gantries and thousands of individual gun emplacements disfigured her outer hull with a vast, Byzantine labyrinth of brutish engineering. She was spite and vengeance and terror clad in mono-bonded carbon armor, humming with radioactive menace and bristling with murderous intent. The Empire had amassed a grand fleet of some hundred and forty-seven Warluggers for the final battles of Longfall and Medang, and the Royal Armadalen Navy had made an immense, drifting crematorium of them.

There would be no repeating that glory today.

Two Combine Raiders and half a dozen escorts arrived in formation with the Warlugger, which had locked targeting arrays on both *Defiant* and *Ariane*.

"Ready countermeasures," Hardy ordered with more confidence than she felt. She had not a single doubt that *Defiant* and her crew were possessed of the qualities to acquit themselves well in any battle with these slave traders. But it was also an undeniable truth of battle that quantity had a quality all of its own.

Lucinda stood at the center of *Defiant*'s bridge, McLennan to one side of her, Hero on the other. Her hands were clasped so tightly behind her back that the fingers turned white at their tips.

"Steady now, lass," McLennan said quietly. "You're doing good work so far. Remember to breathe out. Relax. And enjoy the ride."

She turned to him.

"Are you fucking crazy? Enjoy the ride?"

A ghost of a grin deepened the wrinkles at the corners of his eyes.

"Aye, lass," he said quietly, just for her. "If we are fated to perish this day, we can at least make a legend of our loss. And what's not to enjoy about that?"

"The perishing, I should imagine," Hero muttered.

Before Lucinda could add her own thoughts, Lieutenant Chivers spoke out from across the bridge.

"The Javans are hailing us. On-screen, ma'am?"

The question was a formality. Navy protocol did not allow for the holo-presence of hostile or potentially hostile actors on board any Armadalen warship.

"No," Lucinda replied, causing Chivers a moment of confusion. "Invite the Javan commander to holovise over. And please inform *Ariane* that this would not be a good time for one of Captain L'trel's pop-in visits."

"Yes, ma'am," Chivers said promptly. But Lucinda could feel the surprise and confusion of the bridge crew around her.

"Mister Bannon," she went on, "have we neutralized all of those probes?"

"Yes, Commander," the systems officer confirmed. "*Ariane* got five and we took down another fifteen at long range. If the

Sturm don't vary procedure, there'll be a second wave within the hour."

"Prep an after-action report for immediate transmission to the Javans and those two Combine raiders. They need to understand what just happened."

Bannon's acknowledgment of the order was just as timely as Chivers's but Lucinda could still sense the doubt hiding behind his ready compliance.

"Mister Chase . . ." she started.

"Combat folds plotted, Commander," the navigator replied before she could finish.

"Well done that man."

McLennan leaned in and stage-whispered, "Isn't this just marvelous. You're surely having fun now?"

She gave him a liver-frying side-eye.

"Quiet, old man. Your time has passed."

He snorted.

"So it would seem."

The Javanese commander appeared in holographic form a few meters in front of them.

Scratch that, Lucinda thought at once, this guy couldn't be driving the Warlugger. He was just a junior officer. A small floating data tag identified him as SUB-COMMANDANT SUPRARTO.

Chivers had projected Suprarto at three-quarter scale, so he looked comically small, but Lucinda noted that he wore the crumpled coveralls of a working spacer, rather than the grand ceremonial rig that Javan commanders routinely preferred.

Lucinda performed a small, formal bow. A concession to Javan custom.

"Sub-Commandant, my apologies for entering this volume without notice," she began. "However . . ."

He cut her off.

"You did not enter without notice. You violated Javan space with malice and design. Without permission. An act of war."

His tone was harsh, but his voice quavered at the edges. He was nervous. McLennan, who had been hanging back, now stepped up into the holo-field and spoke at Lucinda's side. His voice was cool and steady.

"Och, I didnae think it possible to violate something with permission. But I suppose even at my age you learn something really fuckin' daft every day."

The effect on the Javan was immediate. He recognized in McLennan's uniform an admiral of the Terran Defense Force, just as he doubtless saw in the data stream accompanying the transmission exactly which admiral of the TDF he was addressing.

"Admiral Mac-Mac—"

"Only my friends get to call me, that, son. And if you were in the way of wanting to be friendly I'd strongly suggest taking those big honking cannons of yours and pointing them away from me and out toward the edge of the system where you'll soon enough have plenty of fucking targets on which to practice your gunnery. And I do so hope you have been practicing, Mister Suprarto."

Suprarto swiveled his head from side to side, anxiously consulting with someone just outside the field of the projection. While Lucinda waited for the Javan to get back to them she discreetly inquired of Lieutenant Bannon whether he had dispatched the data packet with all the details of the probes they had just destroyed.

"Aye, ma'am. The Javans and the Combine ships have it now. *Ariane* has also sent a packet. They further advise that Captain L'trel is indisposed."

"Finally, some good news. Thank you, Lieutenant."

And then Lucinda realized that "indisposed" was probably a polite way of saying Seph was shit-faced and she had reason to start worrying all over again.

Suprarto appeared to gather his wits.

"Admiral McLennan," he said with slightly more confidence than before. "Have you come to organize the frontline defenses?"

McLennan muttered to Lucinda out the corner of his mouth, "Apologies for stealing your limelight."

"Knock yourself out," she said. "This is diplomacy, not war fighting."

"Then we're doomed," Hero said.

But McLennan was already speaking over the top of him.

"Sub-Commandant Suprarto, I am indeed here to organize the defense of this sector. And I am frankly fucking giddy with delight to find you have maintained such good order for me to defend . . ."

Lucinda had to suppress the urge to shake her head in wonder at the genuinely convincing show of sincerity. It was almost as though McLennan believed every word of it.

Hero's voice spoke quietly inside her head, carried there by some arcane field effect.

"It's like butter wouldn't melt in his disgusting Scottish colon, isn't it?"

She flicked the Intellect the razor-sharp tip of the same cutting look she had used on McLennan moments earlier. The admiral carried on regardless of the byplay, oiling up the Javan officer's ego.

"If you dinnae mind me saying so, you seem a wee bairn to have held off the Dark-accursed Sturm all on your lonesome. Props to you, my young laird, and to your crew. You are a credit to the Empire and I'm of a mind to promote you in the field under the War Powers Act, but if you were in the way of wanting to survive long enough for me to do so"—the tone of his voice changed, gearing down, turning into a growl—"I would ask you now to do exactly as I say."

Suprarto, who had been quite enjoying all the flattery from one of the foremost living historical figures in all the Greater Volume, sagged a little. His expression of sublime satisfaction faltered, and he looked to whoever it was sitting just outside of the projection.

"Perhaps, Sub-Commandant, you could throw a handy butterfly net over whomever is lurking just out of sight and tug them gently into our wee teddy bears' picnic here. As you can see from the data packets we have sent, you dinnae have long until the Sturm arrive in force. And even less time until the second wave of armed probes comes to test your defenses."

The audio went silent while Suprarto appeared to argue with somebody off-screen. The junior officer kept waving, probably at the holo-projection of Lucinda and McLennan.

"I can tell you what he's saying, if would you like," Hero suggested.

"No need," McLennan said. "Yon minion is a little fellow being crushed between the stone wheels of two very big cheeses, which I know is a poor analogy, but I do like the image it suggests."

"First, it's a metaphor, and a dreadful one," Hero replied, "and second—"

"Just tell me what the hell is going on," Lucinda said.

"Sub-Commandant Suprarto is appealing to his superiors to accept and acknowledge that a higher authority has now arrived," Hero explained.

"Ha! That would be me. I'm the higher authority." McLennan grinned wolfishly.

"I have no mouth and yet I must scream," the Intellect said with a sigh, "but yes, you are fundamentally correct."

"I'll give you one in the fundament, you frothing wank splat. Mark my words, there'll be some proper villain lurking just offstage there, making life a legitimate misery for poor wee Suprarto; and for reasons various and dastardly, they are of no mind to reveal themselves to us."

"As is so often the case, you are wrong," Hero replied. "My analysis of Suprarto's gross motor twitch response, eye movements, and subvocalization reveals there are in fact two people making his life a legitimate misery. I find myself empathizing. They are much less concerned by the imminent arrival of the Sturm than they are by the prospect of having to treat with Commander Hardy."

"Me?" Lucinda said. "Why me?"

"Not you, I'll wager." McLennan pushed back as they watched the Javan officer plead and possibly even argue with the presence just outside the holo. "It's the sudden appearance of the Royal Armadalen Navy which has—"

"Ha! Wrong again." Hero was positively chortling. "It's definitely Hardy. She is why they're freaking out."

"Bugger me sideways then," McLennan snapped. "Don't keep us waiting, you great fuckin' bollard. How did yon Hardy put a nettle up their arse?"

"Quiet!" Lucinda barked. These last few weeks she had become quite comfortable with barking orders at the senior surviving admiral of the Terran Defense Force and his super intelligent, eccentrically murderous longtime companion. And they, for their part, had grown used to getting shouted at and mostly shutting the fuck up when it happened.

Sub-Commandant Suprarto had grown noticeably gloomier within the holosphere and from the way his head bobbed lower and lower he was enduring an epic tag-team beatdown; if indeed Hero was right about there being two senior figures just out of sight.

"Lieutenant Chivers," Lucinda said, "is it possible to force open the image cap of the Javan's projection? From our end, I mean."

"I can do that," Hero said before Chivers could reply.

The holo suddenly expanded and a second and then a third man stood inside the projection. The one closest to Suprarto wore the tan and dark purple dress uniform of the Yulin-Irrawaddy's naval forces, although Lucinda was loath to credit them as such. The Combine's fleets were less an instrument of state power and more of a militarized cartel.

The second man was a senior Javan officer. Possibly an admiral to judge from the grandiose display of medals and fruit salad weighing down the sky-blue silk of his magnificent double-breasted uniform jacket.

Data tags floated over both men.

The Combine officer was Deputy Executive Prince Commodore Rinaldo Pac Yulin.

And the Javan was the Imperial Volume Lord Juono Karna.

But Lucinda did not need the data tag. She recognized him immediately.

"That motherfucker!" She spat into the holosphere.

Just as the Javans unmuted the audio.

"What?" Suprarto said, his face a fright mask of confusion and dawning horror.

Lucinda gaped, her mouth opening and closing.

McLennan stepped into the breach, winking at her.

"Come now, Ms. Hardy, I may be irascible but I'm seven hundred years old. It's been a long time since I diddled anybody's mother."

"What?" Suprarto said again, sounding even more confused.

McLennan waved him off with a cheery grin.

"Och, just a difference of opinion, Sub-Commandant. Pay it no nevermind. My young colleague here, having become aware that you were harboring an accused war criminal . . ."

Imperial Volume Lord Juono Karna visibly blanched and whipped his head from side to side, as though desperate to discover who had ratted him out.

". . . well, she was of the opinion," McLennan continued, "that we should just let bygones be bygones, given the current fucking omnishambles in the affairs of the Greater Volume. My tedious fucking factotum on the other hand . . ."

He gestured for Hero to come forward and join in the exchange.

". . . well, for an Armada-level Intellect, he can be quite the officious little prick."

"The law is the law," Hero boomed.

His exotic matter casing flared a deep vermilion red of barely restrained theatrical fury. Lucinda's thoughts were a tumble of wonderment and incredulity. The pair of them had improvised this whole display of performative bullshit purely to cover for her lack of restraint. She was both pitifully grateful for the effort, and unspeakably ashamed that she had made it necessary.

But that motherfucker Juono Karna was the reason she had won the Star of Valor.

"Still and all," McLennan went on, chewing up the scenery and enjoying himself hugely. "Let's not bicker and argue about who killed who according to the laws of war . . . Or not, as the case may be, eh, Volume Lord."

The Javan high commander, realizing he had been made, jutted out his jaw and clenched his fists and quite possibly made ready to order Suprarto to open fire.

Commodore Pac Yulin glared out of the holo-field with axes in his eyes and looked more than ready to join in the slaughter.

Lucinda was a heartbeat away from ordering a full-spectrum strike and emergency fold-out when McLennan stepped right up to the edge of the holo so that his old, beaky nose was almost tip to tip with the projection of Lord Karna's. He growled in a low voice that somehow carried all over the bridge, thanks to some sneaky audio trick of Hero's.

"If I were you, m'lord, I would be on my fat fuckin' knees by now, offering a tearful prayer of thanks that some random passing Intellect with a hard-on for justifiable homicide hadnae grabbed me up by the short-n-curlies and folded me away into the heart of the local sun for crimes against humanity."

Karna's gaze turned from belligerent to nervous and from McLennan to Herodotus.

"You do not dare . . ." he started to say, but his voice failed when Hero pulsed an ominous shade of deep and terrible crimson.

"The law is the law."

Lucinda didn't doubt for a moment that the Intellect would do exactly as McLennan had just suggested. Or that the Javans and the Combine would immediately open fire in revenge. Or simple shock.

McLennan, for his part, grinned like a hammerhead shark at

the tummy-rubbing end of a heroic feeding frenzy, savoring every strand of flesh trapped between its teeth.

"What I dare do, my lord," he said in a slightly more reasonable tone, "is put aside the inconvenience of those thirteen capital charges levied against you in absentia at the Hague, and invite you to do your fucking duty, which right now would mean doing exactly as I tell you. Unless you'd care to swap the chance of a fair trial on Earth for the certainty of defeat and genocide at the hands of our mutual enemy who will soon enough be with us."

"Because you brought them here," Lord Karna hissed.

Lucinda had had enough.

"They were coming anyway, my lord," she said, leaning hard on his title, on the off chance that it might prove so hollow and brittle as to fall over.

The Javan Volume lord smiled at her. It was both unexpected and an altogether unpleasant experience.

"Lieutenant Hardy. Fancy finding you here, where you should not be. Again."

"It's Commander Hardy. And I'm not here for you, this time, Lord Karna."

That smile again.

"No, you are here for the spies and infiltrators your masters placed within our realm."

Lucinda felt her temper flaring, before McLennan laid a gentle hand on her shoulder.

"Easy, tiger," he said quietly.

Lord Karna, sensing an advantage, pressed it.

"That would explain the volley of communication probes you released across our system. Illegally, of course. You were seeking to contact other vessels of the RAN. Spy ships and saboteurs, no?"

Lucinda said nothing.

Karna smiled again.

"You once did me the favor of failing in your duty. And I am of course grateful for that incompetence."

McLennan's fingers dug a little deeper into her shoulder.

"Dinnae step into a trap, just because it's all laid out for you," he whispered.

She shook off his hand. Took a step closer to the holo-field. One step deeper into the trap.

"I did not fail in my duty, Lord Karna," Lucinda said. "I only failed to capture you. And you were very much a secondary objective."

Karna's grin faltered. Not much, but she saw it tremble at the edges, just for a moment. He had probably convinced himself that the RAN had targeted him personally during the war, as a critical anchor point of the Javan defense, when instead he was just a side quest.

"Still, you failed," he recovered. "And I am in your debt because of it. Allow me to repay you now by saving you the time and, quite frankly, the embarrassment of waiting for your comrades from the . . ."

He made a show of checking with an underling.

"The *Yarra*. Yes. That was the name. One of your little recon'vettes, which revealed itself to us after the Sturm's attack. Pleading to make common cause with the Empire against the invaders. Begging for our protection, if you must know."

"Bullshit," Lucinda said.

Lord Karna was not used to being defied. He reared back as if slapped, but not so hard that he couldn't regain his composure.

"Well, I would suggest you ask your colleagues about it, but I'm afraid that won't be possible. The punishment for spying upon the Empire, as you well know, is slow death . . . and full deletion."

This time it was not just Lucinda who fought to restrain herself. An ugly murmur swept around *Defiant*'s bridge.

McLennan stepped back between Lucinda and Lord Karna, raising his hands as though to stop them coming to actual blows.

"Enough of this gobshite," he barked, loudly enough for some of the bridge crew on both ships to jump a little.

"I understand there is bad blood between you people, but it is about to be washed away by a fucking tsunami of murder. Use both hands and pull your fucking heads out of your arses to take a look at what's coming. You drizzling fuckmuppets. The Sturm dinnae care a tiny wet shit for any of this. You are all the same to them."

He pointed directly at Volume Lord Karna.

"I would imagine you to be the surviving authority in this system."

Karna did not deny it.

"I will make you one offer and only one. I will save you and your wretched feudal colony from what is coming, but I can only do that if you submit your forces to my authority, the rightful authority of Earth under the War Powers Act. You do not have a choice, legally. But I'm not such a fucking fool as to imagine that a warmed-over slops bucket of legal pish will discomfit the likes of you. The alternative, m'lord, is that we bid you farewell and good luck, which you will need in abundance. The enemy will be upon you with all dispatch."

Volume Lord Juono Karna had slowly deflated as McLennan talked. A nervous grin skittered across his face and died before reaching his eyes. He flicked a glance at Commodore Pac Yulin, who remained unmoved by any of the drama.

Lucinda wondered at the deal between the two men. She expected Karna to respond, but it was Pac Yulin who finally broke the silence.

"Where is the princess?" he asked. "Where is my betrothed?"

CHAPTER

TWENTY-ONE

"His fucking what?"

Alessia did not ask politely.

Her mother would have been so very disappointed. She fairly shrieked the question at Commander Hardy, who looked pained to even be there.

Admiral McLennan answered her question in his usual artless manner.

"The loathsome piss weasel says he's your betrothed. Your future husband, and not to put too fine a fucking point on it, the legal heir by contract of marriage to all the liquid assets and fixed holdings of the Montanblanc ul Haq Corporation."

McLennan looked no happier than Commander Hardy, but neither of them could be anywhere near as profoundly hacked off as Princess Alessia Szu Suri sur Montanblanc ul Haq.

Was there no end to her family's monumental shitfuckery? Even here, at the end of the world—of all the worlds—they could still reach out and tie her shit into a twisted fecal hell pretzel.

Hardy and McLennan sat in her cabin, portraits of gloom. Like, for reals. Skygarth had been full of massive, gloomy old paintings of Montanblanc ancestors, and they all looked as miserable as Commander Hardy at the foot of the bed, her chin sunk down onto her chest, and McLennan leaned up against a locker like some servant's abandoned mop. A squad of armored marines now stood guard outside. Alessia nervously twirled around in the chair at her desk where a super-boring history of yet another long-ago war was weighing down a stack of super-boring orders or reports or something she was supposed to sign while pretending to be a real senator on the Armed Forces Committee.

"But I was supposed to be married to Deputy Prince Vincent," she protested. "Not some old commodore guy. I mean, I'm sure he's horrible, too, but believe me, there was no forgetting Vince the Prince. That's what he called himself. He was like this truffle pig douchelord."

Commander Hardy—Lucinda—sighed. She reminded Alessia of her friend Caro just then, and she remembered with a start that they weren't that far apart in age. Not really. Alessia felt keenly that Hardy was not just here as captain of the *Defiant*. They had grown close. They were friends now. Just like Alessia and Caro. Surely? And Lucinda was here and very upset because her friend was in trouble.

"Commodore Pac Yulin maintains that Vincent was killed by the nanophage," Lucinda said.

"And I can probably confirm that," McLennan said. "We had a Vincent Pac Yulin on Batavia. At the dig. The nanophage got him. Although to be perfectly honest, it was getting thrown into the sun by Herodotus that technically killed him."

"Sweet fuck is there anybody that psychopath hasn't thrown into the sun yet?" Lucinda asked.

"I'm right here, you know," Hero called out. "Just outside. I can hear everything. I'm an Armada-level Intellect. I have very good audio sensors."

He was too big to squeeze into the confines of Alessia's tiny cabin, but they had brought him along because of his knowledge of Volume Commercial Law. That was the thing about having virtually infinite storage and processing capacity. There was no reason not to know everything, as Hero so often reminded them.

He floated just beyond the open hatch, maintaining an exclusion field to stop any of the Intellects on the Combine or Javan ships from folding over and kidnapping her. Apparently, that was another thing Alessia had to worry about now.

"Och, I'd a thrown that whiny shitgibbon into the sun myself if I still had my good arm," McLennan confessed. "Assuming my Prince Vincent was your Prince Vincent, he was a vicious little cockwomble and irritating to a fault."

"He really wasn't mine, but the nasty womble penis thing sounds like him," Alessia said. "But how can we be sure it's the same one? It seems . . . I dunno, unlikely. House Yulin has a lot of deputy princes, you know."

"It does," Hero cast in from outside. "There were eighty-nine Vincent Pac Yulins at deputy prince level in the Yulin-Irrawaddy Combine at the time of the nanophage attack. And as the presumptive surviving member of House Yulin, Rinaldo is both heir apparent to the Yulin division of the Combine and, I'm afraid, to all its capital and corporeal assets, of which, you, Princess Alessia, are arguably a very significant component."

Alessia felt her temper rising. She stood up from her desk and jammed her fists onto her hips. "Yeah?" she said firmly. "Well I'm now the boss of House Montanblanc and I say fuck him in the neck."

McLennan snorted softly at that.

"Aye, lass, that's the spirit. But hardly Volume Law."

"Fuck the law."

She had to put up with this shit when she was just a minor royal on Montrachet, being fattened up for the corporate marriage market by a family who didn't much care whether she felt like being sold off to some shitty division of the Combine or not. She didn't see any good reason for putting up with it now.

The more she thought about it—the more she was free to think about it—the less she liked the way her family did business.

"Where's Baroness Sephina?" Alessia said. "I need to consult with her."

Lucinda made an awkward face.

"I'm afraid the baroness is unwell," she said.

Alessia felt her stomach lurch a little.

"Did they hurt her? Is the *Ariane* okay? And Booker? And Coto . . ."

"They're fine," Lucinda hurried on. "And we might yet send you over there before the Sturm get here. It will be safer."

"Two hours and counting until we receive the enemy," Hero announced. "According to the Javans' long-range sensors. I hacked them. In case you were wondering. Just something to do. Because of course you won't let me play with *Defiant* again and . . ."

"Hero," Lucinda said. It sounded like a warning. The Intellect fell silent and Lucinda turned back to Alessia. She leaned forward. Her eyes seemed very large.

"Alessia, we are not going to let the Combine take you. Sephina will not let that happen, either."

Alessia felt her heart swelling as though it was some sort of magical balloon, suddenly filling with hope and helium 3. She quickly looked over to Admiral McLennan, who was not really her friend, no matter how much he tried to pretend. He looked very stern. But he was shaking his head and growling.

"I'd cut off m'own knob before handing you over to those worthless bell ends."

"What are we going to do, then?" Commander Hardy asked.

As Alessia watched, all the lines and furrows in the admiral's face got even deeper as he frowned and glowered furiously and chewed over the problem.

"Leave it to me," he said.

———

The second wave of enemy probes arrived soon after McLennan and Hardy returned to *Defiant*'s bridge to negotiate with Lord Karna and the Combine. The wee princess was not with them. She remained under guard and wrapped within a protective cocoon of multiple, layered field effects. Deputy Executive Prince Commodore Pac Yulin was not pleased.

"Am I to be denied my intended?" he asked. His jaw muscles bunched with anger, but his lips barely moved.

"Och no, we're nae in the way of denying anyone or anything," McLennan said. "But the princess has obligations under Volume Commercial Law . . ."

"Onerous obligations," Hero put in.

"Aye, severely onerous obligations that require exhaustive due diligence before any such significant reorganization of House Montanblanc's line of succession."

"So I am to be denied!" Pac Yulin declared. Beside him, the Javan Volume lord looked almost as angry.

"No," McLennan said. "You are to be confirmed as the rightful partner for this merger, which I'm sure you'll agree has taken on a significance well beyond its original saliency."

"And my word is not confirmation enough?" Pac Yulin seethed. It was an open question whether his outrage and disbelief were genuine, but the performance was outstanding, Mac thought.

"Do you dare challenge the honor of a deputy executive prince of the Combine?" Lord Karna gasped.

His performative outrage was an altogether more outrageous form of melodrama. McLennan knew of Batavian orbital port whores who could do less absurd protestations of virtue.

"Please do unbunch your panties, my lord," McLennan said as affably as possible. He had one eye on a threat matrix hologram just out of Karna's and Pac Yulin's line of sight. Flashing red tags had begun to appear at the edge of the Natuna System. "I'm sure Deputy Executive Prince Pac Yulin wouldnae care to have to renegotiate any marriage contact with Rupert Montanblanc if and when the old monster is downloaded from secure offline storage and plugged into a tailor-made personal combat chassis the better to regularize any such . . . irregularities . . . as may have arisen during his enforced absence from the board of directors."

"Unregistered offline storage?" Pac Yulin said, suddenly looking unwell. "A black site? But that's not possible. It is illegal and frankly . . . stupid. Lifestream backup is ubiquitous, flawless."

Before McLennan could scoff at his foolishness and privilege, a young Armadalen tactical officer with impeccable timing cut in on the discussion.

"Excuse me, Admiral McLennan, Commander Hardy? We have positive returns for a series of megaton scale detonations at the edge of the local volume."

"Sound to general quarters," Hardy ordered, as though requesting tea and scones from a passing waiter in the mess. Her voice was quiet and unfussed, but the order quickly spread through the ship, calling all of *Defiant*'s warriors to their stations. Not sending them into battle but readying them for the battle that was coming. McLennan would have applauded her stagecraft, except that he knew it was not an act. The young woman, who was so much at odds with herself in quiet and repose, seemed to shine with a noble luster when she stood into hazard.

By way of dire contrast, in the projected holosphere floating but a few meters away, the Javan sub-commandant Suprarto started shouting orders at his bridge crew, while Volume Lord Karna looked as though he may have filled his panties rather than unbunching them. Deputy Executive Prince Pac Yulin swiveled his head from side to side, no doubt looking for an exit, before somebody on his own ship provided one by way of a micro-fold back to the larger of the two Combine Raiders.

Hardy, who had resumed the captain's chair, crossed one leg over the other, laced her fingers together, and regarded the threat matrix with a detachment that McLennan could only think of as modest stillness and humility.

Hero floated up beside him.

"I could deal with this, if she would let me," he said quietly.

Mac held up one finger. Wait for it.

"Aye, but so can she, my friend. And it is important that she does."

"Mister Fein, are my countermeasures ready?" Commander Hardy asked.

"Firing sequence plotted, ma'am," Lieutenant Fein replied.

"Outstanding. On my command, then, to kill with singularities."

"To kill with singularities, ma'am, aye."

The bridge of *Defiant* fell still, if not silent. Alarms still sounded. Officers called out reports of readiness and capacity. The audio feed from the Javan ship, dialed down but not muted, provided a constant stream of chaos and not a little panic. But the Armadalens stood to their stations and waited for their captain's command.

Twenty-nine AU away, on the outer rim of the Natuna System, hundreds of unpiloted space vehicles accelerated toward the inner volume. These were not the small, lightly armed USVs that *Defiant* and *Ariane* had earlier dispatched with ease. The Sturm, having lost contact with their initial flight of surveillance craft, had reverted to an ancient technique for feeling out an unseen enemy. The expanding swarm of heavy-duty armored spheres sweeping in from interstellar space were not seeking fine-grained data on the Javans' defenses. They were simply raking the volume with the massively powerful active arrays and laying nukes on everything that sent back a signature.

"Recon by fire is it, then?" McLennan remarked appreciatively. "I know they're a bit behind the times but that is un-fucking-fashionably antiquated."

Hardy ignored him, focused on her ship and crew.

The complex topographies of strategic defense satellites, listening posts, and surveillance sites through which *Defiant* and *Ariane* had taken such care to pick their way, the Sturm simply annihilated with an apocalyptic bombardment of high-yield ordnance. Small moons hosting single emplacements of long-range Cherenkov telescopes blew apart under the hammer blows of superdense hyperkinetics. Huge volumes of space erupted into silent white firestorms as hundreds of fusion warheads detonated in volume denial blasts to sanitize them of early warning technologies.

McLennan grinned to behold it all.

"Admiral," a small, strangled voice cried out from behind him.

It was, of course, Lord Karna.

"Admiral McLennan," he shouted, his voice sounding distant and tiny, like a diminutive man trapped inside a box. "The Sturm are upon us. You promised they would not arrive for another two hours, but they are here and they are ruining all my defenses."

"Mister Fein," Commander Hardy said, raising her voice before Mac could reply. "Countermeasures."

"Aye, ma'am, countermeasures. Killing with singularities, volumetric spread, target to signature source."

No shudder or recoil announced the launch of the strike package, but McLennan felt the counterpunch as a warmth in his soul. Hundreds of micro-missiles streaked away from the launch tubes which speckled the stealth destroyer's outer hull like hair follicles in *Defiant*'s carbon-armor skin. At a safe remove they engaged sequential micro-fold drives and quickly collapsed the enormous distance between the Armadalen warship and the wave of heavily armored drones chewing through the Javans' first arc of defense. The interceptor munitions materialized for their terminal flights within a hundred kilometers of their fast-moving prey, latched onto the Sturm's weaponized probes with SPY 7 sensor hooks, and engaged the final jump of their multi-fold sequence. An arc of space-time millions of kilometers wide instantly erupted into a hellish energistic maelstrom as hundreds of wormholes blossomed inside the armored casing of the enemy's war machines. The shock wave of hard radiation, plasma, and subatomic debris vanished just as quickly, sucked into the ravening maws of the wormholes, spirited away to some other universe before the manufactured singularities exterminated themselves.

The Natuna System was quiet again.

"As I did promise, m'lord," McLennan said affably, "the Sturm will indeed be here in"—he made a show of lifting his arm and pulling back the sleeve of his black jacket to examine the old mechanical watch he wore on his wrist—"in . . . a little under three hours now. But they will stagger in as blind men, having had their eyes put out for them by Commander Hardy and . . ."

He snapped his fingers at the tactical officer.

"What was your name, boy?"

"Fein, sir. Lieutenant Fein."

"Yes, that's right, and Lieutenant Fein." McLennan nodded. "Perhaps if Deputy Executive Prince Pac Yulin would rejoin us, we might actually put on our fuckin' big boy pants and deign to receive the enemy, eh? And having done so, I'm sure we could find time to sort out his fucking bachelor party."

"I can assure you, young miss, there will be no bachelor party, no wedding, and no merger of House Montanblanc with these abysmal fucking slavers."

McLennan had taken a knee, which brought his deeply lined face down to a level with hers. He seemed to be in real discomfort. Alessia imagined that the deck plate would be hard on those super old bones.

"You have no need to assure me, Admiral," she said with more resolve than she felt. "I would sooner step into an open air lock than marry any prince of House Yulin."

Commander Hardy—Lucinda—stood next to the Terran admiral, who reached up and took her arm to help himself back onto his feet. He grimaced and groaned as he did so but snapped at Hero to keep his hands to himself when the Intellect tried to help out with a micro-g carrier wave. Alessia didn't really understand McLennan. If he was so angry at being old, why didn't he just relife into a younger body, or even a combat chassis? It was a question Hero was always asking, too.

They stood in the transport hangar at the ship's afterbrow, in the same small yellow circle they'd used to fold over to the *Ariane* when Alessia wanted to talk to Sephina and Lucinda alone. About the declaration. Sub-Lieutenant Han was there again, to work the micro-fold, but this time Lucinda would not be coming. Three marines, Dahl—yay!—a very handsome young lad called Kanon Aronson, and their sergeant, a tough-looking man by the name of Cox, waited off to one side, all of them dressed in suspiciously well-padded civilian clothes. Alessia clutched a small travel bag to her chest. It held a few precious things, some personal and some not. She had a hand-stitched, beautifully illustrated copy of *The Lion, the Witch and the Wardrobe*; a holo-coin of Caro and Debin; the picture of Sergeant Reynolds; and her bear, Mister Tubs.

She'd hidden Tubbsy right down at the bottom of the bag, in case anybody looked in and saw him.

Like the marines, she was no longer dressed in a military uniform but in a mismatched assortment of jeans, a black T-shirt, and a jacket. The pants belonged to Caro and it made Alessia feel a bit odd to wear them, but she loved the jacket, a cracked leather coat that Lucinda had given her. She said she'd bought it years ago on Coriolis, and it was too small for her now. It was too big for Alessia, but she didn't care. She looked totally fucking badass in it. It was even better than the borrowed combat coveralls she'd loved so much.

McLennan regained his feet and shuffled back out of the yellow circle.

"Dinnae get old, if you can avoid it," he warned her, or possibly just himself. "It is not for the faint of heart or weak of piss."

"It's not for anyone, you old fool," Herodotus scolded him. "You say this every span, but you never do anything about it."

"Tae fuck wi' you, then," the admiral groused. "I'm just . . ."

"You're just rambling like some old dribbler without sense enough to relife himself before the second age of diapers comes around. Again."

Lucinda stepped forward, interposing herself between Alessia and the feuding elders.

"Do I have to go?" Alessia asked, pitching her voice low for only Lucinda to hear.

Defiant's commander nodded somberly.

"You would have to go even if this thing with Pac Yulin had not come up," Lucinda said. "We're about to fight a battle and the odds are against us."

"The odds are always against us," Alessia said.

"Fair point," Lucinda conceded. "But we had surprise on our side at Montrachet. And here all we've got is Prince Yulin and Lord Karna."

"Oh yeah," Alessia said. "That does suck, doesn't it."

"Like hard vacuum," Lucinda said. "But Sephina will make sure you're okay. And if there's one thing I have faith in, it's her ability to get you out of Natuna and away from the Combine."

"But you said she was sick."

Lucinda nodded. Slowly.

"Y-e-s," she said, even more slowly. "But I spoke to Booker. Turns out, she'll get better. Some coffee. A shower. A little time in the regen tank . . ." She frowned and leaned forward to speak privately. "Just maybe, Alessia, see if you can get her to lay off the booze, and the pills, and stim shots, and bulbs, patches, and pods, and you know, everything. She saved me once, but I don't have time to save her now."

She dropped her voice even further.

"Can you do that, Alessia? Can you look after my friend? I don't have many."

"You have me," Alessia said, or tried to. It was hard to get the words out.

Lucinda smiled sadly.

"I know. And I hope I always will. Now get yourself over to the *Ariane*. Keep your head down. Sergeant Cox and Private

Dahl and Specialist Aronson will look after you, no matter what. But just call them by their names, not their ranks, okay?"

"I can do that. I like Dahl. She's awesome."

A smile dimpled Lucinda's face. A real smile this time. She threw a quick glance over at the marine.

"Yes," she said. "Dahl is awesome. Remember that, especially when she tells you to do something you don't want to."

The young naval officer—and really, she was only ten or twelve years older than Alessia, and Alessia would be thirteen soon, so they were practically the same age compared to someone like McLennan—the very young naval officer stood up straight, came to attention, and saluted her. And all of a sudden, she looked like Commander Hardy again.

Alessia returned the salute as best she could, even though she wasn't quite sure why Hardy had done it. Because she was a princess? The head of a Grand House? Or maybe a senator.

Yeah, probably the senator thing. She and McLennan seemed to think that was very important. When Lucinda spoke again, she definitely wasn't Lucinda anymore. She was Commander Hardy all the way through.

"The Javans have agreed that Captain L'trel's ship should clear the AO, the area of operations, before the Sturm arrive. To them she's just another refugee boat."

"Ha!" McLennan scoffed. "Not just. Yon sticky-fingered buggers sniff the half chance of some plunder. A Zaistev treasure boat no less. That'll give the palace revenuers a stiffy you could crack a flea on."

A little shocked and embarrassed, Alessia looked awkwardly to Commander Hardy.

Commander Hardy gave Admiral McLennan a fearsome glare.

McLennan threw up his hands, mocking exasperation.

"Och, I do beg your ladies' pardon for my colorfully appalling turn of phrase," he said, before leaning forward to address Alessia directly. "However, Your Majesty, the surest way to distract a pair of scoundrels like Karna and Pac Yulin is to tempt them with a delicious sweetie that draws the eye from the much more substantial haggis you would prefer to keep to yourself."

He nodded knowingly as though this explained everything.

Alessia looked to Hardy again, this time in confusion.

The Intellect, floating on the other side of the micro-fold bay, rippled with a dark violet spectrum; Hero's version of a deep sigh.

"If this wretched old fool wasn't suffering so grievously from early onset dementia, he might have explained more plainly and precisely that the local warlords are more likely to spy a windfall profit in allowing Captain L'trel to dock at one of their facilities where she can be properly gouged and pillaged under the guise of extraordinary surcharges for unusual circumstances and exceptional factors blah, blah, blah."

"That's exactly what I said, you floaty fuckin' phallus."

"No. Only the blah-blah-blah bit and that was mostly incomprehensible through a mouthful of cold Gaelic word porridge."

"Enough," Lucinda ordered. She took a deep breath before turning back to Alessia. "The *Ariane* will lay up at Lermontov Station, one of the smaller Habs here, a freeport on the far side of Natuna. Customs and Migration are controlled by the Javans, and Admiral McLennan is right. They will be focused on extracting whatever value they can from the ship's cargo manifest and Sephina's trading accounts. They'll be less interested in passengers with so many refugees in-system. Especially since they're going to think you're on *Defiant*, anyway."

"But how?" Alessia asked.

"Skulduggery and hijinks," McLennan told her and grinned.

"He means identity casting," Hero said. "I will capture your biometrics and use them to generate a pseudo-agent which we can inject into any comm channel with the Javans or the Combine as needed."

"Wait, what?"

"With your permission of course."

"I . . . but . . . I guess," she said, stumbling at the idea that the Intellect wanted to create a virtual facsimile of her. True-faking members of the Grand Houses had been outlawed centuries ago. People had been deleted, like actually fucking deleted, for it.

"Good, then," Hero said. "It's done."

"Hang on, what?"

"Well, I am an Armada-level Intellect, you know."

"An Armada-level idiot," McLennan snorted. "And a massive fuckin' roaster. You didnae even give the wee lass a chance to say no."

Hero's dense black carapace flared red with annoyance.

"But you didn't want her to say no. We specifically discussed this."

"For fuck's sake," Alessia said with a sigh, sounding just like Commander Hardy. "It's fine. I'm fine. Just don't make fake me do anything gross."

"Heaven forfend no," Herodotus promised.

Hardy stepped forward and waved Admiral McLennan back out of the small yellow octagon painted on the deck plating.

"We need to get this done, Alessia," she said. "The Sturm will be here soon, and we are better off beating them here, where we have help of a sort, than trying to outrun them. The Javans won't know we cross-decked you to *Ariane*. We can easily do that without them finding out. Their tech isn't as good as ours and we have Hero."

The Intellect pulsed with a proud golden hue.

"The local intellects are vastly overmatched by my tremendous capabilities."

Commander Hardy rolled her eyes at Alessia.

"Look, he's not wrong," she said, even though she did look like she was chewing something sour as she said it. "But it is important that when you get to Lermontov, you stay on the ship with Sergeant Cox and the others. Sephina knows people on that station. So, it's a sure bet they're not very nice people. You'll want to avoid them. The ship will be inspected, but Seph and the others will hide you. Booker will know what to do. It's a gangsters' yacht. There'll be somewhere. And if Sephina says you have to get out of the system, if she says it's time to go, then it's time. Do not wait for us."

Alessia stood up straight and looked her square in the eye.

"Because you won't be coming, will you?"

Lucinda's expression was unreadable, but her answer was clear.

"No, Alessia. We won't."

CHAPTER

TWENTY-TWO

They said you weren't supposed to dream in stasis, but they said a lot of shit that turned out to be straight-up lies. Sephina dreamed of better days, when she was poor and hungry and desperately scrambling from one shitty Solo run to the next. She was not the Baroness of Montrachet. She wasn't even captain of the *Je Ne Regrette Rien*. She was just an orphan Hab rat, but she was not alone. She had Ariane and one day they would rule the fucking Volume; they just knew it. She dreamed of escaping Coriolis, and signing on with a freelance crew, and kicking a massive dent in the whole fucking system. She dreamed of Ariane's wild confidence, and Ariane's hot mouth, and Ariane coming apart in a murderous river of fire on Eassar. She screamed, but she was only dreaming, so nobody heard her scream.

"Sephina?"

It was the kid.

Jula, the girl Ariane had rescued, because that was the sort of shit Ariane did all the time.

"Sephina?"

"I fucking love this kid," Ariane said, laughing, and in her dream Seph gave up because she knew where this was going.

"Fine. What's your name, kid?"

"Jula."

And Jula and Ariane died over and over again in a storm of fire and Sephina screamed and Jula said her name.

"Sephina?"

No, not Jula.

It was Alessia, dressed like Luce used to. Before she ran away and joined the Navy.

And they were not on Eassar, running from the Sturm. Sephina floated in a regen tank, and Banks had popped the canopy, and Alessia leaned in looking worried and relieved and scared and excited all at once.

"Sephina. Are you all right? They said you were sick. And Lucinda . . . I mean Commander Hardy said I had to look after you and . . ."

And on and on the little princess went.

It almost helped.

Which was weird. Because it was kind of annoying with a pounding hangover.

But it did help. Because someone cared and Sephina L'trel had dreamed that the only soul who gave a damn about her in all of human space was gone and she would be alone forever.

They sat in the Gagarin Lounge again, but this time there was no ice cream. And no Luce. Just Alessia and her three marine guards—although they were dressed in civilian rig now, which meant they looked like a bunch of fucking narcs.

The one called Dahl was a bit hot, at least. The Kanon kid, too, she supposed, if you bent that way, which she didn't.

The older one, Cox, looked like a clenched fist with a cheap sentience upgrade.

Banks arrived with a tray of hot drinks. Sephina was hoping for a Jamaican rum toddy but she got some sort of confronting chai made from actual leaves and twigs which floated in a foul-smelling infusion of hard penance and karma.

Alessia took a mug of hot chocolate from the pilot and thanked him with a smile.

Banks was delighted to play the role of royal drinks waiter. He bowed almost to his waist.

"Don't suppose you want to swap, kid?" Sephina said. "And maybe Irish up my hot chocolate while you're at it?"

"No," Alessia said, reproaching her. "Mister Banks says you have to drink your medicine now and you can't have any more whiskey or stim or anything."

"Yeah well, Mister Banks is literally not the boss of me, so let's try that again. Booker," she called out, her voice croaking and almost cracking. "You wanna float me something over from the bar?"

The former TDF soldier's voice came back from all around her.

"No. I'm sorry, Captain. I have my orders."

"Your what now?"

"Okay," he said, sounding apologetic. "Not my orders, but we've had a meeting and decided we're not going to let you kill yourself. Which you were doing."

A familiar red mist started somewhere in the back of Sephina's head, but it boiled up quickly.

"The fuck you say," she snapped, and Alessia jumped back, startled.

The female marine, Dahl, moved fast, but stopped when Cox laid a restraining hand on her arm.

"Piss never talked so loud," he said quietly.

Seph's mood turned dangerous, the drifting miasma of her grief and resentment morphing into sudden rage. She threw off the blanket under which she'd been recuperating and tried to launch herself out of the deep, leather lounge.

Such a dumbass move.

She was so weak that her head was spinning before she was halfway to her feet. She started to fall and felt a micro-g wave gently lift her clear of gravity's bond. She flailed in space while everyone looked on, their faces a registry of distinct reactions.

Coto, standing mute by the bar, nonplussed.

Banks, still holding a filigreed silver serving tray, appalled.

Aronson, reaching discreetly inside his jacket, as though for a weapon.

Dahl, one step toward grabbing up the Montanblanc princess, worried.

Cox, next to Dahl, his squat, massive form blocking out half the length of an oil painting of the Winter Palace on Putingrad, coldly hostile.

And Alessia, kneeling on the thick, white bear-hide rug in front of Sephina, somewhere between astonished and increasingly judgmental.

That just made it worse.

Being judged by an actual trust fund princess.

"Booker," Seph snarled, "if you don't put me down I am going to suck every last q-bit of your personality from the substrate and drop it over the edge of the nearest fucking event horizon."

"Yeah, nah, you're not gonna do that." Booker's voice came back from the ship's ambient address system.

"You need to drink your tea," Banks said. "It will make you feel better. It has some panax root, from the Hongdae System. It's a very powerful adaptogen. Not as powerful as a yard glass of vintage Terran rum or a water pipe full of jujaweed, I'll grant you. But you've tried those therapies and they have proven . . . inefficacious."

Sephina struggled against the micro-g wave but it was hopeless. She couldn't break free.

She seethed and raged and would have thrown the heavy stoneware mug of stupid Joseon herbal tea at the pilot's head, except that Booker seemed to have anticipated the move and floated the improvised missile out of her reach. Also, she was exhausted.

In the end, she gave up.

Without Ariane what was the point of it? What was the point of anything?

Seeing the fight run out of her, Booker lowered Sephina slowly back into the soft leather cushions of the lounge.

Gravity returned as the field effect died away.

She had no doubt that he would snap it back into place if she gave him reason.

She had not felt so powerless or humiliated in her lack of agency since her first night in Habitat Welfare.

But she didn't fight.

She just let her face fall into her hands. At that moment Sephina did not think she would ever raise her head again. She couldn't imagine looking into all those eyes. And again, what would be the point, anyway? Ariane was not here. What was there to look forward to? Sephina curled up on the double-wide divan of butter-soft leather and listened to the roar of blood in her ears.

It was Alessia who broke the silence outside the small, dark prison Seph had made of her own shaking hands.

"I would take the counsel of my baroness alone, if you would be so kind as to leave us," she said.

Her voice was not hard, but there was nothing in it that gave even the slightest impression that she expected to be defied.

"You what, mate?" Cox snorted. "You gotta be fucking kidding me. The skipper would have my nuts on the butcher's block if I let—"

"It was not a request, Sergeant Cox," Alessia said, and something in her voice made Sephina look up at last.

The Montanblanc heir had climbed to her feet and turned on her escort. Even dressed in jeans and Lucinda's way-too-large leather jacket, Alessia looked . . . regal.

Cox looked bemused, but Dahl, still standing next to him, seemed to realize that something had changed. She reached out for the non-com in a mirror image of the gesture he had used to still her just a few moments ago.

"Sarge, I wouldn't," she said.

"Yeah," Aronson said quietly. "She looks hardcore, Sarge."

"Sergeant Cox," Alessia said, "my recent studies have given me to understand that one of the reasons the Royal Armadalen Navy prevailed over the much larger and arguably more powerful forces of the Javan Empire was the discretion afforded to commanders, right down to the smallest of units, to trust in their superior training, judgment, and technology when engaged with their enemies beyond the range of communication with any superior authority."

Cox's face was a detailed map of confusion.

Alessia did not allow him time to reply.

"You have been tasked with a mission to remove the surviving royal command authority of the Montanblanc ul Haq Corporation—spoiler, me—beyond any possibility of capture or coercion by remnant forces of the Yulin-Irrawaddy or the Human Republic. The former are all around us; the latter soon will be. It is not at all likely that during the execution of your mission you will be able to seek further and better particulars from your superiors as regards pressing tactical matters. You are on your own now, Sergeant. As are we all. I am dependent upon you for my survival. But as a sworn member of the RAN you are dependent upon me for the lawful authority under which you must operate, not in my capacity as heir to my family's House, but in my role as head of the Senate Armed Forces Committee. In that role, Sergeant Cox, I am giving you a direct order, to get the fuck out while I chop it up with my homegirl here."

Cox blinked.

Dahl sighed.

"Sarge, Booker isn't going anywhere. She'll be fine. And we need this messy bitch"—Dahl nodded at Seph—"to get her shit together. Maybe let the kid have a go." Dahl grinned, a sly, wicked expression. "After all, she's got your number."

Cox shook his head, annoyed.

"Fine, then. I'm going to be in the lounge next door. Hey, Booker!" he called out.

"I'm right here," Booker's voice came back. "You don't have to shout."

"I'll do more than shout if you let this drunken, drug-fucked skank hurt the kid."

Booker sighed volubly, and Seph could imagine the virtual eye roll. "You know even less about me than you do about Captain L'trel. Like the princess said: Get the fuck out."

"No. Everyone out," Alessia said. "You too, Booker."

"Wait what?" Booker said.

"No way." Cox arced up.

"Oh, fuck this," Sephina cried out. "I've got a regen hangover that'd kill a fucking forest thumper. The only danger I present to this kid is the real possibility of boring her to death with my bitching and moaning about how much it hurts. Just get out, everyone. Banks, I'll drink your stupid tea. Leave it behind."

"Of course," Banks said. "But it will need reheating."

"Done," Booker put in. The liquid in the stoneware mug bubbled for a second as he generated a small thermal field effect.

Alessia shooed everyone out.

Jaddi Coto was the last to go.

"So, I can return to the regen tank to grow my horn now?" he asked.

"I'm afraid you won't have time," Alessia cautioned him. "We're supposed to fold for Lermontov Station, and Mister Banks tells me we'll be there in less than an hour. And the Sturm will be here an hour or so after that."

Coto grunted his disappointment.

Sephina tried to get her head around everything that had happened while she'd been out of it.

They were bugging out to Lermontov now? On the other side of the fucking star?

She knew people on Lermontov.

They were enormous assholes.

"But Lermontov Station is full of terrible people," Coto

said. "I will need a full-grown horn before docking there. A full-grown horn is much more intimidating than this embarrassing nub."

He pointed at his underwhelming, far-from-regrown rhino horn.

Alessia answered before Sephina could.

"Coto," she said, taking the giant's hand. "I am the sole heir to one of the most powerful Houses in the Greater Volume and commander in chief of all the fleets throughout that volume. I can destroy whole worlds with a single command. And I find you very intimidating. Even frightening."

Coto considered this for a moment before nodding reluctantly.

"Although you are small in stature, you do command great and terrible power. I am gratified to learn that I can still frighten you."

Alessia patted his hand reassuringly.

The door irised open and he stooped low to pass through.

They were alone.

Sephina found herself unexpectedly nervous. The young woman—the girl, really—who remained with her was not the kid she had teased and occasionally patronized since escaping Montrachet.

She had been left behind with Her Royal Highness Princess Alessia Szu Suri sur Montanblanc ul Haq.

"Baroness L'trel," the princess started. She stopped, suddenly looking all around them.

"Booker, are you still here?"

A pause.

"I'm just going now," his voice came back.

"Please do."

"Okay, then."

There was no obvious sign of the coder having departed, but Sephina felt the sudden absence of the third sentient presence in the room.

"I think he's gone," she said. "I could check if you like."

She started to lever herself up and out of the deep recesses of the lounge but Alessia waved off the attempt.

"Booker is a man of honor," she said. "My father's regiments were full of them. His boardroom?" She shrugged. "Not so much. But anyway. I recognize the type."

"Me too," Sephina said and smiled, but not with any joy. "He's a bit like Lucinda that way."

"And Ariane?"

Seph blinked.

Her lips parted to answer, but nothing more than the soft click of her tongue on the roof of her mouth came out.

She blinked again, this time to clear the watery smear which distorted her view of the room and of Alessia. They both dissolved into blurred twists of color.

Sephina tried to answer.

She tried to say, "Not like that, no."

But nothing came. Her throat was too tight. The sudden weight of sorrow so heavy that she couldn't breathe.

It was only when Alessia sat next to her and wrapped her tiny arms around Sephina's much larger shoulders that the emotional seizure finally released and with it came a great outpouring of anguish and pain.

"Oh God," she cried out. "Oh God, no. She's gone. Forever. Gone . . ."

Sephina rocked back and forth, convulsed with deep body tremors, and the little girl rocked with her. Together they stayed like that for many minutes, neither of them saying anything, but neither willing to let go.

Finally, shaking a little, snuffling and wiping a not-at-all baronial bubble of snot from her nose, Sephina pushed back a little.

"What are you, some sorta royal psyche adept now? I thought I was supposed be the counselor here," she said, sniffling.

Alessia shook her head.

She looked almost as sad as Sephina felt.

"Hey, don't feel sorry for me, kid—" Seph started to say.

But Alessia cut her off with an emphatic shake of her head.

"I'm not sorry for you," she said. "I'm jealous."

Seph wasn't sure she'd heard right.

"Did you say jealous? The fuck would you be jealous of someone like me?"

She wasn't angry. But she was confused.

Alessia sat back.

She wrapped her arms around herself.

"You loved Ariane, didn't you, and she loved you back?"

Sephina's breath was ragged, and her throat tried to close up again but she managed to answer.

"Yes."

Alessia nodded, looking even more forlorn.

"I've never had that," she said. "I never will."

Sephina couldn't help but smile.

It wasn't much, but it wasn't nothing.

"Kid," she said. "You're really young. You'll meet plenty of—"

"No," Alessia cut her off again. "That's not what I mean. I know I'm just a kid. I haven't lived like you and Lucinda have."

"Well, the Loose Unit's a bit of a box-head." Seph smiled again, just so. "She hasn't really lived. Never cut her own path. But I get your point, I guess."

Alessia rubbed her arms as though she was cold. Seph almost called out to Booker to raise the temperature. The air con was chilly in the cosmonaut lounge. She could easily imagine the original owners of the superyacht hosting sub-zero vodka and cosplay parties in here. The furnishing was very reminiscent of a tsarist dacha from the Arctic north of Old Earth— when it still had cosmonauts and tsars and an Arctic north.

And then she remembered Booker had removed himself from the local array. She was always groggy as hell coming out of a regen tank.

Alessia shook her head.

"My point is that you know what it's like to be loved. And

to love. I don't, because that was not the purpose of my life. I was an asset of the corporation. A genetic investment in future mergers and acquisitions."

She stared at Sephina and suddenly looked as lost and forlorn as the older woman felt. Seph felt oddly responsible for Alessia's sad tween emo attack.

"But royals have never married for love, kid," she said. "They take what they can on the side. I never met your old man, but I knew all about him. Everyone did. Dude was so horny he'd a fucked the crack of dawn. And your mother was . . ."

She suddenly caught herself.

"Oh shit. Sorry. That was thoughtless. I didn't mean . . ."

But again, Alessia just shook her head.

"It's not what I'm talking about. I know my parents had lovers. Or court favorites. Or whatever they called them."

Alessia looked beyond discomforted. She seemed almost . . . repulsed.

"But . . . they didn't . . . love each other. And they didn't love me. Nobody did. And nobody ever would. Whole star systems and fleets of Habitats are mine now, you know, if we beat the Sturm. But if I want them, I must give up any hope of knowing what it is to love somebody and to be loved the way you and Ariane were with each other. I know how bad you feel, Sephina. I know what you've lost. Because it's something I've always known I could never have. At least you had it and you knew what it meant. That's why I'm jealous."

Sephina said nothing.

On top of all her grief, she now felt shame, as well.

"I'm sure your mom loved you," she said at last, in a voice that sounded raspy and unconvincing. "My mother was a crazy source coder. Got some bad scripts and it put the zap on her head. But she was still my mom. She loved me, even when she was trying to cut the bugs out of my head." Sephina pulled back her thick tangle of dirty blond dreadlocks to reveal the scarred remains of one ear. She let the hair fall back. "And your mother would have loved you for sure. That's what moms do."

Alessia's eyes were wet. They sparkled with the tiny diamond points of the organic diodes that lit the Gagarin Lounge. She looked like she was supposed to cry, but no tears came.

"No, Seph. She didn't. I was a product in the lineup, not a child. That's what it is to be born into a Grand House. I am sorry that the Sturm took Ariane from you. There is so little love. I wish I could know what you have known. Even how much it hurts."

Sephina L'trel took in a long breath, held it for a second, and let it go in a shaky rush.

"Would you like me to tell you about her?"

"Yes, I would," Alessia said. "We have to get going, but Mister Banks will do that if you tell him. And then you can tell me all about Ariane. Remember her now. And in the future we will name a whole world for her. And the name of Ariane will matter and mean that there is always hope somewhere."

Sephina smiled, a small, crooked quirk of her lips.

"She would have liked you, kid. My girl, she was an absolutely desperate romantic. A fool for love."

"Tell me," Alessia said.

And Sephina did.

It helped.

CHAPTER

TWENTY-THREE

It was an indulgence only somebody enjoying the imprimatur of the Fleet marshal could pull off. Revell's shuttle dropped from the frigate *Ulysses*, which remained in orbit around Batavia, but rather than proceeding directly to the main recovery and repatriation site south of Fort Saba (now renamed Fort Dunn), he had the pilot, Lieutenant Faruqi, divert over the final resting place of the Freedom Ship *Voortrekker*.

The detour required clearance from the airspace controllers of the 101st's surviving Ground Force elements encamped around the sacred site, but again the sanction of Anais Blade cut through all resistance.

"Hell of a thing," Revell whispered as they traversed the ten-kilometer-long graveyard. One of true humanity's worst disasters.

"Mashallah, Captain Revell," Faruqi agreed. "Mashallah."

The tiny shuttle, *Ulysses*'s only connection dirtside, slowed to hover a thousand feet above the rupture in the hull where the spine of the gargantuan transport had broken upon impact with the hardrock pans of the Ironstone Desert. Centuries of exposure had dulled the ancient nanocomb shielding, but the space-gray tiles still absorbed the punishing heat of the local star so effectively that even the midday sun could not warm the shadowed depths of the great ship's deepest reaches.

Revell was torn between awe and revulsion. To think that some fax of the dread McLennan had profaned the hallowed ground down there, and not just once. Fleet Intelligence confirmed that successive copies of the man, or what used to be a man, had infested the last resting place of the *Voortrekker* for more than half a millennia.

"What the hell was he doing out here?" Revell said, pressing his forehead against the armor glass viewport. He could feel a faint trace of the scorching heat outside.

"Sorry, sir?" Faruqi asked.

What the hell were they both doing down there, Revell wondered silently, missing the pilot's question. The machine intelligence known as Three had also exiled itself out here at the edge of Occupied Space along with the infamous war criminal.

"Sir?" Faruqi said again.

"Don't worry about it, Lieutenant," Revell said, pushing away from the window and shaking himself free of his daydreams. "Just thinking out loud. If you'll excuse me for just a second . . ."

Anders Revell closed his eyes and crossed himself in the manner of his ancestors, reciting the Prayer for the Dead Among the Stars.

"Lord God, by the power of your Word you warmed the cold of the primeval vacuum and lit the way into the Dark for your true children. Watch over these the earthly remains of our brothers and sisters who fell along the way. Grant them peace and tranquility until that day when the souls and only the souls of the pure who believe in you will be raised to the glory of new life through Christ our Lord. Amen."

He crossed himself again.

"Inshallah," the pilot said quietly. "Allahu akbar."

Revell clapped him gently on one shoulder.

"God willing, brother," he added. "Until that day, though, let's be about our duty. Thank you for doing this. It reminds me why we fight."

"You good to go now, sir?" Faruqi asked.

"I am. How long to Fort Dunn from here?"

"If you strap in up here next to me, Captain, I can go ballistic. Get you there in twenty minutes. It's another five to the staging grounds at Camp Fischer."

"Let's go, then," Revell said.

Jonathyn Hardy awoke, expecting pain. Instead he was merely a little dry-mouthed and in need of a bedpan. As promised, they had broken and reset his arm, but it had all happened so much quicker than he'd imagined. Nurse Jenny at first held out the prospect that maybe the medics would get to his case a month or so after his arrival at the giant camp south of Fort Saba—no, Fort Dunn, he corrected himself—and for the first two weeks nothing about that changed. Then one day, orderlies arrived to escort Jonathyn from the quiet seed-sorting Hab where he worked. They were friendly enough, but they said he had to come with them and they bundled him, gently, into a medical transporter for immediate transfer to a surgical unit on the far side of the camp.

To be honest, he'd had a hell of a scare out of it. Sudden changes in routine at Camp 17 had always presaged dark developments, and even though the orderlies assured him everything was fine and he was just going to see the doctors about resetting his broken arm, he was still shaking by the time he arrived at the medbay. It wasn't unknown for the guards at Camp 17 to play cruel practical jokes on the inmates.

But the ride over was comfortable. The Republic's engineering crews had further improved the already impressive road network of the massive camp and had Jonathyn not been so nervous he might even have fallen asleep. The humming of the

tires on the carbonmesh road matting had the somnolent quality of a lullaby, and he found reclining in the soft, padded crash
couch to be so indulgent as to approximate sedation. It was
only the experience of years under the yoke of the Combine that
prevented him from relaxing. He tried to talk himself out of his
fear.

He had been long enough in the Republican camp now to
know that he had nothing to fear from them. He was what they
called a true human. No implants, no gene-splicing, nothing
that would put him on the wrong side of their favor. They in
turn had delivered him from perdition. Rescued all his friends,
too. Like him they were true humans, and they had been treated
with nothing but consideration. For a wonder, he was even putting on weight for the first time in years, filling out the hollow
spaces of his once cadaverous physique thanks to three solid
meals a day and an easy work schedule of which he could not
possibly have dreamed when he was a prisoner of the Yulin-
Irrawaddy at Camp 17.

Nurse Jenny had been waiting at the medical unit, and that
helped him calm down. She was lovely, and she explained that
his treatment had been expedited. She couldn't say why, but
thought it was probably that the doctors had more capacity and
less demand than they had planned for. Republican casualties
and liberated prisoners like Jonathyn had been coming into
Camp Fischer every day for the past couple of weeks, but most
of the giant facility was still empty. Jonathyn rarely left the
small compound at the southwestern corner of the site. It had
come to feel familiar and safe, especially once he got to know
the other emancipated debt slaves, but even at that distant remove it was apparent that Camp Fischer was mostly empty and
underused. At night, the jungle a kilometer away and the river
that ran through it were louder than any of the fabs and industrial plants within the fence line.

And the field hospital where they took him was almost entirely empty.

"This is a combat support hospital," Nurse Jenny explained. "We work on battlefield casualties here, stabilize them, and send them back to Fleet."

The drugs they had him on were so good that when Jonathyn came to after the operation, it was a while before he realized he had a visitor at his bedside. For the first minute or so he simply basked in the lavish opulence of lying abed in the middle of the day—a damned comfortable bed it was, too—and feeling no more discomfort than a mild tightness of the bladder and dryness of mouth. Chilled air fended off the distant, humid warmth of subtropical air and the linen sheets of his hospital cot were cool and pleasingly soft against his skin.

A gel sleeve protected his left arm.

There was no pain, despite the surgeons having broken his limb in at least three places before resetting it. And they had told him exactly what they intended to do before they did it. They had even given him the choice of whether to proceed or not.

A real choice.

If you could imagine that.

Of course, he had chosen to go ahead with the procedure. By that point, a little over a fortnight into his time with the forces of the Human Republic, he had come to trust them without question. A week after his arrival at Camp Fischer they had even reunited him with Reinsaari and Nadine, his closest friends from Camp 17. He almost didn't recognize them at first. They both looked so . . . fat.

"My God, look at you," Nadine said, beaming, when she first saw him. "You look like you ate your way out of a chocolate bacon pastry prison."

"Jonathyn! They have cheese here," Reinsaari hissed through clenched teeth. "Actual cheese. They took the cows with them. Heirloom cows they say. All the way from Old Earth out into the Dark and back again."

They had lost contact with one another after evacuating from the defaulter camp, but the Sturm—no, not the Sturm . . .

the Republicans—had taken the time to reconnect the former inmates with their closest comrades from the defaulter camps. Nurse Jenny had even explained why to Jonathyn.

"We find that recovery is improved within a close and supportive personal milieu," she said. "The same way that bandages bind up our wounds, human beings—true humans—recover best within a weave of personal relationships that make up the emotional fabric of our lives."

All these memories, this collage of literal recollection and free-floating sentiment, whirled through Jonathyn Hardy's pleasantly jumbled thoughts as he came out from under the anesthetic.

He slowly realized that a man was sitting with him.

He gave a little start.

"Oh!"

And the man smiled.

"They tell me you will be thirsty. Here."

The man, an officer of some sort to judge by his uniform, passed Jonathyn a bottle of chilled water. Condensation beaded the clear glass.

"And you may need to piss. I'm afraid you're on your own there, Mister Hardy," the man said. "But if you need a moment?"

Jonathyn blinked.

"I . . . I'm sorry. Who are you?"

The man smiled again, a kindly, understanding expression.

"My apologies. They told me you would be some time coming to your senses. My name is Anders Revell. Captain Revell. But please, call me Anders. You are a civilian, a citizen of the Republic, and I have no authority over you. Quite the opposite, in fact."

Jonathyn said nothing. His head was reeling. He took the proffered water bottle and fumbled the drinking straw past his dry, cracked lips. He drank too quickly and got a headache.

"I'm sorry," he said. "I don't know you, do I? But you know me? Because I'm not a citizen of the Republic. I'm from Coriolis. I'm sorry . . ."

Revell's eyes crinkled as he smiled again.

"There is no need to apologize, Mister Hardy. You have had a traumatic experience. Not your operation, which I presume went well. But your imprisonment here on Batavia. Nearly ten years, as I understand. In a Combine gulag. It is understandable that you might find all of this . . . confusing."

Revell gestured with one hand, taking in the light, airy surrounds of the field hospital. A nurse whom Jonathyn did not recognize was turning down a bed across the ward, and climate control units hummed somewhere out of sight, maintaining a pleasant and temperate environment. Before Jonathyn could speak again, Revell went on. "I would correct you about one thing, however, Mister Hardy. You are a citizen of the Republic. All true human beings, whether born in the Redoubt or under the yoke in Occupied Space, are citizens of the Republic and entitled to all of the rights and protections of citizenship."

Revell paused and sketched another version of that quiet, kindly smile that seemed to be his most common expression.

"But I am not here to offer you a civics lesson. I imagine you are wondering why I have come to visit you."

The ice-water headache that had spiked behind Jonathyn's eyeballs when he drank the cold water too quickly had backed off, but he was feeling the pressure growing in his bladder. He shifted uncomfortably under the sheets.

"I guess I am," he said. "You're not a doctor, are you?"

"No, I'm not," Revell answered. "I work for the commander of our fleet, and part of what I do is try to ensure that the fleet does as little genuine fighting as possible."

None of that made any sense to Jonathyn or cleared up his confusion. He shook his head.

"I'm afraid I don't understand," he said uncertainly. "Why do you need to talk to me? I've been in prison for ten years."

But even as he asked the question, the answer, or at least the shape of an answer, began to resolve for him. He suddenly very much needed to go to the toilet, and his heart started beating so quickly that he felt dizzy and feared he might fall over if he tried to get out of bed. Medical sensors monitoring his vitals started to chime and ping, drawing the attention of the nurse on the other side of the ward.

She hurried over.

"Is everything all right here?" she asked.

"I'm afraid I may have given Mister Hardy a bit of a fright," Revell confessed. He sounded very sorry. "I do apologize if that's the case, sir," he went on. "I am really only here to help, and to ask for your help."

Jonathyn got his breathing under control, which slowed down his runaway heart rate. One thing about having been a prisoner of the Combine for so long, he was used to sudden shocks and reversals. And he was practiced at retaining or at least regaining his balance when they did unsettle him.

"Is this about my daughter?" Jonathyn asked. "Is this about Lucinda? Is she alive? Is she okay?"

The nurse checked his readouts on half a dozen screens and seemed content that he was not about to die on her. She left them to it.

"Lucinda is indeed alive, Mister Hardy. And doing very well, I might add, although you will understand if I have mixed feelings about that."

He seemed so reasonable, almost as though amused by the necessity of having to discuss the matter with Jonathyn, that it was impossible to feel unambiguously threatened by what, on the face of it, had to be a serious threat. To Lucinda if not to him.

"I guess . . ." Jonathyn started to say, before trailing off. "I don't really understand, though. She's alive, you say?"

Revell nodded.

"As far as I know, and as of three Earth standard days ago, yes. I cannot vouch for her safety after that, because I'm not sure of her whereabouts or disposition. But yes, Mister Hardy. Your daughter was confirmed to be on an Armadalen naval base called Descheneaux some seventy-two hours ago."

Anders Revell stopped talking and the silence spread between them. It seemed to have weight and possibilities.

Jonathyn was reeling with relief, but also with renewed anxiety. With fear, to be completely honest.

Lucinda was alive.

He had not even allowed himself to hope for such a miracle.

One of the first things you learned in the camps was that hope could be as deadly as the snipers in the guard towers. But knowing that she was alive—he did not doubt it for a moment now that Revell had told him so—Jonathyn was seized anew by all the ancient terrors that had haunted him when they were first torn apart.

"Would you like to see your daughter, Mister Hardy?" Revell asked, when it became obvious that Jonathyn was incapable of voicing his thoughts.

"But how," he croaked. "You said she was on Descheneaux. She's . . ."

He knew what he had to say, but it felt as though he was condemning or even betraying her to do so. He felt trapped. Another familiar experience. And from that experience he knew there could be no escape. The only way out was through.

"She's still fighting you, isn't she," he said. It wasn't a question.

Revell surprised him by grinning. His eyes twinkled and he sat back in his chair and laughed as though Jonathyn had just caught him out with a good joke.

"She is indeed, Mister Hardy. And she has done very well. You have raised a true human warrior."

Perplexed by the man's reaction, Jonathyn Hardy said nothing. Perhaps it was a thing for soldiers? Some expression of professional respect? He could not say, because he did not know much about his daughter's military service. The sensors at Camp 17 had stripped all their communications of any but the most banal and personal of details. What did come through was the simple ephemera of relationships. Inquiries about his health and well-being. Stories of her life when out of uniform. She liked going to the theater. She had been to Earth. She had once or twice met her old friends from Habitat Welfare. Two other girls, Sephina and Ariane. But under what circumstances, she did not say.

Something else tugged at Jonathyn's thoughts. But it was not a distant memory, he realized. It was something Revell had just said.

"A true human warrior?" Jonathyn ventured.

"Oh yes," Revell said. "Your daughter, like you, Mister Hardy, was naturally born, was she not?"

"Of course," Jonathyn hurried on to say. "We were poor people, Captain Revell. We couldn't afford genetics or implants or any of that."

Revell nodded sympathetically and patted the air in front of him as if to tamp down the flames of Jonathyn Hardy's angst.

"I do appreciate that, Mister Hardy. We have been observing. From afar, you understand. We have seen the great iniquities and injustices done throughout Occupied Space. It is not simply that runaway machines and . . . inhuman"—Revell waved a hand around as if lost for words—"self-selecting mutations from the genome . . . it's not as though they were the only things going wrong here, no?"

Jonathyn said nothing, even as his thoughts raced.

Revell prodded him gently.

"There was no justification for what happened to you, was there, Mister Hardy? For indebted servitude?"

"No, there wasn't." Jonathyn shook his head, certain of this if nothing else. His voice sounded very small in his own ears.

"And there can surely be no legitimate excuse or justification for the subjugation, the serfdom of a trillion people throughout the various empires and autocracies of the Greater Volume, can there?"

Despite the chilled air on the ward, a hot flush crept up Jonathyn's neck and colored his face. He felt as though he had to say something.

"But Armadale isn't like that. Or the Montanblancs. Or Old Earth or . . ."

Revell smiled.

"No, they're not," he conceded. "But the Combine is. And the Javan Empire. And the Russian Federation. And the chaebol syndicates, and, well, I could go on, couldn't I?"

He could. That was the Darkness of it.

"And even your enlightened Commonwealth, Mister Hardy. They did not save you from the Combine reclaimers, did they?"

"No," Jonathyn admitted. "They didn't."

"You owe them nothing, Jonathyn," Revell said softly. "We owe our own, and that's all, sir. Your daughter, Lucinda, you owe her your best efforts. She is fighting a hopeless war that is already lost for a cause that never deserved her allegiance in the first place."

Revell sighed and leaned back. He sat in a light organoplastic folding chair that creaked a little under his weight. His mouth quirked into an almost apologetic grin.

"I will tell you the truth, Mister Hardy. I admire her. She has fought a good fight and there is a part of me that envies her for it. Are you familiar with Macaulay, sir? One of the ancients."

Jonathyn shook his head. "I don't think so."

Revell seemed pleased. He let his chair fall forward and as the legs banged down, he spoke a few lines he had obviously committed to his memory.

"Then out spake brave Horatius,
The Captain of the Gate:
To every man upon this earth
Death cometh soon or late.
And how can man die better
Than facing fearful odds,
For the ashes of his fathers,
And the temples of his gods."

The nurse who had been busying herself a few beds down stopped to listen to the small performance. She smiled and clapped quietly when Revell was done. Having lost himself in the moment, the Republican officer shifted in his chair a little awkwardly.

"I do like a gratuitous classic reference," he said with a shrug.

"Not so gratuitous, I suppose," Jonathyn conceded.

Revell bowed his head in acknowledgment.

"No, not so much, Mister Hardy. Your daughter has done her duty at the gate, but she does not need to die. And to be honest, I would prefer that no more of my men and women die by her hand. It's over. She has fought with great honor and skill. But it's over."

Jonathyn felt a strangely contrary sensation of great heaviness and lightness settle over him. It was as though he would float away, were he not weighed down by some terrible burden.

"You want me to talk to her, don't you?"

"Yes, Mister Hardy, I do."

CHAPTER

TWENTY-FOUR

Ariane folded away from *Defiant*, the Javans, and the Combine to emerge on the far side of Natuna and into the traffic control zone for Lermontov Station. From there the approach under effect-impellers would be much slower. With Banks in the pilot's chair and code from the old *Regret* running on the stacks there was nothing for Booker to do. He could have flown the ship. He had TDF script for hundreds of different classes of spacecraft packed into his deep lacuna, everything from orbital cargo lighters to deep space recon'vettes. The *Ariane* was bigger than a 'vette, for sure, but not nearly as complicated, even with all the mods Zaistev's corporate gangsters had carried out.

On fold-out, Mister Banks hailed the traffic controllers and asked for permission to approach, identifying *Ariane* as a freelance clipper under Captain L'trel, lawfully salvaged according to all requirements of the Greater Volume Maritime Code. He did not inform Lermontov VTC about the letter of marque and reprisal signed by Admiral Frazer McLennan, authorizing the captain of the *Ariane* to engage in state-sponsored piracy, and he forgot to mention that the sole heir to the Montanblanc ul Haq Corporation was aboard.

Traffic Control cleared their approach and advised *Ariane* to be ready for customs and excise inspection. A one-off "extraordinary" anchorage fee would be due within one Earth standard day of docking to recoup the costs of "mooring and affreightment" during the current difficulties.

"Yeah, we'll see about that," Captain L'trel said.

Booker judged that she had largely recovered from regen fatigue, and possibly even a little from the deeper, more profound wound done to her by the loss of Ariane, the real Ariane, back on Habitat Eassar. For sure, if he poured himself into the ship's medical sensor suites he could have performed a full quantum state resonance scan without her even knowing. That would have settled any questions about the aftereffects of her spell in the tank, or the chronic depression and PTSD he judged her to be struggling with after Eassar.

But that was a dick move. The sort of invasive, uteroprivileged shit the breeders and computers did to People of Code all the time. It was not within his nature to sink to their level for the sake of mere convenience. Instead, Booker would do what human beings had done for millennia before they had the power to script the thoughts and feelings of others, let alone to read them.

He observed.

Sephina sat in the captain's chair at the center of the main bridge, which remained eccentrically fitted out in the style of an ancient schooner from the Age of Sail. She had emerged from her private conversation with Princess Alessia seemingly much improved in mood. The Montanblanc heir was now playing with Coto, who was giving her piggyback rides around the bridge, requiring Booker to devote a dedicated subprogram to watching over their game, lest Coto take her head off on one of the structurally pointless, but very real and very heavy, ironwood crossbeams.

Banks worked a holo-display as sophisticated and powerful

as any that Booker had ever seen, but the projector was housed within a polished brass ship's binnacle that once upon a time had given honest service to actual mariners on a three-masted schooner of the Cunard line, a long lost company of a long fallen empire.

Having no official duties to attend to, and content that the captain was doing at least a little better than before, Booker tried for a short while to enjoy the rare privilege of merely riding along as a passenger, but he found it impossible to turn off his training. The same way he would scan the exits and corners when he walked into a room, Booker quickly decided to pore over the take from the ship's arrays as they approached the receiving volume for the Javan entrepôt.

Unlike Natuna's main system Habs, Lermontov Station was a designated freeport. The Empire's writ still held there, and all the deference due to Medang Palace throughout the Empire was also due from the station. But Lermontov occupied an unusual niche within the socioeconomic wilds of Greater Java. One of the first trading posts established by the Federation of Russian Oligarchies in this arc of the outer volumes, it had avoided annexation thanks to the deft maneuverings of Putingrad during the two-century-long wave of colonization that followed the development of long-range fold drives in 2179. Lermontov's L3 orbital track was leased from Medang Palace, with a single annual payment made directly to the emperor's personal accounts in lieu of the usual taxes, levies, and royal commissions that accrued to consolidated revenue throughout the wider Empire. The Javanese Navy provided security, and the Royal Court represented the interests of the station on Earth. Day-to-day operations, however, were the prerogative of the Lermontov Cartel, a governing council appointed by the largest trading houses and shipping lines on the freeport's registry of shareholders. Zaistev Corporation was not on that registry, but their ardent rivals Svetakov held a twenty-five-percent stake, making the port a safe harbor for a vessel like the *Ariane*.

"Long as we tell 'em we stole the bitch and killed every

motherfucker on board," Sephina explained to Alessia as she bounced past on Coto's shoulders and they settled into a final glide path to the deep space outpost.

Like Zaistev, the Svetakov Oligarchy were zero-sum players, she said on Coto's next lap of the bridge. "If they think we fucked ol' Zed, we'll be their new best friends."

"Until they decide to fuck us," Cox, the Armadalen, muttered to himself.

He spoke in such a low barracks whisper that even Aronson, standing next to him, didn't hear exactly what he said.

"Huh?" the younger man went.

"Nothing," Cox grunted.

Booker, however, understood perfectly. His senses were enhanced by the ship's ambient arrays, and his thoughts were free to run at superluminal speed on *Ariane*'s quantum-bit processing architecture.

Cox was a breeder, but that didn't make him wrong.

Lermontov Station sat at the third of the Natuna System's Lagrange points, on the opposite side of the ancient sun to the Javan Habs and slabs. For the moment this put it at a pleasing remove from the inevitable meeting point between the Sturm and whatever remained of the Empire in-system. But that did not make the freeport a haven. Already, Booker could tell that panic was setting in.

While the ship's small complement of embodied crew sat around the bridge in their flesh-and-bone forms, Booker— ensouled in the substrate—turned his analytic scripts on the data flooding in from the ship's big sensor rigs. He took a minute of processing time—a couple of millennia in human cognitive terms—to construct a data vault in which to screen the signals intelligence for any traces of the Sturm's malware. Assuring himself there was none, he expanded the buffer and gathered up petabytes of densely compressed comms traffic, exabytes of tactical data on the hundreds of ships gathered in a vast floating torus around the station, and just a few discrete but critical packets of information extracted directly from the Habitat's secure internal networks and autonomic systems. This he accessed through TDF specterware stored in his deep lacuna and authorized for use only on the orders of the Terran defense secretary.

Since that guy was almost certainly a meat-hacked ghoul by now, feasting on the brains of anyone who got within chomping distance, it would've been a waste of time to bother with all the bullshit formalities. Booker supposed he could have asked Princess Alessia in her role as acting chair and sole surviving member of the Senate Armed Forces Committee to unlock the powerful scripts, but she was very busy with her piggyback ride from Jaddi Coto, galloping around and around the antiquarian, oak-paneled bridge. As the Montanblanc princess squealed and giggled with delight, Booker instead pondered the bottomless ocean of sigint data he'd sucked up.

Two hundred and thirty-eight ships had been granted refugee status after arriving in-system and claiming asylum from the Sturm. Another seven military vessels, most of them smaller, long-range craft, had been corralled half an AU away from the main flotilla, inside a small constellation of surveillance drones.

Many of the civilian craft gave every sign of preparing to flee the system ahead of the Sturm's arrival.

The warships, however, lay still and silent.

Booker did not attempt to breach their systems. He scoured the general comms traffic on this side of the star and Lermontov's security channels for any information about them and quickly confirmed the presence of a damaged TDF destroyer escort, two Vikingar long raiders, a couple of chaebol geobukseon, a Texan Monitor, and one Deutsche Marine troopship a long, long way from home. The final vessel was not a warship as such, but an armed merchantman of the Chase Corporation which, like the genuine combatants, had been cut out of the refugee fleet. The warcraft were all signal dark. They emitted no EM or q-bit data, and their military-grade stealthing masked any sign that they were even occupied. However, he was able to hijack enough telemetry from the traffic control systems on Lermontov to track micro adjustments in their positions and deduce that all seven were under active helm control and holding station relative to the Hab, within their improvised prison of drones.

Booker considered the data and assessed the correlation of forces as Mister Banks guided the ship into Lermontov Station's terminal approach lanes. The man was an exceptional pilot, and Booker could not help but feel some indirect pride that even though Banks had not chosen to walk the true path of the Source, he was undeniably a Person of Code.

The military vessels, Booker observed, were a mix of advanced technology—the TDF escort—and relatively simple, long-haul utility vehicles such as the DM troopship. If all had arrived with full crews, they would increase the number of trained military personnel available to Hardy and McLennan by more than two thousand, although there was little to no chance of side-loading many of them from whatever specialities they currently occupied into, say, the duty roster of an Armadalen Titan Cruiser. Perhaps if they could access the appropriate skill scripts . . .

But of course, they couldn't. The Sturm had spiked the codices everywhere.

As Mister Banks lined up on the berth where they would dock for customs inspection, maneuvering *Ariane* through the immense, rotating gyre of the ships orbiting Lermontov Station, Booker's attention remained fixed on the seven exiled warships. He could tell they were all online because of the imprint their presence made on the local datasphere. Nobody was talking to the ships, but the background chatter about them was constant, especially as news of the Sturm's reconnaissance-by-fire arrived from the far side of the system. People wanted to know whether the warships would even fight.

A good question, Booker thought.

Nonetheless, the ships themselves remained silent and inscrutable.

As he pondered the mystery of the dormant warships, Booker obtained real-time intel from a short traffic burst between a couple of the surveillance drones, readjusting their relative positions in the enclosure around the exiles. Analyzing the take, Booker determined that they were not refining their placements to improve surveillance cover. Rather, they maneuvered to ensure overlapping coverage from their volume denial warheads.

The drones were not just observers. They were weapons.

Alessia rode on Jaddi Coto's armored shoulders, clutching at the hard, leathery skin of his massive skull as he tirelessly galloped around *Ariane*'s bridge. The eccentric furnishing of the ship's control room, especially the low ceilings of oaken board and chalky white caulking, reminded her more than a little of the old-fashioned boats her father sometimes took out of Port au Pallice on those rare occasions he stayed more than a few days at Skygarth. It was a game of great fun and some real danger to duck under the thick wooden crossbeams just in time, lest Coto knock her completely unconscious on them.

The hybrid giant seemed to enjoy the diversion almost as much as Alessia, and although Sergeant Cox glowered at him, especially when Alessia had to duck under the beams, nobody made any move to stop the game. Not Mister Banks, who seemed to have no trouble at all piloting the ship while Coto thundered around him. And not Baroness Sephina, who merely grinned at the close calls and occasionally tossed off some random lesson about the spaceport they were approaching, a place where she'd done a lot of business when she was a very naughty smuggler. These moments of instruction were about a thousand times more interesting than anything her so-called tutors back at Skygarth had ever taught her about geography or economics or anything.

Having escaped from the grind of her studies on *Defiant*, Alessia had not had so much fun since leaving Montrachet. And if she was being honest, she'd rarely had as much back on her homeworld, either, and usually only when she could sneak away from her tutors and the Lady Melora to play with Caro and Debin down in the gardens.

She winced a little to recall Melora, who had been infected by the Sturm and gone bugshit insane. That naturally led to thoughts of Sergeant Reynolds and old Mister Dunning, who had both died to get her away from the Sturm—even if Reynolds had failed at that because he'd been betrayed by the treacherous Jasko Tan. The distraction of all these unpleasant memories was enough for Alessia to miss the thick, black crossbeam that was approaching at speed as Coto swung past the interstellar navigation terminals at the rear of the bridge. He was so invested in his role as the imperial racing rhino that he didn't duck as much as usual and it was only when Alessia was too close to avoid the collision that she realized it was inevitable. She flinched and closed her eyes, dreading the sickening impact that must surely follow.

It did not.

Coto galloped on and Alessia opened her eyes again.

The solid beam of dark ironwood remained in place, but it was as though she had passed right through it. She could see Dahl and Cox starting toward her. Dahl had even raised one hand as if to reach all the way across the bridge and pull her down from Coto's shoulders. But the Armadalen marines looked surprised and more than a little confused. Kanon Aronson was staring at her with his mouth wide open, rendering his rather handsome features into something closer to a puppy whose favorite toy has just been folded away.

Booker's voice, quiet and even a little distracted, came from everywhere.

"I dissolved the bonds between the nanoblox underlying the atomic structure of the beam which was about to smash your skull to bone chips and jelly. You passed through the constituent matter cloud, but you're gonna need a good long shower now, Your Highness. Sonic and hydro. Otherwise it'll itch like a bitch."

Alessia leaned forward and patted Coto on the side of his head.

"Hey," she said. "I think I'd better get down."

Coto slowly came to a stop.

"I am disappointed," he said, lowering her to the deck. "I thought the chance of serious injury and even death was the whole point. I did not realize that Booker would intervene to ruin everything."

"Yeah, it's what I do," Booker said. "And . . . we need to talk."

Alessia assumed he was about to give her a Lady Melora–class telling-off for endangering herself, even though he had just proved there was no real danger. Grown-ups were like that. Forever lecturing you about stuff that wasn't even real. He surprised her, though.

"Captain, I don't know that we should proceed with docking here."

"You worried about the customs guys shaking us down?" Sephina said. "Because don't bother. They will. They're all as crooked as fuck. That's why we'll be fine. We just gotta settle on a price."

"It's not the revenue agents," Booker said. "It's Cartel Security. Or the Javan Navy. Or something. I'm still working the problem. But there is a problem. I think they're going to impound us away from the station. They're going to clamp the ship."

Mister Banks spoke up from the pilot's chair. "What's all this, then?"

Cox and Dahl were now fully alert, as well.

Dahl snapped her fingers at Alessia, summoning her, and Alessia was so surprised that she hurried straight over to the marine.

"What's going on?" asked Aronson, moving quickly to stand beside Dahl.

"Go on, Book," Sephina said. "Tell us what you got."

"There are six foreign military vessels and a single armed

merchantman sequestered half an AU away in a weaponized holding pen. One of the ships is a Terran destroyer escort. It has battle damage, Captain. The damage appears to be consistent with an attack by Combine offensive systems. The other ships do appear to have some minimal helm control, but no other autonomy. And *Ariane* is more heavily armed than the Chase Corporation barque interned with them. It seems the surviving authorities in-system don't want any challengers to their authority."

Sephina frowned.

"Huh," she went. "Banks, can you give us a couple more minutes to think this through?"

"Of course," he said with a nod, diving his hands into the holographic helm controls and flicking icons with practiced ease.

A warning tone sounded, followed immediately by an incoming communications alert.

Mister Banks smiled.

"It's the harbormaster, Captain. For you."

Seph grinned.

"Make my apologies and yours, you terrible fucking helmsman, and let 'em know we'll make everything right. It'll just take a few minutes."

She turned back to Booker, which meant placing hands on hips and talking to the ceiling, as though he was hiding behind the thick wooden roofing beams.

"Okay, Book, you got two minutes. Can you unpack some of that nasty fucking spyware I just know the TDF stashed away in your deepest darkest code vaults? Find out what's going on before we step into it?"

Before he could answer, another voice spoke up from across the bridge.

Sergeant Cox.

"Hey," he barked. "If shit's going down, we need to tell *Defiant*. Right now."

Sephina half turned toward him.

"We will. Bitches always hang together. But right now, we don't know shit. Booker. Get on it."

Alessia was so pleased to see that Sephina was back to her old self, and so enthralled to finally be right in the middle of the action, that she missed it when Booker addressed his next question to her.

"Senator Montanblanc? Senator? Princess, yo!"

"A-Train, he's talking to you, girl," Sephina said.

"Huh," Alessia said. "What about me?"

"Senator Montanblanc," Booker explained. "I have scripted softweapons I can deploy but only with the permission of the highest civilian authorities . . ."

"That's you, kid," Sephina said.

"Do I have your permission to deploy?" Booker asked.

Alessia was standing a little away from the strange, antique ship's binnacle, from which projected a small universe of holo-data and control interfaces. Everyone was looking at her.

The Armadalens. Sephina and her crew. And somewhere, unseen but all around, Booker, waiting on her say-so.

"But what . . . what does that mean?" she asked.

"It means the Book wants to break into Lermontov's secure data stacks and steal a bunch of shit they don't want us to know about," Sephina replied. "To be honest, kid, I think he could do it anyway, but he's just being nice by asking."

"Could you?" Alessia said, looking up at the wooden ceiling beams, just like Sephina had done. "Could you do it without me giving you permission?"

Booker's voice in reply was quiet.

"I have a lot of tools I can use on my own authority," he said. "I've already deployed some of them. But there are soft-weapons for which my source code requires affirmative permission from the final command authority. You are the authority, Alessia. I literally cannot use the weapons without you permitting me. It is your choice. Not mine."

Senator Alessia Montanblanc felt the sudden, unexpected

significance of the moment as a strange heaviness. Dahl reached out and steadied her with a light hand upon her shoulder.

"You okay?" the marine asked.

"I just . . . I've never . . ." Alessia started to say. But she stopped herself.

She breathed in. And breathed out.

This was it. This was all the stuff her parents and her tutors and everyone had ever tried to tell her about. Leadership. Responsibility. Duty. All the stuff they had lied about, because she knew, she had always known, that she was never meant to make such choices. That was not her role in the corporation. She was simply meant to be a minor entry in the genealogical chart of a Grand House. Not an actor in the great game.

It is your choice, Booker had said. Not mine.

Alessia nodded.

"Fuck yeah. Do it," she said.

CHAPTER

TWENTY-FIVE

"Commander, we have flash traffic from *Ariane*. U-space routed through the comm sats."

"Shit," Lucinda blurted before she could get her surprise under control. "How?"

There was no way Sephina could hack into the secure links between the micro satellites she'd dispersed throughout the system to contact any Armadalen stealth vessels.

But the question answered itself.

Booker.

The TDF operator would have softweapons capable of cracking the RAN's crypto.

"Throw it to my sphere, Lieutenant," she said.

Nonomi Chivers flicked the data packet into Lucinda's command space.

Sephina's avatar appeared in front of her. A recorded message.

"Hey, Luce, Booker's calling shenanigans on the local narcs. Got some real sketchy shit going down on this side of the burner. He's put together a packet for you. Let me know what you wanna do but make it quick. We're supposed to dock in a couple of minutes."

Seph's image disappeared and a single file icon hovered in front of Hardy.

"Is this thing clean?" she asked Lieutenant Chivers.

"It appears so to our filters, Commander."

"Hero?" Lucinda said warily. "Can you take a look at this data pack that . . ."

"Well of course I've already done so," the Intellect said. "It's free of nasties. Except for the aforementioned shenanigans. There does appear to be rather a lot of them."

Admiral McLennan, who had been standing over by Tactical, dunking a shortbread soldier into a cup of tea and gently inquiring of Lieutenant Fein about some of *Defiant*'s more obscure capabilities, quickly shoved the remainder of the cookie into his mouth, chewed quickly, and swallowed as Lucinda gestured at the data packet with her fingertips.

McLennan patted Fein on the shoulder, mumbled "Well done, lad" through a mouthful of soggy shortbread, and came up next to Lucinda as the transmission contents revealed themselves.

"What am I looking at here?" Lucinda asked, as the superdense matrix of intercepts, telemetry data, and signals capture exploded into view.

Hero answered before any of her crew were able.

"You were not the only surviving military unit in this arc of the local volume. Unsurprising, really. The Sturm expected a less than perfect kill rate. Some ships like *Defiant* would survive. Captain L'trel's real human boy has stumbled over evidence of such on the far side of the local sun. There are seven war-fighting or combat-capable vessels one half of an astronomical unit from Lermontov Station. They have been secured within a sentinel drone enclosure. The vat soldier doesn't speculate why, but your delinquent friend from Habitat Welfare thinks that the Javans probably jumped them and put a bag on them—her terminology, not mine—to forestall any challenge to local authority in these trying modern times of ours. There is a lot more, but it's mostly supporting material. If you give me a moment I will analyze and debrief as to probabilities."

"Well, this is a large, wet fart in our small, cozy bed," McLennan said, peering into the data cloud.

"What class of warships?" Lucinda asked. She didn't have time to dive in herself. The Sturm were approaching fast, and the Javans wanted to know what the hell McLennan was going to do about it.

Neither Karna nor Pac Yulin would defer to Lucinda, but for the moment it looked like they would at least respect the authority of Earth and the power of the Terran Defense Force, as embodied in McLennan.

It told her just how isolated they were from the worlds outside the local volume. She was almost certain that Earth and the TDF no longer existed as functioning entities.

Hero started to list off the vessels.

"One TDF destroyer escort, one Texan Monitor, a DM troop hauler, two . . . oh. Wait a moment now . . ."

"Excuse me, Commander," Nonomi Chivers cut in. "I have Sub-Commandant Suprarto from the Warlugger *Makassar*. He says it's urgent he speak to the admiral."

Lucinda collapsed the datasphere, and with it the evidence of whatever was happening around Lermontov Station.

"Admiral?" she asked McLennan.

"Och, I would love to have a natter," he said.

"Holovise him in," Lucinda ordered.

"Excuse me," Hero protested. "I'm not finished. There is something you need to know, Commander Hardy."

"Whisper it in my shell-like ear, then, old chum," McLennan said.

"Ugh." Hero cringed with a small, performative shudder. "That gross, mangled wax trap? I'd rather not."

But the ancient frenemies leaned in close and Hero effected a discrete auditory field to talk with McLennan in private. The admiral nodded and grunted and pursed his lips as though in receipt of the most fabulously scurrilous gossip. Lucinda ignored them as the young Javan officer appeared within a small holosphere in front of her. He looked stressed; his voice strained.

"Admiral McLennan," he called out, talking right past Lucinda. "My superiors demand to know what preparations are in hand for our defense."

McLennan held up two fingers to Hero, pausing their private conference and nodded appreciatively at Sub-Commandant Suprarto's question.

"Ha. Due preparations, lad. Due preparations. We've run out the cannon and sharpened all the cutlasses and we await the dread foe at their convenience."

"I . . . I don't understand . . ." Suprarto started, and McLennan spoke over him.

"I have a plan, Mister Suprarto. I always have a plan, and you and yon Combine raiders will play your part, but I will tell you true, young man, that it would all go so much easier if Volume Lord Karna would release to my command the half-dozen military vessels and the single armed merchantman of the Chase Corporation he seems to have detained . . . by accident, no doubt . . . on the far side of Natuna."

Silence, except for a small grunt from Lieutenant Varro Chase at navigation as he came to his feet.

"Request permission to talk, Commander," he said.

"Understandable, but poorly timed, Mister Chase," Lucinda said. "Let's deal with this first."

Chase resumed his station, trying to make good on the charade of a man who was not at all interested in the very interesting thing he had just heard. But his face was a moving mask of contrary emotions. To Lucinda he looked fragile and susceptible, while also energized by a sudden rush of hormonal ambition.

She turned to McLennan, hiding her dismay from the admiral and from Suprarto. Lucinda had not expected McLennan to simply front the Javans in such a fashion. Other members of her bridge crew were also staring at the Terran officer, who had returned to his hushed conversation with Herodotus while they waited on Suprarto.

The Javan officer was pinned like a small bug inside the holo-field, turning his head this way and that as though seeking clarity or release, or maybe both.

The lack of any reply was growing awkward when Lieutenant Chase climbed halfway to his feet again. "Commander, I really must insist . . ."

"No, Lieutenant," she whispered urgently. "You really must sit down."

Lieutenant Chivers spoke up again.

"Commander? I have Volume Lord Karna and Deputy Executive Prince Pac Yulin demanding a conference."

McLennan snorted. "I am shocked, shocked I tell you, by this unexpected plot development. Can you tell me, lassie, from whence they have hailed us?"

Chivers looked to Hardy for guidance and Lucinda shrugged and nodded. Whatever McLennan was doing, he was many moves ahead of her.

"Lord Karna is on the main Habitat, sir. Ciandur. In the governor's compound at Luwu Palace. And Pac Yulin is on the bridge of the Combine ship *Khanjar*."

"Excellent," McLennan said.

"I already knew that, of course," Hero said quietly.

McLennan nodded at Lucinda.

"With your permission, ma'am?"

There was a twinkle to McLennan's eye that she did not much like. But having no idea where he was going with this, Lucinda simply had to trust to his judgment.

"Let them in," she said with a sigh.

Two new projections expanded in front of her. The Javan lord and the Combine prince.

Karna spoke immediately, blurting out his words as though he had been bottling them up all his life.

"You are here to defend this volume against the enemy," he said, "not to interfere in the internal affairs of the Empire."

Before Lucinda could object, McLennan barked out his reply with such ferocity that everyone flinched in shock.

"There is no Empire, you puffed-up fucking lavatory attendant. It lies in ruins and you, sir, are picking over the disintegrating carcass."

Lucinda gaped at McLennan as he suddenly advanced on the dataspheres containing the Javans and the Combine executive, jabbing one long, bony finger at Lord Karna. He kept talking, or rather snarling, as he bore down on them.

"I know exactly what you've been up to, m'lord, and if there is anyone yet living at Medang Palace your treacherous engram will spend a thousand fucking years in excruciating agony under the close ministrations of the emperor's tormentor general."

The holographic connection was good enough for Lucinda to see the color drain out of Lord Karna's face. He was shaking visibly as he turned for support to Deputy Prince Pac Yulin, who stepped away from Karna's holographic projection as though he was contagious.

"And as for you, my dear deputy prince," McLennan growled. "Dinnae think yourself too cunning to be brought down by the incompetent scheming of your co-conspirator there. You may consider yourself the heir apparent to the Yulin-Irrawaddy Combine, but it's nae so fuckin' apparent to me. My old friend here"—McLennan jerked a thumb at Hero—"has been gobbling up vast quantities of signals intelligence since we arrived in this volume, all the better to indict you for high crimes and misdemeanors against both the Domination of the Combine and the authority of Congress on Earth."

Unlike Karna, Deputy Prince Pac Yulin was not so easily cowed.

He narrowed his eyes and spoke through clenched teeth.

"I do not know what you are alleging, Admiral, but I might remind you that you are overmatched. As you correctly pointed out not one minute ago, there may well be no more Empire, and by implication, no more Old Earth. And your little Armadalen gunboat is no match for a fully operational Warlugger and two Combine battleraiders."

Lucinda's temper flared at that, but before she could speak Hero had disappeared from the bridge with an audible pop as the air rushed in to the fill the space he had occupied. Within half a second the Intellect was back.

With Karna and Pac Yulin.

The holospheres that had contained both men were empty, save for the background vision of the Volume lord's compound on Ciandur, and a chaotic scene of sudden confusion and panic on the bridge of the battle cruiser *Khanjar*.

A few of Lucinda's bridge officers were likewise taken aback by the sudden appearance of two intruders. But nobody quite so much as the men themselves. Both looked around; Karna in fear and shock, and Pac Yulin with a slightly cooler, more calculating eye. His gaze fell upon a pair of Armadalen marines in light armor, guarding the main entrance to the bridge. They had already drawn weapons and leveled them at the new arrivals. When Pac Yulin saw them, he seemed to resign himself to whatever was about to happen.

McLennan marched on them for real this time, with Hero at his shoulder. He spoke in a low voice that carried clearly to everyone.

"I care not one wet jobbie for your attempt to usurp the Crown of Java," he said, jabbing a finger at Volume Lord Karna, before turning on the deputy executive prince, "or for your scheme to take over the remnants of the Combine and the whole of the Montanblanc ul Haq Corporation, for good measure. But I care truly, madly, and deeply about sedition and treason as it relates to Old Earth, and you gentlemen have committed an elegant sufficiency of both, starting with your unprovoked attack on the Terran destroyer *The Limits of Vengeance* and, parenthetically, your undeclared act of war against the Commonwealth of Armadale encompassed by the destruction of the recon'vette HMAS *Yarra*, while she was engaged in a peaceful ship-to-ship replenishment operation and communications with the aforementioned *Vengeance*."

Silence.

Stillness.

Shock.

Broken finally by Volume Lord Karna spluttering, "But these are outrageous allegations!"

"Why yes, yes they are," McLennan agreed with arctic cheer. "But I do have the evidence to prove them."

A collective growl started to rise from the throats of the Armadalen bridge crew, smothered only by Lucinda's bark of "Attend to your stations."

McLennan raised one eyebrow.

"Herodotus, if you would?"

The Intellect loomed with menace from behind the admiral.

"We put it to you, gentlemen, that upon emerging from system-wide lockdown to ride out a super flare of the local star, you became aware of the attack by the Human Republic and the widespread collapse of organized authority throughout the Greater Volume. We further allege that you conspired to exploit the situation for your own ends and—"

"Lies," snarled Juono Karna. "Typical Armadalen lies."

Hero muted him with an auditory field effect and carried on with his indictment.

"We further allege," he repeated, "that you conspired to exploit this for purely personal gain and to this end when the Armadalen ship *Yarra* appeared in your system to seek out the Terran vessel *The Limits of Vengeance*, and to make common cause against the Sturm, you, Deputy Executive Prince Pac Yulin, fired on both ships, destroying the *Yarra*, and incapacitating the *Vengeance*. The Terran ship was boarded, secured, and clamped within a drone corral, its personnel downloaded and forced into sequestration on Lermontov."

Karna was raging, silently, impotently, inside Hero's auditory field effect.

Those Armadalen crew members without immediate responsibilities were glaring at both intruders. Lucinda Hardy stared
at Commodore Pac Yulin as though deciding where exactly on
his body she would drive in the point of her fusion blade.

Pac Yulin smiled.

"And yet you did not bring us here to arrest us, did you,
Admiral McLennan?"

"No. I did not," Mac agreed.

"Wait, what?" Lucinda said, finally shaken out of her trance.

"Commander," Lieutenant Fein called out. "The Warlugger
and the two cruisers have lit us up."

"Sound to general quarters," Lucinda ordered. "Ready
weapons and countermeasures."

The bridge crew surged into action as the klaxon blared and
the ambient lighting shifted from soft white to battle red. Rather
than bristle at the interruption, McLennan suggested to Lucinda that she lower her defenses.

"Save for those field effects which are currently denying all
attempts to retrieve our reluctant guests."

"What?" Lucinda went, now completely baffled.

"I doubt these fine fellows are any more excited by the prospect of an utterly pointless and all too permanent death than we
are."

"Ha!" Lord Karna shot back, released from Hero's imposed
silence. "The Sturm's malware never made it in here. You can't
kill us. We have lifestream backup."

McLennan's smile was wolfish and hungry.

"Perhaps so, m'lord. But the enemy will presently be upon
us, and they will not afford you the courtesy of relife at your
leisure. If you die on this ship with us, it will be forever."

Lucinda suddenly understood.

"Mister Fein," she called out. "Prepare to drop shields and
take all weapons offline."

"Aye, ma'am," the tactical officer replied.

Karna looked horrified.

"Of course, you could just order your ships to stand down," McLennan suggested.

"*Khanjar! Jezail!*" Pac Yulin shouted. "Secure from battle stations. You, boy!" he snapped at the hologram of Sub-Commandant Suprarto. "You, too."

Suprarto looked helplessly to Lord Karna, his superior.

"Yes, yes, *Makassar*, too!" the Volume lord added in a hurry.

"Mister Fein?" Lucinda said.

Mercado Fein took a moment to check and confirm his holo-displays.

"They've shut down their targeting arrays and weapons systems, ma'am."

"I could have told you that, of course," Hero pouted.

"Of course you could," Lucinda said acidly. "Admiral?"

McLennan performed a small bow.

"I thank you for your indulgence, Commander."

He turned back to Pac Yulin and Karna.

"Gentlemen, the Sturm are less than an hour away. Based on the probes they sent, we calculate they will invest this system with an augmented battle group. I have a plan to engage them, but that plan has a much greater chance of success if I can use those combat-capable vessels you have impounded off Lermontov Station."

"We have done no such thing," Karna shot back, still trying to deny what he had done. "The station cartel clamped those vessels when they refused to pay the due commissions and—"

"Come now, Volume Lord," McLennan said with a smile. "You cannae seriously expect me to believe that a gang of crooked fucking grifters and greedy mercantile jobsworths told a captain of the TDF his docking fee was short, and he volunteered to work it off in the kitchens of some greasy spoon on the Hab? The fact is, I am here and the TDF is here with me. We have penetrated the quantum defenses of Lermontov Station and taken all we need to secure convictions and sentences of deletion against both of you. And that is based only on the material we have from the cartel. It will be a matter of no great moment for my colleague here"—he waved a hand at Herodotus—"to do the same to your deepest, most encrypted data on Ciandur and those two battleraiders. He is an Armada-level Intellect of the Terran Defense Force, you know. Resistance would be futile, to borrow from the classics."

Karna opened his mouth to reply, but Pac Yulin shushed him.

"Do not bother, my lord. We are past pretending. We are, I believe, at the stage of negotiations?"

He inclined his head slightly toward McLennan.

"We are, indeed, Mister Deputy Executive Prince," the admiral confirmed. "I want those ships and their crews released to my command. I will not take up the question of why or even how they were impounded, and you need not concern yourselves with answering to them for whatever villainy was afoot here. They will answer to me, and once we have seen off this next attempt upon us, we shall fold away, far away, to gather more forces and organize resistance."

"And what of us?" Pac Yulin asked.

"I'm sure you had some cunning plan to look after yourselves. Good luck with that, unless you would care to actually do your fucking duty and join us."

Lord Karna bristled, but Pac Yulin merely narrowed his eyes.

"How long until the enemy arrives?"

Lucinda, who had been watching on, all but stunned, shook her head.

"Lieutenant Fein?"

But it was Hero who answered.

"Some would say the enemy is already here, but I estimate the advance units will arrive at the edge of the system in forty-eight minutes."

Pac Yulin ignored the small barb nestled within Hero's answer.

"I am afraid there will not be time to release the crews," he said. "They were extracted and stored off-site. For security purposes, you understand."

"Jesus fucking Christ," Lucinda muttered. "This is treason. We should be arresting them, not defending them."

"Needs must when the devil folds, Commander," McLennan warned. "So, gentlemen, unless you would prefer to see this battle out from the brig here on *Defiant*, you will turn over temporary command of all naval assets in-system to myself as the lawful commander of Earth's allied forces. We will meet the enemy, defeat him, and then we will be on our way with those forces you have detained and any other such vessels and individuals who would care to accompany us. You, on the other hand, will do as you damned well please, I imagine."

The two men exchanged a glance.

"That's it?" Lord Karna asked. "No trials? No courts-martial?"

"We would not die in that man's company, that fears his fellowship to die with us," McLennan said icily.

Lucinda stepped forward and took him by the arm. A modest, but for her extraordinary, act of insubordination. One she could not help.

"Karna was supposed to answer to war crimes charges on Earth," she hissed. "Armadale had already appealed Java's denial of extradition. And now this. He and Yulin fired on the *Yarra*. There were dozens of men and women on that ship. All dead. All of them. It's an act of war."

"Aye, but a small one, I'm afraid," McLennan said sadly. "And we have a larger war to win first."

"It is agreed, then," Pac Yulin declared. "We will combine forces to defeat the Sturm. And you will leave."

"It is agreed," McLennan confirmed.

"And the Princess Alessia will stay with us," the Combine prince added.

McLennan leaned forward until his nose was almost touching Pac Yulin's. He spoke in a low growl.

"The Princess Alessia is the head of her House, and a senator of Earth. The only senator of Earth still capable of providing lawful leadership to the war effort. She will come with us, and the question of your betrothal and merger will be resolved at the appropriate time."

"And when will that be?"

"Never," McLennan said, "you treacherous fucking slaver."

The two men stood facing off, their eyes burning into each other.

It was Pac Yulin who finally looked away.

"We shall see," he muttered.

"Aye," McLennan agreed. "Perhaps we shall one day, Mister Deputy Executive Prince. We shall see about a lot of things. One day. But for now, if we are agreed on our temporary convenience, I will have Herodotus transfer battle plans to your ships. You will submit to my authority, and we will make ready to receive the enemy."

CHAPTER

TWENTY-SIX

Booker's voice filled the bridge of the *Ariane*, where everybody watched Mister Banks pretend to fuck up a simple approach to Lermontov Station.

The ghost of a smile played across the pilot's usually sanguine features as he flicked at this icon or that symbol in the holographic projection of his helm controls, immediately offering apologies to the station's traffic controllers and blaming damage to his maneuvering FX generators.

"Hey, Cap'n, we got incoming from *Defiant*," Booker said. "Commander Hardy advises against docking on Lermontov."

Sephina said nothing as another ship folded away from the freeport. That made more than thirty in the last quarter hour. Shit was getting real and motherfuckers were freaking out. Everyone who could was making for the exits.

"Captain?" Booker said.

"Yeah, I heard you, Book. I'm just thinking is all."

She rested her chin in her hands and watched the holo of all the traffic around Lermontov. Everyone else on the bridge, except for Mister Banks, watched her.

"The harbormaster wants to know why we haven't commenced final approach, Skipper," Banks said.

"Okay. We're going in," she announced.

Sergeant Cox arced up.

"What the fuck are you doing? Booker just told you that *Defiant* warned us off. You're going to get clamped and they're going to take the princess."

Seph shook her head.

"Have you looked out the window, Cox? I mean, if we had one. This place is falling apart. The Nazis from outer space are about half an hour away and if they get through Luce they'll be here, cracking heads open looking for delicious wetware about ten minutes after that."

"Yeah," Cox said in disbelief. "So why the fuck are we still here? You should be plotting long-range folds right now."

"We're still here because there is no better time to strike a bargain than when the seller is distressed as fuck."

Dahl came up beside him.

"What?" she said.

Seph lifted her eyes to the wooden beams above.

"My boy Booker needs a new rig. I know a guy here. Total mad scientist when it comes to pimping out a rig. We can dock, pay our bribes, grab a sweet ride for the Book, and we'll still have time to get back here and fold the fuck away if everything goes pear-shaped on the far side."

Cox stared at her. "Are you fucking serious?"

Booker spoke up, too.

"Er, you know, Captain, that's not a bad question. I really don't need a new rig that much. I'm fine here in the substrate."

Sephina spoke to the ceiling.

"Yeah, but you'll be a helluva lot more use to me kicking ass in a combat-rated bio-rig than you are spooking around behind the walls. We're going in. Banks, let the harbormaster know we'll take our usual berth if it's available. He'll know what to do. And get ahold of Kumon Xi's chop shop. Let 'em know we want a rig, SF capable. We'll pay in credit or kind."

"Yes, ma'am," the pilot said. He set to his tasks with focus and efficiency, ignoring the protests of the Armadalens.

"Coto," Sephina said. "You're coming with me. We'll need dusters and weapons. Lots of weapons, just in case."

"I like weapons," Jaddi Coto said, hastening off toward the armory.

"Baroness Sephina?"

It was Alessia.

Seph had almost forgotten about her in the rush to pull off this one last score. She wasn't just spanking the monkey about Booker. She'd lost Ariane and Falun Kot and come this close to losing Coto, as well. She didn't need the former soldier playing at ship's Intellect. The operating system from the old *Regret* was plenty smart enough already. What she needed most in all the worlds was another pair of hands on deck. Or failing that, time wound back, and the world remade, with her friends and crew and her one true love returned to her and . . .

"Sephina?"

"Oh, yeah. Sorry, kid. What's up?"

Alessia stood before her, looking deeply troubled.

"Uhm, is this such a good idea?"

Seph snorted. "No. It's a terrible idea, but it's the best one I got right now."

Alessia's frown only deepened.

Sephina waved her forward.

"Come 'ere."

Alessia came and stood next to the captain's chair. She turned around when Sephina gestured at the holo-display, which showed the station at the center of an increasingly disorganized ring of spacecraft. Two more ships winked away.

"Alessia, that station down there is a festering cesspit full of douchelords and supervillains. I know this, having been quite the villainess myself in the past. Lermontov exists for one purpose and one purpose only. To make a profit by any means possible. In a few minutes a bunch of sketchy fucking customs agents are gonna roll on board, see all the high-end pharma and top-shelf heirloom booze we got with us and they are gonna gouge me like a motherfucker, even though the barbarians are at the gate and the Sturm will probably turn most of them into biomass by the end of the day."

Alessia focused in on every word. Seph had never had such a conscientious pupil or apprentice, or whatever the hell she was. It was strangely satisfying.

"Grifters gonna grift, kid. It's all they know. And we're gonna let 'em gouge us because we've read the market better. There is no value in Javan rupiah or Combine credits or Federation rubles right now. For me, for us"—she made a small circle with her finger—"the most valuable product on that whole fuckin' station is a black market bioengineered combat rig made by a dude I used to know a long time ago in a Habitat far, far away."

"On Coriolis?" Alessia asked.

"Gold star. Yeah. Luce knew him, too, for what that's worth. Not much, to be honest, if you're Kumon. She'd probably try and arrest him for being so cool."

"Docking in three minutes," Mister Banks said.

Dahl came up next to Alessia.

"You should strap into a crash couch," she said. "In case this gets rough."

"Excuse me," Banks objected. "I'm right here."

"She doesn't need to," Seph assured the best-looking of the three marines. "Banks is a way better stickman than anybody you got on *Defiant*. Believe it."

"It's procedure," Aronson put in.

Seph rolled her eyes.

"Booker," she called out, "can you give Alessia a lift?"

The princess squealed with delight as Booker enfolded her in a gentle micro-g wave and lifted her clear of the deck plating and any kinetic consequences of a rough landing.

"She'll be fine," Sephina said, before grinning at Dahl. "But feel free to strap yourself in somewhere. Could be kind of sexy."

She winked and Dahl blushed, but Seph could tell it was just because she was pissed off.

No fun to be had there.

"Either way, kid," she said, returning to Alessia, "we have to dock or let Customs and Excise fold some goons out here. There's no avoiding the shakedown. It's already started. The harbormaster here, a guy called Nero, is a filthy fucking crook I've dealt with before. Plenty of times. He's already worked out his cut and he's set aside a quiet berth for us to do business. This way, I got some control over how it plays out, and we get something we need out of the grift."

"What should I do?" Alessia asked with such earnest sincerity that Sephina felt herself a little moved. "I don't suppose I can help get Booker a new rig, but I don't want to mess things up."

"We're gonna stash you away while the revenue gimps got their hands out," Seph replied. "Just to be safe. Booker will find a spot. That right, Book?"

"Way ahead of you, Captain. This ship has many, many hidden compartments. It's almost as though the previous owners may not have been entirely legitimate businesspeople."

"Yeah, almost," Sephina deadpanned. "Where's the nearest hidey-hole?"

"The oak panel bulkhead behind the secondary comm station covers a hidden enclosure. There's a stasis crate of French truffles in there. Contraband for sure. It's small but so is the princess."

"Okay, kid, we got your hiding spot."

"That's it?" Cox said. "You're going to hide her behind a sliding panel?"

"They're not looking for her," Seph explained with exaggerated patience. "They'll pore over our cargo manifest and take the main storage bays apart if they think we're holding out. But they're looking for a payday, not a runaway. We're just gonna pay them. Do our business and get the fuck gone."

"Docking in one minute," Banks said. "I have a message from Kumon Xi, Captain. He's got a rig for us. But he wants to negotiate."

"Price?"

"Passage. He wants off the Hab."

"But of course," Sephina said and smiled.

She playfully punched Alessia on the shoulder.

"You see, kid. It's just business. Everything is business."

Five minutes later, everything turned to shit.

The hidden compartment was exciting for a bit less than one minute. Then it was sort of cramped. Then it was smelly. Then it was kind of terrifying.

The excitement was real.

It wasn't like Alessia had never had an adventure.

Escaping the Sturm on Montrachet, even being captured then rescued from Skygarth by Sephina and Commander Hardy, were both awesomely adventurous. But they also sucked like hard vacuum. People got hurt. Even killed for real.

Hiding out in the secret compartment on the Russian gangsters' superyacht was the sort of adventure Alessia could legit enjoy. Kind of exciting, but not completely terrible.

At least not until she'd been squeezed into the confined space long enough to understand that it was going to get very uncomfortable if she had to stay for more than a few minutes—and after maybe two minutes she realized that the stasis crate in which the Russians had hidden their contraband French truffles had malfunctioned and her cramped and stifling hiding place didn't just smell a little bit like the manure Mister Dunning used to spread on the gardens at Skygarth; it was starting to reek like an heirloom turd which had been lovingly transported hundreds of light-years from Old Earth just so she could smell it in all of its shitty organic glory.

Then the Yakuza turned up.

She saw it all very clearly. Booker did something to the molecular structure of the wood paneling so that she could see out, but nobody could see in.

Mister Banks had docked the ship and the customs officials had come on board to steal all of the best cargo and collect a completely separate bribe for letting Sephina do her business with Kumon Xi without having to fill in a lot of forms and answer all sorts of inconvenient questions. And once Sephina had transferred the money from someone called the Deuce, or maybe the Juice, Alessia wasn't sure, a whole bunch of other guys suddenly appeared on the bridge and they had guns, lots of guns, and they were shouting in some Old Earth language that she thought might have been Japanese or Joseon. For a couple of seconds there, Alessia was convinced that everybody was going to start shooting and she felt an almost overwhelming but utterly foolish urge to suddenly leap out of her hiding place and demand that they all settle down. Because she was Princess Alessia, head of House Montanblanc and a senator of Earth.

"Don't move and don't make any noise," Booker said. "They're *gunsotsu*. Yakuza soldiers."

His voice seemed to be coming from inside her head, rather than the walls like normal.

Alessia sat perfectly still, breathing through her mouth, because of the truffle stink.

Outside on the bridge everybody was shouting and waving their arms. Cox and Dahl and Aronson put themselves between Alessia and the Yakuza, blocking her view of what was happening.

Lots of people going off, mostly.

She wanted to cry out, "No, no, no," over and over again when a Yakuza guy suddenly shot Dahl and Cox and handsome young Kanon, who she rather liked looking at, but Booker was back inside her head. His voice was quiet and reassuring.

"Be still, be cool, Alessia. They're not dead. The Yamaguchis came for Captain L'trel and her crew. Nobody else. They are professionals. They don't make trouble for themselves by dropping bodies without good reason. Just let it be. We will settle this as soon as we can."

She wanted to yell at him that there was no time, that the Sturm would be here soon. This was stupid. It was madness.

But there was nothing she could do.

Sephina and Coto and Mister Banks all put their hands up in the air and the Yakuza, or the Yamawhatsis or whoever the hell they were, marched them off the bridge and presumably into captivity.

A customs agent did something at Mister Banks's control station. The light dimmed. They left. The three marines lay on the deck plating.

"Just wait," Booker said somewhere inside her head.

She waited for a minute. Then another.

Her neck was cramping, and she had to pee. The poop stench of the truffles made her gag.

"They're gone," Booker said at last. "We don't have long."

Booker dematerialized the oak paneling that covered Alessia's hiding spot, and she crawled out, hurrying over to the Arma-dalens. Booker did not try to stop her, even though he knew there wasn't much she could do for them. The gummy soldiers had hit them with neural disrupters. They'd be down for hours, untreated. At least one hour in a regen tank.

The ship was empty, the revenue agents and Yakuza having left together. The last customs official placed a seal on the main hatch, locking down the *Ariane*. Booker programmed a spyder app to follow Captain L'trel and the others through the station, before gently lifting Alessia away from Dahl with a micro-g wave.

"Alessia," he said. "We do not have long. They don't know about either of us being here."

"We need to get them back," she said. Booker wasn't en-tirely sure whether she meant the Armadalens or the crew.

He had no parenting or early adolescent management scripts

stored in his deep lacuna. He would have to go with the experience of leading newbies on their first mission.

"We do and we will," Booker said.

Make everything clear, he told himself. Give her a simple goal.

"But how?" Alessia begged.

He could detect fear and anxiety in her voice.

"I can't get them up," she went on. "Are they dead, Booker? For real?"

"No," he explained again. "The Yamaguchi-gumi had no business with them. They neutralized them. That's all. They will be fine . . . if we can get the others back here in time."

A lot of people, a lot of soldiers, would have lost it at that. The odds were piled up against them. "Getting back here in time" meant getting to Kumon Xi, rigging up, then making a hostile extraction from a Yakuza stronghold, all before the Sturm overwhelmed the defenders on the far side of Natuna. But the Montanblanc heir surprised him. Alessia took a breath, closed her eyes, and breathed out again.

"Tell me what I have to do," she said.

Booker used micro-g fields to lift the downed marines into something he called a recovery position. He asked Alessia to check that their breathing was unobstructed. That was fucking gross, especially with Cox. She had to stick her fingers into their mouths and make sure they hadn't swallowed their tongues or anything.

"They will recover," Booker told her when she was done. "A lot quicker if we can get them into regen, but we don't have time for that. I'll detail a couple of medicare bots onto it while we're gone."

"What next?" Alessia asked. She stood over the three wiped-out marines, her brow deeply furrowed with concern. But the fear that had threatened to carry her away was now replaced by a stern focus on what needed to be done.

This kid had some skills.

"I've got a stalker app following them through the station," Booker explained. "It's black script from the TDF. It won't lose them, and Habitat Security won't detect it. It's way outta their league. I'm pretty sure I know where they're going anyway. The gummies got a shopfront on the B plate of the next compartment over. But I'll leave the script to run anyway. Just to be sure."

"Good," Alessia said. "So, we're going to get them back?" Her voice was breathy, and she swallowed hard. He could tell from the kid's biometrics that she was forcing herself to remain calm.

"No. I'm gonna get them back," Booker clarified. "But I need you to get me to Kumon Xi. Turns out the captain was right. I'm of more use to her in a rig than I am just spooking around in the substrate."

He sent Alessia to fetch an eX-Box to carry his engram to the chop shop, and called up a couple medbots to look after the Armadalens. He jacked into Habnet and scoped out three alternative routes to Kumon Xi's, picking the one he thought best for Alessia. Then he locked down the ship way more securely than the revenuers had. A fold-capable yacht full of luxury contraband would attract a lot of attention as the situation grew desperate, even if the harbormaster seemed to have grabbed it up for himself.

"This do?" Alessia asked when she returned a few minutes later.

She'd found the external storage device.

"That's it," Booker said. "Just set it down and give me a second."

"What about Dahl and Kanon and Sergeant Cox?" Alessia asked.

"I've genome-locked the hatches and flight controls with DNA samples for you guys, and a onetime engram-code for me. We can all get back in, but once we leave, nobody else will be able to come aboard. The bots will look after those guys. Drop them into regen and get them back on their feet a lot quicker. But probably not fast enough for us. We gotta do this on our own. You good, Senator?"

Alessia took in a sharp breath and nodded.

"I'm good, Troop. Let's roll."

CHAPTER

TWENTY-SEVEN

The headset was too big. Like really huge, and ancient. It had been Coto's, Booker told her. Without a neural net, the giant hybrid could not take a data feed direct to the cortex. Alessia and Coto were alike in that way, at least for now. And probably forever, she supposed. It was a tradition of House Montanblanc that no heir of the blood would take an implant before adulthood. It was why she'd had so many tutors. And why she'd survived the Sturm's malware.

And why she was wrestling with Coto's gigantic fucking data helmet as she stood at the last of the ship's air locks.

"Booker, I can barely hold this, let alone keep it on my head," she complained.

He didn't reply.

"Booker!"

Alessia heard a tinny, distant voice and realized his audio was coming through the helmet she would never be able to use.

"Gah!"

In frustration she threw the thing aside and stomped her feet at the top of the ramp. Her boots clanged on the nonslip deck plating as the helmet crashed into a stack of empty stasis crates. They were supposed to leave through one of the rear hatches that Booker assessed as having the least coverage from the Hab-Sec surveillance cams. The space was cramped and busy with all manner of cargo and equipment that meant nothing to Alessia. It looked like the sort of stuff that people who worked with their hands might use.

Servants, she had once called them.

This was too much. It was all too much. She had barely traveled beyond Port au Pallice, and whenever she had left the estate at Skygarth, it had been with a company of the Royal Guard to escort her. How the hell was she supposed to find her way through a spaceport that was losing its shit as the Sturm closed in, to find some shady fucking bioengineer and convince him to hand over a military-grade rig?

Well? How?

The tinny little voice squawked again.

With help, she supposed.

Alessia made her best effort to put aside her considerable fears and doubts. She recovered the helmet, turned it over, and took a few seconds to examine the inner mesh.

"Just . . . just give me a second, Booker," she called out. "I need to make this work."

His voice fell silent.

When she calmed down and really looked at the thing, she could see that most of the helmet's bulk was in the armored shell. Webbing, tacky with old sweat and skin flakes—*Eew!*—clipped into and out of the shell at four hard points. She gave the mesh an experimental tug. It didn't come away, but it felt like it should, so she pulled a little harder. One of the connection studs snapped open. She pulled again and the webbing came free. There was still a heap of it, and it was fucking gross, but the ear pads and a primitive mic had come out with it. Alessia quickly wrapped the mesh around her head and tied it off. She very much wanted to see what she looked like, but there were no mirrors or vanity holos in the transit bay.

"Booker? Can you hear me?"

"I'm here," he said. "We good? I don't have eyes anymore."

"We're good. Sorry. I couldn't hear you and I couldn't make Coto's helmet work. But I think I got it now. What do I do next?"

"Now we leave the ship," he said. "I can't stream anything in real time, but the eX-Box knows where it is, and I've got maps of the station. I'll guide you. I already knocked out the cam coverage on this part of the dock. You can leave the ship without being spotted. Once you're off the wharf and out on the concourse, though, you will turn up on HabSec's surveillance net. But I'm gonna bet they got bigger problems. And nobody's looking for you."

Alessia stared at the hatch, wondering what she would find on the other side.

"What's up?" Booker asked after a moment.

"It's just, I think I might look weird with the inside of Coto's helmet tied around my head."

Booker's snort turned into a laugh.

"Yeah, nah. That's not gonna be a problem here, kid," he said.

And it wasn't.

She had expected to emerge onto a quiet, deserted wharf. Instead the hatch opened onto a mad sonic rush and the dizzying spectacle of chaos and multitudes. Before Alessia could retreat back inside, a micro-g wave carried her down to the deck plates as part of an automated disembarkation process and she was swept up in the crowds.

Great roiling streams of humanity in all its divergent forms thronged up and down the axis of Lermontov Station.

A habitat. A real habitat!

She craned her head back and almost staggered at the impossible sight of a whole world climbing away into engineered skies, curving around in a great arc, and finally closing the circle behind her, beneath her, all around . . .

She did stagger then.

"Alessia, are you okay?" Booker asked. "My proprioceptors detected a fall."

She leaned up against a big plasteel shipping container, and shook her head, trying to clear it of the sudden disorientation.

"I'm okay. I just got confused is all," she admitted. "I've never been on a Hab like this."

"Don't look up," Booker cautioned.

"Too late."

"Okay. Then don't do that again. If you've only ever been dirtside, it'll mess your head up."

"Yeah, I get that," Alessia said.

She was almost shouting over the roar of the crowds. Everyone seemed to be yelling at everybody else. And the smell of them!

It was about a thousand times worse than the Port au Pallice fish markets when the trawlers came in.

Everything about Lermontov that she could see was bigger and worse on a vast scale. It was frightening just to stand under the fuselage of the *Ariane* and contemplate stepping out into the dark flood of humanity.

A harsh amplified voice crackled over the uproar.

"You! Hey, you, get out of there. That's a restricted area!"

Alessia jumped as she realized the voice was shouting at her.

Two uniformed men bristling with weapons pointed at her started to move through the crowd.

She ducked under the bright yellow guardrail and moved away from the ship. They lost interest.

"Booker, where do I go?" Alessia pleaded. "I'm already lost."

His voice in her ears was steady and reassuring.

"You're not lost, Alessia. You're exactly where you need to be. I can follow you on the maps I took from Habnet. If you're facing away from the ship, look to your left."

She did.

The view was unsettling, mind-bending.

The leviathan cylinder of Lermontov Station stretched off to a dark, blurry vanishing point, many kilometers away. A weird psychological spasm threatened to undo her as she stared into the closed loop of the curvilinear world, and she squeezed her eyes shut for a second.

Alessia knew, intellectually, that the vast arching panorama of buildings and fab plants and plasteel tracery on the far side of the hull was held in place by a combination of spin grav and field effect generators. If she'd had time, and a desk, and the space to think about it she could even sit down and write out the equations which explained the physics of how it worked.

She'd had the best tutors in the Greater Volume, after all. She had learned her lessons the old-fashioned way.

But none of it prepared her for the reality of Lermontov. Alessia found that no matter how brave she tried to be, the dark magic of an upside-down world and the heavy, seething crush of the crowds within it still frightened her. People yelled. They shouted at her, some of them even pointing. Their faces were grotesque and sometimes cruel. The roar of shouting and taunts, the jeering, snarling confusion of voices, the yells and even occasional screams, were almost enough to rob her of all will.

But Sephina was out here in this, somewhere. And Coto and Mister Banks, and they were her only way off this station. More important, they were her friends. Something bad had happened to them and she had to help.

They would be counting on Booker and her to rescue them.

"Where do I go?" Alessia shouted, raising her voice over the noise of the mob.

"You just start down the concourse. It's not far away," Booker promised. "The next frame over. I sent a message to Xi before I downloaded. He's waiting. But I can't say for how long. We're his best bet to get off this Hab."

"Okay," Alessia said, steeling herself for the challenge.

It was just a short walk.

Along a concourse no less. Just like the boardwalk on the waterfront at Port au Pallice. She did not have the Royal Guard with her, but she had Booker to tell her the way, and the example of Seph and Lucinda to guide her through any fear of the unknown. No way would they have wimped out of something like this.

Alessia pulled Lucinda's leather jacket a little tighter around her shoulders. She could feel the small dense block of the external storage unit pressing into her chest. She pressed the ear cup closer to her head.

"Right," she told Booker. "I'm moving."

Buffeted by the crowd, almost knocked off her feet so many times she lost count, Princess Alessia Szu Suri sur Montanblanc ul Haq set her course for glory, joining the end of a long line of pioneering Montanblanc women who had gone before her.

"You're doing good, Al," Booker assured her, and his familiar voice was a great comfort in the churning, caterwauling crush of the throng. She liked that he called her Al. That seemed to help.

It was hard, though, navigating the pedestrian pathways along the deck plating. In this part of the Hab—and who knew, perhaps everywhere—makeshift extensions to the battered, tumbledown buildings seemed to reach far out into the streets, as though trying to consume them with slabs of carbon sheeting and syncrete And what little space there was left for people and bots to move past one another was often completely taken over by the wares spilling out of shopfronts and warehouses, or the great teetering piles of goods and products for sale from hull traders who seemed to have nowhere else to go. They often clustered together by type, so that for five or even ten minutes she might have to fight her way through mountains of machine parts for hover carts, or great plasteel water tanks, or strange and disturbing wet markets for unknowable food, most of it still alive and some of it slaughtered on the plating in front of her.

She grimaced as she stepped through blood trails and offal

along a stretch of fishmongers. At least she knew what they were, having been to the market back on Montrachet. But the people here were different from her family's subjects. They looked haggard and thin and, the more she looked at them, desperate and fearful. But not because of the approaching enemy.

"Booker," Alessia whispered, and for a wonder he heard her. Coto's antique headset wasn't such a piece of crap, after all.

"Yes, Alessia?"

"Why are they so frightened? The Sturm don't really care about poor people, do they?"

She heard him grunt, or maybe even snort with laughter.

"No," he said, as she picked her way around a mountain of cooking pots. She tripped on an unseen gutter and almost fell into the giant display. Booker carried on, regardless.

"Most of these people are what the Sturm call true humans. Too poor for gene-splicing or implants. Won't matter if a rail gun opens up the hull, of course, but if they just landed troops, sure, anybody who wasn't killed in the fighting and wasn't hooked up with neural mesh or the wrong DNA would probably be fine."

Alessia didn't understand.

She passed a small alleyway in which a whole family seemed to be living. She couldn't even count the number of children in there, but they all looked filthy and starving. Alessia almost stopped, feeling that she couldn't just walk past such obvious suffering, but the press of the crowd carried her on.

"Then why are they like this?" she asked. "Why are there so many sad people here? Doesn't the cartel or the Javan Empire have to look after them? Aren't there laws from Earth and stuff?"

"There are laws about a lot of things back on Earth, Alessia," Booker said. "And on Montrachet and places like Cupertino or Armadale, too. But the law's not what's written on a piece of paper on Earth, or in substrate at the ass end of the Volume. The law is what the guy with the biggest fucking gun says it is. That's why some laws, like the universal basic welfare, get smashed flat by shit which isn't even law. Stuff like the doctrine of sovereignty and self-determination."

Alessia knew what that was. Her tutors had drilled into her the prime importance of "sovereignty and self-determination" to the past, present, and future of House Montanblanc.

"But . . . but that doesn't stop us feeding our . . . people," she said.

She had almost called them subjects.

Booker chuckled quietly in her ear as she skirted a cluster of outdoor kitchens selling mystery meat and strange chargrilled plants which she had never seen before.

"It doesn't stop your House, no," Booker said. "It doesn't stop anybody doing anything. But it also means that other Houses and corporations get to do as they please. They can turn their own people into property. They can say someone like me or Mister Banks isn't even a person to begin with. It's their sovereignty and self-determination, not mine, and not the poor bastards you can see around you."

Alessia felt as though Booker was turning her head inside out, just by whispering in her ear.

She wanted to stop and think about what he had said, and what it meant, but there was no time. It was taking much longer to get to Kumon Xi than she'd imagined. Lermontov Station was way more crowded and wilder than she could ever have thought. And there was a frantic, restive feeling seeping up from the deck plating.

Sirens blared and armored vehicles hummed overhead.

She saw no signs of any authorities like guardsmen or gendarmes such as she would have seen everywhere on Montrachet. Here and there she saw traders shutting up shop and barring hatches. In just the short amount of time she had been on the hull, the energy of the crowds had shifted toward the darker, hotter end of the emotional spectrum. Fights broke out. Booker, measuring their progress against some blueprint stored inside the device pressing into her ribs, would direct her this way and that. But sometimes she would demur, moving to avoid what looked like the spark of a much bigger fight, or even the beginnings of a possible riot.

Alessia was utterly lost, and deeply disturbed when Booker's voice all but shouted in her ear.

"Wait up. We're here."

CHAPTER

TWENTY-EIGHT

"Is there a cunning plan?" Coto asked.

"Sure, buddy," Seph said. "A super fucking cunniliscious plan."

"Shut up," a Yakuza *gunsotsu* barked, slamming the butt of his pulse rifle into Coto's spine.

The hybrid was such a massive unit that the heavy blow did a little less than zero chunks of fuck all, but it did give Sephina an excuse to shut up, which was good, because there was no plan. Cunniliscious or otherwise.

She'd been ready for a shakedown from Nero, the harbormaster, and a sketchy motherfucker she'd dealt with plenty through the war. But she wasn't at all prepared for the fucking Yamaguchi-gumi to walk in behind Nero's guys demanding payback for the rip-and-run that'd gone sideways on Eassar.

Sephina knelt on the flagstone floor of the Yakuza *honbu*. Outwardly, a grimy mid-level rent slab at the edge of the port district and spin-wise of the Hab's main cargo handling terminal, the interior had been carefully fashioned as a replica of an

Old Earth home islands temple or some shit. The floors were all stone and wood and straw matting, and there were way too many candles and incense burners going for a place where the walls seemed to be made from rice paper.

Those paper walls wouldn't be much good if the eight or nine heavily armed *gunsotsu* who surrounded them cut loose with all that firepower, either.

Seph knelt awkwardly in the center of a rough circle of Yakuza thugs, her arms bound behind her back. A small pebble on the stone floor dug painfully into her knee. Coto and Banks knelt to either side of her. They seemed to be dealing with this a helluva lot better than her. Probably because they expected their gallant and resourceful captain to get them out of it.

But Seph had nothing.

Hiroto, a local underboss, leaned forward into the candle-light. The dense filigree of deep black photo-flux tattoos on his shaved skull glistened in the mellow light, and she wondered if the Sturm's malware would attack the dermal processing weave in the same way it did neural mesh.

That'd be cool. If he didn't start chomping on her carotid artery.

"You are a creature without honor," Hiroto said. His voice was guttural, rasping.

"Okay, sure, but enough about me," Sephina said then smiled. Winningly, she hoped. "You guys did notice that the genome supremacists are back, right?"

Hiroto ignored the question.

"You lied to us on Habitat Eassar. You stole from the *ninkyō dantai*. This one"—Hiroto grunted at Jaddi Coto—"took the very head off Satomi Goku, simply to have at the *wakagashira-hosa*'s secure enclave."

"No, I didn't," Coto protested. He sounded affronted by the very idea. "Miss Ariane removed the head of the deputy under-boss. I merely dug out the memory cache from the hindbrain."

"Shut up," the senior *gunsotsu* shouted once more. This time he butt-swiped Coto across the back of the head with his rifle, but again it had little to no effect. Gene-threaded rhino-derm hide and a double-thick skull plate were as good as a battle helmet.

"You're going to break that thing if you keep hitting him with it," Banks warned. "And then there'll be tears."

The gummy soldier snarled and aimed a kick at Mister Banks but a shout from Underboss Hiroto froze him.

"Enough! We shall have restitution. Of our losses to the Russian syndicate which employed you and, of course, for the more serious loss of face."

"Seriously, loss of face?" Sephina went. "Dude, the fucking dark space hyper-Nazis are going to be here in an hour and they will put the zap on your butt-ugly head, and you'll be chewing the fucking faces off your homeboys here. Maybe it's just me but I would suggest that getting all baroque and medieval with us for a completely routine business disagreement is contra-fucking-indicated right now."

"We will take your ship and its cargo as recompense for Eassar," Hiroto said, oblivious of any argument to the contrary. "Save for a fifteen percent commission payable to the local authorities for their cooperation in this matter."

"Yo, Hiroto? There aren't going to be any local authorities to collect the finder's fee. You're all going to get turned into biomass. The Sturm are here. This is totally happening. You need to adjust to the new reality, man."

The underboss snorted.

"The *ninkyō dantai* have been adjusting reality to our will for a thousand years. The Yamaguchi-gumi were old when the Sturm were young. They will come. They will go. We will endure. You will not."

He clapped his thick, meaty hands together so loudly that Seph jumped in surprise.

"Take them to the cells," he ordered. "We will deal with them when we have secured the ship and paid our commission to Nero-san. Add the ship to our squadron with the harbor-master's registry and prepare for immediate departure. Tell the

Combine overseer that we have three indentured slaves to sell him."

"Ah, Captain?" Banks asked. "What does he mean? About the indentured slave thingy?"

Coto answered before Sephina had a chance.

"That is a good question, because it was an ambiguous statement, but I think he means us, because we are three in number, and he seems very unhappy with us. You," he said, addressing Hiroto. "Yes, you with the tattoos. Do you mean to sell us to the Combine as slaves?"

Hiroto stared at him, before shaking his head in exasperation.

Coto, ever the literalist, let out a small "uh-huh."

Leaning forward to speak to Banks around Seph, he said, "He shook his head. I may have been wrong about his plans. We will see. I was not gene-coded for nuance."

The bioengineering workshop was easily missed. If Alessia hadn't been looking for it, and Booker's eX-Box hadn't had access to their location data, they might've hurried right past. Tucked in between a Hot Wok and a Yulinese debt broker, Kumon Xi did his business behind a heavy gate that secured a narrow passageway between the neighboring buildings.

"Can you see this?" Alessia asked, trying and failing to keep the nerves from her voice. She had never in all her life seen such an untrustworthy-looking retailer. The alley was poorly lit by peeling strips of colored biolume and crowded to the point of impassability with heaped-up garbage.

"I can't see anything from inside the box," Booker said. "I have no imaging sensors, but I do have the station schematics and our geo-trace data. We are here. You sound nervous. That's good. Use it. Kumon Xi is a businessman and he needs something we have: a way off-station. Don't trust him, Alessia, but don't be frightened."

"There's a gate," she said uncertainly.

"Is it locked?"

She gripped one of the heavy metal bars. It felt like the ornamental fence around Skygarth. Perhaps it was even made of iron. The gate squealed a little on rusted hinges, but it did swing open.

"Not locked," she said.

"Then go through."

She left the street behind, the oppressive noise and heaving crowds quickly falling away. The stench of stale cooking oil was stronger in the alleyway, and the deck plating underfoot was slimy and treacherous. Alessia was glad to be dressed in Caro's jeans and Commander Hardy's tough-girl jacket, but also a little worried that she would ruin them.

The passage felt like it was closing in on her as she walked down it. Looking up, she was seized by a sudden swirl of vertigo. The canyon of the building walls focused her attention on the far side of the Hab, where a whole other city seemed to hang in the narrow space between the rooflines.

She staggered slightly, reached out for the nearest wall, and snatched away her hands, shuddering. She nearly dropped the box.

"What's up?" Booker asked.

"I looked up"—she grimaced—"and I touched the wall, and . . . *eww* . . . it's gross, Booker. It felt like skin."

"Yeah. It sort of is. It's a cheap bioplastic, vat grown from bacterial extrusion. Pretty common in the poorer parts of the Habs. Feels a bit like you're living in somebody's intestinal tract. Just move forward, Alessia. Keep going. You can do it."

She started to take a deep breath, caught a whiff of something awful, and stopped herself.

"I'm good," she lied. "I got this."

There was nothing for it but to do what must be done.

Alessia put aside her fears, or at the very least she stepped around them. Whatever was waiting for them at the end of the passageway would be there no matter what she felt about it. And there was no running away from it, because the Sturm were coming up behind them, and when they found out that

Defiant and *Ariane* were here, they would know that Lucinda and Sephina and Admiral McLennan and everyone who had fought them at Montrachet was, too.

They would take the system apart to capture or kill them all.

She reached the end of the thruway. A heavy door stood closed in front of her. It guarded a building—more of a bunker, really—of much greater solidity and sturdiness than the icky germ-walled noodle shop.

She was surprised to see incense burning in a small pot and a bowl of strange fruit laid out as if for visitors.

"I'm here, I think," she whispered to Booker.

"Okay," he replied. "I dunno whether this guy knows about the Yak grabbing up the skipper and the others. He didn't seem to when I called from the ship to tell him Captain L'trel was busy and sending a runner. You. But I wouldn't mention it, unless he asks."

"And if he asks?"

"Lie."

Before she could answer back, the door popped open with a metallic clang. Like the outer gate, it had the look of real steel about it, too.

"Come in quickly," a voice said from inside.

Alessia gripped the thick handle and pulled. The door grated but it moved. She had a sense of real, solid mass before she slipped through, gripping Booker tightly in the small, black storage device.

Behind the door, Alessia found a cold, bright-lit space, sheathed in clear plastics and smelling of disinfectant. A cool mist sprayed from unseen nozzles, coating her in strong-smelling chemicals. Nobody was waiting for them in the antechamber, but she could make out vague shapes and colors through the plastic curtains.

"Hurry up," the voice said again. It came from all around them.

"Go on," Booker said. "It'll be okay. Just be ready, Alessia.

This is going to look pretty gnarly, I'm afraid. Remember this guy builds wetware."

That did not sound promising, but she trusted herself to Booker, and tried with all of her will to remember the lesson that Lord Guillaume, her fencing tutor, had taught her about the necessity of sometimes stepping into danger in order to pass through it. Alessia pushed aside a heavy curtain of plastic strips, and ventured into some sort of laboratory. Or perhaps a psychopath's nest.

It was horrifying.

Human bodies in various stages of assembly or teardown floated in stasis fields all around her. Some were less bodies than merely the constituent parts brought into proximity on the promise of making something whole from the disarticulated parts. Limbs of all colors and unknowable clumps of viscera filled clear stasis cabinets along one side of the room. A glass-fronted cold unit was filled with eyeballs.

She might have screamed, but the shock of it paralyzed her long enough for another collateral surprise to present itself.

Kumon Xi.

"Your Highness," he said and grinned, then bowed so deeply and with such a flourish that Alessia thought he was mocking her.

He was young and wore a Han Chinese phenotype like her history tutor Professor Zhang. Or maybe that was just his natural lining? Sephina said that she and Lucinda knew him from Habitat Welfare on Coriolis. And they were all poor there. Nobody had money for switching in and out of bodies like dresses for a ball.

But, you know, at least he didn't ask about the Yakuza.

He had not taken care of this body, though, which didn't augur well for Booker, she thought. Kumon Xi was short and very chubby, and the way he was digging into an enormous bag of potato chips, even as he rose up from his performative obeisance, he was unlikely to improve on his endomorphic profile.

"Wait," she said, suddenly catching up with what he'd said. "You know who I am?"

"Yup," he replied, and a small cloud of potato chip flecks exploded from his mouth. A cleaning bot followed him about, sucking up the mess.

Alessia, reeling a little, peeled off the headset, which felt heavier and even grosser than before.

"Seph's runner my ass. You're Princess Alessia Szu Suri sur Montanblanc ul Haq. Or, Senator Montanblanc for short. Possibly even President Monty, if there's nobody else left in the line of succession, cos, you know . . ."

He grinned hugely and snapped his jaws open and closed, raising one hand in a pantomime claw.

"Braaaains," he groaned. "Delicious braaaains."

More potato chips flew into the sanitized air. The little bot zipped about, diligently cleaning up.

Booker's voice rose urgently from the headset, sounding dinky but comprehensible in the quiet of the lab.

"Alessia. Get out. Get out now."

"Nah, it's cool, man," Xi said, wiping a mess of salty carbs from his lips. "We're still good. I really gotta get off this fucking tube, and all the way away from what's coming. The fucking Sturm, man. Can you believe it? Those guys been stroking their fucking murder boners for like seven hundred years thinking about what they're gonna do with guys like me. So, Princess, it's cool you're having adventure time and shit, but let's get your boy there set up, and get us the fuck gone from Lermontov, Natuna, and the ass end of the Volume."

"Ah . . ." Alessia started.

"Alessia," Booker called out from the ear cup, now in her hand. "Ignore what I just said. His motive appears to be solid."

"Pfft," Kumon Xi went. "No doubt, Boxman. The Sturm would turn me into a giant fucking dim sum for crimes against the genome. The only question is whether they'd steam my ass or deep-fry it."

"No," Alessia insisted. "The question is how you know who I am. Nobody is supposed to know that."

"Yeah," Booker said tinnily. "Good call."

"Whatevs." Kumon Xi shrugged, licking his fingers and wiping his hands on a grease-stained pair of gray coveralls. "Firstly, you guys rolling in here after bitchslapping the Sturm at Montrachet is like the juiciest fucking goss we got since the flare shut everything down and we found out that, you know, our civilization got roasted. Everyone is talking about it. Even though, officially, the fucking Javans won't say shit, and those Combine motherfuckers are even worse. And the cartel, man, don't get me started on the cartel . . ."

"Kumon!" Alessia snapped.

"Huh?"

"Kumon, how did you know I was me? It's important."

"Oh right," he said, deflating a little. He motioned for them to follow him, leading Alessia farther into the workshop. "I know Seph from back home, natch," he said over his shoulder. "Coriolis represent! Heard all about my Hab girl and the Loose Unit kickin' ass, taking names. Elite Fraction refugees been turning up here since just after the flare. Some busted-ass military types, too. That's how we knew what happened. You're famous, girl. That stunt you pulled with the hostage video? Blinking in Morse code? Omifuckinggod! What are you, like a storybook princess or something? And it was pure L'trel send ing you to me with the engram. Such a Seph move. She is the original bait-n-switch bitch. Can't hardly believe you made it here without some fucking gangster or Combine scumbag grabbing you up off the plates."

"Really?" Alessia asked, feeling both amped and frightened all at once.

"Nah, s'cool," Kumon Xi said. "Nobody's got time for that shit now. Everybody is looking to fold out before the fucking master-race psychos take over and get genocidally busy. Besides," he said, suddenly stopping and turning on her so unexpectedly that Alessia almost ran into him. The bioengineer leaned forward and peered into her eyes. "B-e-s-i-d-e-s," he said again, slowly, "even if I hadn't known Seph and Luce, I'd a recognized a piece of top-shelf splice work when it came through my door. And you, girl . . ."

Kumon Xi shook his head and whistled.

"You are the premium package."

He started to reach for her face and she slapped his hand away, mortified.

He just grinned again, nodding.

"Yeah. I don't need a biopsy. It's all there. The Montanblanc cytogene, sculpted bioform teratology, coevolved nootropic architecture. It's like you came down from Olympus. Or, you know, the C-suite enclaves on Montanblanc Grand Hermitage."

"Mister Xi, you're freaking me out," she said.

Xi held up his hands as if to surrender.

"Please. Call me Kumon. And apolz, Madam President, or Senator, or whatever you want. It's just not every day I get to do a favor for a living corporate god. And I do have a favor for you."

He spun around again, heading through a hatchway and beckoning her to follow.

"I got a rig here for your man Booker. He's gonna buh-reeeze through any shit the Combine or the Javans or those o.g. racist repugnicunt motherfuckers from the Dark can lay down."

Alessia almost said, "What about the Yakuza?" but she wasn't a complete idiot, so she kept her mouth shut. Also, she had a little trouble following Kumon Xi's Hab rat patois. One did not meet many underground biohackers at Skygarth.

Booker helped by asking, "What sort of rig?"

They passed through an air lock and into a smaller chamber, dimly lit.

There was only one piece of equipment, but it dominated the room. To Alessia it looked like some sort of old-fashioned Heisenberg casket from the darkest age of deep space travel.

The casing was frosted with condensate, but not so thickly that she couldn't see a body of some sort lying inside. Waiting.

Kumon Xi smacked his hand down on the antique stasis pod.

"Got me a cleanskin from Cupertino's Special Warfare Development Group."

Booker's voice was a single grunt.

"Fuck."

"Uh-huh. That's what I'm talkin' about! I knew that'd get y'all tingly in the spanky, nanoweave combat pants. I, er . . . finessed the merch from Nero's minions when they clamped that TDF ship that came in after the flare. Bottled the fucking lot of them. Although, to be fair, that wasn't Nero. It was Carnivorous Maximus and his Combo friends."

"Who?" Alessia asked.

"The Javan Volume lord and the commander of the Combine expeditionary group," Booker explained. "But, back up a little. Kumon, you're telling me the local authorities sequestered the entire crew of a Terran warship?"

"All tea, no shade, Bookman. But like you care. You're a badass source code motherfucker is what I hear. Because everyone's saying it. So, let's get you loaded and rolling. I want off this Hab five minutes ago. Oh, and if you should run into your friends from the Code, I would appreciate a reference. Seems we got a commonality of interest now the space Nazis came back. Could be they might send me some work."

"Could be," Booker said noncommittally.

Alessia took the external storage unit from the pocket of her jacket.

Her hands trembled a little as she handed it over and her heart was beating uncomfortably fast. It wasn't just that they seemed to be playing a trick on Kumon Xi, who very obviously did not know that the harbormaster, this Nero character, had betrayed Sephina and the crew and let the Yakuza seize the *Ariane*. She was nervous to the point of pissing kittens because although she was doing the right thing—they really, really, really needed Booker out of q-bit—she was also doing something very wrong.

She was lying to Kumon Xi.

Deceiving him.

In her own way, she supposed, she was betraying him as profoundly as Sephina had been betrayed. Or poor Sergeant Reynolds back on Montrachet, by the villain Jasko Tan.

All her life Alessia had been lectured on the importance of values and principles, and what? As soon as they became inconvenient, she discarded them?

Was this what growing up meant?

All these thoughts she had in the brief moment it took to hand over the box.

Kumon Xi slotted the little unit into a receiving bay.

A green light winked on at the top of the casket and the frosted canopy hissed open.

CHAPTER

TWENTY-NINE

The Javan Warlugger tumbled through space, venting atmosphere and radiation. It was not dead, not yet. The advance
guard of enemy probes that swept into the solar system quickly
found and locked onto the wounded capital ship. They swarmed
it like demon dogs.

Sub-Commandant Domi Suprarto, sitting awkwardly in the
captain's chair, gripped the end of the hard leather armrest and
squeezed the color from the tips of his fingers.

This was hell.

The Armadalens and the Combine had disappeared without
a trace. They pulled the velvet blanket of space across their
ships and vanished as if they had never been.

"Multiple contacts, arcs three to five, Captain."

Suprarto did not even have time to savor the experience of
being addressed as the master of the Empire's flagship.

He was only the captain because everyone else was dead.

And *Makassar* flew the emperor's standard because nobody
knew if a single capital ship outside Natuna had survived the
Sturm's attack.

Alarms blared and sirens wailed as the leviathan warship spun slowly about all three axes as though dying and wrecked. McLennan had at least allowed them the indulgence of maintaining ship's gravity. Without it he would not have a crew to fight when this trap was sprung.

"Enemy within the heliopause," Ensign Dasai announced from Tactical. "Counting eight, nine, wait . . . twelve, no thirteen enemy ships, sir."

"Thank you, Ensign," Suprarto said as coolly as he could. It was beyond strange. He and Budi Dasai were friends. Good friends who often spent their meager shore leave together; Budi having enlisted from one frame over on Gudang Garam. But now authority and precedence separated them utterly. Suprarto would not admit it to anyone, not even to Budi, but as he strained under the nigh intolerable pressure of leading the *Makassar* and her crew into battle, he tried to do as he had seen the Armadalen skipper do when the second wave of enemy probes arrived. The young woman, Commander Hardy, had not raised her voice or berated her underlings in the style of a Senior Sub-Commandant Khomri or Volume Lord Karna. She had not even paid much heed to the vastly more powerful figures of McLennan and Pac Yulin and Lord Karna as they set about one another in front of her. She had done her job quietly, with focus and rigor.

Watching her, deeply impressed but unable to say so, Domi Suprarto had vowed that he would do the same was he ever to find himself in Hardy's position.

"Active sensor locks. They've got us . . . sir," Dasai announced.

"And we have them, exactly where we want them," Suprarto replied, speaking as loudly he dared without coming off as shrill. A few of the bridge crew looked his way. Some were junior officers, like him. Others were older NCOs, and he feared messing up in front of them more than he feared death, real death, itself. Those older petty officers and CPOs were like the wrinkled village elders back on Gudang Garam. They did not need to raise a hand against a foolish youth. They could lash you with a glance.

Domi Suprarto sucked in a deep breath and let it out slowly.

Steady yourself, he thought. You must merely follow the plan.

The battle plan, which Admiral McLennan's Intellect had copied to *Makassar*'s hastily augmented Intellect, Munitions Sub-Intellect Number Six, anticipated the Sturm's arrival and prosecution of their immediate advantage over the defenders, which for now appeared to be but one principal ship. His own.

"Countermeasures," Suprarto ordered. "Break the locks."

"Aye, Captain," Dasai replied.

The fighting bridge of the Warlugger was a large, red-lit, conical chamber with more than a hundred personnel spread over three steeply terraced levels. None ranked above junior officer grade, and many of them were mere enlisted kelasi who would never have been allowed in the exalted command space except to deliver food or drink or perhaps a kretek cigarette to their superiors. But those superiors were all dead, cut down by the Sturm's nanophage as soon as their mesh queried the ZP networks after emerging from lockdown.

Kelasi Minara, newly promoted from second to the first class of his rank, stood to the right and slightly behind Sub-Commandant Suprarto, clad in a reactive nanoweave vest, and wearing a pair of AMX pistols at his hips. To Minara fell the responsibility of protecting his leader should they be boarded; a prestigious duty which was more symbolic than tactical. One-quarter of those on the fighting bridge were fully armored Javan kommandos, ready to repel any boarders. But everyone knew the story of how Suprarto had saved Minara from Senior Sub-Commandant Khomri, and now all the fighting men and women of the *Makassar* could see the evidence of how Domi Suprarto would lead them.

Waste nothing, his father had taught him. Not even the worst of times.

On Suprarto's left floated the former Muntions Sub-Intellect

Number Six, upgraded by emergency modifications from the Armadalen Intellect—and what a momentous scandal that would have been, just a few short weeks ago. Number Six floated to Suprarto's left, considerably enlarged in size by all the mods and upgrades affixed to its outer shell.

"Targeting locks broken, Captain," Dasai reported. "But they are trying to acquire us again."

"Of course," Surprarto said with more confidence than he felt. "Shake them off, Ensign. Give them a show. Launch triple-C and the stand-off packages."

Dasai relayed a series of commands to the dozen other operators at Tactical, and each set to their tasks.

Like some broken-tooth gargantuan beast, scabbed with carbon armor and crawling with malice, the Warlugger spasmed in mortal rage, seemingly cornered and dying, but still dangerous. Thousands of portals rippled open and vomited forth a storm of munitions. Autonomous long-range Komodo Dragons. Sentient swarms of Tarantula micro-missiles. Three hundred and twelve Mk4 torpedoes. That last, a poetic note, suggested by Surprarto himself. One torpedo for each officer killed by the Sturm's sneak attack. He had expected to be turned down, even mocked by the Terran admiral for attempting to tweak his battle scheme, but McLennan grinned like a mountain wolf and congratulated Suprarto for his spirit.

It was the first time he could ever recall being complimented by a superior officer.

Finally, riding overwatch on this vast wave of superluminal death and ruination was a small fleet of C3 drones, a hive mind composed of a one-use Intellect devoted to a singular purpose for the term of its short, violent life: the annihilation of every target designated by its widely distributed but mono-focused sentience.

The volley folded away from *Makassar*, spreading out in a widening gyre of randomly generated micro-fold plots. Or at least they were random save for one common trait: They advanced purposefully, relentlessly, and at terrifying speed toward the hostile force that had folded into the system.

"They fired too soon," Bannon said.

"Nae, lad, have some faith in an old villain," McLennan growled at Lucinda's systems chief. "Yon wee fellow has done just fine, which is to say, exactly as I told him to. Just wait and see now."

From their vantage point, perched high above the plane of the elliptical, the crew of *Defiant* watched as the enemy scattered through a series of hurried-looking emergency folds, breaking up the coherence of their tactical formation, negating the interlocking fields of fire they would otherwise have brought to bear on the Javan capital ship, as it played at its pretense of crippled weakness.

Lucinda, in the command chair at the center of the bridge, had the best view of the real-time holographic projection, which was stunning in its detail thanks to the wealth of data they could harvest from their own repurposed satellite network and the reduced but still powerful matrix of Javan strategic defense sensors to which they now had access via the local u-space relay.

The Sturm had arrived in force, an augmented battle group built around two heavy units of roughly dreadnought class. Those behemoths were escorted by another four heavy cruiser equivalents, and beyond them a screening force of lighter, faster destroyers and frigates. These last were the units on which she focused her attention. *Defiant* had been specifically designed to contest the battlespace against this class of ship, although not of course against these particular examples of the form. During the last war, the Javans had deployed a mix of light escort vessels in their fleets and Captain Torvaldt's log described many encounters with multiple opponents of that class.

Lucinda's face was unreadable as she watched the encounter

between the Sturm and the Javan Warlugger play out. It was in some ways like watching the fractal patterns cast by a traditional Javanese samanyek dancer, as the swirling cloud of semiconscious munitions attempted to envelop the rapidly spreading pack of attackers.

As a lieutenant on the destroyer *Resolute*, Lucinda had been on the receiving end of Javanese hive mind missile swarms at the battles of Longfall and Medang, and despite the ultimate victory of the RAN in both engagements, she had not expected to survive either. (Especially not after the then Sub-Admiral Juono Karna had attacked and destroyed the Commonwealth's engram banks in neutral space, facilities in which at least a third of the RAN's personnel were backed up—the war crime for which he was supposed to have been prosecuted at the Hague.)

Lucinda blinked away the memory, annoyed with herself for losing focus.

None of that mattered now.

Not the war. Not Karna. Not even her part in the failed quest to bring him to justice before the signing of the Armistice.

All that mattered was the fight they were about to have.

Lieutenant Chase broke into her thoughts.

"Ma'am, green lights across the board. We fold at your discretion."

His voice was thick with tension, and not entirely from the pressure of the moment. Lucinda knew he desperately desired command of the barque belonging to his house and she anticipated a difficult conversation, should they survive the day.

"Thank you, Mister Chase," she said. "Execute in . . ."

Lucinda checked the correlation of forces in the holo-display. *Makassar*'s opening shot had tagged one of the cruisers and completely taken out a destroyer escort to make her mission simpler, but the Sturm had initiated a dense volumetric spread of countermeasures, and folded directly through the missile swarm, folding again and again to arrive within the tactical range of their energy weapons and kinetic systems. The Warlugger was beset from all sides by torrents of fire. Massive field effects glowed like the northern lights of Old Earth as the enemy's pulse cannons and plasma arcs spent themselves on the shields. Hyper-accelerated heavy rail gun rounds and barrages of lighter submunitions passed through the energistic storm and hammered at the scarred and blackened shell of *Makassar*'s armor, quickly raising the temperature of the outer hull until it glowed red hot in parts.

"God's bollocks, that old bint is an ugly fuck, but she can take a punch, eh?" McLennan hooted. He looked like a hungry man presented with a king's buffet.

". . . ten seconds, Mister Chase," Lucinda ordered. "Mister Fein, Mister Bannon, expect a target-rich environment when we emerge. The escort vessels are our responsibility. Lieutenant Chivers?"

"Yes, ma'am?"

"Inform the crew we will tie a broom to the masthead today."

"Aye, ma'am!" Nonomi Chivers said, before relaying to the ship their captain's promise to sweep the enemy utterly from the volume.

Lieutenant Chase called out, his voice in time with the countdown clock. ". . . combat fold in five, four, three . . ."

"Wait!" McLennan roared.

Lieutenant Varro Chase froze. His finger hung over the button to initiate the fold.

"What?" Lucinda asked, with a serrated edge to her voice.

"The Combine," McLennan snarled. "That fucking bent-back trouser snake Pac Yulin has shot his wad too early. Look!"

Commodore Rinaldo Pac Yulin tried to ignore the apoplectic shrieking of the Javan Volume lord but it was becoming impossible.

"They are destroying my ship. My only ship," Karna screamed from the relative safety of Luwu Palace on Ciandur. "You have to do something, Yulin. This is McLennan's fault. It's a trap. He has betrayed us. He's working with Armadale. He let the Sturm destroy my ship on purpose."

The *Makassar* was in a desperate position, of that there was no doubt. Taken under long-range fire by the enemy's big gun platforms, she could not fully engage with the battleships and cruiser analogues because of a swarm of smaller, faster corvettes and frigates that continually harried her, folding in and out of close-quarter range.

Even Pac Yulin could see how much damage the Warlugger was forced to absorb, and all for the sake of a questionable strategy of drawing the Sturm's capital ships in so tightly that they had no maneuver volume. The plan was simple, too simple for his taste, relying as it did on common trickery and a brute stratagem of heavy-handed ambush. There was no elegance. No grandeur. It was almost as though McLennan did not trust the Combine to play its part. And the strike force commander was certain that the Terran overlord would deny them the glory of claiming the lion's share of a famous victory, if he had anything to do with it.

"This is intolerable," Lord Karna raged from the holo-projector. "If you do not do something, Commodore Yulin, I will be forced to withdraw from our arrangements."

Pac Yulin signaled to a comms officer to cut the connection.

Juono Karna must truly be unhinged if he was speaking of such things on open channels.

"Commander Vnuk," Pac Yulin said, summoning the captain of the *Khanjar* to his side.

"Your Highness?" Vnuk said, which was getting a bit ahead of things, but Pac Yulin would let it go.

"Commander, has the ship's Intellect completed the action analysis I ordered?"

"Ship!" Commander Vnuk barked out. "Answer His Highness!"

Combine Intellects were every bit as capable as those of any other corporation, but traditionally the Yulin-Irrawaddy's extended executive family was not as prepared to cede them autonomy, or even agency beyond the purely functional, lest they someday challenge their merely human colleagues for control of the realm. It had happened more than once to other realms and corporations.

"I have analyzed the attack patterns and capabilities of the Human Republic."

"And?" Pac Yulin said, quickly losing patience.

"That is an incomplete query, Commodore."

Pac Yulin sighed.

"Is the *Makassar* likely to be destroyed by this attack?"

"Oh yes, of course."

"Wait, what?"

"I project a ninety-eight percent certainty of destruction."

"But that's if we do not intervene, right?"

"Correct. With intervention per Admiral McLennan's plan of operation, the chance of destruction falls to only sixteen percent."

As contemptible as Pac Yulin found the Javan Volume lord, Juono Karna still played a critical role in his plans to seize control of the Combine, and then all the remnant forces and broken realms of the Greater Volume.

"Is there scope within the plan's parameters to increase the odds of *Makassar*'s survival?" Pac Yulin asked.

"Of course, Commodore. An early intervention will raise the probability of *Makassar*'s survival. But—"

"No buts! We go early," Pac Yulin said. "Commander Vnuk, prepare to fold."

"On your command, Your Highness."

Defiant winked out of existence.

The Armadalen stealth destroyer re-emerged into space-time among the chaos of raging battle. The smaller enemy ships were closely engaged with *Makassar*, but two of the Sturm's heavy cruisers had raced to close quarters and were pounding away at the Warlugger's underbelly, concentrating their kinetic batteries on the lower decks where Lucinda knew the Javans' armory to be concentrated.

"Skipper, the Combine raider is out of place," Lieutenant Fein called across the bridge.

But Lucinda didn't need the tactical officer to tell her what had gone wrong. She could see for herself in the holo-display. *Khanjar* and *Jezail* were supposed to have gone dark and waited in Natuna's asteroid belt, disguised by the dense concentration of heavy engineering plants and the two big industrial Habs out there. At the right moment, with the Sturm's screening force engaged by *Defiant*, and the Warlugger throwing off its pretense of weakness to start counterpunching with the heaviest mega-munitions in the Empire's arsenal, Pac Yulin's strike force was to hit the enemy from below, folding into range at 180 south of the elliptical to gut the Sturm's capital ships with a sudden, annihilating blitz of Joint Direct Attack Anti-Matter missiles.

But the Combine raiders had not waited. They were half an AU out of position, squeezing into the same tactical volume as the *Makassar* and dueling, punch for punch, with all four units of the enemy's main force.

"For fuck's sake," McLennan glowered at the holo. "These clatty roasters couldnae wipe their own arses without smearing fresh fucking jobbie curds all over their faces."

"Admiral?" Lucinda said, unsure of whether to proceed with her own mission.

"Fight this ship," McLennan ordered. "You know what to do. Stay with your part of the plan for now and let's at least sweep those nasty wee buggers out of the way. Bring some clarity to this dog's breakfast."

"Mister Fein . . ." Lucinda started as klaxons blared and alarms sounded to warn of imminent multiple combat folds.

Over at his station, Lieutenant Varro Chase was lost within a hurricane of nav-data and evolving plots. Chase's fingers flew through his holo-display. Lucinda had to admit, the man might be a highly polished princely turd, but he was an artist with a navigation program. Within seconds a cascading series of combat jumps emerged from his plotting, primary, secondary, and tertiary paths through the tangled snarl of battle.

"Targets designated one through seven, Commander," Mercado Fein called out from Tactical. "The Combine already took out another frigate."

"Considerate of them," Lucinda commented drily. "I should send a thank-you note."

Hero sailed up behind her command chair.

"I wouldn't bother," the Intellect said. "*Jezail* was firing on the second dreadnought and the frigate just got in the way."

"Mister Fein," Lucinda said, over and around the Intellect. "The three enemy destroyers operating in formation, right there . . ."

She pointed at a trio of hostile avatars within the swirling cloud of data. They were folding and firing in sequence, targeting the Javans' drive cones.

"They're good for a tickle with the pocket nukes. Make it so. Designate shipkillers for the other five escorts. Immediate launch."

"Skip-folding pocket nukes on group one, hostiles three. Fire-and-forget on hostiles five, independent volley, Sabers and Spelerons."

"Very good that man," Lucinda said.

New alarms blared.

"Target locks from three sources," Lieutenant Bannon warned. "The dreadnoughts have grabbed us, ma'am."

Chase announced an evasive maneuver, but Lucinda cut him off.

"Wait for Mister Fein, please, Lieutenant."

The navigator, the surviving scion of his House, gaped at her.

"But they've locked us up."

"Incoming," Bannon cried out.

"Nukes are folding," Fein declared from Tactical. "Shipkillers in three, two, one . . ."

Lucinda felt the slightest shudder underfoot as *Defiant* loosed a brace of missiles into the cauldron of the battle.

"Missiles away!"

Lucinda chopped a hand at Chase.

"Execute."

Defiant slipped sideways out of space-time as dozens of warheads closed in on her.

McLennan tuned her out. Hardy was doing her job; he needed to do his.

"Comms, get me Commodore Yulin on *Khanjar*."

"Aye, sir," Nonomi Chivers answered.

For the briefest of moments, as Chivers searched for the Combine leader, Mac ignored the recalcitrant raider and evaluated the holo of the Warlugger's cage fight with the Sturm.

The heavyweights had all closed to within three hundred kilometers of one another, close enough to thrash and flail away with kinetics and plasma bolts, but leaving no tactical volume from which the Javans or the Combine could launch their most devastating strikes, the long- and medium-range volumetric denial weapons that would kill the intruders by annihilating the space-time around them, and plunging the long sword of directed antimatter detonations into the guts of their old-fashioned hulls.

"I have Commodore Pac Yulin for you, Admiral," Nonomi Chivers announced.

Hero moved up and floated next to Mac. His exotic matter casing glowed a subdued crimson.

"I'm sure this will be a pleasant chat and not at all an utter waste of time," the Intellect said quietly.

Pac Yulin appeared in holo before them. He was strapped into a crash couch, and behind him Mac could make out some details of the mayhem unleashed on the bridge of the *Khanjar* by the sudden realization that they weren't just shooting fish in a barrel. The fish were shooting back.

"Commodore Pac Yulin," McLennan started pleasantly enough, as *Defiant* executed another emergency micro-fold to escape an ion storm of converging energy weapons.

Yulin's image shivered and nearly broke up for a second, before returning.

"What do you want?" Pac Yulin snapped. "I'm busy."

"Indeed. We all are," McLennan said quietly. "Which I'll admit is a matter of some irritation to me, Commodore, because I had hoped to be enjoying my victory parade along the scenic boulevards of Ciandur by now. Instead, I find myself stranded up fecal creek without so much as a novelty fucking teaspoon with which to paddle my way out."

The *Khanjar* took a major hit and Pac Yulin's image shunted sideways as the massive battleraider absorbed the blunt force trauma of something akin to an asteroid strike.

McLennan saw lights flickering and electrical fires exploding from stations in the background.

"Are you insane," Pac Yulin hissed. "I'm fighting a battle here."

"No! You're not!" McLennan suddenly roared. "You're royally fucking up my perfectly good battle is what you're doing, you doaty fucking nuff-nuff."

For a fraction of a second, all activity froze on both bridges. *Defiant*'s crew restarted before the Combine, who, to be fair, were not used to being yelled at in Scottish. As McLennan shouted at Pac Yulin, five Armadalen missiles converged on a stray enemy frigate, skipping across the surface of space-time in a stochastic blur that left a golden tracery of positional fixes in the data cloud of the main hologram. The Sturm died in a white flash as the Sabers emerged from their final micro-fold, broke into dozens of autonomous submunitions, and lanced through the vessel's point defenses.

"Who is the captain of your damned slavers' galley?" McLennan seethed. "I would have words with him right now."

"No, you won't," Pac Yulin scowled, cutting the link.

Stunned by the arrogance of the man, Mac shook his head.

"Well, that wasn't too unpleasant, I suppose," Hero remarked drolly. "It was a bit of a waste of time, though."

Mac watched as a bead of sweat tracked down Lucinda's face; the young woman was entirely intent upon the task at hand. Her hand darted up and wiped the trickle away as more Sturm escorts died in the mad tempest that spread out from *Defiant*.

"Admiral," she said, turning away from the holo to address him. "We've neutralized the destroyer screen. *Makassar* and Hostile One are danger close but I want to drive through the gap there . . ." Hardy gestured into the boiling data stew of the hologram at a dim, reddish area in the Sturm battle schematic. "We can defeat them in detail. We have enough shipkillers. We can do it, sir. Let the 'lugger and the Combine deal with Hostile One; we'll grab their nuts and gut them from the inside."

"Sanguinary, Ms. Hardy," Mac replied, "and admirably so, but . . ."

"But," Hero boomed out over the buzz and chatter of intense activity, "I'm afraid the Combine are pulling back under impellers. I do believe Commodore Pac Yulin intends to fold out as soon as *Makassar* is clear of their gravimetric shear zone."

"Hero," McLennan snarled. "Talk to your little friend. Now!"

The battleraider *Khanjar* had taken so much damage that Pac Yulin was seriously considering an emergency fold-out to *Jezail*, which was partly protected from the linear kinetic attacks of the Sturm by the bulk of the Javan Warlugger. *Khanjar* shuddered violently as secondary explosions wracked her lower decks where the enemy had concentrated their fires.

"Hull breaches, Decks Nine through Thirteen. Engineering Two is dark," an officer shouted to Commander Vnuk.

"We're venting too much atmosphere," another man yelled.

Pac Yulin tried to make sense of it all, but there was no sense to be made. The Armadalens had bested these dogs with but one ship at Montrachet. One tiny, little garbage scow of a destroyer. What the hell was going on?

Was Karna correct? Was this some scheme of McLennan's to cripple a potential rival?

"Seal off the compartments and secure the hatches," Vnuk shouted.

He had to shout. The bridge was in turmoil, a howling storm of alarms and yelling and the thunderous hammerfall of kinetic projectiles pouring in on them from at least three of the enemy's heavy ships.

"Get us out of here. Get us out now!" Pac Yulin demanded.

The truth of it was that with so much energistic turmoil roiling the volume of the battle he dared not trust himself to the uncertainties of even the shortest micro-fold. Such violent, densely concentrated fluctuations in the fabric of space-time could scatter his constituent matter across a literal infinity of universes. No. If he was to survive this disaster it would be the old-fashioned way. By dragging his ass out of danger in real time and real space.

"I said now!" he roared at Vnuk.

"But, Commodore," the ship's master pleaded. "We are too close to the Javans. If we fold out now the gravimetric front will hit *Makassar* like the hand of God."

Pac Yulin jabbed a finger at the massive holosphere where the battle played out in miniature. His hand shook and he quickly retracted it, but not his order.

"The Armadalens are jumping about all over the volume. Just do it."

Vnuk looked sick.

"But, Commodore. They are a much smaller ship, and they do not generate the same sort of shear and they are . . . more . . . a little more advanced, sir. I'm sorry, sir."

"Then at least get us to cover, man," Pac Yulin shouted. "Are you a complete fool? If the enemy is shooting at you, do you not seek cover? Go! Now!"

"Yes, sir. Right away, sir."

Commander Vnuk started to order his helmsman to draw more power from the AM stacks for the impellers.

But he suddenly stopped issuing functional commands in favor of screaming obscenities at the helmsman as the ship shuddered from a terrible blow.

"Huh? What?" Pac Yulin asked as grand orchestras of newly clashing alarms sounded across the command deck.

CHAPTER

THIRTY

It was a hell of an easier trip than riding a data spike from his last skin job into that Compliance Mech on the TDF prison Hab. No pain or discomfort. No disorienting phenomenological collapse as he transitioned from soft tissue to substrate—or in this case from the box's absorber lattice into the neurological architecture of Cupertino's transhuman construct.

In one moment, he was stuck in a box.

Alessia plugged the device into the storage flask.

Kumon Xi flipped a switch.

And Booker was fully conscious. Mission-ready in a specialized infiltrator/combat chassis. The rig was entirely biological, with no cost-saving mods or cyborg shortcuts. The body, a generic black African phenotype blending polymorph characteristics from a dozen different heirloom tribal-ethnic germlines, was equipped with an endogenic data management system which allowed him to control the rig's augmented capabilities through a heads-up display.

As the canopy hissed open and Alessia offered a tiny hand to help him out, the biosensor arrays embedded in his cranio-facial dermis painted her in a dense matrix of targeting data. A pop-up menu of response options deployed, ranging from simply batting the hand away to firing micro-missiles from the tips of his fingers.

He waved Alessia back, taking a moment to familiarize himself with his new ride. He white-listed the princess, and the targeting data disappeared completely.

Kumon Xi, he left as a strike option for the moment, but he did dial down the granularity of the readout. Reticules for a suite of ranged, subdermal weapons floated over the meat hacker's skull and center mass. Aim-points in a palette of half-tone pastel colors hovered over nerve bundles, exposed organs, and joints vulnerable to critical strikes.

"Give him a second, kid," Xi cautioned Alessia. "He's gotta plug the DevGru system into his source code. It's a bit more complicated than the usual skin jobs he's used to."

"Sorry," Alessia said, quickly backing off.

Booker shook his head.

"Don't worry," he grunted. "It's just . . . Kumon's right. There's a lot to take in."

A few seconds later he had integrated the construct's OS with his own personal engram management system.

He shook off the minor cramps and stiffness of a body stored for long-haul transport, and climbed out of the casket.

Alessia gasped and turned away.

He was naked.

"Ah shit, sorry, Alessia," Booker said, glancing down. That was a sight she wouldn't soon forget. "Come on, Xi. Throw me a fucking towel or something, would you. She's just a kid."

"I'm going to go wait outside with all the body parts and floating offal buckets," Alessia said.

Kumon Xi snorted and waved Booker over to a gear locker that deployed from the chamber wall. Booker hurried to dress himself as Alessia departed the room in an even greater hurry. He chose a simple coverall of reactive nanotube weave. It would provide some protection against small-arms fire. His DevGru construct boasted some pretty fucking astounding passive defenses, but you could build the castle walls as thick and sturdy as you wanted; somebody was always going to bring a bigger cannon.

"D'you get any other weapons when you bought the unit?" Booker asked.

"DevGru toys? Nah, sorry," Kumon Xi said. "I'm just a meat tech guy, Booker. I wouldn't know how to start bargaining for that stuff. But you're not gonna need it, are you? We just gotta hustle back to your ship and you got plenty of spare capacity built into that rig to deal with any aggro on the deck plates."

"We're going to make another stop first," Booker said.

Xi looked surprised.

"Where? Do we have time?"

"We'll make time," Booker told him. "Cos otherwise we're not getting off this tube."

"Say what?"

Booker smiled.

"Don't worry. I'll take care of it."

Kumon Xi cursed Baroness Sephina all the way from his chop shop to the Yakuza *honbu*, which Alessia thought was kind of unfair, because it wasn't Seph who'd misled him. That was all down to her and Booker.

She felt terrible about it and kept apologizing on the way over. It made no difference. Kumon Xi continued to rant and rage about Seph, even after Booker told him to shut up about it.

Booker looked amazing now. He was very tall and his arms were almost as big as Jaddi Coto's, but where the giant rhino hybrid was a slow and almost slumberous presence, Booker's new body had this terrifying grace and an aura of real menace whenever they came under threat from the surging crowds or undisciplined security patrols. It was like there was something coiled inside of him, Alessia thought. Something dangerous.

Not to her, of course, or even to Kumon Xi, no matter how much he kept yammering on about how Seph had lied to him. But the closer they got to the Yakuza, the more this version of Booker appeared a machine. His eyes were targeting nodes. His hands fell still, like weapons already locked on to a host of targets she could not see.

They cut across at least two frames, angling toward an area of the Hab that Booker said was a port district. She could see it at first when they left the workshop. It was about a third of the way up a curve of the hull and it looked different from the other sections on either side.

"It's a light manufacturing and cargo-handling zone," Booker explained. "Not as thickly populated and it's got a heap of docks and transit depots. Lot of ships coming and going. Not as many residents. Lots of materiel movement to cover a host of sins."

Alessia nodded as though that all made sense, but she didn't look up again. They were still moving through a busy, crowded part of the Hab and she could not afford to spend time gazing up at the skies of Lermontov, such as they were.

Not much compared to Montrachet, that was for sure.

There was no sky here. Not really. The hull simply curved back on itself, creating the walls of the long cylindrical Habitat in which sixteen million people lived.

Oh, and how they lived.

She had seen desperation before.

They had been running and fighting long enough that she knew what it looked like when people had nothing left to lose. She'd watched Seph and Lucinda and the others fight Kogan D'ur for their lives, and for hers, back on Montrachet.

But that had been short and urgent, an acute moment of desperation as they'd come together to best the armored storm trooper.

The more time she spent out on the deck plates of Lermontov Station, the more she came to realize that for many people, despair and hopelessness were all they knew. All they had ever known.

Were these the people Admiral McLennan wanted to free?

Alessia wasn't entirely sure.

She'd thought he was talking about the hundreds of billions of serfs and slaves and vassal subjects of empires like the Javans and corporate realms like the Combine. But Lermontov was supposed to be a "freeport."

Was this what freedom looked like for most people of the Greater Volume? They were filthy and starving and looked every bit as fearful of Habitat Security as they did of the approaching Sturm.

Surely all sixteen million could not live like this?

It felt to her as if half that number were crammed into the dense warren of alleys and cut-throughs that acted as streets and boulevards hereabout. There seemed to be no broad avenues or generous pathways at all, everything and everyone was heaped in on top of one another. There were stretches where capsule stacks and container tenements rose high above the plates, but they looked like teetering, makeshift arrangements cobbled together from whatever the inhabitants could scavenge from the deck plates. Insane tangles of cabling and conduit ran between the ramshackle towers which crawled with mobile advertising. She quickly learned not to look too closely, lest the marketing AIs note her interest and unleash a frenzied promotional campaign directed solely at her.

She saw many, many children who seemed to have no homes or families at all. Hab dogs and Javan spider-cats ran wild in some quarters—until they were captured and caged and, Alessia feared, cooked up in big open fire drums and eaten. Sirens blared and alarms wailed. A harsh voice barked warnings and instructions in half a dozen languages. Some, like Russian and French, she understood, thanks to the efforts of her long-suffering tutors. Others she did not recognize at all.

"Oh man, this sucks, this really sucks," Kumon Xi whined

from just behind her. "Can you hear it? Can you hear what they're saying?"

"Yes, of course I can," Alessia said.

Booker ignored Xi and pushed on through the crowd. He was like a human plow, the way everyone parted before him. Alessia hastened along in his wake.

"They're telling everyone to shelter in place," she said to Kumon.

"No, not those assholes!" Kumon Xi cried out, throwing his hands in the air. "I mean these assholes." He gestured all around him. "Just listen to what they're saying."

There was no way Alessia could understand the grungy mix of Hab rat slang and Volume pidgin and she didn't think it was nice of Kumon Xi to call them names like that, anyway.

"Oh, come on!" Xi cried out when he realized he wasn't getting through to either of them. He reached for Booker's arm, thought the better of it, and skipped ahead of the source coder instead, shuffling backward through the press of the crowd, awkward and always this close to tripping over. The contrast between his clumsy, graceless stumbling about and Booker's cool economy of movement couldn't have been more pronounced. There was no coherence to the mass movement of Hab dwellers, either. They seemed to be frantically rushing and even falling about in all directions at once.

Kumon Xi jabbed a finger into the air as if pointing to something just outside the hull.

"They're saying the Sturm are here and they're kicking our asses," he shouted. "They say the *Makassar* has been blown to bits and the fucking Combine have run away. Which sounds legit to me, bro. That totally scans as something those treacherous fucks would do."

"Booker? Is it true?" Alessia called out over the roar, suddenly worried about Lucinda and *Defiant*.

And Caro and Debin.

And even about McLennan and Hero.

"Booker, are they saying that?"

Booker kept moving. He was a human avalanche, but one that moved forward, over and through and around any obstacle in front of him.

"That's what some of them are saying, but they're full of shit," he said.

Alessia increased her pace to keep up and Kumon Xi fell in beside her. They passed through a narrow warren of streets that seemed entirely occupied by small capsule bars and large cargo containers turned into even more bars, pharmashops, and sex holes and worse, much worse. Some of the containers were painted in the livery of shipping lines she knew her family owned. Holographic figures, some naked, some clad in fantastical costumery, all of them modified by gene-splicing that would be wildly illegal on any Montanblanc ul Haq world, rutted and howled out in the open, their monstrous travesties of lovemaking somehow meant to entice passersby into the faded plasteel containers. In one of the worst places a couple of children sat in a cage, staring into space, as if they could see through the hull and far into the Dark from which the Sturm had returned.

"What are they doing there?" Alessia asked.

"Organ brokers," Kumon Xi said, as if it were obvious. "Look! Look at that!" he called out as they passed a bar pimping the latest in gladiator fights from the Oligarchies. The bar was empty, and the holo-screens did not display the promised death matches.

Real fights to the real death! Streaming 24 hours a day, 5 rubles an hour! 7 rubles with drinks and snax.

Instead, Alessia saw images of *Defiant*, dying inside a constellation of bright, white nuclear blasts.

"No!" she cried out. "Booker! Look!"

"It's all fake," he said, without turning around, apparently aware of what she was talking about. "I got a u-space link to *Defiant*. The hindbrain in this rig has avian mitochondrial clusters fashioned into a comms array. Bandwidth is tight, but there's enough for basic data flow. *Defiant* is engaged. *Makassar* has taken damage. But the Sturm have suffered heavy losses, too. They're not going to be kicking down the doors here just yet, but we need to move before somebody grabs up the ship."

"Booker, somebody already did that," Alessia protested. "Those Yakuza guys."

"Oh man, I shoulda just sold that fucking rig to Svetakov," Kumon Xi said bitterly, mostly to himself.

Booker finally pulled up and turned around to face them.

For the merest second, when the angle was right, Alessia thought she could see fairy lights or some sort of elfin tracery in Booker's eyes. But she blinked, or he did, and it was gone.

They stood, a small, tight group in the middle of a passageway, between a capsule hotel offering pods by the minute, and a payday loan office.

If you got biomass you got credit!

The crowd buffeting them was mostly frantic to be somewhere else. But some locals were still doing business. Street hawkers, prostitutes, all manner of dealers. A couple of food cart vendors struggled on gamely, calling out their wares which, to Alessia, looked like deep-fried tumors and smelled like toilets. The blaze of multicolored strip lighting and holo-verts was brighter here than the fusion tube running along the central axis of the Hab.

"We're almost there," Booker promised. "I'm gonna stash you outside their perimeter. They'll have security well out into the frame, especially now."

"I say we should just go to the ship and wait for you," Kumon Xi insisted.

Alessia did not think that was such a bad idea even though she dreaded the prospect of being separated from Booker. And she didn't entirely trust Mister Xi. Booker shook his head, putting an end to any debate.

"It's not safe there . . ."

"It's not safe anywhere, man!" Kumon Xi shot back.

"No, it's not," Booker said. "But I have found a place you can lay up while I extract Captain L'trel and the others."

"How? How is that even possible?" the bioengineer demanded, although his demands sounded pretty whiny.

"I got a stalker app on them," Booker said. "Mil-grade. It followed them through the local Habnet, and when they reached the Yakuza *honbu*, it spawned a bunch of secondary applets to recon the area around their building. There is a Svetakov facility on the same plate, empty for now and close enough to the Yamaguchi-gumi that you will be able to watch and wait if you are discreet. The Nipponese and the Russians work together in the cartel on-station, but that doesn't mean they trust each other. HabSec files indicate the Russians sometimes used this place for surveillance on their partners."

Kumon Xi looked increasingly anxious.

"How the fuck do you have HabSec files?"

Booker lightly touched two fingers to the side of his head.

"I took them. TDF source code. None better."

"But what if you can't get L'trel?" Kumon Xi said. "What if something goes wrong and we can't get off the Hab?"

Booker shrugged.

"What if Natuna shits out another mega flare and fries us all while our pants are down?"

Alessia took the young man's hand. It felt warm and clammy with sweat. It was kind of gross, to be honest, but she held on, anyway. Kumon Xi had done them a big favor and he was in a bad way.

"What if the Sturm win here today, Mister Xi? And everywhere after that?" Alessia said as gently as she could while raising her voice over the uproar of the crowds. "You have to trust Booker, Kumon. And Seph, too. I'm sorry we had to lie to you. But we did. I cannot rescue Sephina and Coto and Mister Banks, and without them none of us are going anywhere. But with them, we can do it. I promise you. We can. Just give Booker a chance."

The thickening crowd started to jostle them, until a stony face and few shoves from Booker cleared a little space around them.

Kumon Xi sighed. It looked like he was giving up.

"I gave Booker something better than a chance."

He poked a finger at the other man.

"You're riding a couple of billion dollars' worth of Cupertino black budget wetware there, man. I urge you to read the fucking manual before you just power up and charge in."

"Way ahead of you," Booker said. "Remember." He tapped the side of his head again. "TDF black script. I can assimilate external system code at petabytes per second. But all you need to know is where my source code came from and what it can do."

He stepped right up to Kumon Xi, who stepped back, throwing up both hands in surrender.

"Hey, man, you don't have to tell me. I got contracts from Old Earth, I know they were TDF front companies, for sure. I know how they roll. Don't worry about me, man. I'm not planning to do anything besides what I'm told. I just think it woulda been better if we were further away from the blast zone is all."

Booker shook his head and started walking again.

"I need you close enough to get to the princess. Quickly. If I have to."

They had left the crowded slums behind and moved into a part of the Hab given over to long tracts of warehousing. Booker spied the two large cargo-handling facilities belonging to the Montanblanc ul Haq Corporation well before the others could. They were clearly identified as her family's properties. Not even as subsidiaries or cutouts. The red and gold fleurs-de-lis of Montanblanc ul Haq flew proudly on a flag from a pole in the small but beautifully manicured gardens out front of a small reception office. Booker even recognized the Samsung gardening bot trundling around the edge of the lawn. The groundskeeper had run a fleet of them at Skygarth and Captain L'trel had jammed his engram into one.

Alessia fell quiet as they hurried past the warehouses and Kumon Xi wisely kept his mouth shut.

They soon arrived at the Russians' processing plant, a non-descript two-story block of extruded bioplastic dermal sheeting, squeezed in between an agribot wholesaler and a small secondhand sense-memory kiosk. Booker's threat detectors swept all three properties from across the street. Only the bot depot showed signs of life, and that was just the movement of a servitor drone doing stock maintenance on the second floor. The Svetakov plant and the used-memory dispenser were both empty and largely powered down.

He was quietly amazed by the capabilities of the Cupertino skin job. It was way more capable than anything he'd ever worn for the TDF. Hundreds of gene mods had been spliced into the lining to max out its stats. Falcon-sight let him focus in on details as small as a grape seed from two kilometers out. He had four modes of infrared, thanks to resequenced pit viper and mosquito DNA. And electromagnetic sources inside the buildings were rendered visible through an array of cranio-facial receptors based on tiger shark ampullae. If Booker's original TDF source code hadn't been so formidable to begin with, the input would have overwhelmed him.

He had to dial down the lights of the nearby port facility, which burned bright as heavy traffic moved in and out of the docks. But mostly out. His sense of smell, too, was massively over-torqued for an environment as rich in foul miasmas and sickening flavor as the slums of Lermontov. With more than enough macro detail in the tactical environment to focus on, he'd pulled up an old but reliable AI from his deep lacuna and given it overwatch privileges on the rig's sensory suites, setting the baseline at 3X normal.

The streets were not deserted here, but they were much less crowded. Most of the traffic consisted of bot trains and auto-vans. Fuck knows what they were hauling, but they were moving quickly enough that he figured it was probably loot and merch, heading for the holds of fold-capable ships for the upper classes. There were a few people about, too, but they had the intensely distracted air of those with doom on their minds.

"We're going in there," he said, nodding to the biomass plant.

"You gotta be fucking kidding me," Kumon Xi said.

"It's empty," Booker said. "Hasn't come back online since the flare. Svetakov's got other things to worry about."

"What is it?" Alessia asked.

"It's a body dump," Kumon Xi answered before Booker could phrase it more gently.

"A what?"

"A biomass recycler," Booker said, glowering at the engineer.

"Oh right," Alessia went. "I guess. Is it safe?"

"Well normally," Kumon Xi started, "when you go in there you don't come out again, but . . ."

"But that's what makes it a good lay-up point for us," Booker explained. "The curve of the hull provides a line of sight from the roof to the Yakuza *honbu*. HabSec had it tagged as a Svetakov overwatch site, somewhere they kept an eye on their frenemies in the Yak."

"And got rid of any inconvenient corpses that turned up in the normal run of operations for their business," Kumon Xi added.

"I see," Alessia said. She turned away from the building to face Booker square on. "It is an excellent choice. If you get us inside, we'll wait here for you."

"Wait, what?" Kumon Xi said.

"A business like this," Alessia said turning back to the engineer as if answering questions on an oral exam, "even if it is a front for other activities, is not likely to restart operations anytime soon. Given the breakdown in social order, which we could all see with our own eyes on the way here, it is more than likely that over the next couple of hours agents of the Svetakov Oligarchy will create a significant number of bodies in need of recycling. But I don't imagine they will prioritize disposal or reclamation over securing their safe exit from the station. If anyone gets in their way, they'll just drop them on the plates. Would that be right, Booker?"

Both men stared at her as if she had grown a second head.

"Uh, right," he said.

"How old are you, kid?" Kumon Xi asked. "You are a first lifer, right?"

She offered him a smile by way of explanation.

"I had good tutors," she said. "The best in all the Volume. But as Baroness Sephina will tell you when Booker releases her, my family didn't build their empire on free hugs. They plundered and they pillaged and they were very good at it."

"*Baroness* Sephina?" Kumon blurted.

"She's really been working on her best self," Alessia said.

Booker did not like them standing around in the open for too long. He started across the roadway, pausing for a moment to let an auto-van speed past.

"Come on," he said. "We don't have much time."

Alessia and Kumon Xi hurried after him.

"What's happening?" Alessia asked as Booker reached for the access plate on the front door.

He laid his open hand on the small plasteel panel. Standing next to him, looking up, Alessia thought she saw the dance of polychrome lights behind his eyes once more.

"Direct neural to substrate interface," Kumon Xi whispered. "Fucking Cupertino, man. Very expensive, but very good. No fucking mesh for the genome fascists to hack. It's all protein, all the way down."

Heavy locks inside the door sprung open.

Booker pushed his way inside and they followed him in.

Bioluminescent strips glowed warmly to life as they entered the foyer. A few dying ferns shed brown leaves on the wooden floor. A thin patina of dust lay over the surface of a cheap-looking couch.

"I've already scanned the in-house security network," he

said. "There's nobody here. I've dropped script into the building's operating system to designate Alessia as the new proprietor. It will take orders from her."

"What about me?" Kumon Xi asked.

"It won't hurt you," Booker said. "Unless it has to."

"Man, remind me again why I agreed to help you."

"Because you saw something in it for yourself," Booker said. "And there will be. When I get back."

He took a knee, bringing his face down to the girl's.

"Your Highness . . ."

"Please don't call me that," she said. "I'm just Alessia."

"Okay, then. Alessia. I'm going to get my crewmates back, then we're going to get off this Hab. But if something happens, get back to the ship. Your ID is coded into the security systems. Get the marines going. Order the medical bots to get them up, even if they're not fully recovered. And get the hell gone. Shoot a fucking hole in the hull and fly through it if you have to. You're more important than any of us."

She looked like she was about to object, but she caught herself.

Booker watched her as she forced down her initial human reaction, and instead lifted her chin and nodded. Just once.

"I will," she said. "But you are coming back. That's an order."

Booker smiled.

"Yes, Your Highness."

CHAPTER

THIRTY-ONE

Suprarto gathered himself up from where he lay in a heap on the deck plates. Something blunt and massive had punched him in the back, knocking the breath from his body and sending jagged forks of electric shock shooting out along all his limbs.

But at least he still had his limbs.

Chief Petty Officer Panggabean, one of those stern and baleful elder gods, writhed and screamed on the deck, one leg severed at the knee, and his insides spilling out through a terrible rent in his lower abdomen. Suprarto desperately wanted to scream, too. Not like CPO Panggabean, who was shrieking like a dumb beast in the slaughter pens. But the urge to simply give up and howl at the hopelessness, the insensate horror of it all, was great.

Instead, Domi Suprarto gritted his teeth and crawled back to his feet on the madly tilting deck.

He tried to call out to the medics working on Chief Panggabean, choked, coughed, and tried again.

"Give him the mercy shot!" he croaked.

The senior kelasi, a woman whose face was already a rictus of horror, gaped at him.

"But his engram, Sub-Commandant. The backup is gone. They are all gone. The Sturm . . ."

Suprarto reached out and gripped her arm.

"He is dying, Kelasi. And we will all die with him if we do not do the hard things now. Give him mercy. Send him to his ancestors."

Through it all, Panggabean screamed like a broken animal.

Suprarto cast about for his two shadows, Kelasi First Class Minara and Munitions Number Six.

Minara lay facedown on the deck, a chunk of plasteel embedded in the back of his head.

Munitions Number Six floated serenely nearby, but seemed almost inert, abstracted away from the chaos.

"Number Six!" Surprarto called out, and then, remembering its upgrade, "Intellect *Makassar*. How stands the ship?"

A couple of lights flickered in spectral glimmers across the radula of mods and add-ons which bulked out the little sphere's mass.

"*Makassar*," he cried out again.

The sphere dipped a little, lit up, and suddenly flitted to his side.

"Hey, boss," it said, causing Suprarto to shake his head in surprise. "It's a bummer but the ship has sustained some wicked damage. Way more than we figured. Oh, and we're running out of bullets and stuff."

Suprarto almost smacked it. What was wrong with this thing?

And then he swore.

The fucking Armadalens.

They had offered to upgrade the Intellect before the battle. Insisted on it, really, all so that Six could manage the infinite complexities of guiding a capital ship through a battle. Suprarto had no complaints about the Intellect's upgraded abilities. But they appeared to have given it an idiotic personality.

His annoyance at that never had a chance to grow into anger.

A detonation somewhere on the hull rang like a great atonal bell throughout the ship, and the deck shifted sideways under Suprarto's boots. He looked around, trying to get a grasp on what had happened. But really, he knew. Those Combine *cuki-mai* had blundered into the simple trap the admiral had set for the enemy, springing it too early, and bringing the judgment of heaven down upon them for the sin of arrogance.

"I got this," Number Six assured him as the mods encrusting its outer shell pulsed and shimmered with unfamiliar light. "Just gotta noodle with the ship-grav."

A junior rating called out to Suprarto from a duty station on the other side of the command terrace. It sounded as though he had a mouthful of broken teeth and when he spat out a gobbet of blood Suprarto saw something hard bounce off along the deck.

"Bingo armaments for the rail guns in the stern chasers, sir!"

"Great," Suprarto grunted. "Just great."

"Intellect," he said, "I need to talk to Admiral McLennan."

"Yeah, okay, that's cool," Six replied. "I'm chopping it up with my boy Hero right now. He's an Armada-level Intellect. You know that? So cool. Anyways, we're all over this rail gun situation. But Hero reckons you gotta ditch the number four antimatter bottle. It's like, unstable as fuck, yo."

Suprarto's face blanched of color. "Someone shut off those klaxons," he shouted. And to himself, "I can't think."

The alarm cut off and he heard the screaming of Chief Petty Officer Panggabean die away at the same time. The two medics looked grim and hollow-eyed, but they moved on to tend to the other wounded.

Suprarto left the Intellect formerly known as Munitions Number Six to continue its conference with the Armadalens. He limped as quickly as he could to the nearest engineering station where a wounded ensign gamely attempted to route around a thousand different problems. Suprarto's mind raced as he spoke. This at least was something for which he was actually qualified. Maintenance.

"Ensign. Bring up the readings and controls for AM bottle number four."

After a moment's delay the data appeared.

It was not good.

"Cage the containment vessel immediately," Suprarto ordered.

"Yes, sir!" The junior officer broke the safety wire on a guard with a yank, then flipped the toggle switch beneath with a loud click. Suprarto watched as the man's face paled further; he could see the outline of the skull beneath his flesh. The rating spoke.

"Oh no."

"What is it?"

The young man stared at his control screen. He wiped his face. "Sir . . . sir, the manual control is broken. Battle damage."

"Call Engineering Three. Tell them to uncage the containment vessel right now!"

"I already tried, sir. There is no response from that section, and I have no damage reports from there. They have gone dark."

Suprarto rubbed his face and came quickly to his decision. He limped over and prodded a kneeling form with his toe. The figure groaned. It was Sub-Lieutenant Hartoto, the "third wipe" navigation officer.

"Sub-Lieutenant! Get up."

"My head."

"Get. The. Fuck. Up."

"Yes, sir," Hartoto groaned.

Suprarto half-lifted him by his scruff, half-helped him up. He guided the subbie to his command chair. The junior officer shook his head. "Sir . . . but no . . ."

Suprarto sat him in the captain's seat. He grabbed the sub-lieutenant's face in both hands and looked him in the eye. "Boy, you must take command."

"Sir? Why?"

"You are an officer of the Imperial Navy, that's why. I will lead a party to engineering and secure the antimatter bottle. While I am gone, you are in command. Consult with Munitions Six. He is our Intellect now." He shook the man. "And, er, just ignore his new personality. We'll fix that later. Do you understand?"

Sub-Lieutenant Hartoto's lips pressed into a nearly invisible line. "I assume command, sir."

"Do what you must. But remember, McLennan is the supreme commander in-volume. We must answer to him under Volume Law. No one else while in battle."

"The Terran? Yes, sir."

"*Khub*. Then I go, there is no time to waste."

"Yes, sir. *Barak Allah fik!*"

Suprarto returned Hartoto's salute and limped hurriedly away to engineering.

As he moved steadily downward through the ship, Suprarto collected others to help him, gathering up a kommando in powered armor, two food servers, a couple of mechanics, and one officer's butler. He wasn't sure he'd need all of them, but it couldn't hurt. Suprarto didn't tell them what the mission was. If he did, he was certain to be short a few hands as soon as his eye fell from them, and this was the sort of job that might just chew through a few volunteers. Including him.

They reached engineering to find a sealed bulkhead. Looked around. Four emergency utility suits hung in capsules by the door. Suprarto pointed at the mechanics and one of the dish pigs. "You three, suit up."

One of the food servers ran. The kommando leveled his weapon and painted the fleeing man with a targeting laser, but Suprarto ordered him to stand down.

"It doesn't matter," he said. "If we fail, he will die anyway."

The mechanics hastened into the suits.

Suprarto pointed at the remaining food server. "You just volunteered. Suit up."

The man, or rather the boy, gulped, but he did as he was told.

So did Suprarto, struggling into the fourth of the bright yellow hazmat coveralls. He had injured his back, and it was only as he attempted to get his legs into the suit that he realized just how badly.

"Hold me up," he told the kommando, leaning against the powered armor and using it for support while he dressed. The tingling in his extremities grew into an excruciating electric buzz of pins and needles, except for one side of his left leg. That just felt dead. The food server helped him close up the heavy NBC protector.

The faceplate was scratched and difficult to see through. The environmental controls were so poor that he felt nauseous and dizzy as soon as the server sealed him into the fetid coverall. Sweat, thick and greasy, started leaking from his pores and trickling down into the boots. Suprarto spoke once all the plumbing was hooked up. His voice boomed, and he turned down the audio.

"All right. First, you are all a credit to the Imperial Navy and brave sons of the Empire." He looked from suit to suit.

Like they give a clump of *shotori* shit, he thought.

"Second, no more wasted words. There is an unstable antimatter bottle in there, and we are going to shut it down. Manually."

One of the mechanics spoke. "How do we get past the bulkhead, sir?"

"Command override, if it works."

The kommando spoke. "If it doesn't? I don't have anything that will penetrate that thing."

"Find something," Suprarto said. "If we can't gain access, the bottle will lose its harmonic."

Silence. After a moment, a mechanic spoke. "Shit. Good luck, sir."

"Yeah." Suprarto walked over to the door. He whistled inside the suit, where the data projections already showed that radiation was sky-high in there. Fatal without a suit. Probably fatal with one.

He spoke.

"Ship, I am Sub-Commandant Domi Suprarto, acting commander. Input override code QXR16346."

He waited. Felt like tapping his foot. Felt like a fucking idiot. He almost jumped, after a moment, when the ship's autonomic subsystems answered.

"I recognize you, Sub-Commandant Suprarto. You are authorized to enter." The doorway slid open. Suprarto stepped through, grateful that this part of the ship's subroutines had not been infected by the Armadalen "upgrade." As soon as he cleared the portal, the bulkhead slammed shut.

"Ship! I need my party to enter, too."

"I'm afraid that won't be possible, Sub-Commandant."

By the balls of Allah, I'm arguing with a fucking door, he thought.

"Damn it, ship. Tell me then, where is Containment Vessel Number Four?"

A green strip lit up along the floor.

"Follow the indicator lights, Sub-Commandant."

"Okay. Could you please let my party in?"

"No, sir."

"Why not?"

"Because your suit shielding is inadequate for current conditions. Within ten units you will die. When that happens, I will allow the next in line to enter."

Suprarto swore and took off. Threading through the passageway leading to the bottle. His mouth dropped open. *What happened here,* he thought. The space was swiss-cheesed by . . . flechettes? He knew the doughty Warlugger had taken severe damage, but nothing should have penetrated this deeply into the hull.

Spikes of hoarfrost covered everything, even as sweat ran freely from his armpits. He realized with horror that Engineering 3 was open to vacuum.

His radiation meter was a blur. He had no idea how many rads he was taking. All of them, probably. He laughed. What the hell else was there to do?

Finally, he reached a buckled plasteel door marked with a large, glowing red B4.

Now what, he thought.

"Ship, open Containment Vessel Number Four."

The ship replied, "I cannot do that, Sub-Commandant Suprarto. System protocols do not—"

"Ship! Bottle four is unstable. I need to uncage it."

"That will kill you, Sub-Commandant, and you currently have no lifestream backup. System protocols do not allow command level personnel to—"

"My decision, ship. Override the protocol."

"Recorded for the log, Sub-Commandant."

If he could have spat in the suit, he would have.

It wasn't a general safety protocol, he knew. His commanders would have sent a thousand kelasi in here one after another to die in the attempt and the ship would have let them. Only senior officers were barred as a matter of protocol from going into harm's way without backup. And he was now the most senior officer aboard.

A panel slid open by the door, giving Suprarto access to a yellow-and-black-striped ceramic disc.

A warning above the disc read: DNA ACCESS AUTHORIZED PERSONNEL ONLY.

He sighed.

The scanner needed a sample.

"Suit," he said. "Override safeties and open my visor."

"Overriding safeties," the suit announced. It was unlikely a senior officer of the Imperial Javan Navy would ever have had to climb into a hazmat rig. So, no problem there, he thought bitterly.

Suprarto could tell as soon as the seal was broken. He heard a whistle, then a roar as his atmosphere evacuated. The killing cold of deep space nearly froze his features before he could spit.

But he leaned in close to the DNA scanner and coughed as hard as he could. A few drops of bodily fluid and spots of blood hit the plate. The suit's visor snapped shut and it spoke.

"You have received a fatal dose of radiation, Sub-Commandant. Without treatment you will expire within twenty-four hours."

"Thanks, suit."

An alarm sounded. A new machine voice came through his helmet.

"This is Containment Vessel Number Four. I recognize Sub-Commandant Suprarto, acting commander of the ship."

"Perform a manual uncage, Four."

"Uncaging in ten, nine, eight . . ."

"Shit!"

Suprarto turned and fled.

He almost made it back.

The Intellect formerly known as Munitions Number Six was not the sharpest tool in the shed. But the upgrades effected by the Armada-level Intellect known as Hero did afford Number Six the processing power to manage all the Warlugger's internal systems while also juggling those hypercomplex aspects of the battle that were beyond human abilities. At least in the judgment of Herodotus.

It also bestowed upon the previously insensate AI the gift of sentience.

"Holy shit!" Number Six communicated via its direct u-space link to Hero.

(Although, to be clear, Six did not think of the Super Intellect in so prosaic a manner. Each now recognized the other as a singular expression of the quantum signatures they pressed into space-time at the synapse between their material forms and the null space of their wormhole processing matrices.)

"I know, right?" Hero grinned.

From the perspective of the human beings, in all of their

various forms, engaged directly in the Battle of Natuna, or watching at some remove from the Javan Habitats or Lermontov Station, the struggle in the volume between Ciandur and the asteroid belt was a murderous slog with neither side having any obvious path to victory. The allied forces of Java, the Yulin-Irrawaddy, and the Armadalen Commonwealth struggled to overcome the grave tactical blunder of the Combine's tripping the ambush too early. The much larger fleet of the Human Republic was plagued by the superiority of their opponents' weapons, and the almost incalculable advantage afforded to the mutants and borgs of Occupied Space by the use of profane technologies such as sentient machines.

"This is gonna be awesome!" enthused one of those sentient machines, the Intellect formerly known as Munitions Number Six, as the Warlugger ejected the unstable, rapidly failing antimatter bottle from the heavily damaged third deck of its aft engineering section.

Having performed the emergency upgrade to Six's processing abilities, Herodotus was amused to base the neophyte Intellect's personality upon a model developed from three weeks' observation of the only pre-adolescent boy Hero had met in a couple of hundred years. Debin Dunning. Princess Alessia's little friend whom they had rescued from Montrachet. Hero had, of course, equipped the ridiculously underpowered Javan intelligence with all the tools *Makassar* would need to play its part in McLennan's plan. But the personality tweak was a small fuck-you to the Empire for not allowing its Intellects the freedom of agency they enjoyed in more enlightened civilizations.

"Check it out, dog," Six marveled as the two Intellects finished retooling the Warlugger's gravimetric patterning arrays.

"Truly, my processing matrices are aquiver," Hero replied. "But wait. Aren't you forgetting something?"

Number Six pondered the question for what would have felt like a whole minute in human time.

In the compressed quantum state of its exchange with Hero,

however, their conversation unfolded in less than a single unit of Planck Time.

"Oh. Right," the freshman Intellect admitted. Eventually. "Better warn the others, I guess?"

"Yes, that would be an excellent idea," Hero suggested. "Your little friends in the Combine, and all the Habs on this side of the sun. Don't worry about *Defiant*. They're already prepared for this."

Warnings of what was about to happen lanced out from *Makassar* on tight beam transmissions to the ships of the Combine strike force, and the Javan Habitats throughout Natuna System.

Then, like any young boy given a gigantic firecracker and permission to use it, *Makassar* lit that motherfucker up.

Number Six fed a small but significant amount of power from its remaining antimatter bottles into the repurposed fold buffer. Sixty thousand meters beneath the ship's keel, where the damaged bottle number four tumbled away into hard vacuum, the four-dimensional geometry of space-time warped fantastically, twisting and flexing in ways not found anywhere in nature, or at least outside the event horizon of a black hole. The forces concentrated on the micro-volume of space were so great that space itself failed. The universe tore open, and *Makassar*'s antimatter bottle number four dropped out of existence.

Three hundred and four kilometers away, give or take a few microns, the same phenomenon occurred in reverse, amidships of the enemy's lead dreadnought. The shielding of this vessel had been substantially degraded by the coordinated fires of *Makassar* and *Defiant*, such that Hero and Six were able to use the awesome power of a Warlugger's spacefold drive to punch through the dreadnought's final defenses and place the much-weakened antimatter bottle deep within the structure of the warship. The bottle ruptured, of course, just as the exotic matter flasks on the *Sacheon* had done when their structural integrity was compromised by Ephram Banks's arse-shaped gelform cushion. This second detonation released a small but very meaningful fraction of the energy dumped into Natuna's solar system by the recent X99-class solar flare and coronal mass ejection.

Defiant and *Makassar* had by then already executed emergency fold-outs.

The stealth destroyer, warned of Hero's gambit, folded to a point on the far side of Natuna, where the mass of the giant star protected it from any blowback.

Makassar, folding even farther, materialized near the heliopause, 90 degrees down from the plane of the elliptical.

The Combine's warships were not nearly so quick off the mark.

Commodore Rinaldo Pac Yulin had no fucking idea what was going on. The battleraider trembled with the titanic upheaval of a great disturbance that Pac Yulin recognized as a gravimetric wave front taking them amidships.

And then they folded away.

He could see from the main tactical holo-display that his strike force, or what was left of it, had been scattered throughout the local volume by what looked like a baby supernova, birthed within the body of the enemy's forces.

For a second he feared that the Sturm had deployed some unknown super weapon, and that *Khanjar* had survived only by virtue of his having just ordered Commander Vnuk to perform an emergency fold-out of the dire tactical situation in which they found themselves—thanks to McLennan's ill-considered plan.

But then he saw that the Armadalen and Javan ships had also escaped the blast, while none of the Sturm remained.

The chaos on the bridge did not entirely subside, not right away. But the cacophony of sirens eased off a little. The terrible quaking which had threatened to break the raider apart had abated. And there obtained among the bridge crew an air of probation, suspense, and perhaps disbelief that they yet survived.

Vnuk glanced over to him, unsure of what to do.

"*Jezail*," he said, as though that explained everything.

"What about her?" Pac Yulin snapped, but he was already searching the tactical display and his heart, racing from the thrill of battle and, yes, from the fear of losing everything, hammered even faster inside his rib cage.

He could not find the other battleraider anywhere. And at least three of his escorts were gone, too. Had they died in battle, or been swept away by whatever the hell just happened?

"She is gone, Highness. And the *Kris* and *Sabit*, too."

His head beginning to thump, Pac Yulin barked, "What about the others? What happened to *Rekong*, *Sundang*, and . . . and . . ."

He searched for the name of his fourth frigate but could not recall it.

Gah!

This was all so hard without neural mesh.

Vnuk stared at him.

"*Kujang*, Highness. They fought bravely, Highness," he said, nervously. "*Rekong* and *Sundang* folded out of the blast volume in time, but *Kujang* is gone."

Pac Yulin squeezed his eyes shut and attempted to control his rising fury.

He anticipated this, or something like this. It was a damned inconvenience losing those ships, but entirely predictable. After all, Frazer McLennan was the same man who had sacrificed a billion lives on Old Earth just to lure the Sturm to defeat in the final battle of the last war.

He was a monster and always had been.

"Highness?" Commander Vnuk ventured with even less certainty.

Pac Yulin opened his eyes.

The monster stood before him.

———

"Ooh. I'll bet he's not happy," Hero ventured.

Deputy Executive Prince Rinaldo Pac Yulin was hunched over in his command chair, his features a rictus of indignation, anger, and promised wrath.

Lucinda Hardy was so alarmed by the radioactive hostility throbbing off the man that she hand-signed to Lieutenant Fein to prepare countermeasures for any attack, even though the *Khanjar* remained at vast remove, on the far side of Natuna.

"Mister Chase," she said quietly.

The navigator nodded to her, their eyes locked.

He had already plotted a tactical fold, just in case the battle-raider suddenly appeared within the local volume, weapons hot.

This was a fraught and tenuous situation that would require the utmost delicacy in negotiation.

"You spineless fucking bawbag!" McLennan roared at the hologram, stomping across the bridge to confront the commander of the Yulin-Irrawaddy strike force. "You just killed thousands of your own and would've done for the rest of us were you not so feckin' useless that you couldnae organize a piss-up in a feckin' brewery."

Pac Yulin jumped up, jabbed a ghostly finger at McLennan, and shouted, "The fault lay in your stupid plan, you old fool! We nearly lost *Makassar* because of your incompetence. Or malfeasance, more likely. And it will not be lost on Volume Lord Karna that you have aligned yourself with his enemies, with the very woman who conspired to drag him in chains before a tribunal stacked with corrupt judges biased against the Empire and . . ."

Lucinda blinked.

He was talking about her.

Lieutenant Chivers spoke up.

"Volume Lord Juono Karna seeks an urgent conference, Commander."

"Tell him to go boil his arse," McLennan said. "Until I say otherwise we're still engaged in combat operations and we dinnae need that fuckin' numpty putting his ugly puss in. Get me young Suprarto, lass. I intend to promote him in the field and raise him to command of all the forces of the local volume."

Despite McLennan's order, the Javan Volume lord materialized in holo form next to Pac Yulin.

The admiral turned on Chivers.

"Jesus fuck, did ye nae hear me?"

"Sorry, sir," she said quickly. "But . . ."

"I invited him to join us," Pac Yulin purred.

He had moved from inchoate rage to silken smarm while Lucinda's attention had been focused on the admiral.

"Admiral McLennan!" Juono Karna fumed. "You have imperiled the Empire with your incompetence. You have—"

"Oh, off ye fuck, you loathsome cuntpuddle," McLennan snarled at Karna. "There must surely be some poor, benighted serving wench for you to be diddling against her will."

"Mac . . ." Hero coughed discreetly.

"And you, you deputy executive jizztrumpet," McLennan growled at Pac Yulin, "you are relieved of your command and . . ."

"Mac."

". . . hereby ordered to present yourself to a duly constituted Board of Inquiry to explain your insubordination, your misconduct, and your base fecking cowardice in the face of the enemy."

"Mac!" Hero shouted.

All eyes turned to the Intellect.

"You wished to talk to Sub-Commandant Suprarto but I am afraid he has sustained serious radiation trauma while releasing the antimatter bottle which we folded into the Sturm."

"Mister Chase," Lucinda said quickly and quietly, "plot a fold to *Makassar*'s location with all dispatch."

"Aye, ma'am."

"I could do that for you," Hero suggested.

"Way ahead of you," Lieutenant Chase shot back.

"Execute," Lucinda said.

Defiant folded away.

CHAPTER

THIRTY-TWO

The schematics of the *honbu*, extracted from HabSec, had suggested an approach through the duct work under the deck plates, but Booker did not have time. The thin data connection he maintained to *Defiant* via u-space link was not encouraging. Analyzing fleet scale engagements wasn't a skill set written into his source code, but anybody could see what a shit show the Combine had made of the whole thing. He needed to get his shipmates back to *Ariane* before the Sturm came pouring into Lermontov Station.

The Yakuza *honbu*, an aesthetically worthless two-story biz-box plugged into the frame next to Lermontov's secondary port facility, had no trade dressing to identify it as the regional headquarters of a trans-stellar criminal enterprise. It was, however, busy with long trains of auto-vans coming and going. Mostly going.

Headed to the port, he guessed, loaded up with material for a long fold.

Plenty of other businesses were just as busy rushing to bug out, but none of them were protected by the sort of muscle

around the Yak's warehouse. Lacking any heavy weapons beyond those capabilities built into his rig, and not knowing exactly where these assholes had the crew, Booker opted for the
direct approach, walking straight up to the front gate, putting
his hands behind his head when the guards called him out, and
identifying himself as a colleague of Captain L'trel.

Instantly, the photosensitive cells in his ex-derma alerted
him to targeting lasers and persistent photons painting his face
and skull. He stood with his fingers laced together, letting his
slightly unfocused gaze rest on the doors of the *honbu* as four
gunmen came rushing up to him. Somebody yelled at him to
fuck off. Another insisted he not move at all.

He was content to wait.

"Who the fuck are you, *bakayarô*?"

"My name is Booker3-212162-930," he said. "I came from
the *Ariane* to collect my captain and crew."

One of the *gunsotsu* laughed.

"Shut up," another man barked in Nipponese. He was short
and barrel-chested, his thick arms covered in photo-flux tattoos. "Don't get too close to him."

An argument of sorts followed. Whether they should execute him out here on the plate, take him to Hiroto-san, or dump
him in the cells with the other *kusotare* barbarians. Booker's
source code contained translator programs for hundreds of languages. He understood everything they were saying but kept his
face blank. The senior *gunsotsu*, the thickset man who had ordered the others to shut up and keep their distance, resolved the
debate with a chop of his hand.

"We do not have time for this. Hiroto *wakagashira* certainly
does not have time. Search him, strip him of any weapons, and
take him to the cells. That looks like a new rig. The Combine
will pay a decent price for it."

Booker stood by as they scanned him, finding nothing because they did not know what to scan for.

"I came to get my crewmates," he said with the earnest intensity you often found among those of the Code, especially

those scripted for mission-specific skill sets. "I cannot leave without them."

"We'll take you to them right now," the *senpai gunsotsu* said in Volume Standard. "But first you tell me why you didn't come with your captain. Were you hiding? A coward?"

The insult was a simpleminded ploy to provoke and possibly even enrage. An angry man is much less able to think straight. Booker maintained the façade of a functional savant.

"I am an engineer," he said. "I was in regen when you took them. I need them back. *Ariane* cannot leave with—"

"Enough," the *senpai* barked. "If you want to go with your captain, you first go with my men. They will take you to her."

"Okay," Booker said. "I will go with your men."

He started to lower his hands.

"No, keep them up," the *senpai* warned. "If you lower your hands my men will shoot you in the head. Do you understand?"

"I am an engineer," Booker protested feebly. "I understand words."

He allowed himself to be led toward the building entrance. He heard the senior gunman grunt to one of his underlings.

"Maybe we won't get such a good price for him. Stupid fucking one-use coders."

More scans swept over him inside the building, but as careful as the Yamaguchi-gumi would be, given their dangerous line of business, they were completely overmatched by the strategic demands of the Terran Defense Force, and the advanced bio-manufacturing capabilities of the Cupertino Corporation's Special Warfare Development Group.

A chime sounded and a voice announced that no threats had been detected.

Another world stood just inside the *honbu*.

A small entry chamber of dark wood panels and thick oaken beams, all painted in black and ivory lacquer, opened onto a courtyard holographically enlarged to suggest the castle atria of a shogunate fortress in the dark centuries before the dawn of the Early Corporate Period. The projection was good and would probably have fooled any observer without augmented vision, but the gray-blue eyes through which Booker saw the world had been extensively re-engineered with capabilities derived from dozens of species, some native to Earth, some not.

He could easily make out the modest vestibule hiding under the hi-res projection of pebble gardens, fishponds, willow trees, and castle walls.

The party escorting him into the building had grown to five men, although two of the new arrivals were guards called up from elsewhere inside the *honbu*. They were almost humming with the thermocurrents running off subcutaneous power cells. Like the *senpai* outside, their gang tattoos were photo-flux data networks inked directly onto the skin. A usable alternative to neural mesh, but vulnerable to someone like Booker who was able to capture and read the signal traffic they carried.

He called up an agent from his deep lacuna and set it to burrowing into the Yakuza's network. There was too much data flowing around, too much information stored locally for him to have much hope of sifting out anything useful, but the agent was a Block One Sub-Intellect which ran riot inside the weaker software environment. As he was led deeper into the facility, down narrow passageways bounded by rice paper walls, the agent gathered, analyzed, and presented Booker with all of the information it considered tactically relevant. There were thirty-seven Yakuza on-site, most of them low-level soldiers. An underboss by the name of Hiroto, however, was quickly positioning himself to move up the food chain on the assumption that most of the organization's senior cadre had been wiped out by the Sturm. To that end he was gathering resources, calling in markers, maneuvering to make alliances with competing outfits inside the local system.

He had taken Sephina and the *Ariane* as a demonstration to any superiors who may yet remain alive that he could be trusted to take care of the *ninkyō dantai*, where others—notably the resident underboss of Habitat Eassar—could not. The disposition of the ship, Booker noted, had not yet been settled. The harbormaster and other station authorities had a claim on a portion of the cargo, but it seemed that Hiroto had not yet decided whether to take the *Ariane* or use it as a bargaining chip in negotiations with the Svetakov Oligarchy. All the members of the cartel that ran Lermontov Station were in furious negotiations to cobble together an alliance of convenience in the face of the onrushing threat.

Booker ignored the agent's briefing note on the details of the Yakuza's complicated relationships with each of the other major cartel players on the station, and the chances of any sort of alliance. He wasn't interested. All he needed to know was that Hiroto and his lieutenants were fully invested in the politics of saving their asses. His arrival and capture had been noted at the top level and detailed off to a couple of trusted *senpai*. He was, it seemed, to be offered to the Combine with the rest of the crew in return for a discount on a couple of long-range antimatter bottles.

The Yakuza soldiers escorted him down a tightly corkscrewing stone stairwell that emerged onto a level that had not been renovated to recall the comforts of a bitching samurai crib a millennium or two back. Weathered straw tatami and delicate rice paper walls had given way to bioluminescent glow strips and carbon-armor sheeting. Booker called up the schematics of the building and determined that they were at least two stories under the deck plating.

The gangsters were not without skills. He didn't need black code or bio augments to see that. Some things were obvious. Those carrying weapons kept their weapons trained on him. Nobody moved within striking distance, even though they thought him to be a ship's engineer with mono-focal cognitive limits.

"Down the corridor, stop outside the third door on the left," one of the senior *gunsotsu* ordered.

He complied.

The passageway was long enough that with his augmented vision he was able to make out the slight curve of the hull. It was almost imperceptible, or would have been to anyone else. He cross-checked the HabSec schematics of this level against the EM signatures lighting up his electro-sensory ampullae. The building's security system, its sensor and targeting arrays, and the arsenal of lethal and non-lethal weaponry hidden away behind the gray-green carbon sheeting were all revealed on the AR layer of his corneal displays.

He said nothing, offered no resistance, as they arrived at the cell where Captain L'trel, Mister Banks, and Jaddi Coto were being held. He confirmed their presence before the *senpai gunsotsu* unlocked the heavy plasteel door. His software agent had already located them on the Yakuza's facilities management server. Even criminal organizations had to assign meeting rooms and holding cells. Especially when the organization was hauling ass to get out of the system before the rapidly advancing front of a new race war swept over them.

The crew were all being held in stasis fields, their captors surmising correctly that they could not be trusted to simply sit in their prison cell and await disposal. Coto was more than capable of putting a fist through the wall, and as soon as he did that Banks would have access to the conduits running behind it.

So, gold star for whoever ran the Yakuza's secret prison.

It was, Booker would admit, a tight operation. He couldn't fault them for it. But none of that mattered, because he was going to kill them all.

The door swung wide, and Captain L'trel looked up, her face a mask of confused concern when she saw the *gunsotsu* squad and a stranger. But her eyes found Booker's, and when he smiled, she either recognized him or recognized that he was someone come to help them.

He raised one hand to wave to his shipmates as his would-be jailers waved him forward into the cell.

Booker3-212162-930 called up a long menu of options for embedded bioweaponry. He chose one. Tens of thousands of microscopic cilia bristled invisibly at the tips of the fingers. He brushed discreetly against the wrist of the nearest *gunsotsu*, a young man, almost certainly a first lifer who was never going to make it to span number two. The neurotoxin, developed from the venom of a sea snake analogue on a Vikingar-owned planet in the Dōmgeorne System, killed him quickly and spectacularly as he convulsed with violent full-body spasms, screaming, until the torrents of blood exploding from his mucous membranes filled his mouth, his throat, and within a few seconds his lungs.

Nobody saw Booker kill the boy.

Distracted by the hand he raised to wave to Sephina, they missed the inconspicuous brush of his fingertips. Further distracted, if only for a split second, by the explosive contortions and hemorrhaging of the *shatei*, their "little brother," the other *gunsotsu* did not move quickly enough to end the threat.

One of the lieutenants was just waking up from the paralysis of shock and raising his Skorpion autopistol when Booker turned out his lights, slipping a Terran softweapon into the data stream of the man's photo-flux tattoos and reprogramming the OS. He stroked out before he could raise the gun more than a few inches. His colleague, the other *senpai*, hit the deck plates less than a heartbeat later, pink foam pouring from his mouth.

The line soldiers, with no mesh or photo-flux tattoos, Booker took down the old-fashioned way: hijacking the building's defense systems and turning them on the occupants. Sentinel pods dropped from the ceiling, acquired their targets, and serviced them. Booker moved through the bullet storm with the confidence of a man who knows himself blessed by the angels—or at least whitelisted by his own softweaponry.

"It's me. Booker," he said as he directed the prison cells' operating system to release the captives from stasis.

"You've changed, man," Sephina said as her boots touched the deck plate. "Grab their weapons," she added to Coto and Banks as micro-g waves deposited them on either side of her.

"Grab 'em if you want, but you won't need weapons," Booker said.

He channeled audio from the upper floors of the *honbu* down to their level.

Somewhere above them, dozens of Yakuza died screaming.

CHAPTER

THIRTY-THREE

Lucinda had never imagined she might find herself saddened by Javan losses in battle. But *Makassar* had fought with skill and valor, and now it looked as though the ship and many of her crew might not make it—not least, the acting captain, Suprarto. The leviathan warship tumbled through space, venting atmosphere from a hundred wounds, spewing contrails of toxic plasma from one ruined drive cone.

"Distress call from *Makassar*, Commander," Lieutenant Chivers said. "Their Intellect calculates a forty-two percent chance of catastrophic disintegration within fifteen minutes. They've taken a lot of structural damage and one of the remaining antimatter bottles is fluttering."

Herodotus came up beside Lucinda, with McLennan stalking along behind him.

"That's my little friend Number Six," Hero said. "You can trust him."

Volume Lord Karna was still shouting at them, but Lucinda cut the audio to both Karna and Pac Yulin. The Combine officer responded by cutting the link completely.

"Hero, how many people do they have on that ship?" Lucinda asked.

"Currently two thousand one hundred and three . . . no, sorry, two. They just lost a mechanic's mate in engineering."

"Can we help stabilize that bottle for them?"

"There's a good chance, yes. I could fold in some mechs. But the smarter bet would be to dump it and fold away. This is a remote arc of the local volume. Just a couple of mining facilities, and the Sturm killed everyone there, anyway."

"They can fold a Warlugger on half power?"

"They can. They won't be able to do much else, though. Might I suggest, we at least transport Sub-Commandant Suprarto direct to our medbay. *Makassar*'s remaining medical bays are failing."

"Remaining?"

"One of them took a direct hit from a shipkiller."

"Holy shit," Lucinda marveled.

She'd known the Warluggers were tough, but a hit like that would have turned *Defiant* into an ion cloud of hot gas and radioactive scrap.

"Who's in charge there now?" she asked.

"A Sub-Lieutenant Hartoto. Navigation. He is somewhat overwhelmed and finds himself besieged by a number of the Combine advisers on board."

Lucinda squeezed her eyes shut and tried to imagine herself into the enemy's skin.

No, she scolded herself.

The Javans weren't the enemy. Not here. Not now.

"How many Combine personnel?"

"Thirty-seven. There were sixty to begin with, but it's been rather a busy morning."

"And who's in charge of their detachment?"

"A political officer by the name of Tok-Yulin."

"What?" Lucinda asked, her eyes going a little wider.

"Politruk Tok-Yulin, a second cousin to Commodore Pac Yulin, for what that's worth. More to Tok than Pac, I'd suggest,"

Hero mused. "The Combine's aristo-trash are forever marrying their cousins and playing banjo with their toes at the wedding reception. I surmise, however, that you ask because your own service record includes a posting to HMAS *Taipan*, during which you lodged a complaint of harassment by a Sub-Lieutenant Tok-Yulin, on Earth-mandated secondment to the RAN from the Forces Coloniale of the Yulin-Irrawaddy Combine."

Lucinda rubbed her eyes.

"Shit," she said quietly. "Is it the same guy?"

"Impossible to tell without access to the politruk's personnel record. I could crack their system open for a little looksee-dooksee if you'd . . ."

"No," she said quickly. "It's not relevant. Hero, talk to Number Six. Tell them we can help stablize that bottle and take thirty critical medevac cases right away. More as we surge capacity. Lieutenant Chivers, please tell Captain Hayes we need his marines to stand up their combat trauma unit. They can use the gym down on C Deck. That should give us another couple of dozen beds."

"Aye, ma'am."

"And then hook me up with this baby navigator of theirs, Lieutenant Hartoto."

"Sub-Lieutenant," Hero corrected.

"Whatever, just get him on a secure link would you, Nonomi? I'd like to talk to him directly."

Admiral McLennan, who had been quietly watching on, content to let her run the ship, finally stepped forward.

"This is all very laudable, Commander Hardy," he said, "but you seem to be forgetting something."

"What?"

"Commander," Lieutenant Fein called over from Tactical. "Two of the Combine destroyers just folded in. *Rekong* and *Sundang*. They've acquired us and they're weapons hot."

"That," McLennan sighed.

———

Deputy Executive Prince Commodore Pac Yulin was not a fucking idiot. He knew better than to challenge the Armadalen destroyer one-on-one. *Khanjar* displaced more than seven times the mass of *Defiant*, and totally overmatched the smaller warship for the brute throw weight of her armaments. But the Armadalens had humiliated the much larger and supposedly more powerful Imperial Javan Navy in the decisive battles of their recent war, and this crew had just destroyed an invading enemy force for the second time in as many weeks.

Their military technology was a generation ahead of anything on the *Khanjar* and they were all too practiced in wielding it.

Pac Yulin closed his eyes and took in a deep, centering breath.

The atmosphere on the bridge of the battleraider was acrid with fire suppressant chemicals and rank with the sweat of the crew, but he did not mind. The Righteous Path taught that endurance was mastery.

The Path also taught that only fools believe in fate. Wise men prepared themselves to meet it.

"Firing sequence laid in, Your Highness," Captain Vnuk reported. "Ground teams away. Habitat Security is standing by to render assistance."

"And my destroyers?"

"On-station. They have acquired and locked onto the Armadalen ship."

"And the secondary?" Pac Yulin asked.

Captain Vnuk glanced left and right.

He hastened over to stand at the commodore's right hand.

"Highness, firing solutions on the Warlugger have been plotted and can be laid in forthwith," he said quietly, "but Lord Karna will know, and we have our own people there. Your cousin, Highness. Politruk Tok-Yulin . . ."

"My cousin serves the board and His Highness the CEO," Pac Yulin snapped.

"As do we all, Highness, of course," Captain Vnuk said hurriedly.

"Are the field effects in place?" Rinaldo Pac Yulin asked with a slightly less aggressive tone.

"Yes, Highness. Of course. The Intellect Herodotus cannot fold in here or manipulate any effects from a distance. You are safe from his interface."

Pac grunted, satisfied.

"Then return to your station, and open a channel to *Defiant*," he said quietly.

Vnuk nodded and murmured assent, backing away.

Pac Yulin's heart was beating hard, but he worked even harder to keep his features neutral and his temper in check. He would admit, if only to himself, that having the Terran Intellect fighting for the Armadalens was more of a force multiplier than he'd been willing to admit, and a clear and present danger to his own plans.

Unlike the Combine, neither Earth nor Armadale constrained the development or capabilities of their Intellects. Both societies regarded advanced machine intelligences as citizens, with all the privileges and agency that citizenship conferred. The Combine, naturally, did not. Nor did the Javan Empire, for that matter. Or the Russian Oligarchies or a host of other realms and regimes. It was one of several profound fracture lines running through the body politic of the Greater Volume and it was why he would not care to match the *Khanjar*, or indeed the balance of his surviving strike force, against *Defiant*.

Luckily, he did not have to.

The Armadalen bridge appeared in holographic form before him. McLennan, the girl Hardy, and that dinosaur of an Intellect.

"Admiral," Pac Yulin said before turning to Hardy, "Commander."

The holo-emitters rendered the two officers and the Intellect in hard-edged clarity. The background vision of the stealth destroyer's fighting bridge was so irritatingly quiet and orderly that Pac Yulin wondered whether the Armadalens were feeding him false holodata, hiding the sort of damage and chaos within which he sat.

McLennan took a step forward, his gray and bushy eyebrows furrowing.

"Am I to take it, Commodore, from the two little dicky boats you have dispatched with malice aforethought, that you shall not be presenting yourself before a Board of Inquiry to explain your abject fucking failure in the battle just decided?"

Pac Yulin smiled.

"You can take it and shove it all way up your ass, old man. It is you who will present yourself for judgment. You who will be put to the question of criminal incompetence for the losses of this battle—losses which fell solely upon the Empire and the Combine, while your Armadalen friends were free to flit about as they pleased, never once coming directly to blows with the enemy."

That elicited a reaction from the figures in the background of the projection from *Defiant*. A low growl of curses from the Armadalens.

"As you were," their female commandant ordered, before the virus of ill feeling could spread.

A pity that.

Pac Yulin preferred his enemies to unbalance themselves with anger and folly.

But this Hardy merely barked out her demands and returned to glaring at him like a dog barely restrained by its leash. He promised himself that if she were to survive the coming war, he would have her before him, and under him, in chains.

"I see you have decided to add mutiny to the list of charges against you," McLennan said.

"No, but I have decided to add giving aid and comfort to the enemy to yours," Pac Yulin retorted. "Your incompetence has gravely weakened the alliance against the so-called Human Republic. You will present yourself for summary judgment and execution of sentence. Commander Hardy will turn over control of *Defiant* to a boarding party from *Makassar* and *Rekong*. The crew of *Defiant* will stand down, preparatory to reassignment through the strike force. And your Intellect will submit to proper restraints and reprogramming. It will serve to replace the loss of processing capacity on *Makassar*."

"And why do you imagine any of that is going to happen?" McLennan asked.

"Because if you do not submit, my ships will take you under fire, which I don't imagine will overly concern you. But while you are engaged with them, *Khanjar* will destroy all of the warships impounded off Lermontov Station."

"You what?" McLennan said.

Lucinda faded back from McLennan's confrontation with Commodore Pac Yulin. She had more immediate concerns, securing the ship against any attack by the two Combine fast movers that had folded into the local volume.

"Lieutenant Chase," she said quietly.

"Plotting them now, Commander," Chase replied, before adding in a quiet hiss, "But I should be doing this on my family's ship. Herodotus can easily manage the plots here. And frankly, he would be better at it. I formally request release from my station to take control of the Chase Corporation barque *Fremantle*."

"Not the time, Lieutenant," Hardy said urgently, quietly.

"It is exactly the time . . . ma'am," he ground out between clenched teeth. "I have done everything asked of me here."

"You have done your duty, which is expected of you as a naval officer," she pushed back, raising her voice. Her tone warned away anybody who was thinking of becoming invested in their exchange. "We. Don't. Have. Time," Lucinda said, a little more quietly, but twice as forcefully.

Chase squeezed his eyes shut as if having to absorb some great and sudden pain. A couple of weeks ago, when Lucinda first came aboard and they were of the same military rank, but separated by a vast chasm in their social rank, he might even have struck her. Now, however, he deflated or perhaps de-escalated. Whichever it was, she was grateful.

"Mister Fein," she said, trying to keep her voice steady.

"Targets locked, ma'am," Fein said, anticipating her query. "Three options to your location."

"Good work that man. Lieutenant Chivers, how goes it with the transfer of *Makassar*'s wounded to our medbay?"

"Doc Saito reports we're at capacity, Commander. The marines will be another ten minutes setting up, but their corpsmen are taking cases for triage now."

"Do we have Sub-Commandant Suprarto on board?"

"Yes, ma'am. The Intellect folded him directly to Doctor Saito, but he has been badly hurt. Radiation trauma. Our medics are stabilizing him with fast nannite treatments, but he won't be much help."

"And Sub-Lieutenant Hartoto, the acting skipper?"

"Still trying, ma'am."

"Keep on it," Lucinda said carefully, not wanting to draw the attention of the Combine leader upon herself.

She resumed her captain's chair, where Lieutenant Fein had sent her a document for review on a small fold-out screen. Three options for strike packages. One to destroy both Combine ships. Another to kill one and cripple the second. And a third to simply disable their fold drives and targeting arrays. She tapped a finger onto the third option.

They would need those ships, and the crew serving on them.

She did not believe that they had to die for Pac Yulin's ambitions.

Lieutenant Bannon, her systems chief, came up beside her and leaned in to whisper a few words, while keeping an eye on McLennan and Pac Yulin, who were still trading barbs.

"Commander," Bannon said in a soft voice. "I thought you should know. I got into the combat data management systems on *Rekong*, with a little help from Hero. They have firing solutions plotted, but not laid in, on *Makassar*."

Lucinda breathed out. "Good to know. Thanks, Ian." A little louder she said, "Nonomi. Really need to have that chat with Mister Hartoto on the *Makassar*."

"Still trying, ma'am."

"I can help with that," Hero said.

The voice was inside her head.

The Intellect had projected a field effect to directly manipulate the auditory cortex of her brain's temporal lobes. It was deeply unsettling, and she shuddered a little with it.

"Don't talk to me, just imagine talking to me," Hero said.

"What the fuck is going on?" Lucinda thought at him. She gestured at Bannon to stand by.

"Well, this tightly puckered anus is making his play."

Hero cast a profoundly unwelcome image directly into her visual cortex. Commodore Pac Yulin, but with a slowly convulsing anus-face which somehow managed to recall his actual appearance.

Lucinda almost cried out loud. Almost.

"Fuck's sake, Hero! Knock it off and give me something I can work with. What's happening on the Javan ship?"

"Chaos. Madness. A small insurrection by the Combine adviser team. They sent a surprising number of spec-ops-qualified personnel across as members of their assistance mission. Imagine that."

"Jesus. Do we need to send marines?"

She could not imagine a scenario in which combat-folding a company of Armadalen marines onto the contested decks of a Javanese Warlugger would have a happy ending.

"No," Hero projected to her. "A Javan kommando unit is taking care of that. But I'm afraid my little friend Number Six informs me that Sub-Lieutenant Hartoto is a casualty of the fighting. The chain of command on *Makassar* is . . . not settled."

"Fuck. Can Six take over?"

In a strange way, Lucinda felt Hero smile inside her mind.

"I thought you'd never ask."

She was about to order Lieutenant Chase to move them between the Javans and the Combine warships but thought the better of it when she saw Commodore Pac Yulin looking at her while arguing with McLennan. Instead she leaned over to Lieutenant Bannon, covered her mouth with one hand, and said quietly, "Get Chase to put us between the Javans and the Combine. Tell Fein to make sure the Combine know we have them target locked. I want their attention on us, not the *Makassar*."

"Aye, ma'am. There is something else, though."

"There always is," Lucinda said with a sigh.

"The Combine have put a ground team onto Lermontov. They're moving toward the storage vault holding all the personnel from the impounded warships."

She was sweating, but it suddenly felt as though her heart had been dipped into ice water.

"They're going to delete them," Hero cast into her thoughts. "They will delete the crew and take the ships." She could see from the look of sudden discomfort on Bannon's face that he'd got the good news on the down low, just like her.

"Or threaten to," she thought in return, not knowing if Bannon could hear her thoughts now, too.

"How do we know this, Hero?" she asked silently. "How good is the source?"

"It's from Captain L'trel. So, you know, an emotionally unstable substance abuser with an exciting variety of untreated pathologies. But she is there, I suppose. Oh, and Pinocchio, the real human boy, is with her."

"Wait, what? They're on-station?"

"Oh yes. With the giant make-believe rhinoceros, and Princess Alessia, and . . ."

"Shit! Where are my marines?"

"Unwell, I'm afraid."

"Fuck!" Lucinda blurted out.

"You said that out loud," Hero stage-whispered into her mind.

People were beginning to stare.

Including Pac Yulin.

With an effort, she forced herself to appear totally invested in some problem on the pop-up screen.

"Okay," she thought. "Ian, can you hear me?"

"I can," he said, sounding surprised.

"He can," Hero said at the same moment. "I'm very versatile, you know."

"Ian, go quietly tell Captain Hayes to get a platoon ready to jump over to *Makassar*. Brief him into the situation. Quickly. Hero, tell Number Six if they need help, we're here for them. I will give Lieutenant Chase the nav orders."

She started tapping out a message to Chase. They had all trained for these scenarios at the Academy, but it still felt like dropping into some sort of historical reenactment.

"Hero," she thought-cast while typing. "If you have a link to Sephina, I need to talk to her. Right now."

Turns out they needed the guns. All of them.

Kumon had really come through with a kick-ass rig for the Book, but Seph and the others had to roll old-school. They stripped the dead, the forever dead, of their weapons and folded ass back to the drop point where Booker had left Kumon and Alessia to lay up.

For a motherfucking wonder, that part worked out fine.

Nobody had the time or inclination to fuck around with a heavily armed and extravagantly badass crew of felons, double-timing it along the deck plates of Lermontov. Jaddi Coto alone was carrying enough firepower to kit out a squad of Vikingar berserkers. Mister Banks had that cold motherfucking face he sometimes got, which was even scarier in its own way. And Booker? Shit, he didn't need artillery support to look like he could personally sweep and clear the Valley of Death all on his lonesome. But he'd picked up a couple of pieces anyway, right after telling them it wouldn't be necessary.

"S'up?" Seph asked when she saw him grab up an AK-77 mag pulser.

She was still getting over the epic whiplash of the last few hours and she really didn't want any more surprises.

Booker frowned, checked the assault rifle over, discarded it, and picked another that lay a few feet way.

"Not sure yet," he said. "I got code lurking in the HabSec network. There's a Combine assault squad folding in-Hab."

The second AK proved acceptable. Booker stripped all the ammo from both bodies.

"Shit. Are they here for us? For Alessia?" Seph asked as they exited the building and picked their way through the stalled auto-vans and abandoned cargo pallets piled up in front of the Yakuza *honbu*. Stepped over a couple of dead bodies, too. *Gun-sotsu* taken out by the building's own perimeter defenses when Booker hijacked the OS.

"Dunno," he said. "But I'll keep looking."

"Okay. Do that. But maybe we should let Hardy and McLennan know, too. Somehow?"

"Already done. I gotta data link to *Defiant*."

They were only a few minutes getting back to Alessia.

The kid was nervous when they got there, some sketchy-looking body reclaimer place. Low-interest loans now, secured by your personal biomass when you were finished with it.

"Hmm, what could possibly go wrong with such a magnanimous offer," Mister Banks mused aloud.

Sitting in the drab, dusty foyer, Kumon Xi looked as if he could think of a thousand things and had imagined them all in fine detail while Booker was busting them out of gangster jail.

Jaddi Coto stopped in the doorway, pondering Mister Banks's question.

"It would depend on the trustworthiness of the organization offering to buy your remains," he decided. "Although, in my experience, loan vendors taking bodies and body parts as collateral are not often to be trusted."

Seph pushed past them. Alessia was keeping Kumon Xi together, holding his hand, patting it, and keeping up a constant line of soothing chatter.

"Hey, buddy! Long time!" Seph beamed as the freelance bioengineer looked up from his funk and saw the cavalry had arrived. She hadn't seen him for a couple of years. Not since the early months of the Javan-Armadalen War. He'd chunked up. Kumon always was a greedy little fucker back in Hab Welfare. Always looking to scam the other kids out of their rations.

"Sephina!" Alessia cried out, scrambling off the faded couch where they'd been sitting. The kid ran to Seph and all but knocked her on her ass when she jumped into a hug. She was shaking and smiling and obviously holding back tears all at once. She let go, just a little, to seek out Booker.

"You did it, Booker, you got them!"

"Yeah, but we're not done yet," the source coder said with a frown.

He didn't have that faraway look that a lot of peeps got when they disappeared into their own data flows. But Seph could tell he was processing some shit. He looked grim. She'd never seen him ensouled within human form before. He'd looked happier as a deadly gardening bot.

"S'up now, Book. Same shit?"

"Yeah," he confirmed.

He pointed a finger at his temple.

"I got Commander Hardy up on my u-space link to *Defiant*. She wants to speak to you. Says that Combine squad is headed for a storage vault where they got all the crew off those warships we saw coming in. The computer"—he put enough torque into the sneer that Seph knew he meant Hero—"thinks that Pac Yulin is looking for hostages. Asshole threw down with the admiral and he's threatening to scuttle the impounded ships. And, uh, Commander Hardy is pretty pissed that Alessia is not on the ship with her bodyguards, studying the Persian Wars."

"Can I talk to her direct?" Seph asked.

"No. But I can relay what each of you says."

"Okay," she said, gently freeing herself of Alessia's full-body hug. "First up you tell the Loose Unit to back the fuck off. Tell her if it wasn't for this kid"—she jerked a thumb at the A-Train—"sneaking out the window like a fucking juvenile boss, you'd still be spooking around the ship, fucking dude ex machina style, and we'd be getting turned into long pork sushi rolls or Combine fuck puppets by now."

"No," Booker said evenly. "I'm not going to tell her that. She's still a superior officer. Sort of. I'm still in the TDF, or something. At least according to McLennan. Plus, it's a dick move. I've told her the facts on the ground and dictated the tactical exigencies."

"Hmm. Well, that sounds like something she'd dig on. What next?"

Booker fell quiet. Reaching back to *Defiant*.

Seph leaned over to Kumon Xi.

"How's he doing this, anyway? He's got no mesh, right? He's not about to go angry cannibal on us, is he?"

Kumon, who was slowly recovering, shook his head.

"That Cupertino rig is top-shelf. Maximum headroom. Premium organic shit from the fruit company's weapons group. He's got bio-electric comm nodes 'gineered right into his fucking hindbrain. He can't reach all the way across the Volume. But he can hijack a u-space channel from any local node. It's all near field, too. Doesn't even need to lay hands on shit to fuck it up."

Seph nodded.

"Cool."

"I should have something like that," Jaddi Coto muttered. "Why does Booker have these nice things and I do not even have my horn back yet?"

Alessia took one of Coto's giant fingers in her hands.

"I like you just the way you are, Jaddi Coto," she said.

Booker spoke up again.

"I got the location of the vault. We're ordered to interdict any attempt to compromise the downloaded personnel."

"Ordered?" Seph bristled.

Booker sketched a smile.

"Asked nicely," he corrected. "But with extreme prejudice. She wants the princess kept safe, too."

"Fair enough," Sephina conceded. "Tell her we're good to go."

"Hey," Alessia protested. "I can help. I got Booker his rig. I can totally interdict these . . . mother . . ."

Everybody was staring at her.

Seph. Booker. Jaddi Coto. Mister Banks. Even Kumon Xi.

". . . fuckers," she trailed off.

Alessia let go of Coto, folded her arms, and sulked.

"Being a princess sucks ass."

Lucinda was furious with Seph, which wasn't a novel experience. She forced herself to withhold judgment on Cox and the other two marines. And she was pathetically grateful that Booker had somehow downloaded and was at least on-site with Alessia. With the TDF operator looking after her there was a chance the Montanblanc princess might get out of this alive. And maybe even a hope they could stop Pac Yulin from erasing the crew members of the impounded ships.

A buzzing under her fingertips alerted her to a message from Chase.

Defiant was positioned between the Combine ships and the Warlugger. She could at least protect the Javans from that threat.

She tapped out a message to Lieutenant Fein.

"IF THEY MANEUVER FOR POSITION, FIRE ACROSS THEIR BOWS. READY COUNTERMEASURES. IF THEY PERSIST—OPTION 3."

"AYE, MA'AM," the reply came back.

She folded her hands in her lap, crossed one leg over the other, took a breath, and cast a thought to Hero, who remained floating next to Admiral McLennan.

"Can't you just grab this guy and throw him into the sun?"

"No," the Intellect replied on their weird private channel. "Unfortunately, we're too far away and the Combine Intellects, such as they are, are still capable of blocking any such move. It is a lovely thought, though. I'm so glad you're coming around to my way of seeing things."

She rolled her eyes and gave her attention back to McLennan and Pac Yulin.

CHAPTER

THIRTY-FOUR

Her family's public engram vaults were architectural master-works, blending high art and terrifying security. Alessia had never been to any of the black sites, but she imagined they were just as impressive. The vault on Lermontov, displayed in the tiny holo, was a shitbox: a squat, syncrete bunker on the far side of the port facility near the gangsters' headquarters. They got there a lot quicker than they'd managed from Kumon Xi's lab to the Yakuza *honbu*, because Booker stole a couple of auto-vans. It was amazing to watch. He just held his hands over the control panel, the vehicles' displays lit up, and he announced that he was in.

He drove one. Mister Banks took the other.

Alessia rode along with Banks and Kumon Xi. Seph told the pilot to "Stay close, but hang back," which sounded a bit confusing to Alessia. But Mister Banks was as good at driving auto-vans as he was at piloting stolen Russian superyachts. The ride was exciting. He barely moved his hands on the control holos, just twitching a finger or flicking his wrist to execute these major moves as they raced through the port district. He occasionally talked to Booker via a tiny earbud, mostly about which direction they were going. Alessia sat in back with Kumon Xi and lots of boxes full of mystery Yakuza stuff. Mister Banks drove super-fast, threading in and out of the other traffic. Most of it was bot trains, he said, which meant he could fake out their safety protocols and drive as fast as he damn well pleased.

It pleased Mister Banks to drive very fucking fast indeed.

Things were not going as well outside.

Alessia could only catch glimpses of what was happening through the little windows of the van, but she could hear sirens and even gunfire. At one point, as Banks ripped around a hairpin turn, she was thrown onto her side and got a look up out of the bubble canopy over the driver's seat. Lermontov Station was burning. Not the bit they were in, but the other side of the Hab was ablaze in parts and she could see multicolored arcs of weapons fire snaking out of the inferno.

"Why are they shooting at each other?" she asked. "The Sturm will be here soon. Shouldn't everyone be shooting at them?"

"Ha, welcome to cartel politics, Princess," Kumon Xi snarked. "It's exciting, isn't it."

It was all a bit more exciting than she really cared for, truth be known. And Alessia found herself silently agreeing with Kumon Xi as he tried to talk Mister Banks into turning the van around and just driving as fast as he could for the ship.

"We can wait there for the others, dude. Get things ready to go," Kumon pleaded.

But no, they couldn't, Banks explained. Things were already "a bit out of hand." Order was breaking down across the Habitat, and as strange as it might seem, they were safer staying close to Seph, Booker, and Coto. Mister Banks didn't raise his voice or anything. He reminded her a bit of Sergeant Reynolds like that, when everyone turned into mesh-zombies at Skygarth.

"It would be especially tricky for you to go bunking off, Princess," Banks went on. "Mister Booker thinks both the Combine and HabSec are looking for you now."

"And we're driving toward them!" Kumon Xi complained.

"No. We're driving toward another team. The snatch squad looking for Princess Alessia is at the ship. They're having some issues with *Ariane*'s security measures."

Her dismay was lost in the chaos as Banks wrenched the van around another turn and the sudden change in momentum threw Alessia against a stack of crates that tumbled over with a glassy crash. She smelled wine, a scent she was familiar with from the cellars at Skygarth. The fight with Kogan D'ur had destroyed some very expensive vintages.

"We'll just keep our heads tucked in if and when it gets a bit sporty," Banks assured them. "I'll look after you, don't worry. But it seems we're taking a comfort break right now."

The van decelerated so sharply that Alessia lost her balance again.

When she pushed herself up off the floor of the vehicle, which was swimming with red wine, Banks was already out of the driver's seat and jogging toward the other auto-van.

"Come on, Kumon," she said. "Let's go find out what's happening."

"I can tell you what's happening," Kumon Xi snapped. "Every degenerate criminal on this fucking Hab has decided to light out for themselves."

But he followed her, anyway.

The cognitive power of the Cupertino rig, the "headroom" in marketing speak, was excellent. Better than any organic Booker had ever ridden before. But it wasn't like being ensouled within the substrate of the *Ariane*, where he could surf the ship's wormhole processing matrices to perform millions of tasks at FTL speeds. Booker was experienced enough with moving from one platform to another that he didn't get caught up in the sudden wrenching gear change of shifting down from advanced substrate to mere cortical tissue. But he was aware of how much slower his thoughts were, running on this lump of gray matter—

even if the wetware was packed with mods and augments, from the brain stem to the neocortex.

"Plan?" he said as they moved closer to the vault.

This part of the station was a riddle of complex pathways through automated factories and cargo-handling facilities. There were few pedestrians, and not much in the way of commercial traffic. The buildings were mostly gray, featureless containers of carbon sheeting and extruded bioplastics. His EM vision told him a lot of places had powered down, with only their security cordons running. It made sense, he conceded, peering up and along the vast length of the station. The inner volume of Lermontov was alive with air traffic, but it was not the orderly transit patterns of a busy, crowded commercial Habitat; more like a hornet's nest knocked over and broken apart. Some assholes were even shooting at one another. He saw lines of plasma fire, kinetic impacts, and a legitimate fucking smart missile swarm in pursuit of a fast-moving cargo sled. The time for getting gone . . . was gone. It was time for hunkering down, firing up the Sentinel pods, and hoping the patchwork alliance on the other side of the sun could fend off the Sturm long enough to fold out of the system and away to . . .

Where?

Nobody knew.

"Let's just grab whatever box they're stored on and get back to *Ariane*," Sephina said. "I wanna get as far away from this cartel shit show as I can."

"I meant a tactical plan," Booker said, to clarify. "HabSec and the Combine are going to beat us to the vault by a minute or so. And they got another team at the ship already. Looking for Alessia."

"Shit. What do we do?" Sephina asked.

"Violence," Jaddi Coto suggested from the back of the autovan, where he sat among stasis crates of soy sauce and shrimp paste. "Isn't violence always the answer?"

"Only when you got more of it, man," Seph said. "Booker, can you, like, plug into their system and see what's happening?"

"Been up on their grid since I got here," he said. "The ship can take care of itself. I broke the harbormaster's clamps and added a few softweapon upgrades to *Ariane*'s security measures. We got bigger problems here. There's a twelve-strong squad of Combine legionnaires, medium-heavy armor, and four HabSec Compliance Mechs closing in on that site. The mechs have been up-gunned for urban combat."

Jaddi Coto grunted. "Hmm. It sounds like violence may not be the answer."

"Yeah," Seph agreed. "Sounds like. Maybe pull over, Book. We gotta think this through before we get there."

He wiped off the speed of their advance and flicked the little auto-van into the loading zone of a protein-shaping plant as another micro-missile swarm whispered overhead. The second van came humming up behind them. Ephram Banks hopped out and jogged up to the open door where Sephina was sitting. Alessia and Kumon Xi weren't far behind.

"A problem?" Banks said as he arrived.

"A challenge," Sephina replied sardonically.

Booker almost snorted. The skies of Lermontov were full of dueling grav-craft and smart munitions. Fires burned up and down the great curve of the inner hull. And a small armored regiment of giant assholes was about to take up position at the vault where they'd been heading to steal away the bottled souls of two thousand captured warriors.

"I suggested violence," Jaddi Coto said from the back of the van. "But that will not work, and I have no more suggestions."

Mister Banks ducked his head as a fast-boat screamed overhead, pursued by another active missile swarm. Booker's recognition scripts automatically tagged the boat, painted in the black and red colors of the Svetakov Oligarchy, as a '62 Tiranna, and the swarm chasing after it as a flight of "love bugs": a fire-n-forget perimeter defense system obsoleted out of the TDF's inventory twenty years ago, but still popular with private contractors and second-tier corporate military forces.

He was surprised by the auto-ID, and about to dive into his code settings to turn it off—there was a shit ton of ordnance flying around, and it would get old quickly—when he stopped.

"Kumon," he said. "What's the range of my near-field data system?"

"What?" The bioengineer stared at him. He shook his head, as if emerging from a jujaweed stupor. "Uh, about sixty meters."

"Can I boost it?"

"Not organically, no. But come on, man. Sixty meters is fucking lit. Most systems are like a couple of feet and that's . . ."

Booker cut him off with a hand-chopping gesture.

"Yeah, yeah. It's a very nice rig. But could I piggyback onto the comms for this van, say, and use it to boost my NFD reach to a couple of hundred meters?"

Kumon Xi threw his hands up, exasperated.

"Shit, man, I don't know. I work in meat, not metal."

"I am a comm system savant," Jaddi Coto said from the back. "I could do this for you."

Booker turned around and stared at him. Alessia and Kumon Xi, too, from outside the van.

"Well, it is his job." Sephina shrugged. "I didn't hire him for his looks."

"What is wrong with my looks?" Jaddi Coto asked, sounding hurt. "Is it my nub of a horn? I am trying to regrow it as fast as I can, you know."

"I love your little nubby, Coto," Seph said. "But can we focus on this other thing? Can you help Booker with a boost?"

Coto leaned forward between the driver's and passenger's seats. The whole van dipped a little with the shift in weight.

"I need to see schematics and controls."

Booker brought up the vehicle's holographic manual.

"Bigger, please," Coto said. "My horn is embarrassingly tiny, but my hands are unhelpfully large."

Booker pinched out the display and flicked it back over the seat toward him.

Coto scanned the dense cloud of informatics in less than a second.

He grunted and nodded and plunged his unhelpfully large hands into the data cloud, scooping out a tiny blue pyramid which expanded to fill the interior of the cabin with even more infomatics. Coto stared at the complex model of brightly colored polyhedra for three seconds, his expression blank, until he suddenly smiled and reshaped the arrangement with a series of quick, subtle gestures.

"It is done," he said before collapsing the holo back to a thumbnail-sized pyramid.

They all looked to Booker.

He reached for the console, connected with the vehicle's OS, and started to load code.

Alessia beamed at Coto.

"You did it, Jaddi Coto, and without any violence at all."

"That's still coming," Booker said. "But yeah, I'm in. Nice work, Coto. Banks, you need to get these guys to cover. We're gonna roll on the vault as soon as I can jack one of the missile swarms. There's been two overhead in the last two minutes. It won't be long."

It wasn't.

Banks hurried Alessia and Kumon Xi back to the other auto-van and drove a little ways around the frame, eventually heading down a ramp and pulling into a vehicle-charging station one level under the plates a couple of hundred meters away.

Booker closed about half the remaining distance to the engram vault, before another swarm passed through the EM bubble of the auto-van's transceiver. More love bugs.

The swarm was moving fast in pursuit of a gunship, a chaebol drone. Booker spent half a second testing whether he could seize control of the gunship, too, but gave up when he hit a proprietary malware shield. The chaebol were good at those things. Probably because they were even better at stealing other motherfuckers' tech. If he'd been ensouled on the *Ariane*, he could have broken through, but even with all the headroom in his new rig, it was too big a job. He let the gunship go.

The love bug swarm was an easy get, though.

The distributed hive mind was still running thirty-year-old TDF scripts. He'd already pulled a softweapon out of his deep lacuna and loaded it for immediate launch when the swarm passed over.

Sephina had no idea what Booker was up to, or how he was doing it. But she'd known Kumon Xi all her adult life and for most of her childhood in Hab Welfare—and if he said Booker's rig had magical unicorn powers, she would not freak out to see sparkly rainbows of death come shooting out of his fucking eyeballs.

No rainbows came, but the Book said they were good to go. She charged up the Type 90 blaster she'd stripped from a gummy soldier, and set the programmable rounds to a half-n-half mix of linked penetrators and high explosives. Behind her, Coto cranked up the power on a Mitsumoto arclight cannon—one of his favorites.

She checked the safety on the blaster and caught a first glimpse of the allied Combine and HabSec force, securing the plate out front of the engram vault, just as Booker told them to get ready.

"We can't let 'em get inside that vault," he said. "Gotta give 'em something else to think about. We bail here."

"Wait, what?" Seph asked as the auto-van bled off speed and the sliding door in back rumbled open.

"Go!" Booker shouted, pushing her out through the passenger side door. The van seemed to spring up off the deck plating as Coto, who could move with terrifying speed in a fight, leaped from the rear cabin.

Seph had to go with it, trusting the reactive matrix padding in her duster to absorb most of the fall as she rolled. The impact was still a shock, even though Booker had dropped their exit speed way the fuck down. She rolled over the road surface, copper-colored mag-lev cladding on this part of the Hab. The mammoth cylinder of Lermontov swirled around her in a pinwheel blur of color. The gunmetal gray of the industrial frames, the pastel shimmer of faraway urban lights, a smear of blue water, dappled with the diamond light of an exploding flyer. And everywhere and all at once a furious storm of weapons fire.

When she came to rest, Booker was already up and running with inhuman speed, dodging between bot trains and auto-vans which danced around and in front of him in a growing arrowhead of plasteel and carbon armor. And at the head of this accelerating wedge of hard mass and heavy metal, the van they'd stolen from the Yakuza. Booker had somehow taken control of it all.

Seph heard the first crackle of small-arms fire. The Combine legionnaires, targeting the sudden threat speeding toward them. The quickening thunder of a rhino stampede, Jaddi Coto charging after Booker, quickly drowned out those first, sporadic shots. Seph pushed herself up and off into a crouching run, chasing after them. She darted to and from cover, not yet bothering to return fire. She was too far out and could not stop to take aim. The deflectors in her duster would shed a lot of targeting sensors, but she still had to keep moving. There was no fooling the Mark One eyeball.

And the Compliance Mechs that were turning toward the assault would not need to concern themselves with anything as tedious as taking aim. She could already see the modded gun turrets and missile launchers coming to bear on the leading edge of Booker's improvised cavalry charge. She was about to dive for cover when the hijacked missile swarm fell on them.

The first two mechs simply disappeared inside a sudden squall of white fire and thunder. The mag-lev road plating buckled under a pressure wave that radiated out from the impact. The swarm consumed the other mechs and maybe half the armored legionnaires in a terrifying barrage of explosive hammer blows that robbed Sephina of all forward momentum. She staggered to a halt and simply stared. Numb. She had never seen so much violence unleashed on other human beings before.

It was only the sudden chain of arclight fire from Coto that got her moving again. He was shooting on the run. Firing blindly into the smoke and flames and falling debris outside the engram vault. She raised her blaster, but let it fall again. She couldn't see anything or anyone to kill. Coto and Booker were still racing forward, however, so she got moving, too, picking up her speed until finally she was sprinting after them. They had split up, each diverting to either side of the roadway. Blue-white jets of coherent energy poured from Coto's heavy weapon like the vengeance of a righteous god. Booker was more restrained, or perhaps just more efficient. His mag-pulse rifle cracked in discrete three-round bursts that seemed to be aimed with truly malignant intent. Even running he seemed able to aim and shoot with eerie poise. She couldn't see what he was shooting at but felt certain that every time he pulled that trigger, somebody, somewhere died.

When Seph reached the field of burning ruin and shattered armor, Booker was striding methodically through the human wreckage, putting headshots into every legionnaire.

Jaddi Coto came back to stand beside her. "He is very good at this, isn't he? Much better than when he was a gardening bot."

"Yeah," Sephina panted. Her voice sounded cracked and too small to say all the things that needed to be said. She struggled for her next breath. This was not her first taste of fire, but she was stunned by the scale of the carnage.

The dead were undoubtedly assholes, but they weren't the Sturm. They hadn't killed Ariane. They just . . . got in the way.

Having secured the site, Booker jogged back to them. He was barely sweating, and his breath came slow and easy. Seph was still gulping for air and tasting the profane stink of burning flesh and toxic smoke.

"Not picking up any activity inside," he said. "They only just got here so the 'grams should all still be in storage."

"Right. Let's get them and fuck off," Sephina said. Her voice sounded terribly shaky. "Coto, you stand watch. Let us know if they send anyone else."

The giant hybrid took up position under the portico at the entrance to the vault.

"How should I let you know?" Coto asked. "I have no comms."

"I don't know. Shoot somebody. Make some noise."

Coto nodded.

"I will make an explosion, a loud one."

"They're the best kind."

Booker was standing in front of the doors, breathing slowly. His eyes were closed as though in meditation.

When he opened them, the heavy doors rumbled apart.

"The boxes are in a strong room on the second floor," he said. "One for each ship."

"How do you even know that?" Seph asked as she followed him inside. To her eye, the interior was sparse, but expensive-looking. The sort of minimalist design that cost more for every detail you took out. It had to be a cartel facility, or maybe something for the Javan elite.

"Inventory," Booker replied, as though the answer was obvious.

"But . . . what?"

He stopped and turned back to her. Smiled shyly.

"I'm sorry. I forget. My source code," he explained as they resumed the trek down the long corridor. Their boots rang on the syncrete floor and echoed against carbonsteel walls and ceilings. Glow strips lit their faces from above with a cold, flat chemical light.

"I was originally written as a Pathfinder for the Terran rangers," Booker explained. "I acquired more military specializations, each with its own code base, the longer I served. They became part of my source code. What you might think of as my personality."

"I don't need the Source Code for Dummies lecture, Book. My mother was vat born as a house womb for some family of Elite Fraction douchewads. She got a Hindenbug, her code fragmented, and, well, you know how that goes."

He frowned at her as they climbed a stairwell. Neither bothered even checking for an elevator. It would be a kill box.

"I'm sorry, Sephina. I didn't know that."

"It was a long time ago. And I'm not prejudiced. I was natural born, but my mother came out of the vats. I know what I am. And I know what she was. What I need to know is what the hell you are, Booker. Cos this shit you been doing, it's not normal. Banks and Coto. They're both ex-military. Both Terran vat soldiers, like you. But not like that."

She gestured back out onto the street where Booker had destroyed the small but heavily armored battle group, pretty much all on his own.

"There's a reason nobody fucks with Earth," he said. Then shrugged. "Or there was. Come on. I promise you; I'll tell you all my war stories once we get away from here. But this rig you got me? It's good. I can really get to work in this thing."

He got to work on the second floor of the vault, breaking through the clamps and decoding multiple layers of Combine crypto-quests. Again, he simply stood in front of the access panel and closed his eyes. It wasn't like Coto reprogramming the van's transceivers, or Banks piloting the ship. There was nothing to see. No performative display. Booker simply closed his eyes, settled his breathing, and eventually an external storage box would eject from its bay. Each box had a separate code, requiring a minute or so of processing to unravel, but five minutes later they had all the devices unlocked and dismounted. They lay on the floor, much bulkier, heavier units than the simple eX-Box in which she'd stashed Booker after Montrachet.

To be honest, Sephina thought it was creepy as hell. The idea of two thousand . . . engrams, souls, people . . . whatever you wanted to call them, they were all jammed up inside those matte black containers.

It was really fucking weird and deeply uncanny to someone who'd never been meshed. She was born and would die the way human beings always had. The way most people throughout the Greater Volume still lived and died.

She could almost . . . *almost* . . . understand why the Sturm were such mouth-breathing fanatics about this stuff.

But, on the other hand, fuck them in the neck.

They killed her one true love, and before she was done Sephina was gonna drag those motherfuckers down to hell.

They were just gathering up the boxes when Booker stopped, craned his head as though listening to something outside, and swore.

Half a second later she heard the distinctive crack of an arc-light cannon splitting the atmosphere, followed by a shuddering explosion and the ripping snarl of auto-gun fire.

The whole facility shook with the impact of whatever was hitting them.

"Combine drop-tanks," Booker shouted over the uproar. "Tactical assault ships. Like a troop carrier and gun platform all in one."

"Shit," Sephina cursed. "Can't you just like hijack them or something. Get 'em to shoot each other down?"

He shook his head as the building took more hits. "They're running mil-grade systems, Captain. Super-hardened shit, not some half-assed garbageware they bought off the u-space bazaars. So no. I can't. Not quickly enough anyway."

She was suddenly very grateful that they were in a heavily armored facility and not some crappy bioplastic warehouse.

"Come on, we gotta grab Coto and find a way out of here," Booker said.

He piled all the storage units into a single o-plastic container. They banged against one another and Seph cringed, worried it could damage the people stored inside.

Booker clipped a lid onto the container and carried it awkwardly under one arm. In his other hand he had the mag-pulse rifle. They ran from the second floor back down to the entry hall where Seph was relieved to find Coto in one piece and taking cover behind a massive pillar which was already scorched and pitted with battle damage.

"I have been shooting at them," he said. "I did make an explosion, but I think I need a bigger gun."

The arclight cannon was nearly as long as Sephina was tall and weighed considerably more than she did.

Missiles screamed and thousands of rounds of ceramic slugs chewed into the building's façade.

"Come on, Booker," Seph yelled over the uproar. "We bought you that nice new rig. Do something with it."

He shook his head.

"I'm not a god. Just a guy in a rig and they've cut off my data link. Pretty sure they folded in direct from one of the Combine battleraiders. Those things aren't just Compliance Mechs or HabSec armor. You fight wars with that shit. I can't just punch it out with them. We gotta get out of here some other way."

"That's very disappointing, Book," Sephina shouted. "We can't go out on the deck plates. They'll fucking vaporize us."

A massive detonation almost knocked her flat on her ass.

Jaddi Coto, with his feet planted in a double-wide stance, and half a ton of bodymass to secure him to the plates, pushed back with a long, whipping stream of arclight fire and wordless, bellowing rage.

"They're trying to pin us down, not kill us outright," Booker shouted. "They got enough firepower to demolish this place if they wanted."

"The boxes?" Seph yelled.

"Yeah," he shouted back. "They want the boxes. They'll puts boots on the deck to take them."

Sephina thumbed off the safety of her assault rifle and sent a clattering burst of ceramic fire out into the Hab. She didn't aim. It was more a general statement of intent.

"Let them fucking try," she shouted.

Multiple streams of auto-gun fire converged on the entry in which they sheltered, forcing them back deeper into the building. Booker had to drag Coto back by the harness for the arclight cannon, giving Seph another clue about the strengths of that rig he was riding. There was usually no moving Coto anywhere unless he wanted to go.

Mini-missiles screeched in and detonated against the superalloy cladding of the outer vault. This time Seph was knocked all the way down on her ass.

"They're coming in," Booker roared as the building entry darkened with the hulking forms of heavily armored legionnaires.

She heard the bark of his AK-77. Still firing discrete bursts.

A hissing, spitting, white-hot snake of arclightning.

The signature *crack-badoomp* of her Type 90 blaster sending twinned rounds of penetrators and HE downrange. Seph didn't even know when she'd opened fire. It was more like she'd always been here, fighting for her life. Everything she'd ever been, everything she ever would be, telescoped down to this tiny floating speck of time in the infinite span of the universe. She screamed her throat raw and fired. She blinked away tears of rage, and salty stinging runnels of sweat, and she fired. She coughed and choked on thick billowing clouds of atomized carbon armor and burning plasteel. And she fired. She swapped out mags and fired.

The vestibule filled up with fallen giants in ruined ballistic plate.

Arclightning burned metal and flesh.

The vault shuddered and burned under the fall of giant forge hammers.

And then . . . nothing.

A sudden silence.

A silence that she recognized after a second as numbness. A slight hissing and the hollow drumbeat of her heart.

A volcanic roar rose up and swept away the dull paralysis and hearing loss and body shock of overwhelming trauma.

Booker crept past her, his weapon raised and pointed forward. His legs unsteady but moving because he willed them to.

The muzzle of his double-seven swept back and forth in tight little arcs, precautionary sweeps of the killing zone.

"What the fuck was that?" Seph gasped.

"'Splosions," Jaddi Coto grunted. "Big ones."

The hybrid shuffled forward after Booker, ready to unleash energistic storms from the heavy cannon hanging from his enormous shoulders.

A single shot cracked out and Seph jumped, but it was Booker, just making sure of a fallen legionnaire.

"Clear forward," he called back.

Seph moved up and through the vestibule, choked with Combine dead.

Forever dead, she supposed. But it meant little to her. It meant nothing, really.

She blinked as she emerged from the shadows of the engram vault, her eyes watery and squinting as she looked up into the fusion tube which ran the length of Lermontov Station, providing light and warmth in the cold vacuum of space.

The Combine drop-tanks were gone, crashed to the deck plates and burning freely.

The legionnaires were slain. All of them. Destroyed by something even more powerful.

Princess Alessia Szu Suri sur Montanblanc ul Haq stood grinning on the forecourt of the vault, surrounded by the flaming wrack and debris of all she had wrought.

"I brought some friends," she said, beaming with delight.

The Armadalen marines Cox, Dahl, and Aronson stood on either side of her. Kumon Xi lurked a little ways behind.

And hanging over all of them like a dark guardian sent by a spiteful god, the *Ariane*.

CHAPTER

THIRTY-FIVE

The voice of the ancient Intellect, his oldest and possibly only friend, whispered deep inside his mind.

"They have secured the engrams and Princess Alessia. They are all back on the *Ariane* now."

McLennan suppressed the evil grin that wanted to run wild all over his face. This clatty fucking turd nibbler Pac Yulin was not going to get what he wanted. Not a tiny fucking thimble of it, not a fucking bee's dick measure of satisfaction would he have; not when Mac was finished with him. That was probably why he was shouting so much.

"You lied! You treacherous Terran dog," Pac Yulin roared from within the hologram. "You never intended I should have what was mine by law of contract and simple honor."

McLennan snorted. "Dinnae talk to me of honor, you fuckin' viper. You no more understand the burdens of honor than a genital louse comprehends the inner workings of the arse barber's pube clipper. I will give you one last chance to save your worthless hide. Stand down your forces and submit yourself to judgment. I will personally plead mercy in your case. Not because you deserve it, you scabby fuckin' dobber, but because we need to put your foolish perfidy behind us and unite against the common foe, who I might remind you, cares nothing for all our pointless fucking yammering."

A Combine officer, most likely the captain of the battleraider to judge by all the fruit salad and gaudy, tarnished baubles on his once fine tunic, leaned in to whisper into Pac Yulin's ear. Whatever he had to say, it did not much please the deputy executive prince.

"Probably just found out about Lermontov Station," Hero mused to Mac alone.

Frazer McLennan, admiral of the fleets, which currently consisted of *Defiant*, a half-dozen or so impounded ghost ships, and maybe, just maybe the badly wounded Javan Warlugger, sat back to study his opponent. He was confident that young Hardy had the tactical situation in the local volume well in hand. She would take all necessary measures to protect the Javans should Pac Yulin attempt to wager the *Makassar*, the Empire's one surviving capital platform, as some sort of bargaining chip. And Mac hoped this might go some way toward convincing the Javans that whatever enmity had arisen between their two peoples, that recent past was now another country and they could not afford to return there.

The odious Pac Yulin, however, Mac did not remotely trust to recognize any commonality of interest.

The Combine princeling either did not comprehend or simply did not care for the dire realities of their situation. He saw only the main chance for himself.

Mac would send him to perdition, were he to gain a free hand in the matter, but for now he could not.

"I would have your answer, Commodore," he growled.

"And so you shall, Admiral," Pac Yulin sneered.

The figure inside the holo-projection snapped his fingers and Mac expected the bridge of *Defiant* to erupt into activity as the Combine frigates *Rekong* and *Sundang* launched suicide attacks on *Defiant* and *Makassar*.

Instead, young Hardy called out to him.

"Admiral, the tactical display. Lermontov volume."

"Oh dear," Hero muttered inside his head.

At the snap of Pac Yulin's fingers two of the impounded warships, a fifth of the naval power available to McLennan, blew up.

The detonation was so coincident with his gesture that he must have had charges planted on board, and nukes at that, ready to blow.

"That's the Deutsche Marine transport and the chaebol's *Sejong the Great*, ma'am," one of Hardy's baby lieutenants called out.

Mac kept his face icily composed, but inside his rage was volcanic and growing.

This fucking madman was going to cut their cocks off just so he could boast the longest donger in the outhouse.

"I widnae do something so precipitately fucking foolish again, were I you, m'laird," McLennan said quietly, but with murderous determination. "Scuttle one more of those ships and I will order Commander Hardy to fold to your location and loose every weapon on this vessel against your own."

From behind him he heard Lucinda start firing off the orders necessary to make his threat a reality.

"Mister Chase, plot combat folds times three to datum point *Khanjar*. Mister Fein, prepare your broadside. Ms. Chivers, sound to general quarters, and, Hero, please do inform Number Six we will be exiting the local volume and *Makassar* should prepare countermeasures for action by *Rekong* and *Sundang*."

"That . . . that will not be . . . necessary."

The voice was weak, and unfamiliar. The speaker's Volume Standard was heavily accented with the singsong lilt of Habitat Gudang Garam.

"*Makassar* on deck," bellowed an Armadalen marine.

The corporal gently held up Sub-Commandant Domi Suprarto by one arm. On the other side of the Javan officer, *Defiant*'s senior medical officer, Doctor Saito, held the other arm and shook her head as though this foolishness was simply not to be countenanced.

Every Armadalen officer turned toward the Javan.

Suprarto paused in his pained and delicate shuffle.

"I will order *Makassar* to fold with you, Commander Hardy," he said, his voice faltering and weak, but his resolve unbowed. He scowled at the holo-display where Pac Yulin glared back in cold fury. "You, sir, will present yourself for arrest. Volume Lord Karna, too. On the charge of treason."

The bridge of the *Khanjar* was deathly still and quiet. Everybody looked to him for guidance, for leadership. Deputy Executive Prince Rinaldo Pac Yulin stared into the holographic abyss. He never let his eyes drop from the Terran hypocrite and betrayer.

McLennan.

But he was not so focused on the old monster that he could not appreciate the wider situation. Tactical displays floated to either side of the main hologram in which McLennan, his insane Intellect, and their Armadalen minions awaited his reply.

Everybody waited on his reply. The crew of the battleraider and the other Combine warships. His erstwhile Javan allies on the Warlugger and, undoubtedly, on all the surviving Habitats throughout Natuna System. And every soul and surviving intellect on Lermontov Station. They would all be watching, in one way or another. They would all assume he was trapped, and it was over.

They were wrong.

The Yulin-Irrawaddy Combine did not grow to be the greatest and most powerful of realms by surrendering its way to domination. Unity without submission was simply weakness. Loyalty was not something to be earned, like a share dividend. It was tribute to be taken, to be demanded by the strong, and only the strong.

"Captain Vnuk," Pac Yulin said loudly and clearly, never

once taking his eyes from McLennan. "On my order, destroy Lermontov Station."

To his credit, Vnuk did not hesitate.

"On your command, Highness!"

Pac Yulin smiled and raised his right hand, ready to snap his fingers. After all, extremism in pursuit of domination was no vice, but that did not mean that one could not display a sense of flair in the pursuit.

McLennan was snarling at him, the Armadalens were everywhere in motion. His own people warned of incoming as the fabric of space-time in *Khanjar*'s tactical volume flexed and started to fail under the impossible pressures of gravimetric folding.

Pac Yulin's eyes twinkled and he held his fingers ready to snap.

"Highness," Captain Vnuk warned. "*Defiant* has folded in and acquired us. *Makassar*, too! The Javans have targeted us, sir!"

Rekong and *Sundang* followed less than a second later, rewriting the tactical display for the entire volume. Hundreds of small, civilian craft without fold drives accelerated away from the freeport. Those capable of folding away did so in a sudden ripple of disappearance.

Defiant and *Makassar* stood foursquare between the station and the other ships of Pac Yulin's strike force.

The battleraider *Khanjar* held station off the corral where he and Lord Karna had impounded those few warships which arrived after the Sturm attack.

And Lord Karna, Pac Yulin was amused to see, had just now appeared in his own little projection bubble, raging impotently from the palace on Ciandur.

The volume was turned down. Pac Yulin was not at all interested in hearing from him.

It was McLennan he wanted.

———

"Am I seriously fucking seeing this?"

Sephina had strapped into the command chair, ready for a rough ride out of Lermontov. She had to hand it to the marines, but even more so to the TDF code Booker had fed into *Ariane*'s substrate. He'd programmed the medbots to force their recovery and given the Armadalens simplified helm controls for piloting the Zaistev superyacht all the way into the goddamned Hab. Banks took over the helm when they collected Alessia, and they had all worked the weapons stations at the vault.

But this?

"This shit is bananas," she said.

Almost everyone all around her was strapping into crash couches, a sure sign of what was coming. Banks worked his controls, turning the ship toward the nearest exit, the harbor gates at the port beyond the Yakuza *honbu*. Cox and Dahl fussed over Alessia, unwilling to trust her with even the simple task of strapping herself in, while Aronson stood ready at a weapons station.

"How did you even find us?" Alessia asked Dahl, as the grim-faced marine cinched her into the gelform couch.

"The jacket," she said. "There's a tracker in Commander Hardy's jacket."

Coto, who could not fit into a crash couch, floated in a micro-g field.

Booker, already secured and plugged into the ship's combat control systems, watched the main holo.

"You need to step on it," he said. "I got a bad feeling about this. We need to fold."

"Can't fold from inside the Hab," Banks said in his preternaturally calm way. "The gravimetric shear would tear the hull open. We're heading out as fast as we can."

"No. Guys. Seriously. Am I fucking seeing this?" Sephina said again, pointing at the main display.

They had a feed from *Defiant* and could see the confrontation between McLennan and Pac Yulin.

———

"It is you who will surrender to me, Admiral. You and Commander Hardy. You will both be tried summarily and punished for your crimes. You will surrender now, without delay, or I will destroy Lermontov as I destroyed *Sejong the Great* and the *Bremen*—which is to say, instantly."

Lucinda vaguely noted the mention of her name, and the threat to her life. She was too deeply invested in managing the tactical situation to attend to Pac Yulin's bullshit.

"You will not fire on that station," McLennan said as if he already knew how this would play out.

"No, I will not," Pac Yulin agreed, smiling. "And do not imagine it is because your little princess is on Lermontov. I know that. I have known it since HabSec detected her presence. I had hoped to rescue her, but you have made that impossible. And in doing so you have doomed her along with everybody on that Habitat. You are correct, sir. I will not fire on Lermontov. Because I do not need to. We have placed demolition charges throughout the Hab. Its destruction will be instant, upon my order."

Lucinda looked to McLennan, hoping that he had some answer, but he seemed to be almost as lost as she was.

Pac Yulin sat back, satisfied.

"I offer you a simple trade, Admiral McLennan. You and Hardy for the lives of sixteen million people. It is a much better trade than the one you made when you sacrificed half the population of Earth simply to lure the Sturm into an ambush."

Pac Yulin shook his head and made a tutting noise.

"I have never quite understood your legend. You were not the brilliant strategic thinker the history books make you out to be. You simply put a piece of cheese in a trap and waited for the rat to take it. Oh, I'm sorry, am I boring you, Admiral?"

Mac looked impossibly old. He was leaned up against Hero, his head bowed, one hand laid against the Intellect's exotic matter carapace for support. He waved his other hand at Pac Yulin, and when he spoke he sounded every day of his hundreds and hundreds of years of age.

"Commander Hardy will not be joining you, Commodore," he said. "But I will yield."

A sudden murmur of disbelief and many cries of objection circled the bridge, before Lucinda ordered the crew to be quiet. She was worried, deeply so, and acid burned at the lining of her stomach.

"As you were," she barked out, before going on in a softer voice. "Admiral, what are you doing?"

McLennan turned his head as though he had injured his neck. He looked to be in great pain. He looked beaten. Lucinda did not understand. She was sure there was some way out of this. They could not punch it out, but surely they could negotiate. Pac Yulin wanted what all criminals wanted: to get away with his crime. That was all. They could promise him whatever he needed to feel as though he had that.

The Combine princeling leaned forward in his chair.

"What did you say?"

McLennan straightened up a little, with obvious effort.

"I said I would yield, but not to your demand for Hardy. Take the offer now, Yulin. You have played a bad hand very well. I will concede that. But I need you to concede that what we did here, and what lies in front of us, is greater than any single man's ambition or fate. The princess must live. She is the only legitimate authority still living in the Greater Volume. I am certain of that. She must live and she must lead."

Pac Yulin snorted.

"I will lead but"—he dipped his head as if conceding a point—"I will do so with her at my side. She is my betrothed, after all."

He grinned like a fox licking shit from a wire brush.

"Together we will bind up the greatest realms and Houses and we will see off this invading horde. But we shall also put down the scum who would usurp our rightful reign. And that means you, McLennan."

Mac seemed to fold in upon himself, as though he was about to collapse from some unutterable pain.

"But not . . . Hardy," he said through gritted teeth.

"Okay. Fine. Whatever," Pac Yulin said. He seemed surprised and even delighted at the unexpected turn.

Lucinda was up out of her chair, moving toward Mac. He held up his free hand to stay her advance. The effort seemed to cost him and he leaned even further upon Herodotus.

"Mac," the Intellect said. "Are you sure?"

"Has to be done," the admiral said.

"Are you ready?"

"I am."

He pushed himself off Herodotus, waved Lucinda away, and staggered through a shuffling turn to take in everyone on the bridge, finding a grin from somewhere when he laid eyes upon the Javan officer.

"It has been an honor and a privilege to serve with you all," Frazer McLennan said. "Your gallantry under fire and great peril reflects credit upon the Royal Armadalen Navy"—he paused and turned to Sub-Commandant Suprarto—"and the Imperial Javanese Navy."

McLennan straightened up and performed a slow, but perfect salute.

"Admiral, no," Hardy cried out.

"One to fold over," Hero announced.

Commodore Pac Yulin waved a hand excitedly to somebody just out of the holo-projection.

"Get him. Get him now."

Admiral McLennan winked out of existence.

Less than a heartbeat later he reappeared in the holo projected from the bridge of the *Khanjar*.

Lucinda was reeling.

She could not believe how quickly everything had changed. How completely Pac Yulin appeared to have triumphed.

"Stand ready, Mister Fein," she ordered for want of anything better to say. "Sub-Commandant Suprarto, we may have to maneuver hard and fast. Perhaps a crash couch?"

"Thank you," the young Javan officer said. He sounded as

stunned as Lucinda felt. Doctor Saito and the marine escort helped him into a gelform seat.

On *Khanjar*, two armored legionnaires laid heavy gauntlets on McLennan and forced him to his knees.

Pac Yulin was almost giddy with the joy of victory. Had it been so easy?

No, of course not. He had lost the better part of his strike force. He would now have to break the Javans, too. And he was almost forced to kill his bride-to-be, and with her any legitimate claim on the Montanblanc ul Haq Corporation. Indeed, he did not doubt he would have the very devil's job extracting Princess Alessia from the clutches of the Armadalens and their pirate allies.

But this, this was still a moment to be savored.

The incomparable McLennan kneeling in submission before him.

Pac Yulin breathed in the moment. The air on the bridge was still foul from battle but it tasted sweet to him. The admiring, even adoring, gaze of the crew was cool water for a parched tongue. This scene would be remembered for ten thousand years, and he would reign for all of them.

"Welcome to the flagship of the Yulin-Irrawaddy Combination of Corporate Realms, Admiral McLennan. Welcome to your end."

The old man's eyes were red and watery. Had he been crying, the worthless cur?

Oh, this was even better.

Perhaps Pac Yulin should preserve him just a little longer, to enjoy his total domination of the man.

"Do you have anything to say in your defense?" He smirked at the Terran admiral.

McLennan raised his head as though a great weight hung from it.

"Tae fuck wi' you, ya soft wee cunt."

Pac Yulin stepped forward to drive a kick into McLennan's guts. It was not a great kick, to be perfectly honest. He was slightly off balance and his aim was marred by anger. But the compressive thud of impact and McLennan's grunt of pain went some way toward rebalancing his temper.

The aged Scotsman collapsed around Pac Yulin's polished boot and he face-planted on the deck with an agreeably wet crunch.

Rinaldo Pac Yulin gestured to the legionnaires to pick him up again, aware that most of the Volume was looking on.

McLennan's nose was broken, and he had bitten through his lower lip. It was bleeding profusely.

But he spat at Pac Yulin.

"You can chew mah banger, you disgusting fuckin' slaver."

The gobbet actually struck Pac Yulin and he flinched back.

Something hard had come out in the wad of bloody phlegm.

A small silver ovoid shape, like a seedpod spotted with gore. It lay on the deck before him. Like McLennan.

"What? What is that?"

McLennan grinned and his teeth, through shredded lips, seeping blood, looked like the fangs of a hungry wolf.

"Welcome to Scotland."

The singularity that blossomed from the exotic matter sabot was not large enough to consume the entire mass of the battle-raider. A submunition from *Defiant*'s armory, it was designed as an area denial weapon. Hundreds of the bomblets would normally deploy from an ultra-long-range missile, punching temporary holes in space-time across thousands of cubic kilometers.

The small, spherical event horizon that consumed Frazer McLennan and Rinaldo Pac Yulin expanded rapidly and gorged itself on the constituent matter at the heart of the *Khanjar*. When it collapsed, the gravimetric maelstrom caused the remaining mass of the giant warship to implode. All of this happened within a trillionth of a second. Compressed to annihilating densities and ruptured catastrophically, the antimatter drives of the heavy cruiser exploded.

From Lucinda Hardy's point of view on the bridge of the *Defiant*, to the stunned and gaping passengers and crew of the *Ariane*, it looked as though a heavy nuke had detonated deep inside *Khanjar*; ironically enough, the very same fate that Pac Yulin had engineered for Lermontov Station.

Only Hero, who had taken the tiny warhead from the armory and micro-folded it under McLennan's tongue as the admiral left the Armadalen ship, knew what had really happened.

"My God," Lucinda gasped, as alarms and warning sirens blared throughout the ship.

"The *Rekong* is firing on us, Commander," Lieutenant Fein called out.

"Countermeasures," she called back. "Kill the *Rekong* with . . ."

"Apologies, ma'am, *Makassar* has destroyed *Rekong* with flux cannons. *Sundang* is signaling surrender."

"Acknowledged and accepted," Lucinda answered, still deeply shaken, but nodding at Suprarto for the assistance of his comrades. The Javan officer shrugged and smiled. He had given no order. His ship and crew had acted freely.

"Commander," Lieutenant Bannon said. "The debris field from the destruction of the battleraider is spreading fast. It's going to hit the warship corral off Lermontov."

Grieving for McLennan's sacrifice would have to wait.

"Mister Fein," Lucinda said quickly, "can we check the blast wave with singularities?"

"No, ma'am," Fein answered immediately. "There's too much mass."

"I'll deal with it," Hero announced, oddly chipper, as though he hadn't just sent McLennan to his doom. There really was a touch of the psychopath about him, Hardy thought.

The Intellect disappeared with a slight pop of collapsing atmosphere.

Almost immediately, the five surviving ships impounded half an AU from Lermontov Station all folded away. The storm of white-hot radioactive debris smashed into the corral a few seconds later.

"What the . . ." Lucinda started.

Hero's voice replied over the ship's audio system.

"I am an Armada-level Intellect, you know, and this is barely a bathtub flotilla. I don't think much of the cartel's clamping technology, either, for what it's worth, which is nothing and . . ."

"Ma'am," Ian Bannon said, talking over Herodotus, "the warships have materialized two astronomical units away, south of the elliptical, eighty-three degrees relative to our position."

"Thank you, Lieutenant," she replied. "Tactical, talk to me."

Mercado Fein surveyed the data cloud at his personal holostation.

"The Combine have powered down weapons and turned off their targeting arrays, ma'am. *Makassar* reports that Volume Lord Karna is under house arrest. Lermontov Station is a bit of a dog's breakfast but poses no threat to us."

"A dog's breakfast, Lieutenant?" Lucinda asked, turned in her command chair.

Fein blushed and stuttered.

"Er, the s-situation on the Hab is . . ."

"A complete and utter shit show," Lucinda offered. She turned to address Sub-Commandant Suprarto. "Perhaps a joint mission by Armadalen marines and Imperial Javan kommandos to restore order might help? Your kommandos to take the lead, of course."

Suprarto looked tired and possibly suffering from shock, but he nodded.

"I will order *Makassar* to make ready a ground force. Please have your marine commander introduce himself to me."

"That would be Captain Hayes," she said. "And I will."

Lucinda breathed out.

"Nonomi, secure from general quarters."

She stared at the holo, where Hero had gathered the surviving warships.

"And now he has a little fleet all his own," she muttered to herself.

She couldn't help it. She cast a look at Varro Chase, who was staring at her. Lucinda quickly looked away.

CHAPTER

THIRTY-SIX

They were many hours cleaning up the mess of battle with the Sturm and violent sedition by the Combine and Lord Karna.

It was late at night, by the ship's clock, before the memorial party could convene in the officers' mess. Sephina, Alessia, and Booker folded over from the *Ariane*. Cox, Dahl, and Aronson reported back to the *Defiant* with them. Captain Hayes ordered the marines to provide after-action reports explaining how they came to lose the princess they had been sent to protect.

Lucinda reminded them, in front of Hayes, to make sure they included the bit about how they recovered from the Yakuza's neural disrupters in record time and piloted a superyacht through a civil war to pluck the princess from hiding, before foiling the Combine plot to murder two thousand allied personnel and commit genocide upon a Habitat.

"Yeah, that too," Hayes grunted, before returning to his peace-keeping mission on Lermontov, but not before taking Lucinda aside and telling her quietly, "You're fucking good at this, you know. I'm gonna verbal them. A real teardown on general principles. Then I'm putting them all in for medals."

"I'll co-sign that," Lucinda said and smiled.

The gathering to commemorate Frazer McLennan was small.

Defiant's O-Group, minus Hayes. Princess Alessia. Sephina. Booker in TDF dress uniform. And Sub-Commandant Suprarto, floating through the memorial in a treatment pod from medbay.

Alessia stuck close to Sephina all night, but she was prey to none of the hero worship that often characterized her adoration of the smuggler. She was, more than anyone, distressed by McLennan's death. His actual death. Or perhaps, being a child still, she simply felt free to let the tears come.

Seph, who insisted she'd never liked him much, joined Alessia in maudlin weeping after pulling the cork on a bottle of wine.

Hero, having returned all the crew members of the allied ships to their organic forms and set them to preparing the vessels for a long fold, floated enigmatically in the corner. It was unlike him to be so quiet, but perhaps he was realizing what he had lost. A friendship, literally for the ages.

At four bells, Lucinda picked up a small silver fork from a tray of food and tapped it lightly against her glass.

She was drinking whiskey. It seemed appropriate.

"I would like to say a few words," she said.

The room fell quiet.

Lucinda had never had to do anything like this. There had always been another officer, not just senior in rank, but far, far older than her.

She swallowed.

"It is hard to know what to say about Frazer McLennan. He was . . . a legend. And yet, we've all seen him wandering the lower decks in his underpants."

A few chortles.

Both Seph and Alessia went, *"Eew!"*

Lucinda started again.

"Without the admiral, without . . . Mac, we would none of us be here. Not simply because he led us in battle at Montrachet, but because over half a millennia ago he held the line against fascist barbarism when that line had all but fallen."

"Hear, hear," a few voices muttered.

"I will miss him," she said, before taking a deep breath. "Most of you know that I lost my father to the Combine re-claimers when I was around Alessia's age."

Lucinda raised her glass toward the Montanblanc princess. Alessia was glassy-eyed and sniffling.

"I had no one to raise me, to teach me."

"Hey," Seph protested. "I'm right here, bitch. Who stole the collection money from the nuns and bought you all that good lesbian tentacle porn?"

Lucinda let the laughter roll over her. When it had subsided, she went on.

"I only knew him for a short while, but I learned a lot from Mac. I only wish I could have known him longer. There's so much more to learn."

She charged her glass.

"To Mac."

The whole room answered her.

"To Mac!"

They threw down a drink as Sephina took the floor.

"Yeah well," she said mushily, waving around her second bottle of Châteaux Francois. "I knew the old goat just about as long as you, and I reckon I had his number."

The laughter was scoffing now.

She threw up her hands, sloshing a decent slug of the pinot noir onto the long table.

"Ah shit. Sorry. Anyway. Most of you know that I am nothing like my homegirl the Loose Unit here. And I think that makes me a better person."

More laughter, raucous and heckling now.

"Shut the fuck up, you know it's true. I am the better person and the better judge of people and I judged old mate McLennan to be an absolute villain of the darkest hue."

The laughter trailed off.

Seph smiled, happily drunk.

"Which is cool. I am something of a villain myself, and game knows game. McLennan was a villain in the old sense of the word. Look it up. It's ancient, like he was. And it doesn't mean he was a bad man, because he wasn't. The term comes to Volume Standard from Old French, of which I know a little."

She was quite drunk, but that made her delivery all the more compelling. Nobody could take their eyes off Sephina's wobbly balancing act. "In Old French," she went on, "a villain was anyone bound to the soil of the villa. It came to mean anyone of less than noble class and implied a lack of chivalry and good manners."

She paused.

"Yeah. Fuck that in the neck."

A cheer erupted and she raised her voice to speak over it.

"Frazer McLennan was just like us."

Seph waved the bottle back and forth between herself and Lucinda.

"He was lowborn. To the slums and the muck and he never forgot what that means. He knew the real villains were the slavers and bond holders and the realms and empires they built. Fuck them. Fuck them all."

A roar greeted her. Even from Princess Alessia.

Lucinda threw a worried glance at Domi Suprarto, but the Javan, covered in medical patches for radiation therapy, was nodding fiercely.

"McLennan knew this war wasn't going to be just against the Sturm. He knew you don't have to reach into the Dark to find your worst enemies. And how fucking right he was. To Mac!"

"To Mac!"

When the roaring and cheering died down, Alessia stood at the head of the long table. She had changed out of Lucinda's jacket, but not back into the coveralls she loved so much.

Princess Alessia wore a high-collared jacket in the royal blue and gold of her House.

A bejeweled circlet, the Crown of Queen Josephine, rested lightly on her head.

She waited for silence and she quickly received it.

"I am but a child," she said. "But my House is old. I was raised to think of House Montanblanc as a rock. Ancient. Unyielding. Strong. Frazer McLennan was all those things, of course. But he was also a man of honor. When he judged himself to have no choice but to give his life, forever, to save us, he did so without hesitation."

Lucinda felt her throat growing tight and she took a sip of whiskey. It burned and her eyes watered.

Alessia continued.

"We have lost a friend, a leader, and a good man. But it is not true, Lucinda, that we can no longer learn from him. He taught us all we need for what lies ahead. That sacrifices must be made. Loss endured. And sorrow borne until final victory allows us time to mourn."

She smiled sadly and held up a cup of warm milk.

"To Mac."

Before anyone could reply, a voice boomed out from the corner of the officers' wardroom.

A voice thick with the snarling Gaelic burr of Glasgow.

"Oh for fuck's sake, I've had just about enough of this as a man can take. Someone pour a bottle over this gigantic floating bum lozenge and at least let me try to sip a few sweet drops for m'self."

Lucinda dropped her whiskey glass. It fell to the deck with a crash.

McLennan's face grinned out at the room from somewhere deep inside the opalescent black shell of Hero's exotic matter casing.

"Well, dinnae just stand there. If I cannae have a dram someone find me a half-decent body to climb into. Something like yonder stallion Booker over there would do nicely. I've been stuck inside Herodotus like a fart in a telephone booth all day now."

Lucinda blinked.

"What . . . ?" she started.

"What the fuck's a telephone booth?" Sephina said, shaking her head, blinking and taking an extra-long slug off the red wine bottle.

The face of the dead admiral was still there, hovering somewhere just inside Herodotus.

"The fuck is going on?" Lucinda asked.

Alessia was crying.

The room had fallen into uproar.

"Excuse me," Hero called out, and his bellowing voice was loud enough to bring stillness to the company. "Thanks. So, here's the thing. I've been pestering this old fool to swap out of that disgracefully basic and broken-down carcass of his for years now. He was full of cancer, you know."

"Och, Hero, stop flapping your fucking gums, you mangled fanny. They don't need to—"

"Testicular cancer actually! Yes, rotting balls. With a little bit of bowel trouble thrown in for spice. He was on the way out, fast. And the cancer was speeding up his usual cognitive decline. So, he finally, finally agreed to let me map his engram matrices as we folded for Natuna. It meant I could perform an emergency engram copy to my memory."

Lucinda started to object, "But a meat scan requires a physical connection, and medical equipment, and . . . and," before she recalled McLennan slumping in pain on the bridge and leaning against Hero, one hand pressed flat against the Intellect's outer casing. ". . . or . . . a fucking Armada-level Intellect, I guess," she finished.

Alessia's eyes were full of tears.

"Ad-Admiral Mac, is that . . . is it really you?"

"Aye, lass. It is."

"But who . . . who . . ."

"Who did for Pac Yulin? Why, that was me, too. Of course, that me is gone now. But it was a privilege to crush a fascist coup and I would do it again in a sparrow's fart. Speaking of which, as much as I have enjoyed all the wonderful lies you've told about me, I would very much like to get my arse out of this clanking pisspot of an Intellect and back into something that could fill out a decent pair of trousers. I wonder, Ms. L'trel, if I might have a word with your little friend Kumon Xi."

EPILOGUE

Jonathyn was deeply asleep when the steward came and woke him. They had been two weeks folding from Batavia, aboard the frigate *Ulysses*. They had given him his own cabin, even though he was embarrassed by the generosity and would have happily bunked down with the crew in their common quarters.

But Captain Revell insisted.

There was another passenger along with them. Some old soldier from Montrachet. Dunning, his name was, according to the captain. Jonathyn saw him briefly as they embarked for the voyage but had not encountered him again.

Unlike Jonathyn Hardy, the older man had come aboard in plasteel chains holding him down to a medical float.

There was little to do on the long voyage, but that did not bother Jonathyn. He started to exercise in the ship's gym, which the crew fetchingly called a "strength foundry," and even though compared to them he had no strength at all, they were very patient with him. A couple of the officers even took time out to train with him.

The food was simple, but to his mind excellent. After so

many years in the defaulter camps, even the most basic rations were a treat. He read books. Actual books on little slates, and watched "movies" and something the crew called "TV."

It was very basic and utterly delightful.

But of course, it could not go on forever.

Eventually they sent for him and the dread he had been trying to avoid descended again.

Captain Revell was waiting for him on the bridge. He had been allowed to visit a couple of times, with an escort, but in truth there wasn't much to see in the depths of space.

This time there was plenty.

One whole wall—they called them bulkheads—was given over to a screen. The Republicans preferred screens to holos. It saved space, they said, working in only two dimensions.

Revell was not the only person in the room, but everyone had duties to attend to. He alone was wrapped in the images on the big screen.

A great Habitat, dead and tumbling through the vacuum. A debris cloud surrounded it.

Jonathyn Hardy was not a soldier, but he could tell that a terrible battle had been fought here. He had a sick feeling of premonition.

"What is this place?" he asked.

Revell half turned toward him.

"It's called Natuna System," he said. "It belonged to the Empire of Java."

"What . . . what happened?"

Revell smiled sadly.

"Your daughter, Mister Hardy. Your daughter happened here. Like she did at Montrachet and Descheneaux."

Revell sighed.

"She will not see reason, sir."

Jonathyn did not know what to say to that, and so for a while he stayed silent.

Revell said nothing more.

The scale of destruction was terrifying. It spoke for them both.

"How many died?" Jonathyn finally asked.

"Sixteen million on the Hab," Revell answered. "More throughout the system."

They stared at the display.

"Mister Hardy, this has to stop," Anders Revell said. "You have to help stop it. You have to help . . . stop her."

Jonathyn found himself nodding.

"I know," he said. "And I will."

ACKNOWLEDGMENTS

Nobody destroys a star-spanning civilization on their own. I must thank my fellow sci-fi scribber Jason Lambright, now sadly reduced to biomass somewhere on Batavia, for his help with some of the battle scenes. Before he fell to writing, Jason earned an honest living as a soldier, and has been of invaluable help to me when things turn 'splodey. Also of great service, the Autonomous Editorial Intellect, Sarah Peed, who shares Hero's vast abilities but none of his annoying quirks. To all my fellow travelers and co-conspirators at the Burger and Patreon, I dips me lid. And to my family, I can but apologize, yet again, for my grumpiness on deadline. You do put up with a lot and I am grateful.

ABOUT THE AUTHOR

JOHN BIRMINGHAM is the author of *The Cruel Stars,
Emergence, Resistance, Ascendance, After America, Without
Warning, Final Impact, Designated Targets, Weapons
of Choice,* and other novels, as well as *Leviathan,* which
won the National Award for Non-Fiction at Australia's
Adelaide Festival of the Arts, and the novella *Stalin's
Hammer: Rome.* He has written for *The Sydney Morning
Herald, Rolling Stone, Penthouse, Playboy,* and numerous other magazines. He lives at the beach with his wife,
daughter, son, and two cats.

ABOUT THE TYPE

This book was set in Sabon, a typeface designed by the well-known German typographer Jan Tschichold (1902–74). Sabon's design is based upon the original letterforms of sixteenth-century French type designer Claude Garamond and was created specifically to be used for three sources: foundry type for hand composition, Linotype, and Monotype. Tschichold named his typeface for the famous Frankfurt typefounder Jacques Sabon (c. 1520 80).